BOOKS BY GORE VIDAL

NOVELS

Williwaw
In a Yellow Wood
The City and the Pillar
The Season of Comfort
A Search for the King
Dark Green, Bright Red
The Judgment of Paris
Messiah
Julian
Washington, D.C.
Myra Breckinridge
Two Sisters
Burr
Myron
1876
Kalki

SHORT STORIES

A Thirsty Evil

PLAYS

An Evening with Richard Nixon
Weekend
Romulus
The Best Man
Visit to a Small Planet

ESSAYS

Rocking the Boat
Reflections upon a Sinking Ship
Homage to Daniel Shays
Matters of Fact and of Fiction

GORE VIDAL

KALKI

A Novel

Random House New York

Library of Congress Cataloging in Publication Data
Vidal, Gore, 1925-
Kalki : a novel.
I. Title.
PZ3.V6668Kal [PS3543.I26] 813'.5'4 77-90248
ISBN 0-394-42053-5

Manufactured in the United States of America
2 4 6 8 9 7 5 3
First Trade Edition
A limited edition of this book has been privately printed.

FOR KUKRIT PRAMOJ
who first told me
of Kalki

ONE

1

$\mathbf{W}$HERE TO BEGIN?

A week has passed since I wrote that first sentence.

I am sitting at the big table in the Cabinet Room of the White House. I have been asked to give my version of what happened. I have also been requested to avoid the historian's best and closest friend hindsight. This is not going to be easy.

For some minutes I have been staring out the window. It is late autumn. Brown leaves are falling. A year ago I was in Los Angeles, dead broke. Now I am at work in the White House. Is this a success story? Try again.

Beside my typewriter is a logbook. I have taken it with me on every flight that I have made since I won the International Harmon Trophy for my contributions to world aviation. The first woman to be so honored was Jacqueline Cochran, back in the fifties. She was married to a millionaire who indulged her love of flying. I had no money behind me.

In the back of the logbook I write down phrases, sentences that appeal to me. Although I was an engineering major at the University of Southern California, class of '64, I was very much into what used to be called the humanities—as opposed to the inhumanities of science, machinery. A year ago September I wanted to start my life over. To go back to school. To get my doctorate—in Pascal. A lot of women my age were going through the same sort of crisis. Operation Last Chance. One afternoon I went down to USC and stood for a while in a long registration line. Although I looked younger than thirty-four, I didn't look seventeen. Within a yard or two of the registration desk, I fled. I had developed a nosebleed.

I have always wanted to know everything. To be everything. Master of not only the one but the other of the two cultures. At home with Ronsard. At home with Heisenberg. Yet when I "wrote" my book, it was ghost-written by Herman V. Weiss, hack. According to the publisher, I was not at home with the muse. I am still not at home.

Here is a quotation from Horace: "Born under the malignant influence of change."

I like that. I don't know who or what—*whom* or what Horace was referring to but that phrase certainly describes the state of the world as of last year.

Another quotation. This is from Diderot. I prefer him to Voltaire. "The first step towards philosophy is incredulity." Under this sentence I wrote "last words." Whose? Diderot's? I've forgotten. But those words, first or last, describe my own state of mind all last year. In fact, if incredulity can be measured in steps, I was wearing seven-league boots that February afternoon when I met Morgan Davies beside the pool of the Beverly Hills Hotel.

There! I've done it. I've found a place to begin.

But, first, who is Morgan Davies? And, second, who am I? "You must put the reader right there, Teddy," as that cliché master and structuralist H.V. Weiss used to say to me. "Put him in your shoes."

To be in my shoes or seven-league boots last year, you would have to have been Theodora Hecht Ottinger, known as Teddy, aged thirty-four, test pilot, native of San Diego, graduate of the University of Southern California (degree in engineering), winner of the International Harmon Trophy, breaker of records and men's self-esteem (if you happened to have talked to an envious male colleague) and author, with H.V.W., of the best-seller *Beyond Motherhood* (lousy title), a candid look at my life and hard times as a flier, woman, mother and would-be know-it-all. In spite of H.V.W.'s overexcited style, the book made a big impact. A lot of women admired the way in which I had deliberately removed myself from the bioreproductive track or trap that nature had created for me and which I had loyally served by giving birth to two children. In perfect health and with maximum publicity at the Marie Stopes Clinic in Daly City, I underwent a bilateral partial salpingectomy, better known as "Band-Aid Surgery." Two tiny incisions were made in the pelvic area. My tubes were cauterized and I was, literally, Beyond Motherhood. The occupant of a new category. For me, at least. Unfortunately, I was still a woman in a man's world, and the battle went on.

For two years I was a celebrity. I appeared on every important television and radio show in the U.S. and Canada. I never discussed fashions, menus or Ms. Onassis. I talked about overpopulation. The defense budget. Flying. The magic of flying. (I had wanted to call the book *Gravity Defied*, but my editor Morgan Davies said no.) I am only alive at the controls of a plane. But I enjoy designing, engineering. In '68 I tested the Lockheed 1011. I persuaded Boeing to drop the variable-geometry (or swing-wing) aircraft in favor of the fixed delta-shaped wing and tail plane. Then came the Harmon Trophy. Feminists hate the word aviatrix. I love it.

Eighteen months ago the curtain fell, as H.V.W. would say, on my act. I appeared on *The Merv Griffin Show*. Someone mentioned Indira Gandhi. I said that I thought she was the greatest woman of our time. I received a lot of hate mail. *Beyond Motherhood* was remaindered. I was no longer asked to go on television or even radio. But I was not sorry. I thought Ms. Gandhi's campaign to sterilize the Indian male was the bravest and most extraordinary act of any political figure up to the appearance on the scene of the person that I am now working for here in the White House.

Am I coming through on the page? Can the reader see and hear Teddy Ottinger? I hope so. Because I cannot for the life of me see the reader. For reasons which will soon be obvious.

One more line from the logbook. *"Qui veut faire l'ange fait la bête."*

Pascal. Is it apt? I hope not. After all, I did not set out to make an angel of myself or anyone else, much less a beast. I only wanted to exist. To function. To be accepted in the way that a man with my ability is accepted. From the look of my logbook, I read a lot of Pascal in the sixties. I suppose reading him was a prophylactic against the counterculture. It is strange, come to think of it, that the daughter of two practicing Christian Scientists should have been so drawn to a Christian mystic.

I am considered beautiful. Although dark-haired and dark-eyed, I resemble my idol Amelia Earhart. My father was at USC with Amelia. He was in love with her. He followed her to Boston when she was doing social work at Denison House. She told him, no, nicely. She became world-famous. She vanished over the Pacific in 1937, seven years before I was born. I always wanted to be like her. She wore men's clothes. So do I. After I won the Harmon Trophy (my third mention of that prize —am I unusually vain? like a man?), aviation circles began to buzz with rumors that I was a dyke. *Beyond Motherhood* was my answer to that rumor. In a dozen furious pages, I took the bisexual route, along with Joan Baez, Kate Millett, Susan Sontag and other worthies of the day. In a discreet way, I told all. As a result, my husband Earl Ottinger, Jr., not only divorced me but got custody of the children as well. I discovered that a lot of men hated me. Most women were admiring but kept a distance.

Why am I creating a false impression?

The truth is that I made up my mind in high school that I was going to be the world's greatest flier. I was fascinated by Amelia Earhart. Collected pictures of her. Read everything that I could find about her. After a lot of hard work in what was very much a man's world, I got my wish. I was the best pilot in the world. I was also tough as nails. But I was an anachronism. In an age of near-total automation a pilot like Amelia, like me (even one like the wealthy Mrs. Odlum) is irrelevant. And yet because there was something so archaic about being a flier in the sixties and seventies, a lot of people found me interesting, particularly the men who admired me but kept a distance and the women who hated me.

As I write this, I am wearing a belt that Amelia gave my father forty years ago. It is narrow, with blue and white checks. I could have loved her. But fate played us a dirty trick. By the time I was born, she was dead. In a funny way I believe that Amelia crashed her plane for both of us. I suppose that is why I have never feared death in a plane.

Change is not, necessarily, maleficent. Even so, as I made my way to the pool of the Beverly Hills Hotel, I was aware that things appeared to be changing for me, and for the worse. I was broke. I owed two months' alimony. Yes, I was the one who paid the alimony. Nobly, I had insisted on that proud right. As a result, I was a national heroine for more than a week—to the men. Women wrote me ugly letters. I was not, apparently, a pussycat.

Who was Morgan Davies? Morgan used to work for Clay Felker. Who was Clay Felker? He published some magazines in New York and Los Angeles. Several excerpts from *Beyond Motherhood* appeared in one of those magazines. Morgan was also the one who brought H.V. Weiss into my life. When Clay Felker lost control of his papers to an Australian (a subject of endless interest to the press and no one else), Morgan Davies became managing editor of *The National Sun*, a lurid newspaper dedicated to corrupting the morals of the lower IQs. I dated Morgan a couple of times but we never made it. He was too fat. He also had difficulty breathing. Asthma, he said, but it was plainly emphysema from too many cigarettes. I dislike being around people who smoke. During the period when Morgan and I needed each other, we got on well. Now it looked as if Morgan needed me again. He had asked me to meet him "Right away."

Beggars cannot, I thought to myself in the style of H.V.W., be choosers. I found myself resenting the sunbathers beside the Beverly Hills Hotel pool. Everyone looked so pleased to be there. Merv Griffin was in one of the cabanas. He said, "Hi, Teddy!" I thought his politeness was very sporting. After all, the ruckus over Indira Gandhi could not have delighted his various sponsors.

I sat in a deck chair beside Morgan, who was wearing trunks with a flower motif. He was talking into a telephone. Something he did well. The blond Swede or Norwegian who was in charge of the pool area said, "Hello, Ms. Ottinger! We haven't seen you in a long time."

"I've been testing planes," I said. It was always necessary around Hollywood to remind people that you were still in demand at whatever it was that you were celebrated for. No one was allowed to fail within a one-mile radius of the pool of the Beverly Hills Hotel. If anybody had, the resulting tidal wave would have drowned the guests.

7

"California's so boring," said Morgan. Then he gave me an approv-
ing nod. I was wearing my test pilot's jacket with TEDDY OTTINGER in
Day-Glow on the back. Tacky but effective in establishing a readily
recognized logo. I was a commodity. I was for sale. I was also on the
shelf.

Morgan took the *Sunday New York Times* off his lap. (That means
it was a Sunday afternoon when we met. Must try to establish the exact
date of what turned out to be, literally, an historic meeting.) He let the
newspaper fall in sections to the cement pavement—plop, plop, plop.

"So what've you been up to, Teddy?" Then he stopped and—an old
annoying habit—played back what he had heard me say to the pool
attendant. "You've been testing planes, you said."

"Yes, Morgan." It was hot in the sun and I took off the windbreaker.
I was pleased that he tried not to stare at my blouse. The Ottinger
breasts were—are—celebrated. After three years of yoga, I remade my
body. In the image of . . . ? Who knows? Each of us is so many people
all rolled into—none?

"I guess," said Morgan, "testing planes is still a good business. Those
new appropriations for the military . . ."

"You guessed wrong." I told the truth, not wanting to. "As far as
Defense goes, everything's unmanned or unwomaned. We have the
MIRVs. We have the MARVs. We have the Cruise missile, and now
the M-X. Except for the B-1, there's nothing new that requires flesh,
a brain, me. So all I can do is check out planes for all the airlines that
are going bust." Wanting to say nothing, I had said too much.

Just past the tall sick palms at the edge of the pool, the exhaust of
a half-dozen jets was making a kind of tick-tack-toe in the dusty brown
sky over Los Angeles. I realized that the jets were burning up the ozone
at the top of the sky. Even so, I loved them.

"Tough," said Morgan, obviously pleased that I was not doing well.
I watched the sweat trickle between his pendulous breasts. They were
covered with wispy gray hairs. The nipples were coyly inverted. He
began to wheeze. Homeopathically, he inhaled a cloud of cigarette
smoke, coughed, and said, "What's happened to that movie you were
going to star in, about what's-her-name?"

"Amelia Earhart. It's been postponed. There's a problem with the
script." The problem with the script was Shirley MacLaine. She had
said that *she* was going to make her own film of Amelia's life. My friend

and producer Arlene Wagstaff wanted to buy her out. But Shirley had said no.

"You were quite a writer." Morgan covered his chest and stomach with the Travel Section of the *N.Y. Times.*

"I wasn't any writer," I said. "It was all 'as told to' that shit Herman V. Weiss you found for me."

"Wasn't Herman Clay's idea originally? Anyway, old Herman did a good job. But if you don't want to work with him again, you don't have to."

A message chimed loud and clear. "You want me to write a new book? *Beyond Beyond Motherhood?*"

"I love it!" Morgan patted my arm. His hand was sticky with baby oil. "And you can tell the world all about those chicks that you ball."

Men are obsessed by women who do not need them. Before I could respond in elegant kind, the telephone rang and Morgan talked for what seemed hours on the riveting subject of whether or not the President would drop the Vice-President in the coming election. Or was it the other way around? The so-called power brokers of that day never knew what was important.

Anyway, I had got part of the message. Morgan was not interested in a sequel. I started to feel gloomy. With good reason: I was an out-of-work pilot with debts in the vicinity of one hundred thousand dollars, with two kids aged nine and eleven, with alimony to shell out at the rate of one G per month, not to mention the various extras for the children, including plastic surgery for Tessa's harelip, an operation that was *not* covered by medical insurance though I had been told by the company that it would be. In real life I was never allowed to get more than a yard or two beyond motherhood.

The one bright spot in my life was Arlene Wagstaff, aged forty-two plus. Plus only God knew how many years. But Arlene wore most of those years well, and in public. As of last February, she was the highest paid salesperson on television. She was also a household name, and image. Arlene's masterpiece was the Jedda Coffee Commercial where she is first discovered as a typical listless housewife, complete with neurotic frown. She tries to vacuum the floor. She fails. As she crumples into a chair, a kindly neighbor brings her a cup of Jedda coffee. Arlene drinks the coffee, with astonishing results. No longer catatonic, she is full of energy and pilots her vacuum cleaner like a jet. The income from that one commercial kept us both in comfort.

No, Arlene and I were not making it. We were more like sisters. Like sisters who really need each other. She was the breadwinner. She was also an alcoholic. I am not. I monitored the margaritas. Nursed the hangovers. Hid the pills at midnight.

"What do you know about Hinduism?" Morgan gave me his shrewd managing editor–*cum*–power broker stare. He once said that the greatest moment of his life was when he had been able to elect as governor of New York someone named Carey or Curry. At least Clay Felker thought big. Well, bigger. I never really liked any of them.

"The gods all have a lot of arms. And heads. Cows are not eaten. Souls transmigrate. I hate curry."

Morgan pressed the Travel Section close to his stomach. People kept looking at us. Some recognized him. Some recognized me. As there were no bona fide movie stars beside that pool, we had no competition. Merv Griffin had left.

"Then there are those kids with the shaved heads," I said. "You see them on Hollywood Boulevard. They chant *Hare Krishna.* They wear yellow dresses. Sandals. Or sneakers without socks."

Morgan nodded. "Yeah. Those are Hindus. One kind, anyway. It seems there are a lot of kinds."

"Like our own Christians. Once, twice, thrice-born . . . and even unborn."

"I don't think that remark is in good taste, Teddy," said the editor of *The National Sun.* Morgan liked the President. I thought him a creeping Jesus. The President, that is. Morgan was Judas in anyone's book.

"There's an American guy living in Nepal. In Katmandu. He's a Hindu. In fact, he says he's the Hindu messiah. He goes by the name of Kalki. Maybe you've seen some of his disciples. They're all over the place, handing out leaflets. And white paper flowers. Free!" Morgan gave me a pamphlet that he had been sitting on. Across the top of the cover was the word "Kalki." Under "Kalki" was the not entirely encouraging message: "The World Is Ending." The pamphlet's general appearance and texture had not been improved by the pressure and the humidity of Morgan's huge buttocks.

"I've seen them," I said. "And I remember wondering why they didn't ask for money. Most religions are rackets."

"That's what got me curious, too. That and the fact nobody knows much of anything about Kalki. So far, there's been only one skimpy AP story. Some of the local disciples have been interviewed but they don't seem to know much about him. They just repeat the party line. How the end of the world is on its way, so get your space together. Which is not what we call hard news. So far, Kalki's never granted an interview to anybody. He just preaches the word in his ash . . . what do you call it?"

"Ashram, a monastery." I suddenly recalled that I had seen the Kalki ashram on Santa Monica Boulevard. The building had once been a radio station. Somehow I had taken for granted that the huge KALKI on top of the building were the call letters of some new FM outfit.

Morgan looked at me keenly, steadily, as befitted an admirer of H.V. Weiss. "Three weeks from now Mike Wallace is going to interview Kalki for CBS's *60 Minutes.* Kalki has only just agreed to do the interview. So here's my proposition. I want to beat CBS. I want you to get to Kalki first. I want you to interview him for the *Sun.*"

Morgan took the Travel Section of the *Times* off his stomach and there, as I knew it would be, was the front page of the section printed backwards on his belly from the sweat.

As the sun dipped behind the striped canopy of the poolside bar, I thought longingly of a bullshot. "I am not," I said, "exactly the first person you would think of to do a piece on Kalki, or anyone else. I'm a pilot, not a journalist."

"Kalki's real name is Kelly." Morgan covered himself with a towel. I was glad. Ill-arranged flesh depresses me. "Jim. John. Jack. Something-or-other Kelly. I'll give you our file on him. I'm afraid it's pretty thin. He was in the army. Served in Vietnam. I mean Nam. Then he settled out there." Morgan pointed west, toward Malibu, Catalina, Asia. "He went native. Then, last year, out of the blue he said he was Kalki."

Something sparked in my head. I *had* read about him. I opened the pamphlet. On the first page there was a picture of a good-looking young man wearing Hindu clothes. Kalki. "He's supposed to be god, isn't he?"

Morgan nodded. "Yes. He's on record as being the final incarnation of the god . . . somebody-or-other. His mission is . . ."

"Eschatological," I said, made happy by each syllable of that useful word. Before Morgan could ask what the word meant, I set out to impress him with the width and the breadth and the depth of my newspaper reading. "He's got an ashram in Katmandu. He's surrounded by hippies. They all take drugs. Kalki's real name is James J. Kelly. With his appearance on earth, the human race will end. You see? I have total recall." I do. Once I have read something, it is forever on file. Thank God, most of the files are securely locked. You can go mad from too much remembering, particularly of the endless flow of mindless images on television, of the dark caravans of words that cross the pages of newspapers to invade and ravish the delicate house of memory like killer ants.

"Good girl! So how would you like to write about him?"

"I'm a test pilot, Morgan."

"You're the best-selling author of *Beyond Motherhood.*"

" 'As told to' Herman V. Weiss. Get him. He's teaching structuralism and semiology at San Fernando State."

"I want you."

"Why?"

"Because, Teddy," and the voice was grave, urgent, sincere, *"he* wants you."

"Who does?"

"Kalki. He himself said, last Monday, by Telex to the Los Angeles bureau of *The National Sun,* that there was only one writer in the world, at this time, that he would allow to interview him, and that writer—personality—aviatrix—and gorgeous gal was the one and only Theodora Hecht Ottinger, and I am an absolute fool for telling you this because now you can really hold me up. But I don't care. I need you, Teddy. It's as simple as that. After Mike Wallace, this guy is going to be all over the media. That's why I've got to get to him first. And the only way I can do that is with you."

"Does he know I can't write?" I cannot think why I thought this detail worth mentioning. No one else could, either. I was able to read the odd page by Joan Didion, the even page of Renata Adler. But no more. I did read Michel Foucault. But then I have never stopped studying French. As of last February, all the arts were running down; entropy was sovereign.

"I'll buy you a writer," said Davies, or "snapped Davies," as H.V.W. would have written.

"I don't know . . ." I began, or rather ended. I knew perfectly well that I was, again, in luck.

"Teddy, honey, this can be really big. I've also got a tie-in with Doubleday. They'll give you an advance for a book. It couldn't be simpler. All you have to do is turn on your trusty tape recorder and let him talk. You'll make history."

"Why?"

Davies narrowed (H.V.W.) his small eyes. I noticed that they were red from smog. Last February you could hardly breathe in L.A.

"Because," said Morgan, "Mr. Kelly says he's god. Because there are some big-money people financing him who think he's god or say they do. If they've got other reasons, find them out." Morgan's nose for who's getting money for what was almost as sharp as Clay Felker's. "In the last year, he's picked up an enormous following in India, which is pretty remarkable when you consider that he's an American. You'd think that they'd resent an ex-G.I. claiming to be a Hindu god. But they don't. Quite the opposite. Millions of them are busy purifying themselves, getting ready for the end of the world."

"Maybe he really is god." I thought this funny.

Exhaust from the jets made a trapezoid over the palms. "But if he's god," Morgan was reasonable, "what does he want? He'd have every-thing anyway."

"So had Nelson Rockefeller but he still wanted to be president. Gods are always up to something. They want you to live by the Golden Rule which, being all-powerful, they don't let you do because it spoils their game." This was particularly true of the original god of my parents, that testy old curmudgeon Jehovah. Some years before I was born, mother and father Hecht gave up Jehovah for Mary Baker Eddy, a bungalow outside San Diego and a social club that catered only to the goyim. At least we kept our noses. My father died, confident that death did not exist. It's my theory that Mary Baker Eddy did not exist because death does. That is for sure.

"Anyway," Morgan was back on his usual track, "the main thing is the money. Where is it coming from? How can he afford to send those kids out on the streets, giving away pamphlets, flowers; and refusing money?"

"O.K., Morgan. I'm hooked. I'll be Theodora Ottinger, newshen.

The Oriana Fallaci of West Hollywood. But why? Why, with all the professional journalists buzzing around, does he want to talk to me?"

"Well, he says he read *Beyond Motherhood.*"

"Then maybe you should send him Herman V. Weiss."

"No. It's you. And only you." Morgan replaced his professionally keen look with a genuinely puzzled one. "Look, kid, I'm as surprised as you are. I even sent him a Telex. Will you accept any other name journalist? But the answer was Ottinger or nobody."

"So it's Ottinger. O.K." We shook hands, greasily. I rubbed the baby oil off my hand with a corner of Morgan's towel. He said he would deal with my agents at the William Morris office. He said he would get me all the information that he could find on Kalki.

Across Morgan's chest was printed YOUR CARIBBEAN HOLIDAY in reverse.

2

"HI, MA!" TESSA GAVE ME A BIG HUG. THEN I SHOOK HANDS WITH my ex-mate Earl Ottinger, Jr. "Where's Eric?" I asked.

"Over at the doctor's. He's having allergy tests."

"That's the third set."

"He needs them, Teddy. He's high-strung. He's been through a lot. We all have."

I reminded myself not to make a scene about money in front of Tessa, an attractive child. There was almost no trace of the harelip; and I was glad that some of my vanished money had been well-spent. Then Tessa left Earl Jr. and me to what H.V.W. would have called our own devices.

"Martini?"

I said, yes, as they were already made.

I looked around the room, hardly able to believe that I had spent eight years, the better (that is, worse) part of my married life in this house overlooking the side of a dusty hill behind which was the Pacific Ocean and residential Santa Monica.

I am not a heavy drinker but I polished off one whole martini in about two swigs. Earl Jr. had that effect on me.

"How are things at the office?" I asked, as I used to ask every day at the witching hour when he would come home tired from—he said —the realtor firm where he worked but actually drained of what little basic energy he possessed by one or another of the employees of a certain massage parlor on Melrose whose regular client he had been since '68. I know. The proprietress was a former Rockette from New York and friend of Arlene's. She told us how the girls thought Earl Jr. was a joke; told us how sorry they felt for me. They were good girls. I am not at all sure that I ever really liked men.

"Lousy," said Earl Jr., from habit. He looked puffy but, thank God, he was no longer wearing beads, and his hair was cut short. Last February we were well into the counter-counter-culture en route to the counter-Carter-counter-culture, or a lot of Evangelical Christian nothing. I will note for future historians of our culture what I heard a year and a half ago at a party in Long Beach. A girl came up to the man I was talking to and announced: "Hi! I'm Bettina. I'm Pisces. I'm into health food, water sports and bondage." I knew then—in a blinding flash—that the Great Anarch in the sky was all set to let fall the curtain. Johnson? No. Pope, Alexander. As it turned out, universal darkness did not by any means bury all. But now I must withdraw from the verge of forbidden hindsight.

"You always say it's lousy. But real estate is having a boom. I know. I read the papers."

Earl Jr. just stared at me, full of hate. Of course, I couldn't blame him. One day I was Mrs. Earl Ottinger, Jr., wife, mother and home-maker (and only part-time test pilot and trophy winner). Then willy-nilly, the operation, the book, the divorce. Overnight I was the new Amelia Earhart. I had left behind me husband, children, tubes. In that *anno mirabilis* I was the ninth most admired woman in the world, according to the Gallup Poll.

Earl Jr. never really accepted any of this. But then I never really accepted any of him. My one-time shrink Dr. Mengers is positive that I became a test pilot as a means of escape from the earth, from my own fecundity, from Earl Jr., from the children I never wanted. Yet I must have felt *something* for him once, I thought, staring through the martini's first comforting haze at my ex-husband's pale double chin.

Tears came to my eyes. There were tears in his eyes, too. Love? Tenderness? Regret? No. It was the red-alert smog, creeping up the Santa Monica Canyon from the Pacific Freeway. Carbon monoxide from the tens of thousands of cars as they crept from south to north, from north to south, bumper to bumper.

We wiped our eyes and blew our noses with the paper cocktail napkins that I had bought at a sale three years earlier; and cursed the smog.

"So how's Arlene?" Earl Jr. hated Arlene and suspected the worst.

"Still trying to produce the Amelia Earhart story."

Earl Jr. sneered if a sneer is pursing the mouth as though something has got caught between two teeth. "Don't," he said, "hold your breath."

"Don't worry. I won't."

"I see where you're supposed to be lecturing at USC on zero-population growth." This was meant to be the beginning of a quarrel. We always disagreed about overpopulation and the maintenance of a proper balance within the biosphere. Earl Jr. thought that there was plenty of everything. I knew that there was plenty of nothing. Except people. Since there were four or five billion too many of us last February, whenever I got the chance I gave my pitch, which, basically, is the subtext of *Beyond Motherhood*. Dr. Paul Ehrlich, Dr. Barry Commoner and Teddy Ottinger, Test Pilot, were the chief prophets of that day. We spoke to the deaf. But we spoke.

"I'm canceling," I said. "I've got a new job."

"So when are you going to settle down?" Earl Jr. did his best to make me feel guilty. Occasionally he succeeded. After all, he was the father of my children and a lot better father than I had ever been a mother. Even in the old days I was always on the go, studying engineering, aeronautics, testing planes, leaving Earl Jr. to see the kids through their chicken pox and so on. But then they were *his* children, too. He had wanted them. I didn't. I suppose that that was what made me the permanently guilty party in my own eyes. Out of conventionality, I had gone against my own nature. But you have only the one life. If you can find it, live it. I did. Do.

"No wedding bells for me, baby. Ever. I've gone that route." Having hurt his feelings, I quickly added, "Not that being married to you wasn't wonderful. It was. Really. And truly. But you have to be yourself, no matter what."

"Well, nobody can say you haven't been a success in that department." Earl Jr. was bitter. I was pleased. We had begun a familiar quarrel. There is something soothing about hearing old reproaches. Constants in a world of change.

But then I let go my end of the familiar quarrel. I had other things on my mind. "I'm not so sure about the success part. At the moment . . ."

"You're two months behind on the alimony, Teddy."

"That's what I wanted to talk to you about, Earl Jr. I'm broke . . ."

"But not too broke to be having a high old time up there on Sunset Plaza with Arlene and her dyke friends."

"Women without husbands are not always dykes." In the old days the dyke-line used to really lay me out. No longer. In the land of the vibrator, the bisexual woman is queen; and the heterosexual man on the ropes.

"You know," said Earl Jr., "that both kids need psychiatric care, and that costs money."

"No shrinks!" I was firm. "For one thing, I can't afford it . . ."

"So you *won't* be making the February payment on time?"

"Sue her!" When I heard that voice, I spilled half a martini onto my new denim trousers. Mrs. Earl Ottinger, Sr., my ex-mother-in-law, entered the room like a rabid terrier, yapping and moving about dangerously. She was quite capable of taking a bite out of my leg. I believe that she was one-fourth Negro or black. But even after *Roots* on television, I never had the nerve to mention the unmentionable. She came from Baltimore. She despised "the coloreds." Earl Ottinger, Sr., was deceased. He, too, had been a realtor, after a career as a warrant officer (junior grade) in the Air Force. Why am I writing all this down? The Ottingers no longer matter to me. To anyone. Am I sentimental?

"Well, hi, Lenore," I said.

"Go to hell!" Mrs. Earl Ottinger, Sr., had been beside herself when I divorced Earl Jr. "The cauterizing of the tubes, yes. Why not?" That had been her line at the time. "If you want to stop having babies, fine. But never forget that you will always be the mother of my grandchildren and Earl Jr.'s wife! No Ottinger has ever been divorced in history." When I made history, Lenore never forgave me.

Over the martini shaker we had one of our three-way battles. As always, I made up my mind that I was never going to see either of them again. They were deeply awful. Each in his own peculiar way.

"You should come back home." Although the second martini usually had a soothing effect on Lenore's nerves, the terrier-bite was as sharp as ever. "The children need you. In the worst way."

"They've turned out very well, Lenore," I spoke with a raised temperature (what H.V. Weiss would have described as "warmly"). "Thanks to you. Thanks to Earl Jr."

I let drop a bucket or two into the deep well of my insincerity, and poured the contents of that far from lonely well over the enemy. They lapped it up. Feigned or not, flattery is sure-fire. I praised them into silence.

We looked at one another fondly. Then Earl Jr. broke the magic spell. "Teddy's unemployed," he said.

" '. . . wild blue yonder, flying *high* into the sky . . .' " Lenore sang the Air Force song. Those had been happy days for her, following her husband from air base to air base during World War II.

"I'm going to India," I said. "Next week."

That stopped Lenore's singing. Earl Jr. blinked his eyes.

I told them about my meeting with Morgan Davies. Neither of them had heard of Kelly or Kalki, but then neither of them had heard of Horace, Alexander Pope, Pascal, Diderot, Heisenberg's law or entropy. Their lives were spent, successfully, repelling information. They were perfect "clears," to use Scientologist jargon.

When I was finished, Earl Jr. struck. "Lenore," he always calls his mother by her first name, something I could never get used to, "has got the big C."

The awfulness of that statement shadowed the room.

"That's right." Lenore looked very pleased with herself. For a lot of people cancer was a sort of status symbol. Not for me. If I find so much as a pimple anywhere, I go into shock.

"Actually, we don't know if it's the big C yet," said Lenore, settling into a third martini, full of pickled onions. "They operate at Cedars-Sinai next Tuesday. At seven A.M. on the button. Then they'll know. After the biopsy, they'll know."

"But that's just terrible" was the best I could do.

"I know." Lenore was now wearing a strange half-smile, as though she knew something we did not know. Perhaps she did. "I think it's diet," said Lenore, "the way this thing is going around. Not enough roughage in what we eat. Mrs. Hendon—you remember Mrs. Hendon? From Sherman Oaks? She had *her* mastectomy in August and she is positive . . ."

I told Earl Jr. that the first penny received from Morgan Davies and *The National Sun* would go straight to the kids. On the other hand, I didn't want either of them to go to a shrink because "They are not disturbed," I said. "But they will be by the time one of your primal screamers gets through shouting at them."

Earl Jr. just pursed his lips and said, "Considering what *you* did to them, I don't see how they can very well avoid not being disturbed."

In waltz time, the two of us did a few steps of that familiar number while Lenore withdrew to the kitchen. I could hear her talking on the telephone to Mrs. Hendon in the Terminal Ward.

I got away before Lenore came back to the living room. I have never really been into death. Or water sports. Or bondage. I am not Pisces but Libra.

3

M Y LAST DAYS IN L.A. WERE HECTIC.

Morgan Davies gave me newspaper stories on Kelly-Kalki, books on Hinduism, a researcher named Bruce Sapersteen. Mr. Sapersteen was in the New York office of *The National Sun*. He rang me at Arlene's house, and offered to come out "to the Coast," the Easterners' phrase for California. But I said, no, not yet. Sapersteen said that he would send me whatever he could even though "there isn't too much. In English, that is. There's a lot in Hindi of course." My antennae had quickly picked up the message that Bruce Sapersteen was a clone of H.V. Weiss.

"Suppose Kalki really is god? Then what do you do?" Arlene was sitting at the edge of her gall bladder–shaped pool. Large imitation gallstones on the bottom lit up at night. Arlene's sense of fun had been shaped back in the forties, the decade into which I was born.

In the morning light and without make-up Arlene looked remarkably good, despite the piece of triangle-shaped adhesive tape between her eyebrows. She called this sticking-plaster "a frownie." She had a positively mystical belief in that tape's power to smooth out the frown lines that had once been entirely if not permanently eliminated by silicone injection in Brazil. The lines had come back, thanks to sun and booze and near-sightedness. Although most of Arlene's professional career depended upon her ability to read Teleprompters and cue cards, she refused to wear glasses in public. Contact lenses terrified her, even the soft plastic ones.

"But I don't believe in god," I said. Arlene had started on the first of the day's many margaritas. She had been warned by her doctor to give up tequila in the morning. He begged her to switch to a good, light, refreshing breakfast wine from the Napa Valley. He himself owned shares in a vineyard. He would sell her his own brand. "But wine," said Arlene, firmly, "gives me gas."

"Oh, everything's god." Arlene looked about her at everything. In this case, everything was the redwood screen around the pool that she had had painted yellow, a patch of smog-brown sky, dusty hibiscus bushes, the dead bird that the Japanese gardener kept forgetting to take out of the small cactus garden.

"Or nothing."

"That's very metaphysical." Arlene liked to remind me of the good education that she had had in the Midwest. But, as she was the first to confess, she had forgotten everything that she had ever learned, along with all the millions of words that she had been obliged to learn as actress, singer, pitchwoman. As a girl she had wanted, she always said, to be a veterinary. But show business had seized her by her beautiful throat. In the late forties and early fifties, she was an almost-but-not-quite movie star. Now, in never-too-late middle age, she was the highest paid TV pitchperson, after Barbara Walters. A total celebrity. "Anyway, he looks nice in his pictures."

"How can you tell?" I asked. "We've nothing to go on except a lot of hazy wire-service pictures." I opened the Kalki file. There was not one clear shot of him. He looked like anybody, with long hair and a beard.

"I have a hunch he's cute. And you know my hunches." Arlene flashed me the Wagstaff smile and I felt, as always, that I was suddenly inside a TV commercial. There is a sense of unreality, of double exposure, living with someone whose face you have seen all your life on television, selling appliances, acting, chatting. Public and private, inner and outer grow confused, blur.

"Why don't you come with me?" I gave her a gentle pinch on the inside of her thigh. As of last February, that inner thigh was as taut as could be, thanks to surgery. Over the years what Arlene had not had lifted could never have fallen. In her own way, she had dealt gravity if not a death a body blow.

"You know I can't. You're sweet to ask. But I'm taping all next month. Then there's *The Gong Show*. I'm committed through March. How long do you think you'll be gone?"

"I don't know. I shouldn't think more than a week or two. Morgan's in a hurry. He wants the story before CBS."

"But *what* story? I mean, so the kid says he's god. Christ, between here and Carmel you can find a couple thousand freaks who say the same thing."

"But *why* is he saying it? And where's his money coming from? And then—why me? Why will he only talk to me?"

"You're gorgeous! And you're mine! So divine!" Arlene brayed what turned out to be the lyrics of a song that she had once sung with the band of Tommy Dorsey.

Arlene was well into the second chorus when the telephone by the pool rang. It was Earl Jr. "Well," he said accusingly, "Lenore has got the big C. They removed . . ."

At length and in gruesome detail, Earl Jr. described Lenore's trials and tribulations at Cedars-Sinai. I did my best to block out what he was saying. Arlene told me later that while I was holding the receiver with one hand, I was compulsively massaging my breasts with the other, searching for lumps.

I do recall thinking, everything's out of control: population, the weather, the cells of each and every body. Things seemed to be converging in a disastrous way. Arlene had had leukemia for six years. She was in a state of remission. We never mentioned the subject. But it was always there. Then there was me dead broke because there weren't any planes to test due to the recession or depression. There was. . . .

As I put down the receiver, I was suddenly glad that I was going to India, to Nepal, to meet an American who said he was Kalki, come to end the world because, I said out loud, "Things can't get any worse."

"What can't, Teddy?" Arlene frowned beneath her adhesive frownie.

"Life."

"Oh, that! You need a man. *I* need a man."

"That's the last thing I need."

"It's the first thing I need. But I'll settle for the second. And the third." Arlene chuckled, as she pulled off her bra, pulled down her pants. Not a scar anywhere on that God knows how old yet still trim brown body.

With a languorous sigh, Arlene spread her legs, as though tempting the sun to rape her. Then she went to sleep in full view of the Mexican maid who was preparing the vegetable and nut salad we always had for lunch. As the maid stared at us through the kitchen window, there was no expression at all on her heavy Aztec face. But then she was used to seeing Arlene in the nude. Arlene liked people to see her with no clothes on. She even liked people to watch her make love because "Let's face it, sex is one of the few things I do really well now that my golf game has gone to pieces."

Arlene had had no life except in public and on camera. Was I attracted to her sexually? Yes. Most people were. "Thousands have tried," she used to say with a wicked grin, "and none was ever allowed to fail!"

TWO

1

MORGAN DAVIES TOOK ME TO THE AIRPORT IN HIS CHAUFFEUR-driven limousine. "Part of my contract," he said proudly. He was always competing with Clay Felker. I never knew why.

But Morgan had been generous to me. I was solvent. I was also puzzled. "I still haven't a clue about Kalki." Whenever in doubt, be honest. You will not be believed.

"I thought you paid a visit to that ashcan on Santa Monica Boulevard."

"Ashram. Yes. I spent a day there. They all believe he's god on earth. But I still don't know why."

"What about drugs?"

"I didn't see any. Or smell any."

I had found the whole experience puzzling. Kalki's disciples (or mandali, as they liked to be called) were absolutely convinced that the end of the world was at hand and that they must purify themselves not only through prayer but through abstention from meat, sex, alcohol and drugs in order to be reborn in the next cycle of the human race. The really holy ones would become Enlightened like the Buddha and achieve Nirvana, which is nothing at all.

"Does this really appeal to you?" I asked Neil, a former gym instructor. He had red hair on forearms that resembled a tarantula's legs. There were absolutely no vibes between us. We were seated in what had been the control room of the radio station. On the other side of a plate-glass window was a large studio from which symphony orchestras used to broadcast. Now the studio was filled with ordinary-looking men and women wearing gym clothes or blue jeans or bathing suits. Each sat in the yoga lotus position. A record of George Harrison playing the sitar provided background music. Foreground music was provided by a man in a yellow robe. He chanted in Sanskrit. I had the same discouraged feeling that I had experienced while attending an e s t meeting the year before.

"That's not the point." Neil offered me a vapid Scientological smile. "I mean it doesn't have to appeal to you. You're the one who's got to measure up, 'cause the show's over. That's why Kalki's here. This age of man is about to end. We gotta purify ourselves." Definitely not a religion of hope. But then, to be fair, Christianity was never exactly a barrel of monkeys when it came to the here and now.

Neil saw me to my car. "I sure envy you, getting to meet *him*," he said. I had told him about my mission.

"Any messages?" I asked, flashing a smile of Weissean fun.

But Neil won the round. "You can't send a message to *the* message." Then he gave me a white paper lotus. "This," he said, frowning, "is a symbol of our Lord Vishnu." I was fairly certain that he had learned the speech phonetically because key words like "symbol" had obviously not been explained to him. "Who was born of the lotus. When the lotus has come to all men, this world will end. There's also," he added in his own voice, "a number printed inside that leaf there. If your number's chosen, you can get a cash prize. So watch the papers. Cash prizes are being handed out from now on, until the end." I asked when that would be but Neil said that he had not been told.

Cultural note for future historians: The mood of most of the world last year was eschatological. Things were running down and entropy was on the warpath. Because of this prevailing mood, those sects that promised to save a few souls from the coming disaster were popular. That day in the ashram on Santa Monica Boulevard I decided that

Kalki was a sort of Hindu Jehovah's Witness. I was impressed by Neil's happiness, and certitude, and stupidity. Of such are made kingdoms of earth if not of heaven. Kalki was a shrewd operator.

At the airport Morgan kissed me on the lips. "I love you," he lied. "Beat CBS. That's all I want, Teddy." Morgan was not an ambitious man.

En route to Hawaii, there was a thump in the seat beside me. I had been joined by a tall, lean, elderly Indian—from India. He wore a dark pin-stripe suit. He gave me a big smile. The top row of his teeth were as white as only plastic can be. The bottom row were yellow and scraggly. The whites of the eyes were pale gold while the irises were dark bronze. Thanks to H.V. Weiss, I describe—and describe. Particularly important characters. Is this an important character in my narrative? Yes.

"No smoking." He spoke with a British accent.

"No smoking?" I did not catch his drift at first.

"This is the No Smoking area and they have put me in a Smoking area. I hope you don't mind." I said, no, I did not mind, assuming that he was mad, or lying, or both. The First Class section was entirely empty except for us. He had his choice of a dozen seats not next to mine.

"Allow me to introduce myself, Madame Ottinger. I am Dr. Ashok. My card." The card said *R.S. Ashok, Ph.D., Professor of Comparative Religion, Fairleigh Dickinson University.*

"How do you know me?" I asked, entirely out of vanity. I wanted him to say that he had caught me on *The Merv Griffin Show.* I wanted him to criticize me for praising Indira Gandhi. I would then be able to do thirty or forty minutes on birth control and on the need for drastic measures. This would get us halfway to Honolulu. I set him up. But then he set me down.

"I could say," the white and yellow teeth shone in the dark face, "that I recognized you because you are, very simply, the greatest aviatrix in the world. Or that I know your name because it is clearly marked on the small paper banner attached to the back of your seat. But I will tell you the truth. I am on this flight because our mutual friend Mr. Morgan Davies told me that *you* would be on this flight."

"Morgan brought me to the airport. He never mentioned you." When there is no doubt to be in, go straight to the point.

"Dear Morgan was not certain whether or not I could get a booking."

I said nothing about the empty First Class section.

"In any case, we have, if I may say so, similar missions. I, too, am in hot pursuit of the false Kalki."

"Why false?"

"Come now, my dear Madame Ottinger, surely you . . . well, to begin with you are not, I trust, a Hindu."

"No. I'm nothing."

"Which is to say you are *some*thing profound." He twinkled. "I am less so. I am a Hindu. A Brahmin. I belong to the highest of the four castes."

"Yes. I know. The Brahmins are the priests. Then comes the warrior class, and so on. I've done my reading." In the two weeks that I had spent reading the Upanishads and other Hindu holy texts, I had not come across a single line that I wanted to put in my logbook.

"Then you must have an inkling of the exquisiteness of my dilemma when, suddenly, out of the blue, a foreigner, a Westerner, a born Christian, a white man announces to the world that *he* is the final avatar of Vishnu."

"The final what?" In my reading I was still following the endless adventures of Rama and of Krishna . . . proto–comic strips that must have given pleasure to preliterary (not to mention pre–cathode tube) generations. Nothing ever really happens to these incarnations of Vishnu, except adventures. The Vishnu story is not like a human story. But then perhaps god stories are different from the other kind. Am I telling a god story? Wait.

"Avatar means a descendant . . . no, not a descendant, really, more like a reincarnation of Vishnu, who is *the* god."

"A drink or beverage before lunch?" An altogether too cute stewardess joined us. I ordered a Coca-Cola.

"Vodka on the rocks." Dr. Ashok gave me his gold-white smile. I did not take it. "You see, I am not really a good Hindu. I eat meat. I drink alcohol. Even so, I am forever a part of the eternal cycle. I also," he said, in exactly the same tone, "admire Arlene Wagstaff more than any other lady on television."

"Do you?" I was icy. "I'll tell her." I knew he wanted me to show surprise. To ask him how he knew that we were friends. To wonder just *what* he knew. But I was the Snow Queen. "Now, Dr. Ashok, tell me why you are so certain that J.J. Kelly is not the last incarnation of the god Vishnu."

Dr. Ashok's crest was if not fallen aslant. But he was game. He began to lecture me, a mean revenge. "To date, Vishnu has appeared on earth nine times. The last time was more than two thousand years ago, when he appeared among us as Gautama, a Nepalese prince. In due course, this prince understood everything and so was known to the world as The Enlightened One, or, in our language, the Buddha. You don't have Russian vodka, miss?"

"Only Smirnoff, sir."

Dr. Ashok sighed and drank Smirnoff. "The tenth incarnation of Vishnu will not take place until this cycle of creation is at an end. This present cycle is known as . . ."

"The age of Kali." I took pleasure in being able to quote from *Hindu Mythology* as easily as he. "Sometimes known as the age of iron," I added. Although I no longer menstruate quite as I did before, I occasionally feel something odd when my old time of the month is at hand. Is it an actual cramp? or just the memory, the shadow of a cramp? Whatever it is, I felt it with Dr. Ashok. In fact, I can never think of him without that spectral pain.

"Just so," Dr. Ashok hissed, more like a Japanese than an Indian. "In any case, the age of Kali has roughly one hundred and thirty-five thousand *more* years to run. Ergo. Ergo." Dr. Ashok liked those two syllables so much that he repeated them a third time, "Ergo, Mr. Kelly cannot be Kalki. He is *premature.*" For some reason that word so delighted him that he had a fit of the giggles which did not end until he inhaled vodka. Then he had a coughing fit. I smiled compassionately. And did nothing. I do that well.

"Sorry, my dear Madame Ottinger. I was overcome. Overwhelmed by your countryman's pretension."

"But aside from Kalki's being pre . . . ahead of schedule," I didn't want him choking again, "a lot of what he has been doing seems to fit the legend." I held up my copy of *Hindu Mythology.* "It says here that the last incarnation will be a white man on a horse."

"You have misread the text." Dr. Ashok took his first round. "It will be a man of no known color who will mount a white horse. Then Kalki will draw his sword . . ." Dr. Ashok shut his eyes. He seemed unnaturally pleased at the prospect. "The sword will blaze like a comet and the wicked will be destroyed and the dark age of Kali will be at an end while the dread Yama—that is, death—will reign until the human race has begun a new cycle, a new golden age in which the Brahmins have regained their original ascendancy and purity has been restored. Naturally, I am telescoping all this for you in order to help you in your—uh, researches."

"Whenever I am told something that I already know, I feel secure. For this renewed sense of security, I am in your debt, Dr. Ashok." This time no bucket plumbed the well of insincerity. I made no effort to be pleasant. I had never been as suspicious of anyone as I was of Dr. Ashok on that flight to India. Everything about him was wrong. He knew too much; also, too little.

Dr. Ashok hummed what I took to be a mantra of some sort. He was getting drunk. "You probably," he said at last, "want to know why I am returning to India."

"Actually, I would never have asked."

"You are well-bred. I can tell." Dr. Ashok's eyes strayed to my breasts. I held my breath. "I am on leave of absence from the university. A certain government is interested in Mr. Kelly. They asked me to find out what I could."

"Whether or not he is an incarnation of Vishnu?"

"Good heavens, no! Perish the thought." He was now wolfing down those too dry, too salty peanuts peculiar only to commercial aircraft. "I don't for one moment accept his claim. Let us be logical. Vishnu would *never* return as a *white* man." Dr. Ashok's voice was freighted (H.V. Weiss verb) with emotion. For an instant I almost changed my policy; was almost compassionate as I imagined Dr. Ashok trying to hail a taxicab in Atlanta. But not even the thought that he might have been a victim of Jim Crow appeased me. I practiced dynamic tension with my thighs.

"If Vishnu should return he would be a Brahmin, like me. No. No," Dr. Ashok laughed, a bit crazily. *"I'm* not Kalki."

"I didn't think you were. You have no white horse." I offered him a little joke. Had he been forced to ride in the back of a bus? Use lavatories marked COLORED?

But Dr. Ashok was not listening. "The Hindu religion is being viciously, perhaps criminally, exploited by an ex-American soldier, deeply involved in the sale of narcotics."

"He *sells* drugs?" This was new. I had been reasonably convinced that the Kalki ashram on Santa Monica Boulevard was clean as the Weissean whistle. Since I am a nonsmoker of anything, a whiff of pot on those depressing premises would have set my inner alarm bell tolling.

"He sells ganja, as they call hashish in Nepal. Also, cocaine, opium and white heroin . . . so much stronger than Mexican heroin, popularly known as 'brown sugar.' After all, your Mr. Kelly . . ."

"Not mine, Dr. Ashok."

". . . began his career in the Medical Corps of the American army in Vietnam, the traditional launching pad for many a would-be entrepreneur of drugs."

"Name one other?" From the beginning, I found it impossible to take Dr. Ashok seriously. He did not ring true, to continue with that inner bell of mine. But I could not get him to answer questions, offer proofs. He was now hurling rhetorical questions at me, much the worst kind.

"Why has the unsavory Mr. Kelly surfaced now? Where was he during that dark period from 1968 to date? And did you know that almost four years before your superb armies withdrew in moral triumph from Vietnam, the banner of the great American Republic carried reverently in the arms of that wily diplomat and patriot for all seasons, your Ambassador Martin, Sergeant and Specialist with a superior Five rating James Joseph Kelly vanished into the bush. And are you aware that after eight years in the wilderness, as your so clever holy book would have it . . ."

"Not *my* holy book, Dr. Ashok. Pascal, yes. Jesus, no."

But Dr. Ashok had no interest in hooking his sentences onto anything anyone else might say. He was a self-starter. ". . . such a good book, too!" Dr. Ashok smiled sweetly, softly, sincerely, referring, I suppose, not to Pascal's *Pensées* but to the New Testament of somber memory. "In any case, your now *Mr.* Kelly appeared one day at the Blue Moon Tea House in Katmandu and announced to the comatose inmates that he was Kalki. Dear Madame Ottinger, I ask you—why?"

This rhetorical question seemed to call for a brief answer or sound, which I made: "A nut?"

"Yes." Not understanding me, Dr. Ashok handed over his last package of dry salted peanuts.

"No. I meant crazy."

Dr. Ashok took back the nuts. I suddenly realized that his kinky gray hair was not his at all but a wig. I remember thinking that men are more vain than women. We keep up appearances in order to survive. They do it to prevail. Yet why was I shocked when I read that John Wayne had had his face lifted? More to the point, why am I now asking rhetorical questions like Dr. Ashok? Confusion.

"There is a long tradition of holy madmen, and it is quite possible that he is mad. But the overriding question, dear lady, is to what purpose, and to whose benefit?"

There was a long pause. He stared at me. The golden eyes narrowed. Actually, they did not really narrow. I keep falling into Weissisms. Dr. Ashok's eyes had a tendency to pop whenever he wanted to rape your attention. The eyes were now as round as those Spanish gold doubloons that were found by two surfers north of Trancas last year. The doubloons turned out to be counterfeit. The surfers were for real.

I was being forced to support the monologue with a line or two. "Since I have no way of knowing, why ask me?" I managed a snapping sound.

"Who most resembles the pseudo-Kalki?"

"The true Kalki." I thought that pretty good. I could also see that I was beginning to get on Dr. Ashok's nerves almost as much as he was getting on mine.

"The true Kalki is thousands of years in the future. They are separated by a wall of time. And there is something that likes a wall, as your great poet Edgar Snow once wrote." Dr. Ashok suffered from a mild form of metaphasis. He made Spoonerisms. "No, I see your Mr. Kelly as a political pawn . . ."

"A moment ago you had him in the drug business."

"Put the two together!" Dr. Ashok clapped his hands. "Now we begin to see a picture emerge. Should a foreign power want to undermine the West, what better way than to corrupt and weaken the citizens with drugs? What better way than to offer them a false religion which tells them that the end of the world is at hand? After all, who would ever enlist in your proud military services if he was stoned?"

"Who would if he was not?" As a test pilot, I had worked with the American Air Force for nearly ten years and I was confident that the United States could not win a war against anyone. Between alcoholism and incompetence, the American military was out of the running. Luckily, the Russians were in the same fix. Few people understood that for thirty years the balance of power had been maintained between East and West not by nuclear weapons but by vodka. Needless to say, I was not about to pass on any of this to a civilian with a curly gray wig.

Dr. Ashok ignored my aside. "A society weakened by drugs and by a false belief in the world's magical end could not protect itself against communism. The pseudo-Kalki is an agent for . . ." Dr. Ashok stopped. "We must find out, dear lady. Is it Russia, China, Vietnam or Korea?"

"Or is it Cuba? The CIA . . .?"

At that moment the 747 started to shiver and yaw, and the captain's voice on the intercom said, "Well, folks, we've just hit a bit of Clear Air Turbulence up here and the seat-belt sign has just gone on and so will all flight personnel return to their seats."

The plane lurched from side to side. I was scared to death. I always am when someone else is flying. But Dr. Ashok kept right on drinking; and never spilled a drop. He also continued to explain, and explain. He suspected that Kelly was a Soviet agent. He thought it suspicious that Kelly should be in Nepal, a buffer state between the Soviet's enemy China and the Soviet's supposed friend India. He likened Kelly to the Reverend Sun Moon, another messiah at work in the United States. The Reverend Sun Moon was thought to be paid for by the government of South Korea which was paid for by the American Congress whose members, in turn, were given kickbacks by the South Koreans.

Dr. Ashok was one of those people who like to relate anything to everything. I am the opposite. I only recognize demonstrable connections. On the other hand, I have a suspicious nature. I knew that Dr. Ashok had been, somehow, assigned to me. I assumed that he intended to use me to get information about Kalki. From the beginning, let me state for the record, I was certain that he was an agent of the CIA. Who else would wear such an obvious wig?

2

I WAS EXHAUSTED UPON ARRIVAL IN NEW DELHI. THOROUGHLY DISORI-
ented (or, to be exact, disoccidented), I drove with Dr. Ashok from the
airport to the hotel. The narrow streets were crowded with dark simian
people. Dr. Ashok kept waving to them, as if he was the Dalai Lama.
The moon was still bright in the western sky. The dawn was pale pink.
The air smelled of wood smoke, curry, shit. If a psychedelic trip in any
way resembles common report, New Delhi qualified as one.

There were pink flamingos on the pale green lawn of the Oberoi
Intercontinental (née Hilton) Hotel. Pink from the rising sun's colors?
or was I just hallucinating and there were no flamingos, pink or otherwise? or lawn?

I went straight to my room where I found four beautiful girls in saris.
They were just standing there, giggling, doing nothing. I suppose that
they were maids, or foreign agents, or figments of my imagination. I
shooed them out of the room. Fell into bed, fully clothed. Slept.

Six hours later the telephone beside the bed rang. I held the receiver
over my head. From far away I heard the voice of an American girl
pronounce what seemed to me to be the following nonsensical syllables:
"Mrs. Ottinger? This is Lakshmi."

I was still trapped within a nightmare of pink flamingos, Dr. Ashok's
yellow-white teeth, and Arlene standing beside the gall bladder–shaped
pool. Arlene was wearing Dr. Ashok's teeth around her neck and
nothing else except the Jedda Coffee listless housewife's neurotic
frown. As the ringing of the telephone began, one of the flamingos
curled its neck and became a telephone. Nervously, I held the
flamingo's beak to my ear. The flamingo whispered: "I am the wife of
Kalki. I am downstairs in the lobby."

"Don't get too near those flamingos," I said. "They can be dangerous." Then I woke up; canceled the reference to the flamingos; told
the wife of Kalki that I would join her as soon as I had showered and

dressed. Literally. That is, I wore a dress. I was in too fragile and distraught a mood to play butch. I felt as if I had the dreamer's power to walk through walls.

In the lobby, beneath a potted palm, a blond American girl in a purple sari stood, holding a white lotus in one hand. A real lotus. No lucky number inside. Behind the girl a vitrine displayed ugly necklaces of brass.

As I stepped out of the elevator, she came toward me. When I put out my hand, she made a steeple with her hands, and bowed. This was my first experience with the Hindu pranam, or greeting. I just bowed.

"Pranam," said Lakshmi.

"Hello," said I.

"Sit down, Mrs. Ottinger."

"Thank you . . . Mrs. Kalki?"

"Call me Lakshmi."

"Call me Teddy."

We sat side by side on a sofa. Most of the guests were at lunch. The lobby was self-consciously exotic: Benares brass, bright ceramic tiles, potted plants whose fronds rustled in the arctic air of a malfunctioning air-conditioning unit. In a decade of flying at great speeds between one point and another, I had got to know most of the world's international hotels and I had come to hate the way in which they always managed to strike an unholy balance between American discomfort, as prescribed by St. Conrad, and whatever the hideous local color required. The Oberoi Intercontinental in New Delhi was par for the course.

Strangely enough, despite all my travel, as of last year I had never been to Paris, the one city that most excited my imagination. I could have gone several times, en route to somewhere else. But I thought, no. I'll wait until I can go there when I am in love. Last summer I finally made the trip. But I am skipping ahead. Enough to say that I was sufficiently romantic to want to see Paris not through the windows of a Hilton Hotel, but through the eyes of a lover. I am sure that in a previous incarnation I was French. At USC I got a prize for a translation that I had made of the first two chapters of *l'Homme qui rit.* What would my life have been like if I had taken my master's degree not in engineering but in French literature? if I had not married Earl Jr.? if I had . . . been someone else, obviously. *"Console-toi, tu ne me chercherais pas si tu ne m'avais trouvé."* Pascal again: Console yourself, you would not . . . never? have looked for me if you had not found me. I would never have been this "hateful" self (his word, not mine), if that self had not found me.

Lakshmi smiled. She was shy, or seemed to be. "Did you," she asked unexpectedly, "bring your pilot's license?"

I was surprised. "Yes. But I'm here as a journalist, not . . ."

"Can you fly a Learjet?"

"Of course. But I'm here to interview your husband."

"Of course." Lakshmi was a slender version of the young Grace Kelly who haunts *The Late Show*. "But Kalki would like you to help him. As a pilot . . ."

"God needs help?" My inflection was Arlene's, doing ethnic. "I'm sorry. I hope that wasn't tactless." From the beginning, I found Lakshmi attractive, as a woman and as . . . Lakshmi.

The smile did not waver. "God requires many things of us, Teddy. We've just bought a Learjet. It's here at the airport. I came down yesterday from Katmandu to claim it. But the pilot's got dysentery. And the copilot's incompetent. It's really a godsend, your being here. You will help us, won't you? You'll fly the *Garuda*. Please."

"I'm easily persuaded." By a beautiful girl, I said to myself. "What is the *Garuda*?"

"The original Garuda was a great bird on whose back the god Vishnu used to fly. I thought we should give the same name to the Learjet. I hope you'll like us."

Before I could declare myself a devotee, we were interrupted by Dr. Ashok. Smiling his villain's smile, he came toward us, wig askew.

"Madame Ottinger! You are awake! And you have found each other!" Dr. Ashok threw exclamation marks at us; plainly, he was school of Weiss. I was more than ever convinced that he was some sort of government agent. For one thing, he had recognized Lakshmi. Yet I had not come across a single mention of her in the press, much less a photograph.

To my astonishment and Lakshmi's chagrin, Dr. Ashok started to drop slowly and creakily to his knees.

"Stop!" Lakshmi's low voice was very hard; except of course no sound has any tactile qualities outside H.V.W. land.

With an arthritic crackle, Dr. Ashok locked his knees; began a slow and no doubt painful ascent, all the while intoning: "Pranam, oh Queen of heaven. Oh . . ."

"There will be time enough for that in Vaikuntha."

Vaikuntha is the heaven where the god Vishnu and his wife Lakshmi live, according to the invaluable *Hindu Mythology.*

Did I take any of this seriously at the time? No. For one thing, I was suffering from both jet lag and culture shock. For another, I had never had the slightest interest in Christ (Scientist or magician), Mohammed, Moses or any of the other beloved gods of the human race. I won an exchange in class with the head of the French Department at USC. I had said that Descartes had failed to establish the existence of god. *Je pense, donc je suis* is not a truth but an aside. Descartes wanted to establish a causal proof for god's existence. He does this by arguing that since man is finite and god infinite, how could someone finite imagine the infinite if the infinite (god) was not already *there?* Easily. We have no experience of eternity but we have no difficulty in imagining it, true or false? I like only what is demonstrable. For instance, if Amelia Earhart had not existed, I would have stayed on the ground and taught philosophy.

"I go to Katmandu, oh ocean-born, oh mother of the world. There I shall attend your consort who is imperishable, who is endless, who sleeps on water . . ."

Despite our restlessness, Dr. Ashok managed to recite quite a few of the several thousand titles of the goddess Lakshmi and of the god Vishnu, whose last reincarnation was thought (by some but not by me) to have occurred some thirty-five years earlier when J.J. Kelly was born in the Irish district on the Industrial Canal near Lake Pontchartrain just outside the greater New Orleans area.

"All are welcome, Dr. Ashok." Lakshmi gave a brisk nod, ending the conversation in the Hindu style. With every appearance of true worship, Dr. Ashok backed away, head down. I remember thinking that if he was acting, he was doing a dismally good job.

"He is your enemy." Lakshmi spoke casually.

"Yours, too, I would guess."

But Lakshmi did not answer. Instead she stared at me for what seemed a long time. My face felt hot. I must have blushed, something rare with me. Then she said, "Let's look at the people." An odd way,

I thought, of saying, "Let's go for a walk." But then she was a deity. Or thought she was one. The same thing? *Je pense. . . .*

The hour or two that Lakshmi and I walked about the old quarter of New Delhi determined my future. I fell in love with her. I am susceptible. Arlene thought me promiscuous. I am not. Except in the mind. I stay out of bed as much as possible. I *may* be frigid. Certainly I like essence more than substance.

Lakshmi talked very little, and what she said was never very interesting. I did not care. I was euphoric. I liked best her silences. Those were the moments when we really got through to one another. My father said that Amelia was like that, silent for long intervals.

We visited a Hindu temple where only monkeys lived. The monkeys were extremely intelligent, and very bad-tempered. A guardian at the main entrance gave us each a stick. "They bad monkeys. Bite. You hit, missy." He grinned, showing teeth every bit as dangerous as monkey fangs.

Lakshmi led me through a small courtyard into a roofless stone chapel where each inch of wall space had been covered with intricate carvings. The monkeys were everywhere. They sat in circles. They swung from ruined windows to the ground and back again. They watched us carefully. Some held out their hands for food. Others pulled at our clothes. Only when threatened with sticks did they back off. They chattered not at us but among themselves. This was disquieting. They were hostile, self-aggrandizing.

"Here I am." With the lotus, Lakshmi touched a carving of a smiling girl, holding a lotus, too. "I was born of the sea." The rest of the carving was hard to make out beneath the bat-droppings and the lichen.

"Like Venus. You look like Botticelli's Venus."

"Perhaps I inspired him, too." Lakshmi gave me a Botticelli smile. Was she serious? I could not tell. She tapped the lotus in the carving's hand with the lotus in her own hand. As the lotuses touched, I half-expected to see a sunbeam or bolt of lightning or whatever it was that entered the Virgin Mary's ear on a certain interesting occasion. In my own skeptical way, I was getting in the mood.

Suddenly a large female monkey dropped down from the ceiling. She clutched a sick-looking gray-pink baby in her arms. Chattering shrilly, she pushed the baby toward Lakshmi who, gently, touched the baby with the lotus. The monkey was silent. The baby stirred. Then—with a leap upwards—they were gone.

Impressed, I asked the sort of question that one could only ask in a state of culture shock, jet lag, love: "Are you really a goddess?"

"Are you really surprised?"

"I'm not religious. I enjoy proofs of god. They can be fun." I started to quote Descartes but thought better of it. Any mention of my French masters used to send Arlene straight to the TV or "family" room, as the realtors call it, complete with "wet bar."

"I don't think we're very good at proofs." With her stick, Lakshmi tried to clean the figure of a four-armed god. "And I don't think we're exactly fun."

"What are you?"

"Queen of heaven." At least this was the sort of out-of-sync day on which statements like that could be made and not seem entirely loony. The setting helped. "And if you accept us . . ." Lakshmi paused, smiled. The eyes were palest hazel, like those of the Botticelli Venus.

"What happens?

"We will admit you to Vaikuntha when the age of Kali ends." Lakshmi sounded like Arlene promising to come up with a pair of tickets for *The Hollywood Squares.*

"When does the age of Kali end?" I remembered to be the inquiring reporter. I was also genuinely curious. Who would not be?

"When it is time."

All the monkeys in the immediate vicinity were staring at us. Had the word spread that a goddess was on the premises? They were unnaturally silent. I felt uneasy.

Lakshmi had finally cleared the carving that she had been scraping at with her stick. "There he is—Vishnu." I saw the outline of a young man with four arms. He wore a crown. "In one hand he holds a conch shell. See?"

I scraped at the dirt with my stick. "Yes. Why a conch shell?"

"When Vishnu appeared on earth the eighth time, he was called Krishna. At that time there was a demon who lived in the sea, inside that shell. Krishna killed him." Lakshmi pointed to a round object in another hand. "That is the quoit, a weapon. The next hand holds a club. And—see? The last hand holds a lotus, as I do."

"Why the lotus?"

"When Vishnu lay sleeping upon the waters—from which I come, from which all of us on what is now this earth come—a lotus grew from his navel. And the lotus gave birth to Brahma. And Brahma created the world."

This was all a bit rich for somebody acquainted not only with the mild confusions of Mary Baker Eddy but with the seventeenth- and eighteenth-century notions of deity as an extension of mathematics. At USC I had mastered that cycloid which so obsessed Galileo, Descartes, Pascal. Looking back, I realize that the pure mathematics which had brought Descartes to god had brought me to engineering. "I thought Vishnu was god."

"Everything is god. Nothing is god."

Since I was in love with her, I disguised impatience. I had a job to do. "How," I asked helpfully, "did the universe start?"

"There was—before time—a supreme god called Prajapati. He had —and he has—three aspects. Brahma, the creator. Vishnu, the pre-server . . ."

"Where is Brahma these days?" I knew the answer. But I wanted to hear what she would say. Any variant on *Hindu Mythology* might be a clue.

"He sleeps. He will not awaken until it is time to re-create the world."

"And the third god?"

"The third aspect of the one god is Siva, the destroyer." Lakshmi frowned. "There are those who would put him higher than Vishnu."

"So where is Siva now?"

"Here . . . there . . . everywhere. Always waiting."

"For what?" I wished that I had had time to wash my hair before our outing.

But Lakshmi did not answer. Together we crossed the ruined court-yard. In silence, the monkeys watched us; among them, the mother monkey. As we passed her, she stared up at Lakshmi with agate eyes. The baby's eyes were shut. I could not tell if it was dead or sleeping.

Lakshmi reached out and touched the large monkey's head. I could almost feel the long tusks closing on that white hand. To my surprise, nothing happened. "They are our friends," said Lakshmi. "When Vishnu appeared on earth as Rama, he married Sita . . . an earlier incarnation of me. When the demon-king Ravana kidnapped Sita, there was a great war between Rama and Ravana. In the war the monkeys fought side by side with Rama, and the demon-king was destroyed, as he always is. Since that time the monkeys have loved us, and we have loved them." Well, Mary Baker Eddy thought that pain, disease, old age and death were "errors."

We were now outside the temple. Everything was so totally unreal that I gave a tip to what I thought was a beggar but turned out to be a very angry monkey with yellow fangs and eyes like Dr. Ashok's. Then, having made that mistake and just barely avoided getting my leg bitten, I used my stick on what I thought was a particularly vicious-looking monkey only to realize, too late, that it was a beggar with no legs.

Lakshmi got us into a taxicab before we were lynched by an angry group of men and monkeys or, rather, two angry groups since the monkeys did not like the people thereabouts any more than the people liked the monkeys.

I was not loved by either faction that strange day.

3

THE NEXT MORNING LAKSHMI AND I DROVE OUT TO THE NEW DELHI airport, where, miraculously, she was able to get me checked out by the authorities in less than an hour. "I have influence," she said. And she did. We were then driven by jeep across rutted runways to the area where private planes were kept and serviced.

A dozen mandali were waiting for us. Most were white Americans. They looked ordinary. Not a pair of wild-eyes among them. Yet they bowed low to Lakshmi. Although she was careful to introduce me to each of the mandali, I did not register a single name. I was interested only in the airport, in the maintenance crew, in the cows that had strolled, somehow, past the wire fence and onto the runway.

As a pilot, I made a fuss about cows on the runways. I was ignored.

Several thousand years ago India was suffering (as usual) from over-population. Question in the rulers' minds: to eat the cows or to use them for agriculture? Agriculture won. The cow was made sacred. No one could harm a cow, much less eat one. The cow was the original tractor. The result? too many people plus too many cows. Having achieved the worst of all bad worlds, India was a macrocosm of what had gone wrong with the human race as of last February.

While the indolent and unbelievably dirty maintenance crew lounged about, I went over the *Garuda* with H.V.W.'s fine-tooth comb and so discovered beneath a tarpaulin in the baggage compartment what looked to be a set of batteries but was, in fact, a time bomb.

I've always been fascinated by electrical devices of any kind, including those intended to trigger explosives. This was a sophisticated piece of work and, plainly, not of Indian manufacture. I turned to the crew chief, a small thick man with a murderer's face. Yes, there is such a thing as a murderer's face. Look in any mirror. I turned my flashlight on him. Made him blink. "What's this?" I held out the bomb case. Luckily, I was too frightened to be afraid. This sometimes happens in the air, during an emergency.

"Battery," he said. "Extra battery. Very useful. No extra parts in Katmandu. Very expensive."

"I don't think we'll need it." I smiled. "You can have it." I offered him the bomb.

"No, no." He was terrified, proving that he was in some way an accomplice. *"Need* battery," he said, backing away.

"Battery go boom-boom," I said. I made as if to throw the mechanism at him. With a yell, he hightailed it out of that baggage compartment, and all our lives.

I set to work. Aware that the least mistake would translate us all into the polluted haze over New Delhi, I detached the triggering mechanism. Obviously, I did not make a mistake. I kept my mind entirely on the work at hand . . . except for Amelia. When I am in a tight spot, I think of Amelia taking off from Lae, New Guinea. I think of her navigator, Fred Noonan; he is in the back of the plane, drunk. I invent dialogue for them. The crash or the secret landing is only a few hours away. Sometimes I think I *know* what she said, what he replied. I think she crashed the plane deliberately. She had more guts than I.

As I took the bomb off the plane, Lakshmi said, "We're late." I was startled to see that it had taken me an hour to dewire and defuse the mechanism. Time can stop.

"I'm sorry." I was cool. "There was a problem. It's solved now." Not wanting to alarm them, I left it at that.

The flight crew was watching me with H.V.W. impassive faces. I went over to a rusty tin barrel filled with monsoon rain water, and let the bomb sink to the bottom. I then drank a bottle of sickly-sweet orange soda. My hands were shaking now. Lakshmi looked at me curiously. She knew something was wrong. But asked no questions.

Shortly after noon, we were airborne.

I had not been in a Learjet for over a year and though it is not my favorite aircraft, I was happy to be forty-five thousand feet above those fierce monkeys, those ambling cows, those starving people. Antoine de Saint-Exupéry wrote, somewhere, that the natural aviator is a fascist. This is not, literally, true but I know what he means. When you fly alone, you are no longer a part of the human race. You are outside, above, beyond. Only you and the cosmos exist. Or so you think. I can see how easy it must be for a flier to drop a bomb. There is nothing, really, beneath you except the villain gravity. All that matters to the flier is the delicate blue-black film through which he peeks at a cosmos that does not appear to be peeking back.

I was delighted to see the Himalayas, steaming like dry ice in the sun. At such moments I always wished I could capture for others what it is like to be . . . well, wind, sand and stars; and quasars, too; and other suns. But I am just a natural flier, no more. From all accounts, de Saint-Exupéry was not only not a natural flier, he was a lousy pilot who was bound to crack up, and did. But he knew what it was like to decorate with words the cosmos.

Lakshmi joined me in the copilot's seat. She wanted to know what had delayed our take-off. I told her. I asked if this was the first time that there had been an attempt on her life, or on Kalki's.

"Yes, it is the first time." Lakshmi sounded serene. "But according to Kalki, there will be other attempts." Although Lakshmi was smiling, I saw that the lotus had withered in her clenched fist. I asked her who she thought had put the bomb on the plane. She shrugged. "As the age of Kali ends, there will be horrors." She said no more.

I asked why I had read nothing about her in any of the stories of Kalki.

Lakshmi was amused. "Because I'm one of the revelations."

"When are you due to be revealed?"

"Very soon."

As quickly as I could, I got her from vague essence to homely substance. "Where did you first meet Kalki?"

"When we emerged from the sea together, on the blossom of the lotus." I turned to look at her, and caught her smiling at me, an impish little girl smile; quickly, she put on her grave goddess look.

"I was thinking more of the here and now . . ."

"New Year's Eve, 1970. In Chicago." Lakshmi was startlingly brisk. "I went to a party at the Drake Hotel. I was with a boy that I thought I wanted to marry."

"Were you from Chicago?"

"No. Silver Spring, Maryland. My father was a lobbyist in Washington. For the Cuban sugar interests. But then Castro took over Cuba, and that was that. Luckily, there was enough money to send me through American University. Then I had two years at the University of Chicago. I was a graduate student. Nuclear physics. But when I met Kalki at the Drake, that was that."

"You quit school."

"I quit everything. I haven't seen my family since. I've had no connection with anyone from my old life, except Geraldine O'Connor. You met her at the airport. We've known each other forever. Kalki likes her, too. She was at American University, too. But then she transferred to M.I.T. She . . ."

I broke in, politely. I was not interested in Geraldine O'Connor, whom I had not noticed at the New Delhi airport. "What was your real name?" I was excited. I had never really thought that I would be able to find out anything useful for the *Sun.* Now I had actually beaten CBS to the (in Weissean lingo) punch. I had met Kalki's unknown wife.

"I was christened Doris. Doris Pannicker. Two *n*'s. One *c.* "

"So you weren't really born of the sea . . ."

"The first time, yes. But this last time was a mess. By Caesarean section. My mother never forgave me."

"Did you marry Kalki in Chicago?"

But the easygoing Doris Pannicker was suddenly replaced by

Lakshmi, queen of heaven. "You must ask him," she said. She stood up. "I want you to meet the others."

One by one, the mandali came and sat beside me in the cockpit. They were all fairly uninteresting except for Geraldine O'Connor, Lakshmi's particular friend. Geraldine had wiry red hair, freckled skin, a good figure.

Geraldine told me that she had taught biochemistry. She also had a doctorate in biophysics. She had done original research. In genetics. "I was about to get tenure at M.I.T. when I quit, and joined Kalki."

Kalki was plainly tolerant of Woman Scientist. I wondered what sort of degree *he* had got from Tulane. Had he taken a course in comparative religion? From someone like Dr. Ashok? Did he know Dr. Ashok? My mind was busy making links out of not much.

I asked Geraldine how M.I.T. had responded to her departure. She laughed. A nice sound. "To abandon tenure? That's unheard of. I am now a non-person in the university world. But then all of that is kal."

"Is what?"

"Kal is the Hindu word for yesterday. Kal is also the Hindu word for tomorrow."

This jibed nicely with the impression that I had been getting of Hindu culture. "Kal explains why they have neither history nor science. Everything happens in the present, or not at all."

Geraldine replied with the phrase that sums up the thousand names of the god Vishnu who pervades the entire universe: "Sahasra-nama."

I liked Geraldine. I loved Lakshmi. I feared the unknown Kalki.

Katmandu airport is one of the world's worst airports. But we were lucky. Visibility was good. No stuffed cloud broke us up on descent. Amelia once told my father that when it came to flying she feared neither mountains nor water, only jungle. "To crash in an African jungle!" she shuddered. "And survive . . ." Yet water claimed her. Or was it a desert island?

I taxied to a stop. A half-dozen jeeps containing soldiers were waiting for us on the runway. The soldiers had machine guns at the ready. As we disembarked, they surrounded the plane.

Lakshmi greeted the senior officer. He saluted her. Then, most respectfully, he showed Lakshmi, Geraldine and me into an old Cadillac. The other mandali were taken away in a bus.

"We've booked you into the Ananda Hotel," said Lakshmi.

"It's where all the spies stay." Geraldine grinned. "You'll love it."

I wondered what she meant. Was I thought of as a spy or double agent? I was, of course. But then doubleness, literally, duplicity *(dupli-cité, duplicitatem)* is a part of journalism, according to Morgan Davies. And a half of life.

Because of our police escort, we did not have to go through the usual formalities of entering a country. We were treated like royalty. Also, like prisoners.

Lakshmi said that she would arrange for me to meet Kalki the next day.

Geraldine pointed out the sights of Katmandu, as seen from the airport road. The principal monument was to—whom else? Conrad Hilton.

THREE

1

I SIGNED THE ANANDA HOTEL REGISTER. THE CLERK KISSED MY HAND. He was Hungarian. He gave me a cable from Morgan Davies, which read: BEAT CCC LOVMRAM. I interpreted this as "Beat CBS. Love, Morgan." I did not have much time.

The lobby was crowded with all sorts of people, mostly men, many of them Caucasian, none of them tourists. Business was the order of that Himalayan day. Beneath a gilt-framed photograph of the fat young man who was the current king of Nepal stood my non-Caucasian nemesis. "Welcome to Katmandu!" Firmly, Dr. Ashok shook my so recently kissed hand. The wig appeared to rest upon his eyebrows. The effect was cretinous. He radiated treachery.

"How did you get here so fast?"

"Magic carpet, dear Madame Ottinger. So much faster than the *Garuda* and—dare I say it?—so much safer."

Obviously Dr. Ashok had known about the bomb. Did he put it there? I was now certain that he was a CIA agent. I was also certain that he found me sexually attractive. I smiled at him. A woman instinctively forgives a good deal in a man who is sexually attracted to her (*pace*, Greer, Millett, Figes). On the other hand, attempted murder is not among those things instinctively forgiven except by the advanced masochist. I would rather give than receive pain.

"We are," said Dr. Ashok, "surrounded by secret agents."

"You fit in nicely," I said. And he did. The Chinese agents all wore steel-rimmed spectacles. The Russian agents looked like American businessmen, as did the American businessmen, pursuing the glittering dollar even here at the end and the top of the world. The CIA was represented by Dr. Ashok, who invited me to lunch. He knew Katmandu well, he told me. "You will need some local color for the *Sun.*"

As we walked to a restaurant in the old city, I noticed that there was smog, even here. But the climate was bracing. Despite the altitude, there is never snow in Katmandu. Had it not been for the smog, we could have seen the high Himalayas beyond the city. In those mountains, there is only snow, ice.

I enjoyed the ancient part of the city. I intended to take notes as we walked, but there was too much to see. Temples, statues, pagodas, round altars to the Buddha called stupas. Colors vivid, mostly scarlet and saffron. Smells pungent, cinnamon and sandalwood. Shapes intricate. . . .

The people were tall, pale-skinned and slant-eyed; in appearance they were more Chinese than Indian. Every last one of them was either beginning, in the middle of, or ending a bad cold. Much hacking, spitting. I wished that I had allowed Arlene's doctor to give me a swine-flu shot.

Dr. Ashok stopped in front of a building made of dark wood. Heavy carved beams supported a high peaked roof covered with yellow tiles. Wooden lattices covered small windows. Suddenly the lattices of a second-floor window were thrown open. A small girl leaned out, screaming. The more she screamed, the more delighted was not only Dr. Ashok but the Nepalese passerby. Then adult arms were wrapped about the child, and she vanished from view.

"A goddess," said Dr. Ashok. "When they find one, they lock her up for life in that palace. The previous goddess dropped her body some while ago, and it's taken them all this time to discover her new form. Naturally, the reincarnation is a bit distressed at first."

"How can they tell that the child's a goddess?"

"Astrological signs. Physical signs. Oh, our . . . their priests are very good at that sort of thing. Nepalese gods are always, as you say, kosher, unlike certain self-proclaimed gods." Dr. Ashok chuckled. What is the difference, I once asked H.V. Weiss, between a chuckle and a laugh? Between a giggle and a simper? Between. . . . It was no use. Despite Weiss's enrollment in the current school of French structuralists, he knew nothing about words. But then very few professional theorists of language are at home with language. I noticed this phenomenon when I heard Noah Chomsky lecture. He found it difficult to express himself in words. Perhaps he knew too much about them to want to put them to work.

The Blue Moon Tea House was a series of small dirty dining rooms, separated from one another by glass-beaded curtains. The clientele was mostly Western hippies (the old word—was there a new one?) or Asiatics pretending to be Americans gone native in Asia.

"There used to be many more of these types." Dr. Ashok indicated a half-dozen stoned Americans who were got up in sixties costumes. Katmandu was like a science fiction time-warp, a bit of preserved American time. "Fortunately, the Nepalese Government has been taking a hard line—well, a *harder* line on drugs. The riffraff are mostly gone. Or transformed like your Mr. Kelly."

We were served a watery vegetable soup filled with curry. There were also slices of fried bread. A truly unpleasant meal. We drank beer. "What," asked Dr. Ashok, "is your personal impression of Doris Pannicker?"

"You mean Lakshmi? She's nice. She's intelligent. She believes Kalki is god. They all do."

"I am, my dear Madame Ottinger, going to level with you. I am not a professor at Fairleigh Dickinson University in New Jersey. That is my cover, as we say. Actually, I am a special agent of the Central Intelligence Agency of the United States Government. Sometimes known as The Company. My credentials." Under the table, Dr. Ashok flashed what could have been any document with a photograph of himself attached. For the first time, I suspected that he was *not* with the CIA.

"I liked your first cover, Dr. Ashok, so much better than this one."

Dr. Ashok paid no attention. He had begun what I took to be a carefully prepared aria. "I need your help, dear lady. The United States needs your help. It is our suspicion that J.J. Kelly, late of the U.S. Army Medical Corps, is not only a key figure in the drug traffic that emanates

47

from the so-called Golden Triangle northwest of whose hypotenuse you
and I are presently seated in Katmandu but that, simultaneously, and
perhaps at cross-purposes, he is working with the Soviet Union's secret
service, the KGB, whose intention is not only to cause as much friction
as possible between China and India *vis-à-vis* Nepal but also through
the planned infiltration by Kalki's religious organization of the United
States to further demoralize the United States not only through increased drug traffic but by a deliberate weakening of the proud Protes-
tant work ethic that has made your Republic the wonder of the earth
through the propagation of Hinduism—the one true religion, as I
believe, but a religion not applicable to those who serve at the altar of
Moses, Jesus and the Rockefeller family. This is Jason McCloud, of the
United States Drug Enforcement Administration. Do not look surprised, or move to greet him. Simply stay as you are. He has taken the
chair to your left. Pretend you are old friends. An agent of the KGB
is present in this room."

As casually as I could under the circumstances, I turned to the left.
Next to me sat a large black American man. He was dressed in a blue
suit, with a vest.

"McCloud," the black man said.

"Ottinger," I said.

McCloud showed me *his* credentials in front of everyone. He was
obviously not given to secrecy.

"Important you infiltrate the Kelly compound." McCloud talked
through clenched teeth. In imitation of a popular television actor,
whose name I still can't think of.

"I have explained." Dr. Ashok lit a joint. I was mildly startled.
Should a CIA spook light up in the presence of what those who revere
the agents of the DEA would call a narc? Somehow Dr. Ashok seemed
lacking in tact. After a deep drag, Dr. Ashok passed the joint to
McCloud who inhaled deeply. For the first time I thought that
McCloud was what he said he was. It is well known that DEA agents
are, to a man, drug addicts. I refused the joint.

McCloud—dreamily—filled me in. "This guy Kelly set himself up,
up here, in 1968. He's the head man of a really sweet operation. He
has agents in Kabul. In Dacca. In Vera Cruz. His American dispersal
point is New Orleans. We've got a good overall idea of how he operates.
But there are missing links. That's where you come in, Ms. Ottinger."

"But let us not forget the political implications of the Kelly operation." Dr. Ashok was, if anything, more oily than ever as a result of the hashish, or ganja. "Naturally, our dear friend McCloud is obliged to think only in terms of the drug traffic. And of course that is a most important part of the equation, let me say, right off, anticipating, Jason, your natural defense of the Drug Enforcement Administration whose thousands of agents are everywhere on earth rigorously rooting out and promoting the sale—I mean suppressing the sale of drugs both hard and soft. And what a job all of you have done! Not only collectively but individually, in the agreeable yet keen-witted person of special agent Jason McCloud, the terror of the Golden Triangle, the scourge of the northwest hypotenuse."

Overwhelmed by this rich tribute, McCloud's eyes rolled up, showing the whites. They stayed up. A truly alarming effect. He was stoned out of his head.

A bit late in the game, I realized that the Blue Moon Tea House was what used to be called an opium den except that instead of opium-pipe smokers, the customers were hashish smokers.

"Good night, sweet Jason," Dr. Ashok crooned. "And fleets of angles see thee to thy breast. The local ganja is very powerful . . . may I call you Teddy?"

"No," I said, with as sweet a smile as I could summon. I was very definitely getting a contact-high in that smoky room.

"I am crushed. You are a very beautiful woman, as well as a world-renowned aviatrix. Why do you think your Mr. Kelly has allowed you to interview him?"

"I don't know. Would you stop puffing smoke in my face? I'm getting dizzy."

Dr. Ashok carefully stubbed out the joint. Then, thriftily, he put the roach in his pocket. "We have had some difficulty infiltrating the Kalki ashram, a fine example, by the way, of thirteenth-century Nepalese architecture. What we are searching for is the link between your Mr. Kelly and the KGB."

"Destroyers of youth," said Jason McCloud, the whites of his eyes still gleaming in the dark face. "Predatory playground pushers." McCloud gnashed his teeth. "Marijuana is a halfway house to something worse." He was sound asleep.

"A truly intrepid and devoted narc." Then Dr. Ashok turned to me.

Falseness blazed in his golden eyes. "The CIA, my dear Madame Ottinger, would be forever in your debt—as indeed would be a grateful nation—if you were to act as our eyes and ears within the Kelly or the Kalki camp."

"No, thanks." Dr. Ashok was beginning to tire me. The smoke in the room was giving me a headache. "I'm a correspondent for *The National Sun*. I am not a spy for the U.S. Government."

"There can be only one loyalty for you and for me and for all Americans, and that is The Free World. To serve that noble but constantly endangered entity, particularly now when the powers of darkness are, even as we speak . . ."

"You speak," I said.

But he did not hear. Words continued to cascade from dark blue lips. ". . . now met in spurious battle here on the Himalayan heights with those of light and the issue is nothing more, nothing less, than the soul of man, the meretricious atman itself." I was pleased that he did not know what meretricious meant. I was pleased that I knew that atman is the Hindu word for soul.

"I pledge allegiance to the flag of the United States . . ." McCloud's eyes were now shut. In a deep and thrilling voice he recited the pledge of allegiance to the flag.

My grip on reality was loosening. I felt unreal, the way that I always felt when Arlene was drunk and I wasn't. I had the same sensation with these two zombies. "What have you got on Kelly?" I asked, tired of rhetoric.

"James Joseph Kelly is thirty-five years old. Only two years older than your own lord Jesus was at the time of his terminal misadventure atop high Golgotha."

"Not *my* lord Jesus. I'm an atheist." I wanted to quote Diderot but could not recall the exact French. I've always envied the confidence of those *philosophes*. They thought that they could know everything. They even dared to write an encyclopedia. Did Amelia speak French? She wrote poetry. I've read some of it. She wanted to be everything, too. Or am I re-creating her in my own image?

"You are to be congratulated." Smooth as silk was Dr. Ashok. "Not much is known of Kelly until 1964 when he went into the U.S. Army at the age of twenty one, a recent graduate from Tulane. Now the mystery begins. Since Kelly was a premed student and a protégé of the brilliant Associate Professor Giles Lowell, M.D., he would have been able to avoid the Vietnam war—or 'police action,' to properly designate that valiant attempt to save Southeast Asia for the free world. Kelly could have gone on to medical school. Or he could have become an officer in your—in *our* army. Instead, he chose to enlist. He chose to join the medical corps. He chose to go to Vietnam. He chose to remain a mere noncommissioned officer. Why? I think I know the answer. He took drugs. He sold drugs. Ergo, for a humble enlisted man, the medical corps was the place to be if you wanted, secretly, to acquire an unlimited supply of drugs, particularly in colorful wartime Saigon."

McCloud's head was now resting on my shoulder. Dr. Ashok helped me prop him up against the wall. No one paid the slightest attention to us. The other addicts were eating poisonous-looking cakes. Addicts crave sugar.

"There are some gaps in Kelly's military record. For instance, he was on some sort of special assignment in '65. Army Intelligence refuses to tell us what he was doing. Imagine! As if, in time, they can hide anything from The Company! But we are not really interested in ancient history, no matter how amusing. What we want to know—and this is where I pray that you will help us—why has he suddenly become a religious cult figure? Why is he pouring his own money from his own drug syndicate into Kalki Enterprises, which is paying for hundreds of ashrams all around the world? Is he using, as we suspect, his potentially enormous influence as a religious figure to subvert the American way of life in order to serve an alien creed based on inhuman collectivism?" The wig had receded, like the tide. Intelligence had again taken up residence on that dusky brow. Dr. Ashok removed from his pocket a small silver box.

I made neutral sounds. "According to the people close to Kalki, he really thinks that he is Vishnu reborn. He really thinks that the end of the world is at hand."

Before my startled eyes, Dr. Ashok took from the silver box a pinch of cocaine. He sniffed. Then he put the box away. We might have been at a show-biz party in Bel-Air.

"For the sake of argument, dear lady." He sneezed. "Let us say that Kelly really believes that he is Kalki and that the world will end when he mounts his white horse. Incidentally, we have just learned that he has indeed bought a white horse. It will arrive in Katmandu Sunday from the stables at Jaipur. Kelly cannot ride but I suppose that he'll take lessons. Anyway, let us say that he is sincerely living out the legend of Kalki, why then would he incorporate himself in the state of Delaware, as Kalki Enterprises? Why would he buy the Jefferson Towers apartment house, a stone's throw from Washington D.C.'s Vatican-owned Watergate complex? Why is he investing heavily in choice Los Angeles real estate? Why are his followers, even as we speak . . . as *I* speak, spreading out across the United States, preaching the gospel according to Kalki while beating up the followers of the Reverend Sun Moon? Answer me these questions, and you will be a hop, a skip, a jump ahead of The Company, and a truly great or greater American."

"Read the *Sun*. I've got to go. Is Mr. McCloud dead? I think he's stopped breathing."

Dr. Ashok felt McCloud's pulse in a most professional way. "McCloud lives. And dreams. Dear lady, consider yourself on our payroll, too. And remember that only the sky above is the limit for those of us who work for The Company." To my amazement, Dr. Ashok began to stuff twenty-dollar bills into the pocket of my jacket. "A first payment. A sign of trust. A valentine, dear Madame Ottinger." It was February 14.

I finally stopped him not only from corrupting me in the name of the U.S. Government but from getting in a covert feel or two. "Take your money." I put the wads of cash back onto the table. I felt noble. I also felt stoned. Perhaps I was.

"I thought you were a patriot." Dr. Ashok looked at me mournfully. The wig had slipped forward again, driving out intelligence.

With some difficulty, I got over and around McCloud, whose face was resting on the table.

The air was blue with ganja smoke. *Blue* Moon Tea House?

In the first dining room an American girl was sitting alone. She wore granny glasses and a sunbonnet. She was crying, and drinking mint tea. She had a bad complexion.

In the kitchen someone was playing a flute.

2

THERE WAS A NOTE FROM LAKSHMI AT THE HOTEL. "A CAR WILL PICK you up at ten o'clock tomorrow morning and bring you to the ashram." She had signed herself with a drawing of a lotus.

The car arrived not at ten o'clock the next morning but at noon. As a result, I was again trapped by Dr. Ashok who seemed less oleaginous than usual. He had also developed a tremor of his hands. Withdrawal symptoms?

As I stepped out onto the terrace in front of the hotel, Dr. Ashok detached himself from a group of American secret agents (or Rotarians or salesmen) and greeted me in Chinese.

I told him that Chinese was not one of my languages. He apologized. Then he made his pitch. He wanted to wire me for sound so that everything said at the ashram could be monitored by the CIA head-quarters in attractive downtown Katmandu. I declined. Dr. Ashok did not seem surprised. At this point I was fairly certain that he was out of his mind.

I excused myself. Sat at a table on the terrace. Ordered tea which never came. Watched squads of Japanese tourists, marching through the traffic, photographing one another. As I tinkered with my tape recorder, "Do not approach" was writ large on my face.

The car arrived from the ashram. The driver was Nepalese. I was positive that I was being kidnapped. For some reason, paranoia blossoms luxuriously in the Himalayas. I saw myself chained to Mount Everest, raped repeatedly by teams of abominable snowmen, assisted by the odd Sherpa.

The outskirts of Katmandu are like the outskirts of any city in the world. That is to say, ugly, raw, disorganized; cement-block metasta-sised. But the countryside was green and rolling, and on a good day

(which this particular one was not) you could see the Himalayas, spar-
kling like masses of quartz and crystal.

I dislike descriptions in books. Why do I feel obliged to describe
Nepal? I suppose because it really was different, and unexpected.

In the old parts of Katmandu the houses are made of dark red brick,
rather like the eighteenth- and nineteenth-century houses you see here
in Georgetown. But the Nepalese houses have small latticed windows,
peaked roofs of yellow tile supported by carved beams that overhang
the narrow streets. . . . But I've already written that description. I am
convinced that several million miles of home movies which no one has
ever willingly looked at have taken the place of millions of pages of
descriptive prose that no one has ever willingly read. My favorite writers
Diderot, Voltaire, Pascal almost never describe anything.

I arrived at the ashram, unraped. The ashram was a large red-brick
mansion set in a grove of tall feathery-looking trees. Dr. Ashok was
right. The house was beautiful. At the main door two Nepalese policemen stood guard. They looked jumpy.

Geraldine came out to meet me. The policemen stared first at her.
Then at me. They seemed hostile. My paranoia was now in full gorgeous bloom. Between the hijinks at the Blue Moon Tea House and
the attempt to blow up the *Garuda,* I was no longer the entirely
intrepid Teddy of legend.

"Pranam, Teddy."

I pranamed right back.

Geraldine was wearing a green silk sari, to set off her red hair. I
thought her sympathetic. But my heart belonged, to paraphrase Arlene's favorite song of the distant forties, to Lakshmi.

Together we entered a long room with dark beams of carved teakwood. I found the effect unsettling. For an instant, I thought I was back
in L.A., in a neocolonial Spanish room, that last resort of those house-
wives of my generation for whom French provincial had somehow
backfired. In my homemaking days I was strictly Bauhaus. Earl Jr. was
French provincial, all the way.

"Kalki's meditating," said Geraldine. "Everyone is. Except me. I've
been waiting for you all morning."

I explained why I was late.

"Then stay for lunch. I hope you like rice. That's all we ever have."

I started to switch on my tape recorder. But Geraldine shook her head. "Kalki allows no tape recorders."

"Can I take notes?"

"If you like. But it won't make much difference. I mean, all that you will get from him is, well, a wavelength. He sends and we receive. If we can, of course. Sit down."

We sat side by side on a long bench. I felt as if we were waiting for a train.

"How long have you been here?" I asked, doing my best to be a professional journalist. My only problem was that although I usually asked the right questions, I almost never listened to the answers.

"I've been here just a year. It's been absolutely fascinating. I have my own laboratory."

"Genetics?"

"Yes. I've been trying to isolate certain . . ." Geraldine stopped. She did not elaborate. Because she thought that I would not understand? or because she was afraid that I would? "Anyway, the real challenge is getting the right equipment up here. That's why I went down to Delhi with Lakshmi, to pick up a new kind of laser." Geraldine frowned. "Lakshmi said you found a bomb . . ."

I nodded. "Who do you think put it there?"

"I don't know. Kalki has enemies. It could be so many people. He's incredibly popular in India. So the old-fashioned Brahmins hate him. He even has secret missions inside Red China and the Chinese wouldn't like that if they knew . . . and they must know."

"But why murder us instead of Kalki?"

"Kalki was supposed to be on that plane. At the last minute he decided to stay in Katmandu."

"This is not a safe sort of business, is it?"

Geraldine smiled. "Well, there are bound to be people who don't want the age of Kali to end. I suppose they think that if they kill Kalki, life will go on as usual. But it won't."

Before I could get her to explain what she meant by that, a gong sounded deep within the house.

"Kalki is in the audience chamber." Geraldine's voice was suddenly reverent. She got to her feet. Took my arm. Led me to the double teakwood doors at the end of the room, which opened automatically.

Both Geraldine and Lakshmi were fascinated by electrical devices. Lakshmi had herself installed the doors. The three of us were definitely unwomanly, as womanliness was defined in those days.

The audience chamber was the same size as the waiting room. Against one wall was a dais about two feet off the floor. Behind the dais was a life-size wooden statue of the god Vishnu. In each of four busy hands, he held one regulation conch shell, one club, one quoit, one lotus. The statue had been painted a ghastly dark blue . . . Vishnu's official color.

On the dais, Kalki sat cross-legged. He was staring straight ahead. In theory, he could see us because we were in his line of vision but actually he did not see us, according to Geraldine, because his atman or spirit had left the body.

Did I believe any of this? Of course not. I had a job to do, nothing more.

As Geraldine and I lay side by side on the expensive Persian carpet in front of the dais, I had plenty of time to examine Kalki. He wore a saffron yellow robe with a rope belt. The upper body was lean. The crossed bare legs were thick and muscular, and covered with golden hairs. Unlike those Y.M.C.A. Jesus Christ photographs of him that I had seen, Kalki was clean-shaven. The curly dark blond hair was cut short. The eyes that looked out into farthest space were a deep blue.

I could feel my latent heterosexuality slowly beginning to assert itself. Kalki was sexually attractive to me. He was blond. I am dark. That fact alone was enough to set our respective cells to vibrating. Opposite needs opposite. But I had not yet heard the voice. With men, the voice is all-important. I can respond sexually only to a certain pitch. Lacking that pitch, I am cold. With women it is not the voice but a certain curve to the inner thigh. Arlene had it. I hoped that Lakshmi had it, too.

We must have lain there for ten minutes, waiting for Kalki to join his body again, and us. Finally, he took a deep breath. He blinked his eyes. Geraldine whispered in my ear, "Touch his foot. A sign of respect."

Gingerly, a favorite H.V.W. adverb, I touched Kalki's right big toe. The skin was rough and dry.

Kalki looked directly at me. Then he smiled. "What is there," he asked, "beyond motherhood?"

"Freedom," I said. This was not exactly the first time I had answered that question. "You can be both a woman and a man."

"Tiresias."

I was surprised that he knew who Tiresias was. I don't know why but I had thought that Kalki would be a bit on the stupid side. Instead, he was quick, knowledgeable, attractive. And the voice? For me, an aphrodisiac. He spoke with a slight Southern accent, which I found pleasant, so unlike a recent president's gabble or gobble. But, best of all, Kalki's voice was a baritone that shaded off into bass. I was now turned on. The dial had been switched. All systems go.

"Pranam," said Kalki, and began his pitch. "I am the avatar." Kalki's manner was reasonable. "I am the highest of the high. The divine beloved who loves you more than you love yourself. Before me was Zoroaster, Rama, Krishna, Buddha, Jesus and Mohammed. Now I have come. Atcha. I am here. I am the ultimate avatar, the last incarnation within this cycle of time. On the day that I mount the white horse, the sword Nandaka blazing like a comet in my right hand, I shall destroy the wicked. At my approach the flesh of this world will fall away like grass before the scythe, and the age of Kali will be no more. Then, in the stillness of the void, I shall re-create the human race. The golden age will come again. For I am Kalki. I am Vishnu. I am the highest of the high. Before the creation of the universe, I was. After the last star burns out, I am."

Kalki stopped, as unexpectedly as he had begun. He seemed not at all interested in my reaction. It was plain that he had made the same speech many times before.

I was overwhelmed, by physical lust. With an effort, I remembered my mission. "When," I asked, "will you mount the white horse?"

"Tomorrow. I'm taking lessons." Kalki was perfectly casual.

"I meant when will you . . . well, end the world?"

"When I do." Kalki was obviously not giving away any secrets. "Now . . . Teddy?"

"Please," I said. "Call me Teddy."

"On earth there are, at any given moment, Five Perfect Masters. I believe that I have found three. Before the end, I must find the other two." Kalki gave me a long as opposed to short look.

"What is a Perfect Master?" I asked.

"One of those who attend to the spiritual governance of the world.

Before the age of Kali, they were easy to recognize. Even as recently as Moses, it was not hard to tell who was a Perfect Master and who was not. But now that all things human have deteriorated and fallen apart, the Perfect Masters are as demoralized as everyone else. It is now possible for a Perfect Master to live and die completely ignorant of his own identity."

I got the point. I was being auditioned for Perfect Masterhood. I played along. I had no idea why Kalki would want to enroll me in his movement. Perhaps this was a standard come-on, or put-on. Certainly he was a marvelous seducer, and I was ready to be seduced. I mean literally seduced. Kalki's religious message interested me even less than Mrs. Eddy's progress reports from the lab of Christ Scientist.

"Do you know Mike Wallace?" Kalki asked.

"No. But I've watched him on television."

"I've never seen him. But then I haven't looked at American television in years. Anyway, he's interviewing me for CBS."

I told him that Wallace was a good performer; that the program *60 Minutes* had a high rating. I could not believe my own ears. There we were in the Himalayas, Teddy Ottinger, Test Pilot, rapping about Mike Wallace's television ratings with the ultimate avatar of the god Vishnu. Blown was my mind.

A gong sounded from yet another part of the house.

"Lunch," said Kalki. He stood up. He was shorter than I expected. But he held himself very straight, and when he moved it was like (yes, H.V.W.) some great cat.

As Kalki gestured for us to follow him, I saw that he was wearing a gold bracelet set with a single large cabochon ruby, the jewel Syamantaka (yes, *Hindu Mythology*), worn always by the god Vishnu. Kalki had yet another mark of the god: in the center of his chest grew a single blond tuft of hair, a sure sign of divinity. I assumed that he had shaved off the rest of the hair on his chest in order to conform with tradition. I was entirely skeptical. I was also entirely attracted to Mr. Kelly.

There were twenty or thirty people at lunch. We squatted on mats in a circle. I was at Kalki's left. On his right was Lakshmi, who greeted me like an old friend. Between Lakshmi's inner thigh (imagined) and Kalki's voice (heard), I was in a state of rut. Beyond Motherhood does not take you Beyond Eros. Quite the contrary.

The mandali at lunch were a mixed crew. Most were Americans.

They seemed like businessmen. The sort that you see at air shows, making deals. The only religious-looking mandalin was an ancient white-bearded Indian. He was benign, withdrawn, holy. I was positive that he was a Perfect Master. But Geraldine told me that he was an accountant from Madras, come to see Kalki on business.

The whole ashram had been wired with Muzak, and we were obliged to listen to the rise, fall and ultimate dispersal of those singing icons of the sixties, the Beatles. I preferred the sound of Joni Mitchell, but she had not yet made it to Katmandu.

Young . . . acolytes? in yellow robes served us mounds of rice and cooked vegetables. Occasionally Kalki would murmur the Hindu word for peace: "Shanti." Otherwise, he did not embarrass us (me) with his godliness. He told me that he had been checked out in a Cessna. "But I've never flown a jet. I want you to teach me how to fly the *Garuda.*"

"Vishnu ought to be able to fly the *Garuda* without lessons." I wanted to get a rise out of him.

Instead it was Geraldine from whom the rise came. "Kalki," she said firmly, "can do anything." She sounded as if she meant what she said.

Kalki smiled. "Well, I can certainly take a few lessons in how to handle a jet." I was glad that he had not based his performance on Moses or Jesus or one of the other bad-tempered gods. Vishnu was obviously a likable creator, despite the four arms.

"We'll go for a spin," said Kalki. "Right after lunch." But this was not easily arranged. First we had to get through to the Katmandu airport. That took an hour. Then the maintenance crew had to be alerted; authorities were appealed to. It was five o'clock before we were able to take off.

Meanwhile, several hundred Indian and Nepalese pilgrims had gathered outside the ashram. They made a circle around a crumbling stupa, covered with rambling roses not yet in bloom.

Lakshmi and I stood at a window and watched as Kalki walked . . . no, glided toward the stupa. At his appearance the pilgrims prostrated themselves. They seemed ecstatic, but in a low-keyed way. They made a strange sighing sound.

Kalki mounted the stupa. He raised his arms in blessing. Then he spoke Hindi. The voice was low, beguiling. Some of the worshipers wept. Some moaned. Some laughed nervously. Many touched his feet, a sign of worship.

I asked Lakshmi what he was saying.

"He is describing the end of the age of Kali. He is telling them how to purify themselves. He speaks beautiful Hindi. And of course he knows Sanskrit, the original language of the gods."

"I'm sure he didn't learn Sanskrit as a premed at Tulane."

Lakshmi laughed. "God can speak in every tongue. And of course god's been living in Nepal for eight years."

Kalki gave a final benediction. Then he was gone.

"He'll meet you in the car. What do you think?" Lakshmi seemed truly interested in my reaction to Kalki.

"Well, he's very attractive."

"Oh, dear! And you're very attractive, too." Lakshmi was filled with Weissean rue.

I was rueless, to neologize. "Do you really think I'm attractive?" Despite my boldness, I don't think she got the message. She simply saw me as another good-looking woman who might have designs on her husband.

"Of course I do. You know," she added . . . no, divided. "We are celibate. It is part of the purification." Like a sister, she put her arm around me. I shuddered with excitement. "You are going to have a role to play in the sacred story," she kissed my cheek, in a chaste way. I nearly screamed. "I can tell."

"What sort of role?"

But Lakshmi only smiled. She smelled of jasmine.

I joined Kalki in the back of the old Cadillac. Torn window curtains had been drawn. The driver was separated from us by a glass partition. As we drove out through the main gates, the guards saluted. They seemed even more jittery than before. Again I had the mixed impression that in Nepal Kalki was both a kind of royalty and a prisoner.

I asked Kalki if he had studied Sanskrit in school.

"No. But languages are easy for me. They have to be."

"Have to be?"

"Yes. For what I have to do."

"Were you always Vishnu?"

"Always."

"And did you always know who you were?"

Kalki's dark blue eyes suddenly glittered as a ray of sunlight blazed through a hole in the window curtain. "No," he said. Then he grinned, "Yes."

"Yes and no?"

"Or no and yes."

"I don't follow you."

"I don't lead."

"But you have to—well, *teach* something."

"I have come not to teach but to awaken." This was very fast.

"Awaken to what?"

"The end."

"When will that be?"

"Soon."

"How?"

"When I mount the white horse, sword in hand. Do you believe in me?"

I didn't quite know how to answer. I did not of course believe a word that he was saying. Nevertheless, I was picking up a sort of strange vibration from him. It could have been religious. But I suspect that it was only . . . only! sexual. Fans of St. Theresa of Avila think that the two responses are not unlike. "You ask for a lot of belief."

"I must."

"I'm curious about one thing." Conscious of his body next to mine on the seat, I was somewhat short of breath. "Why do you go to all this trouble if you are going to bring the world to an end? I mean, why not just shut everything down quietly? And then start all over again or whatever you have in mind. I mean, why preach? Why make laws if everyone is going to be dead anyway." Kalki smelled of sandalwood, of blondness. The sweat of blonds is different from ours.

"I no longer make laws." Kalki stretched his legs. I was moist. "In the past, I laid down principles. I made laws. But since the beginning of the human race, no more than a handful ever followed in my way. Now, for the tenth and last time, I am here. And it is too late for laws. The most I can do is to help you purify yourself, to help you achieve serenity, to help you come close to me."

Kalki stared into my face, as though it were a map on which an X marked where the treasure was hidden. "When I was the Buddha, I showed the way to enlightenment through the obliteration of all desire, and, finally, of the self. I shared with those who would follow in my way the knowledge that the 'I' does not exist, that there is only Sunya, a beautiful emptiness, a void in which all things are, and no more. But as the Buddha, I failed. Before I was the Buddha, I failed as Krishna. Before I was Krishna, I failed as Rama. Though as Rama I destroyed the demon-king Ravana who tried to steal my wife. Except for a few souls I am forever veiled from man by his own curtain of ignorance."

"But if you are really god, you can take the curtain away whenever you like."

Kalki did not answer that perennial question. By and large, querulous gods never do come up with an answer to: well, if you don't like evil, why did you invent it? I think de Vigny got it right: *"J'aime la majesté des souffrances humaines."* Yet I know that if I were god I would not enjoy human suffering no matter how majestic. Quite the contrary. But then I would not have gone to the trouble of inventing the human race.

"The curtain will fall on the last day." Kalki was flat. "Meanwhile, I evolve, too. Even though I am, in essence, eternal and changeless, I shall not be complete, as Kalki, until the day that I mount the white horse, and the human race comes to an end."

"To begin again?"

"As I choose."

I will say that there is nothing like talk of the end of the world to diminish sexual desire. At this point I was . . . what? I must be absolutely precise. This section of the story is crucial. Crucial is derived from crux. Pertaining to the cross. I thought he was either mad or a great actor, or both. I was chilled by the matter-of-factness with which he spoke of the end. The End. Yet I have been conscious of the process of ending all my life. The first and unbreakable law of our estate is the second law of thermodynamics: everything is running down. But I could not conceive of someone just switching off the engine.

At the airport, we boarded the *Garuda.*

"I've always wanted to be a good pilot." Kalki strapped himself into the copilot's seat. I explained the instruments. He was quick. You only had to tell him something once.

Aloft, I let him take the controls. He was well-coordinated. He told me how much he had liked *Beyond Motherhood,* particularly the parts about flying. "That's why I wanted to meet you." He was simple, direct, charming. God?

We talked about aviation. I told him some of the problems women had had to face, as fliers. During the Second War Jacqueline Cochran and Nancy Love (I met her once, a beauty) had trained a number of women fliers to test and ferry planes for the American military. There were more than a thousand women pilots enrolled as Women's Airforce Service Pilots or WASPs. Predictably, the men were furious. In 1944 Congress disbanded the WASPs. Thirty years later, thanks to my efforts, among others, women could fly for the American military as well as for the commercial airlines. Our finest victory occurred in September 1976 when ten women were accepted for the pilot-training program at Williams Air Force Base near Phoenix. I was made an honorary member of the Order of Fifinella, founded by the surviving WASPs. I always loved being with those women. Some had known Amelia. We were sisters. Kalki was sympathetic.

I let Kalki take us up to forty thousand feet. I set a course for Mount Everest, smoking like dry ice in the sun. I see that I have used the same simile before. H.V.W. would not repeat it. I will.

"Who," I asked, "put the bomb in the *Garuda* yesterday."

Kalki seemed not to be interested. "The Indian Government. The American Government. The Association of Southeast Asian Nations. Who knows? Who cares?"

"Do you know Dr. Ashok?"

Kalki nodded. "What do you think of his wig?"

"Unconvincing."

Kalki laughed. "They are all after me. The CIA, the Drug Enforcement Administration . . ."

"Why?"

"Why not? I am their fate, and it is only human to try to avoid fate, which is death."

"Dr. Ashok thinks you are in the drug business."

"Perhaps he's right." Kalki was imperturbable.

"That seems like an odd thing for god to do."

"There are no rules, except those that I choose to make." I felt for the first time Kalki's coldness, and by coldness I do not mean an H.V.W. word. I mean, literally, something inhuman or nonhuman. There was a space inside him that was beyond zero, a level at which he could not respond to anyone in any usual way. I have noticed that same quality in animals. Neutrality. Distance. Otherness.

"What shall I write about you, for the *Sun?*"

"That I *am* the sun . . . also, stars, moon." Kalki gave me a charming grin. "Write anything you like."

"You are the end . . ."

". . . and the beginning. And the middle. You're an attractive woman, Teddy."

"I've already written that you are celibate." Some of the chill began to go.

"There are always special dispensations. God may enter you yet. You may be chosen."

"Is this an invitation?" I did want him.

Kalki wanted me. But the response was cryptic. "When you went beyond motherhood, you came to me."

The rest of our conversation had to do with aviation. He had never heard of Amelia Earhart. I told him all about her. She had had an unhappy marriage with a publisher and publicist called George Palmer Putnam. If she did kill herself deliberately on that last flight, G.P. (as she called the husband) was the reason. I used to daydream that Amelia was my mother.

Late that night Bruce Sapersteen rang me at the Ananda Hotel. I assumed that every spy in Katmandu was listening in. One becomes accustomed to the absurd very quickly.

"I'm in New York," he said. I tried to visualize him. From the voice he sounded young. I began to attach red hair to his head. Sideburns first. Then tight curls at the top. I turned him into a young version of H.V. Weiss.

"I've seen Kalki," I said. While the telephone lines from New York to Katmandu crackled and whispered with the recording devices of a dozen agents, I gave him the beginnings of the first story for the *Sun.* I had a fair idea how Morgan would play it. Old-fashioned: "Dr. Livingstone, I presume." With me as the intrepid Stanley at the top of the world. Sapersteen was pleased. I had laid on a lot of local color. "I'll write it up," he said. Always "as told to," I thought to myself, never "as told by." My destiny, until now.

"The big question," said Sapersteen, "is who put the bomb on the *Garuda.*"

"Kalki doesn't seem to care."

"That's funny."

"Not if he thinks the world is coming to an end."

"Has he given you a date on that yet?"

"No. But it's pretty soon, I think."

Then Bruce Sapersteen, Researcher, actually came up with some research. "Kalki Enterprises has just hired Madison Square Garden for the night of March 15. There's to be some kind of rally. Find out . . ."

"That's what I'm here for." The connection was then broken. Like everything else, the telephone companies of the world were in a state of increasing entropy during those last days of the age of Kali.

The next morning, as I was waiting for the car from the ashram to pick me up, I had one more go-round with Dr. Ashok. He was on the front terrace, talking to a group of Chinese men. When he saw me, he loped over. "Dear Madame Ottinger!" The usual ceremonious nonsense. "We have just learned that Kalki will arrive in the United States two weeks from now. He will hold a rally in Madison Square Garden in New York." I assumed that he had listened in on my conversation with Sapersteen. "At this rally, he will announce that the end of the world is about to take place. He will then give the exact date." Dr. Ashok looked so crazed that, for the first time, I thought him not only sane but possibly serious despite the essential frivolity of his alleged employer the CIA. "While you're at the ashram, you must *find out that date!*"

I was soothing. "I'll do my best."

"Dear lady!" Dr. Ashok crooned somberly into my ear: "Think of this as a quest. On the order of the Golden Goddess or the White Bough." It was quite obvious that confusion entirely reigned in that disordered mind. I thought, sadly, of all my tax money wasted on the likes of Dr. Ashok, of Jason McCloud.

For the next few days I was able to avoid Dr. Ashok. Meanwhile, Kalki avoided me. I saw him only in public, receiving pilgrims. Against my better (is there a worse?) judgment, I was impressed by the ease with which he talked Hindi, Chinese. He had star quality, an element often alluded to in Arlene's circle of show-biz friends, none of whom possessed it. I know that I have a touch of it. So has Arlene. Amelia personified it.

Lakshmi apologized. Told me how busy Kalki was. Suggested that I attend some of the classes "to get at least a notion of what we're all about." I did as requested. And spent many boring hours chanting incomprehensible Sanskrit mantras. Quite a few featured om, a mono-syllable meaning the Hindu trinity. American novices particularly dug om. Somehow or other, these various incantations would help us to merge with the infinite at The End. I have always found the infinite unappealing as an abstraction.

Approaching my own wit's end, I was saved by Geraldine. Just as I was coming out of class, om-ed into a state of imbecility, Geraldine appeared. She wore a white laboratory smock. She put her arm through mine. "You've suffered enough," she said, with an attractive smile. "Let's go for a drive."

And so for a drive we went, in a dusty Volkswagen.

A clear, cool but not cold day. Brown winter fields. Occasional farmhouses. Clumps of odd-looking trees, as well as familiar conifers. Small temples or shrines to this god or that. Most often, however, the holy places were sacred to the local boy made good, the Buddha, the last incarnation but one of Vishnu, currently at home in the golden flesh of J.J. Kelly.

"Are you enjoying yourself?" Geraldine sounded a bit like a hostess.

"No. I haven't talked to Kalki since the first day."

"There's probably a good reason."

"There's also a lot of pressure on me." This was true. Morgan himself had rung. The first article was a success. Where was the second?

"Not if you give up the story."

"Give it up? What's left of my career is riding on this assignment."

"There are other careers."

"There are no more planes for me to test. There are no more records for me to break." I spelled it out.

"I've always been a fan of yours." Geraldine said this so simply that I fell more or less in love. I was unusually susceptible those days in the Himalayas. Given to crying jags at sundown. And Valium.

Geraldine stopped the car. We were at the top of a small round hill that contained a small round crater filled with dark water that gleamed like polished metal.

"There," said Geraldine, "is the source of the Ganges River."

"I am impressed." I was. Even if this dark pond was not the true source, the setting was—word? numinous. She showed me the spot

66

where the lake overflowed, became a stream that promptly vanished among fir trees. I thought of cold green woods, of melted snow, of water falling, of grand confluences. Then, suddenly, there it was: the Ganges, the bisector and nourisher of all India. A river that had been holy ever since it "first flowed from the toe of Vishnu," said Geraldine with an absolutely straight face.

"Please!" I might have been sharper if she had not so sweetly declared herself my admirer. "I mean, do you really believe that sort of thing?"

Geraldine sat on the tall grass. I sat beside her. The dampness was not unpleasant. "This is the beginning," she said. Was she deliberately ambiguous?

"From the toe of Vishnu?"

"I *believe* in that toe!" Geraldine gave me a sidelong glance. I had no idea if she was serious or not.

"Let me interview you," I said. "Tell me, Professor O'Connor . . ."

"Geraldine."

Progress. "Do you really believe that the world is about to end and that Kalki will take the whole lot of you to heaven, sometimes known as Vaikuntha?"

"The world will end."

"Date?"

"I've not been told."

"Method?"

"I've not been told."

"Will the sky open up? Will there be angels with ladders . . ."

"You're being silly."

"I'm trying to find out how Kalki means to get rid of us."

"He will preside over the end, in the same way that he presided over the beginning." As lunatic as our conversation was (to me), I was struck by Geraldine's certainty; also, by her intelligence. Sitting beside that dark pond which may or may not have been the source of the Ganges, may or may not have flowed from Vishnu's toe, I began to waver in my skepticism. I did not believe Kalki was god. But I did think that anyone clever enough to have enlisted someone like Geraldine might be clever enough to set off, let us say, a nuclear reaction that might kill everyone, including himself. Question: why? I asked it. But Geraldine was not about to tell me anything beyond the official line. I let my arm rest on her shoulder. To my delight, she let it remain there. More progress.

We were both quiet, listening to the wind comb out the fir trees. Then she said, "Teddy." This was the first time that she had used my first name. "Kalki wants you." Retrogression.

"Like Jesus?"

"Like what?"

"You know. Like those signs that say 'Jesus wants you.' "

"Be serious."

"Jesus isn't serious?"

"Jesus isn't at all. He was. But Kalki is. Kalki is the living avatar. He can save you."

"Wow!"

"If you're not interested." Geraldine shrugged my arm from her shoulder. This was blackmail.

Wanting to cry, I laughed. "Of course I'm interested. But why me?"

"Why *me?*"

"You believe in him."

"So will you. Anyway, what matters is what *he* wants. So—here is your chance."

"But what am I being offered? Paradise? And what must I do in exchange?"

Geraldine stared hard at the pond. So did I. From time to time, the dark waters were set to rippling in the oddest way. Were there monsters beneath the surface? Abominable sea serpents?

"What," I asked, surrendering, "am I supposed to do?"

"Drop the story." That was to the point. I knew then that all the rumors were true. Dr. Ashok and McCloud were right. Kalki Enterprises had nothing to do with religion; only drugs, money.

I said the obvious. "I need the job."

"Kalki will look after you."

"What am I to do for money?"

"In a very short time, there will be no such thing as money."

"But what about between now and then?"

"He'll pay you what you want. That's no problem." As Geraldine spoke, I had a vision of thousands of playground pushers taking the nickels and dimes of addicted children and sending them off to Kalki

Enterprises, incorporated in Wilmington, Delaware.

"Aside from believing in Kalki, what will I have to do?"

"Fly the *Garuda* for him."

I was not prepared for anything so practical or anything that made so much sense. One design was at last plain. Morgan Davies wants an interview with Kalki. But Kalki does not give interviews. Morgan boasts of having published *Beyond Motherhood* by the best pilot in the world. I am no longer modest on page, or off. Kalki then agrees to be interviewed by Teddy Ottinger not because he intends to give her an interview, but because he wants to hire the aforesaid world's best pilot. In a sense, I had been had. But then I was all set to have him. So there we were. The mystery of why Kalki had agreed to be interviewed only by me was a mystery no longer.

Instead, a valley of decision had, as it were, opened up at my feet. "I'll think about it."

Together Geraldine and I walked along the ridge of the hill. Just beyond the lake, a ramshackle wooden temple was elevated from the dust by worn steps of soft stone. Red and gold banners flapped from poles. Dirty fat priests greeted us. So did dirty fat puppies who appeared to live inside the shrine itself where, through splintered lattices, I could just make out the gilded statue of the Buddha, smiling his famous I've-got-a-fivefold-secret smile. If one is going to be a god on earth or his surrogate, then I suppose that the Buddha's way was the best: neutral self-absorption in non–self-absorption. I remember wishing that Kalki would imitate his predecessor. I could not imagine the Buddha at Madison Square Garden, on television. But then the Buddha was an example. Kalki was the end.

A priest kicked a puppy. It rolled like a fur soccer ball down the steps of the shrine. Everyone laughed. The other dogs were not intimidated.

Geraldine said a prayer in front of the shrine. The priests were surprised, pleased. They were even more pleased when she gave them money.

On the way back to the Volkswagen, I asked the crucial question. Crucial to the *Sun,* anyway. Drugs.

Geraldine's response was cool. "I've heard that, too," she said.

"So much smoke . . ." I began.

"No fire," she ended. "Look, everyone wants to discredit us. The other churches. The American Government. The Indian Government. Even the Nepalese keep threatening us. Luckily, we've got the money to pay them off."

"From where?" When in doubt, ask direct questions.

"Pilgrims. People who believe. There are millions of them now, all over the world." Geraldine was not one to let from her bag the stray, the inconvenient cat.

"Hardly millions." I tried to recall some of Sapersteen's research. Tens of thousands, perhaps . . . more than South Korea's gift to human credulity could claim but fewer than, say, America's order of dusky Moslems. Yet all the research figures showed large revenues, important investments, a constant tide of money going out but never, plausibly, coming in. Was there, somewhere, a billionaire who believed in Kalki, and paid the bills?

As Geraldine was not about to give anything away, I played a religious card. "Will these millions of believers be saved, too?"

"When the new cycle begins, all things will be new. Those who have purified themselves will go on, as always. They will be born again. A happy few will attend Vishnu in Vaikuntha."

Whenever Vaikuntha was mentioned, my attention span would snap. It snapped.

In silence we approached a tall dark shining stone that stood by itself in a field. Geraldine bowed to the stone. She hummed a mantra. I took a good look and saw that the rock had been carved into the shape of a phallus. "Oh," I said.

"It is the linga. The emblem of the god Siva." Geraldine frowned.

I was eager to show off my reading from *Hindu Mythology*. "Siva is one of three aspects of the one god who is three." My grandfather Hecht was a rabbi, very Orthodox. "The Trinity!" he used to whisper. "What hard work to think that one up!" He always whispered when he mentioned Christianity. He thought that the Cossacks were just around the bend, even in San Diego. He died shortly after my parents converted to Christian Science. I am convinced that the Trinity in white smocks and armed with hypodermic needles was . . . were? too much for him. He had been born in Luxembourg. He had tried living in Southern California but could not endure the sun. He moved back to Ohio. Where he died. In Dayton. Why Dayton? I don't know. The

Wright brothers came from Dayton. He had been a widower most of his life.

"Siva sprang from the forehead of Vishnu. He is blue-necked, horrible, divine, moon-crested, three-eyed." Geraldine recited some of the traditional epithets used to describe Siva. I was fairly certain that she was *not* putting me on.

"Who," I asked, "is more important, Vishnu or Siva?"

"Vishnu!" Geraldine looked grim. "He *must* be!" And that was all that she would say. I noted the urgency of the *"must."* Obviously there was some sort of competition between Vishnu-Kalki and Vishnu-Siva. But . . . no hindsight.

For the first time I found Hinduism attractive. Well, *moderately* attractive, and basic. I liked the idea of depicting as god human genitalia. Christians had done that in the twelfth century. God the father was the penis, the son was the scrotum, the holy ghost was the ejaculation. Jews did not go in for that sort of thing. In the Old Testament sex was only for kings, and reproduction. There were no images. For us, there was nothing graven except, most dangerous of all, the word.

3

THE NEXT DAY I WENT TO THE ASHRAM. I ASKED TO SEE KALKI. Not available. Geraldine? The same. Lakshmi? She had left a message for me. Would I join one of the morning classes?

I did, gloomily. A class full of young and interchangeable Americans. They all had the same set smile; and stared at you with the same unseeing pair of uninhabited eyes. They were like androids, waiting to be switched on. Instinctively, they seemed to know that there were altogether too many where they came from. Yes, the seventies were a perfect time to start a religion. If you are born knowing that you don't

really exist, that there's nobody home, why, then let god—any god—
fill up the empty space.

While om-ing in unison with the others, I kept my sanity by staring
out the classroom window and so was able to observe the arrival of the
CBS television crew with their cameras, lighting and sound equipment,
air of importance. Everyone was excited, and pleased. Even the Nepalese police were smiling, delighted by this invasion from the twentieth
century.

Mike Wallace wore a brown suit, a yellow shirt, a dark tie. He carried
a clipboard. He was talking to the director or the producer of the
program. All in all, I decided that it would not be a good idea for us
to meet. The night before, I had talked to Morgan in New York.

"The second piece is a lulu!" Morgan actually said things like "lulu."
"We've gone and beat CBS to the punch. Keep it up, Teddy." I told
him that I might be able to keep it up better if I were allowed to read
"my" two pieces. He thought that very funny. Anyway, 60 Minutes
had been aced.

Although I seldom watched television, I did enjoy Wallace. Odd
cultural note in re television: those who did a lot of it, seldom watched
any of it. Arlene was an exception. She watched all day long. But then
she drank at the same time. Even so, she had her preferences. She was
a loyal fan. She had known Wallace in the fifties and thought him
sound; that is, conservative. The only important row that Arlene and
I ever had was when she made a television commercial for a presidential
candidate called Ronald Reagan.

As my head began slowly to dissolve from om-ing, a girl tiptoed into
the classroom. "Lakshmi will see you," she whispered. "Go to the
Room of the Goddess."

The Room of the Goddess was Lakshmi's inner sanctuary. Only a
select few were allowed to attend her there. The room itself was
undistinguished except for an ancient bronze statue of the goddess
Lakshmi who possessed, I was relieved to discover, the regulation set
of arms and legs. Hindu gods tend to busyness.

Lakshmi was curled up on a cushion between two charcoal-burning
braziers. It was a nippy day.

"We've been neglecting you. And I'm sorry." I melted. I was constantly melting in the Himalayas. I attributed my condition to the

altitude. This could explain my love of flying. Altitude, speed. Gravity escaped. Earth transcended, and denied.

"I find the classes interesting." I lied, as one who loves.

"Geraldine told you our . . . plan." Lakshmi was not entirely at ease, which was appealing.

"Yes, she made me an offer. Price was not mentioned." I am good at business.

Lakshmi was not. "This is not just a job. It is a life. It is also a future life."

"But I'm not exactly a believer." Should I call her Lakshmi. I decided not to.

"You will be, if we want you to be." There was no nonsense about that. She sounded eerily confident.

"Are you so convinced of Kalki's persuasiveness?"

"In a way." Lakshmi smiled. Then she played atomic bomb to my unsuspecting Hiroshima. "The world will end on April 3." Lakshmi was matter-of-fact. H.V.W. would have had her voice tremble or even go shrill. But she was composed. It was as if she had just given me the date of a party she wanted me to come to. "I wasn't supposed to tell you that. Please don't tell your newspaper. I'm taking a chance. But then I'm assuming that you'll join us. There's not much time left. Only a few weeks."

"When you say the world will end on April 3," I always cling to the hard fact, if there is one, "do you mean there will be a nuclear explosion?" *Hiroshima, mon amour.* "War? or—what?"

"Kalki means. I don't. All I know is that he wants you with us at The End. And after."

Through the thick stone walls, we could hear the CBS television crew as they set up their equipment. "I need more power!" someone shouted. Who does not, I thought. I am physical, not metaphysical. Logic is my strongest point. I can usually see any argument's flaw. I saw this one's. "Should the world really end, what is the point of my taking this job? I'll be dead along with everyone two days after April Fools' Day."

"This is not an April Fool," said Lakshmi. "The Iron Age *will* end, which means that the world we know will end, except for a few. Kalki has decided."

"Except for a few." Even now, that phrase sounds and resounds in my head. This was the first clue. I fished: "If there are survivors, that means there won't be radioactivity. The fire won't be nuclear."

"What fire?"

"I thought that the age of Kali would end in fire."

But Lakshmi did not rise to this or to any other proffered bait. She simply sat there on her cushion; and waited.

"If what you say is true, I'd like to survive. Naturally. But I am not a believer in endings. Things always go on. There is only change. How much will Kalki pay me to be his personal pilot?"

"Whatever you ask."

"A contract that will be binding *after* April 3?" I made my little joke. Lakshmi made hers, as it turned out. "Yes," she said.

We left it at that.

Together we went down to the courtyard where the taping was about to begin. Wallace and the producer stood next to a dais. They were going over notes. Nearby a diesel generator had been installed. Energy was in short supply almost everywhere last February.

"Where's Kalki?" asked the producer.

"He's in make-up," said the director. He was staring through a viewfinder at the door through which Kalki would make his entrance. "He'll be here in a minute." The director was tall, and very blond. He was about my age, maybe younger. He wore horn-rimmed glasses; red, white and blue sneakers. He had large red hands. I remember everything from that day. In close-up. In slow motion. On wide screen. With stereophonic sound. I am now not consciously selecting details. They select themselves. I just put them down.

Lights were turned on. The red brick wall of the ashram glowed. A sound man put on a set of earphones; then he twisted the dials of the recording equipment. I turned to Lakshmi, to tell her that I thought I had met the director before. But Lakshmi was gone. She came and went, like that. Mike Wallace cleared his throat.

The door beside the dais opened and Kalki stepped into the fierce light. Everyone stopped talking, moving . . . breathing? For a moment, he stood in the doorway. He seemed afire in the yellow robes. The eyes were startling; not only for their amazing blueness but because they had the unusual quality of seeming not to reflect but to generate light.

"Pranam," said Kalki. As he gestured, the ruby bracelet sprayed fiery particles in all directions like the promised fire.

Wallace joined Kalki at the door. They talked in low voices. I tried to listen; heard nothing. Then the director said, "O.K. Places everybody."

Kalki went inside the ashram, and a man with a clapboard stood between the camera and the door.

"Start rolling," said the director.

The man with the clapboard declaimed in a high self-conscious voice, "Kalki interview. End of the world. Take one." As the man stepped out of the camera's range, Wallace stepped into the lights.

"Cue Kalki!" shouted the director.

The door opened. Kalki was again framed by the doorway. Again he said pranam. Again the ruby flashed. Again the eyes were a source of light.

Kalki sat on the dais, and Wallace sat on a stool beside him. The interview began. Unfortunately, I was not able to hear what was said. But I could tell that Kalki was cool and serene while Wallace looked ill-at-ease. It was as if a mischievous decorator had placed a wooden Indian next to a golden Buddha.

The taping ended. Kalki and Wallace went inside the ashram. I was about to go look for Lakshmi when the director turned to me and said, "Hi, Teddy! Remember me? I was technical director on *The Mike Douglas Show*. In Philly, you remember?"

I remembered. Again I was melting. I think, now, that I was having a nervous breakdown in Katmandu. First Lakshmi. Then Geraldine. Now a man, wearing horn-rimmed spectacles, red, white and blue sneakers. Seven years earlier I had chatted with him for all of five minutes when I was in Philadelphia promoting *Beyond Motherhood*. Now here we were together, atop the world, and I was in heat.

"I had a drinking problem then," he announced. Yet I had showed no more than polite interest in him. Perhaps he had sensed my unfocused lust, no, hysteria. I tried not to howl as he continued to drone, "Nearly lost my job. Peggy left me. Took the kids. Now I'm Alcoholics Anonymous." While he talked, he kept looking at me, lecherously, which naturally turned me off, so sweetly are we made. A bird in hand is no bird at all, though the bush burns. "I read your first interview with Kalki. It was swell. But they were pretty upset at CBS. This was going to be *their* first. You know what I miss the most? Beer. Draft beer.

Funny, because I never drank the stuff before I was A.A."

"Try ganja."

"I did. Last night. But it's dry, and I'm only into what's wet. Let's have dinner tonight. I'm at the Ananda, too."

I cooled his ardor with briskness. Brusqueness, too. I asked if *60 Minutes* was interviewing anyone other than Kalki for the program.

"No. He's the whole show. For his segment, that is. He's quite a performer. I got a hunch that when New York sees what we got today, this segment'll run maybe ten, ten and a half, maybe eleven minutes, you know, an in-depth study like the one with the Queen of England."

That night I went to bed early, carefully avoiding the CBS crew; the director with sneakers. The telephone rang twice. I let it ring. I had a good cry. What, I wonder, is a bad cry?

The next morning when I was told that Kalki wanted to fly, I hit some sort of emotional peak. Because I wanted to fly. To break barriers. To murder gravity.

I wore a jump suit, Kalki wore his yellow robes. Otherwise there was nothing at all exotic, much less godlike about him. He looked a bit like pictures of the young Lindbergh who, of course, looked like the young Amelia whom I resemble, in the darkest way. We look for reflections of the self in the other. I asked him if he had enjoyed the interview with Mike Wallace.

"It was necessary." He was offhand.

"For your work?"

"For the human race. At this point I must be seen by all, heard by all. They must be able to prepare." Kalki banked to port. "If you want a contract," he said, "I will give you a contract." But he grinned when he said this, as if the world really was coming to an end and we were just playing games.

Circling illegally over Chinese air space, I changed the course of my life—of history, too. "All right," I said.

Kalki nodded. He did not seem surprised at my decision. "I want you to go back to the States tomorrow."

"I thought you were hiring me as a pilot."

"I am. But I have other work for you to do."

"Such as?"

"I want you to keep on with this story about me. That way you'll be in a position to find out what people are saying about me, what they're doing."

"You mean the narcs?"

"You'll know what I mean." That was that.

We spent two hours in the air. I was in a marvelous if too volatile state. As I circled Mount Everest, I was perfectly happy. Whether Kalki was god or a con man made no difference. We were at the top of the sky.

I even felt good when we came down, and I turned the plane over to the maintenance crew. The dented Cadillac was already on the runway. Kalki said something to the driver in Hindi. Then we got in back. Kalki stretched his legs, shut his eyes, appeared to sleep.

Half an hour later the driver turned off the main road and drove us through dark woods to the bank of a fast-running stream, where he parked the car. Across the water, several hundred men and women in bright clothes stood, expectantly, around a smooth old altar. They paid no attention to us. Kalki was now awake.

"What are they doing?" I asked.

"You'll see."

A procession appeared from the woods. Men in scarlet and saffron robes were dragging a goat by a metal chain. Someone beat a drum, at random. A tall thin yellow man blew what looked to be a conch shell, a loud discordant honk. I looked at Kalki. He had gone rigid, legs still outstretched. Afraid that he was epileptic, I looked in my handbag for something to put between his teeth, to keep him from biting his tongue. I had a cousin who was epileptic. "Grand mal," he would say, proudly, keeling over, with froth at his lips. But Kalki was merely in some sort of trance, and I put away my comb.

Two men placed the goat on the altar. The goat tried to kick free of the ropes that bound its legs. Animals know. I shut my eyes. Then opened them again just as a priest slit the goat's neck with a knife. The crowd dipped rags into the fresh blood that gushed upon the stone altar. Again the horn sounded and the drum was struck.

Kalki came out of his trance. He said something in Sanskrit or Hindi. Then he tapped on the window that separated us from the driver, and the car started. He turned to me. "I have accepted the sacrifice."

"It was grisly," I shuddered. "I ought to give up meat. I hate how we treat animals. How we betray them. We look after them. We feed them. We treat them like pets. Then we murder them. What must they feel at the end?"

"But this was ritual."

"I don't like blood."

"You are blood. That's what these people know, and you don't. For one instant, they were in a proper relation to the universe."

"Which is about to end."

"The cycle, yes. The universe, no."

How shall I write the rest of what happened that day?

I have no fear of flying, to make the obvious play on the title of a typical woman's book of the seventies, a period when Jewish princesses became queens of popular fiction just as the Jewish princes had reigned as kings in the decade before. But I am once removed from Jewry by the antiseptic Christ Scientist. I cannot use the tricks of my sisters. They were interested in freeing themselves of the stereotypes of Jewish princessdom, which they confused with all womanhood. This is not unnatural. We start with ourselves. We have no choice. But then we move out. They started with themselves, and did not move at all. They told us that they were telling it like it is. Then played it like it always was. They would have men the way men (they thought) had women. Boldly. Without feeling. Aiming always for the big O, and nothing else. The way, curiously enough, I almost always dealt with men, except those first weeks with Earl Jr. at USC. I fell in love with him, not knowing that that was *not* the normal thing to do. What is normal? What can be described. Whatever love was, I felt it (or, more to the point, thought that I felt it) for Earl Jr., and married him, and was happy never after. But then my *tendresse* is reserved for my own sex, as nature intended.

In the beginning women spent most of their time together, back at the cave, raising children, making clothes and dinner, inventing the wheel and fire. While the women created and procreated, the men were out hunting, and bonding. Oh, that male bonding! But then we had our own kinds of bonding, too. We were the special ones. And we have known it from the egg. After all, it was a woman who first made the connection between her own cycle and that of the moon. It was a woman who realized that if her cycle was that of the moon's, then the moon must follow obediently the coursing of woman's blood. So from uterus to sky would go the command: wax moon, wane moon. Raise the tides and lower them. In the womb all fetuses begin as female. Maleness is an afterthought.

Close to the end, things were confused. Women wanted "liberation." Of the sort that I had made for myself. In their "fictions" Jewish princesses tried to become Jewish princes. The result was not erotic. They tried to describe the genitals of men in the same way that they thought that men described those of women. But their maiden hearts were never in those descriptions. Girls who feared flying tended to race blindly through zipless fucks. The masculine image was dealt with and done with in sentences that never rang true because sex itself never interested these ladies. How could it? Only they themselves interested themselves. As a result, the only time their sentences would wriggle with life like so many electric eels was when they felt obliged to describe, in detail, their own personal charms. Beginning with voluptuous bodies, exquisitely depilated; ending with piquant faces, nose-bobbed and teeth-capped.

After the obligatory inventory of beauty, it was time to nosh. Never have so many dreadful dinners been described in such sensual detail. Where the true shape of a scrotum was not possible for them to describe upon the page (how can you describe what you can only look at without seeing?), the preparation of a shrimp remoulade, a lobster salad (defiantly the princesses gorged on nonkosher delicacies), a sumptuous casserole served on Royal Crown Derby, by candlelight—yet.

I am taking my time to get to the point because I have never known a satisfactory way of describing the sexual act. H.V. Weiss was a devotee of the pre-princess technique a.k.a. the Hemingway earth-moved syndrome. There is a good deal of that in *Beyond Motherhood,* a book I have never been able to read straight through. Except for the descriptions of flying, it is Weissean and of no merit.

I shall not describe Kalki's genitals. That is a major decision. The princesses would think this a cop-out. I will note that he was not circumcised. At the time I wondered if this was a sign of godhood. Certainly the reverse was a sign of Judeo-Christian godhood as opposed to the Hindu creative principle which requires an unmutilated male.

As far as I could tell he had not shaved his chest. The single tuft of hair was authentic. Like Lakshmi he smelled of blondness, which always attracts us darknesses.

How would I rate him as a lover? In the last days of Kali the male performance was constantly being measured on a scale that tended precipitously to slide. Kalki knew exactly what he was doing and what he was doing took me into account. This is rare with men, or so I've found. It is common with women; hence, that love known to my rabbinical grandfather as "Sapphic." He liked to use Greek words to describe the sexual perversions of the goyim. If he could see me now! Or even then, as we lay side by side on a blanket that Kalki had (thoughtfully?) found in the back of the car, which was parked near the temple that Geraldine and I had visited. The driver was inscrutable.

I pulled up my trousers. Kalki pulled down his robe. I laced my boots. He slipped on his sandals. It was chilly, though the sun was shining and there was not a cloud in the sky.

"Well," I said. And left it at that.

"Contented?" God granting favors was not so different from man giving, graciously, of his virile energy.

"Why not?" I put on my test pilot jacket. "It's cold here."

"That pond . . ."

"Sprang from your big toe. Geraldine told me."

Kalki pushed the golden curls out of his eyes. Yes, he appealed to me. Even so, at the glorious moment some seconds after entry when like a great sneeze my body shook with uncontrollable ecstasy (oh, Weiss, what have you done to my word-maker?), I thought not of the sweating smooth blondness that held me in wiry arms but of Lakshmi, receiving what I was receiving. I *was* Lakshmi, for an instant. And happy.

"You don't believe in me." Kalki was more sad than irritated.

"No." Better to be honest.

"Well, you will. In time."

"What about Lakshmi?" This was stupid of me. But women do that sort of thing. Darken the mood. Presage calamity. Not that I was in love. But he might have been. I am writing nonsense. Kalki wanted sex. So did I. It was nothing more or less than the Himalayan effect. I was susceptible. I was also in heat. He was in rut. Most men are most of the time or so they think, which is the same thing. Even before I read Kate Millett, I hated D.H. Lawrence.

"Lakshmi is my wife, forever." Not even H.V.W. would have had a character make such a statement. On the other hand, the sentiment would have been bobbing around in the stew of his worn phrases. "Lakshmi is my wife, forever." Kalki meant that literally . . . assuming that he was god, which I was not about to assume that cold bright afternoon beside the alleged source of the River Ganges.

"I don't know why I mentioned her. I'm sorry."

"Which do you like best, men or women?" All men want to know this, confident that you will say men.

"Women," I said, half-lying. "But each case is different. I've never had sex with god before." I teased him. He took it well. Hand in hand we walked back to the car by way of the Siva phallus.

Kalki murmured something as he passed the dark shining stone.

"What did you say?"

Kalki grinned. "I was talking to myself. That is, to one of my selves. Are you ready for The End?"

I stopped. Up ahead was the shrine to the Buddha. The long red and gold banners were snapping in a wind from the northeast, I noted. Force of habit. I have an inner barometer. Can predict weather with some accuracy.

"No," I said, "I want to go on."

"Everything goes on. But in a different form."

"I'd like to stay in this form as long as possible."

"Perhaps you will."

"Lakshmi said that a few will survive. Is that true?"

Kalki nodded. He seldom looked at you when he spoke.

"Can you give me a hint of how you are going to end the . . . cycle?"

"Can't you see the signs?" He did not answer me directly. "The air is poisoned. The water is poisoned. The people . . ."

"The people reproduce geometrically, agricultural resources increase mathematically, if at all. I had a chapter on that in *Beyond Motherhood.*"

"Then you can see that the human race is in its terminal phase. Well, I have come, as prophesied, to purify."

"And to destroy?"

"The age of Kali is the age of iron. The age of iron is the age of evil regnant. So it will end, with me, astride a white horse, which will be the trick of the week because I'm scared shitless of horses."

We both laughed at that. There was not much else to laugh at.

"God should be able to ride a horse, or do anything else he wants to do."

"But at the moment god is incorporated. I wear James J. Kelly's body. I am limited by his flesh. How did you like him, by the way?"

"Nice," I said, meaning it.

"His body liked yours." Kalki smiled. "But no woman has to be *told* that.

On the way back to the ashram, we resumed our previous relationship: interviewer with evasive celebrity. I asked him about Dr. Ashok.

"Dr. Ashok is a man of parts. And plays them to the hilt."

"Is he CIA?"

"If that is what he plays." This was no answer.

"Jason McCloud."

"A narc." That was an answer.

"Do you deal in drugs?"

"Would I tell you if I did?"

"I don't know. You might trust me, now that I'm an employee."

"You are also working for Morgan Davies of *The National Sun.*"

"I know when you are planning to end the world. April 3."

Kalki was not pleased. "Lakshmi told you?"

"Yes. She wanted to impress me. To show how little time there was left."

"Will you print the date?"

"No. Will you tell me about the drug business?"

"No. There are more important things for you to know."

"Such as?"

"Go to New Orleans. You'll meet one of the Five Perfect Masters there."

"How?"

"He'll find you. Don't worry. Take things as they come."

That was the end of that. The Katmandu interlude was over. I came down from the mountains. I fell out of love with Lakshmi, with Geraldine. I stopped crying in the night. I threw out my Valium. I had been in a state, all right. But by the time that the 747 landed at Los Angeles, I was myself again.

Kalki was not god. I was certain of that. I was also reasonably certain that he was in the drug business. I had yet to find the connection between a drug syndicate and a new religion. Obviously there was one. I did not believe that Kalki would switch off the human race on April 3, as desirable a happening as that might be.

What did I really think at the beginning of last March, without hindsight? I thought that Kalki was out of his skull. But I also thought that he might really think that he could do what he said he was going to do.

One curious thing: No matter how rigorously I bathed, I continued to smell his blondness on my body. This lasted for a week. Stigmata? I hoped that Arlene would not notice.

FOUR

1

ARLENE AND I MADE LOVE FOR TWO HOURS THE DAY THAT I GOT back from Asia. Though groggy with jet lag, I was my true self again. I was out of the mountains.

I have never understood why Arlene and I were a duo, as the gossip columnists used to say. Arlene had no interest in aviation. I disliked show business. Arlene never read a book. I did, and do. She was old enough to be my mother. Well, answers to questions come at the end of sentences. My Christ Scientist mother was a monster. A line from the logbook, by Jules Renard: "There is nothing harder to look at than the face of a mother you do not love and for whom you are sorry." Except that I was never sorry for her, only for myself, the only child. I escaped into books, flying, engineering, French literature. I did not go . . . I *fled* to school. Anything to get away from home.

One bright afternoon in my twenty-fifth year, Mrs. Hecht thoroughly cleaned the two-bedroom condominium in Santa Ana that she had bought after the death of my father. She then prepared herself a cup of tea and settled down in an easy chair just opposite the television set, which was broken. The repairman was due any minute. During the any minute, she spread a newspaper over her lap, placed a plastic bag over her head and suffocated.

The television repairman found Mrs. Hecht early that evening (he had been delayed). Headline of the newspaper on her lap: TEDDY OTTINGER WINS INTERNATIONAL HARMON TROPHY. I had killed her. My success had killed her. She was a jealous woman, no doubt of that. Once, at bridge, she had tried to strangle her partner. She did not have many friends.

Shortly after my mother's death (which she did not believe in but I did), I started to take up with older women. Earl Jr. never suspected. But then neither did I. For a long time I did not realize why I so much enjoyed the company of Hilda Barefield, of Renée Dubilier. It was Hilda who seduced me, finally. I never looked back. After *Beyond Motherhood,* Arlene and I lived together openly. Surrogate mother? Why not? She also paid the bills.

"I hope you told Mike Wallace that I think he's a pussycat." Arlene wrinkled her nose the way that she did whenever Jedda Coffee was given her after a bad experience with the Other Brand. I never allowed her cuteness to cause me a moment's distress.

"I didn't get to speak to him. Has the show gone on yet?"

"I don't watch, angel. You know that."

I have still not been able to sort out satisfactorily the events of last March. My main recollection is one of panic. I was also suffering from a recurrent nightmare that I had never had before, or since. I am backstage, in a theater. I am the star of a play. The curtain has gone up. I am waiting in the wings for my cue. Suddenly I realize that I don't know what the play is about. I have not learned the lines. I try to slip out the stage door. A stage manager brings me back. He shoves me out onto the stage. Lights blind me. Applause deafens me. Then an actor finishes a speech. He turns to me, expectantly. My cue. I try to speak; but no sound comes. Silence. I can just make out the audience on the other side of the lights. They watch me, expectantly. As the silence continues, they are the ones who break it. They whisper to one another. They are angry. Then I wake up, in a sweat. Yet I have never acted in a play. In some mysterious way, Arlene and her actor friends must have transferred to me their own anxieties. So many other things are contagious, so why not nightmares? For me, the events of March were like pieces to a puzzle that I could not fit together. Or a play whose dialogue I had not learned.

I did not see Earl Jr. or the children. But I spoke several times to my former worse half on the telephone. Sample conversation: "So you're back, Teddy." Earl Jr. was accusing. Emphasis on the word "back."

"How are the children?"

"Do you care, Teddy?" Earl Jr. escalated more rapidly than usual. But then I was behind with the alimony payments.

"Of course I care."

"You haven't asked about Lenore and the operation."

"How is she?"

"After they removed the right breast, they had to go back in and remove all the lymph nodes from under her right arm. Three of those nodes showed signs of malignancy. Lenore's staying with me now in your old room and is undergoing chemotherapy at the hospital. Her hair has all fallen out, Teddy. Lenore's beautiful thick hair." If ever Mother Nature designed a classic fag-hag plus fag-son team, it was Lenore and Earl Jr. But Mother Nature is famous for her humor. Despite appearances, Earl Jr. was doggedly heterosexual while Lenore had no time for fags.

I married too young. That is the usual cop-out, and is usually true. Earl Jr. and I had, at the most, four good weeks together. I used to think that everything was my fault until Hilda convinced me that we are what we are and whatever I was, wife and mother was not a part of the initial psychic blueprint. These things are no one's fault. My father always said that I should have been a boy. I will not dwell on the implications of that opinion. He was an intelligent man. He made fiberglass boats until he was conned into selling his patents to a large corporation. He died poor. Although I was fond of him and he was proud of me, I could never forgive him for not marrying Amelia Earhart. I am sure that he could have. He had been interested in aviation at the time. He was also a do-gooder. He joined her for a time at Denison House in Boston. They worked with the poor. But he was too self-effacing, and she was too restless. Finally, she took to the sky for the fun of it. *The Fun of It* was the title of her best book. He told me once that Amelia was so blond that her eyelashes were white. Dark like me, he was turned on by blondness.

I told Earl Jr. that I was sorry about Lenore's hair but glad that the operation had been a success. I promised him that I would pay him his alimony as soon as I got around to depositing my first check from Kalki Enterprises. Then I talked to the children. They sounded fine. I said that I would see them at Easter, as soon as I got back from New York. Obviously I did not take seriously Kalki's prediction. In fact, I had insisted on a three-month contract, from the first of March to the first of June. Kalki had agreed. But he had also added, with a catlike grin, "I don't think you'll hold me to it."

On my second day back in L.A., Bruce Sapersteen came to see me. He had flown "out to the Coast just to meet *you*, Teddy!"

I received him in Arlene's library, a room in which the only books were a leather-bound set of *TV Guide* from the first issue to date. Reputedly, Arlene was in every issue, something for *The Guinness Book of World Records*.

Bruce Sapersteen was tall, dark, willowy. In every way the reverse of my mental image of him. The telephone is the great deceiver. Sadly, I dyed black the carroty curls that I had given him; removed the bushy sideburns; smeared evenly the pink freckled skin with Acapulco Sunbrown pancake. He was almost a decade younger than I. Columbia School of Journalism. *Village Voice. The National Sun.* The pieces that he had written in my name sounded like Tom Wolfe on a very bad day. I suppose that this was a slight improvement on H.V. Weiss's tightly coiled Hemingway-type prose; but not much. When it came to "as told to" collaborators, my cup had a tendency to overflow.

"You're a lot better-looking than your pictures, Teddy." This is always an acceptable opening. If I did not warm to him, I did not grow any chillier.

"Thanks, Bruce. I read your pieces. I thought you'd be younger."

"Thanks, Teddy." Like most journalists, Bruce seldom listened. "We've got a great thing going, you and me. Morgan's happy; circulation's gone up. Everyone's following our lead. We ought to be able to squeeze a lot more out until he blows it."

"Blows it?"

"Kalki says he's going to give a definite date for the end of the world at Madison Square Garden. When that day comes, Kalki's out of business. Want a snort?" Bruce produced a cocaine snifter. I shook my head. He sniffed. Then, nose pink and runny, he brought me up to date. "We've nailed down the drug connection. The lawyers are going over it right now. Soon as they give the green light, we're off and running."

"What kind of proof have you got?"

Bruce opened a notebook. "After Kelly left the army, he went to Thailand. In Bangkok he became associated with the Chao Chow Overseas Chinese Community, one of the principal drug syndicates in the world. The Golden Triangle is their turf. Kelly's worked with them ever since, peddling not only white heroin, but heroin-3, our old friend brown sugar. Kelly has a partner in New Orleans, one Giles Lowell, M.D. Take notes." I took notes. "Together they own something called the New Orleans Tropical Bird and Fish Company. Along with legal consignments of birds and fish from Latin America, they receive consignments of drugs, which are then dispersed all over the country. Morgan wants you to go to New Orleans. Describe the shop. Interview Dr. Lowell. Then just sit back and leave the writing to us." Bruce closed the notebook, very pleased with himself. A single drop of clear liquid clung to the tip of his nose.

"Anything to oblige," I said. "But what is the connection between Kalki the god and Kelly the drug merchant?"

"I don't know."

"So that's for me to find out."

"That, and the date of the end of the world. When we know those two things, it's fat thirty time." Bruce had obviously been impressed by journalism school. But then so was I. By schools. If the line at the registration office at USC had been shorter last year, and if I had been looking better and not got a nosebleed, I would have enrolled in graduate school like half the intelligent women that I knew (and quite a few that were not so bright). Yes, I would have gone back to school. I would have started all over again, and got my doctorate, and had a second life, if that first go-round could properly be called a life at all. Beyond motherhood—a Ph.D.? Anyway, the line at the office had been too long. I had split. Now I am in the White House. Yes, this is a success story. So far.

I did not tell Bruce that I knew the magical date. I also did not mention that I was under contract to Kalki Enterprises. I felt no disloyalty. Without me, there would have been no story of any kind. I was just a front, and knew it. And did not care. Morgan and I were using each other. But I did wonder at the coincidence. Kalki had wanted me to go to New Orleans, to meet a Perfect Master. Now the *Sun* also wanted me to go to New Orleans. Had there been collusion? If I was not in a paranoid state, I was on the border.

The drop fell from Bruce's pink nose. He seemed not to notice. Last year a lot of people that you met were sniffing coke. I didn't dare. If my reflexes are not swift, I am out of business. Dead.

"We've made a reservation for you at the Lafitte Hotel. In the French Quarter." Bruce gave me an envelope. "Ticket. Vouchers. Morgan says watch your step. You may be walking into the middle of a tong war down there."

This was too much. I crossed the state line into paranoia. "I didn't know there were any Chinese in Louisiana."

"That's not what I meant. Last year when Kelly went public with all this messiah shit, he broke with the Chao Chow syndicate. That's why he is going to get hit." As Bruce spoke, I saw again the bomb at the back of the *Garuda*. I wanted to go to the bathroom. "The Chao Chow have taken out a contract on him. It's with this underground Chinese society called Triad. Triad's got people all over the world. Hit men. You pay. They kill. Couldn't be neater. The latest word out of Hong Kong is that Kelly is going to get himself hit some time in April. April," said Bruce with a coke-inspired giggle, "is the cruelest month. Get it?" I got it.

2

NEW ORLEANS WAS LIKE EVERY OTHER AMERICAN CITY IN THE AGE of Kali. The air was dark with smoke from oil refineries. There were too many cars, people, crime, violence, anomie. As a result, Kalki was catching on. Also, while I had been in Asia, the so-called Lotus Lotteries had become a national pastime. Lottery, of course, was a misnomer. In a lottery you buy a ticket and if your ticket bears a lucky number you win a bundle. The white paper lotuses were not bought but given away. Then, each week, the press announced the winning numbers, and cash prizes were doled out by Kalki Enterprises. Kalki was now a household word. Although no one understood where the money was coming from, everyone enjoyed the Lotus Lotteries.

The contemporary New Orleans note was struck by the taxi driver who took me in from the airport. He was white, middle-aged; he was from New York and believed. . . . But let him speak for himself: "I never pick up the coloreds."

I pointed my silence in his direction. Although it struck the back of his neck, he was impervious.

"You think," said the driver, "that maybe I'm prejudiced or a bigot. Well, I wasn't until last year when I picked up these two black guys and one pulled this gun on me and said, you drive out to the edge of town to where this unfinished high-rise was. Well, I kept on telling them how I had only a few dollars which they could have but, no, they weren't interested. 'We gonna kill you,' one of them kept saying. So when we got to this deserted building site, they told me to get out of the car and the one with the gun kept saying, 'We gonna kill you!' "

"What happened?" I was interested in spite of myself.

"I got shot twice in the stomach and then they ran away. Well, I was lucky because I was able to crawl over to the car radio and call for help. Here. My clippings." Mounted in a small gold picture frame were two short newspaper items. "Cab driver shot" was indeed the story. I was impressed.

Just as we turned into Canal Street, I saw the first of the Kalki billboards. There was Kalki's face, thirty times as large as life. In color. Beneath the face, "The End." And that was all. Twenty thousand similar billboards had been set up all around the United States as a sort of teaser for Kalki's appearance on CBS's *60 Minutes*, which in itself was a trailer for the rally in Madison Square Garden. Since talking to taxicab drivers was the hallmark of the higher journalism, I asked the driver what he thought of Kalki. "I don't," he said firmly, "pick up the coloreds any more." He repeated the story of the shooting without so much as altering a word. From that epoch I remember only two things vividly. The cabdriver with the thick neck. And the television director with the red, white and blue sneakers and a hankering for draft beer. Memory is a mystery.

The Lafitte Hotel was a brand-new hotel that did its best to imitate the gracious hotels of yesteryear. I imitated the gracious aviatrix of this year. I asked for messages. There were none. I tried to ring Morgan Davies. He was in conference. I rang Dr. Giles Lowell. He was out of town. Not a good beginning.

The legendary French Quarter was definitely ominous. At all hours of day and night, people were drunk, stoned. But some of the houses were charming, and the fancy ironwork balconies lived up to expectation. Not all the magnolia trees were sick. One or two had produced a waxy yellow flower, shyly unfolding in the acrid air.

At the end of Dauphine Street was a large two-story wooden house with an iron gallery at the second floor. A discreet sign announced: NEW ORLEANS TROPICAL BIRD AND FISH COMPANY.

Through street-level windows, I could see hundreds of caged birds. Parrots, cockatoos, myna birds . . . I have now run out of tropical birds' names though as a girl I had been a devoted bird-watcher. But nothing as exotic as those scarlet, green, yellow, blue creatures had ever come my way in Southern California.

The birds stared through the windows at me; eyes as bright and as fixed as those of their saurian cousins. Beaks opened and shut but no sound came through (bulletproof?) glass.

I put on an amiable, stupid smile, and went inside. I knew my part: Suburban housewife wants to assemble an aquarium for her young son in order to teach him nature's way of balancing an eco-system, or once the big fish have eaten up all of the little fish, they fight with one another. Backwards Mother Nature spells "Dinner."

The main showroom occupied the whole downstairs of the house. There were a number of what looked to be customers. But I took nothing at face value. I assumed that the narcs were the ones who seemed most interested in the tanks of fish, in the cages filled with birds, while the pushers were those who came and went, looking businesslike. I studied each face covertly, fearful of finding a Chinese face attached to the sinuous body of a tong killer. But there were no exotic faces in the shop.

On the other hand, the shop itself was not only exotic, it was a trip,

as the addicts say. Lights inside the fish tanks cast swirling water
reflections upon the walls while the discordant screams of the birds
managed, quickly, to give me a blinding menstrual-style headache.

I sat on a chair next to a door marked PRIVATE, and shut my eyes.
I tried to screen out the psychedelic effect, only to find that the rainbow
colors went right on blazing and writhing behind my shut lids.

"Can I help you, miss?" A woman's voice.

I opened my eyes. A small what H.V.W. would call mousy woman
was looking down at me—suspiciously? Nervously? Nothingly? I was
now in the highlands of the state of paranoia. I had no idea how I
seemed to her. I could have been a legitimate customer taken ill, or an
illegitimate customer suffering from too much brown sugar in my tea.

I prayed that my stupid smile was on straight. "I have a headache.
That's all. The birds are so loud."

"I know. I really hate them." She had a thick Southern accent. She
was nervous. "And I have to work here."

"That must be awful for you."

"I like the job. It's just those awful birds. But can I help you, miss?"

"Well, I don't know. I wanted to start an aquarium. For my son.
He's ten. That's a wonderful age. When you're still so open and yet
so . . ."

"But you're not from New Orleans." She had spotted *my* accent.

"Surely, you don't have to be from New Orleans to have a tropical
fish tank." I could feel my stupid smile slipping toward my chin.

She gave me a pin-sharp look. Had I said a code phrase? "No, I guess
you don't."

"Actually, my husband and I have only just moved here from
near Sacramento where we used to live. Marysville, the town is
called . . ."

At that moment the door marked PRIVATE opened and out stepped
Jason McCloud. He looked very natty in a conservative gray flannel
suit. He carried an attaché case. I tried to become invisible by widening
my cretin's smile. Our eyes for a moment locked in the best Weissean
tradition. Then the lock was swiftly broken. Showing more white to his
eyes than was absolutely necessary, McCloud fled, nearly upsetting a
birdcage. The cage's occupant screamed irritably.

"Do you know each other?" asked the girl.

"No, I don't think so." I almost said that they all look alike to me, the sort of thing Arlene's friends liked to say seriously to one another as a joke. For them Ronald Reagan was really and truly America's last white hope.

"Is that Dr. Lowell's office?" I pointed to the door marked PRIVATE.

"Yes, it is." The girl frowned. "But he's not here. Do you have an appointment?"

Just as I was about to play Teddy Ottinger, Investigative Journalist, able to plumb the deepest throat in order to get that scoop or beat or whatever they call it, someone at the front of the store called out, "Mrs. Kelly!" The girl excused herself.

I was in luck. The girl proved to be Estelle Kelly, first wife of James J. There had been no mention of her in any of the stories about Kalki; she was a non-person, as they used to say in the people's paradises of the East. But non-person or not, there she was. I took her to lunch. I did my best to charm her.

Shy, bad-tempered, nervous, Estelle Kelly was not easily charmed. At first, I did most of the talking. I was careful to spread as much truth around as possible. I told her that I was Kalki's pilot, that I wanted to meet Dr. Lowell, that I was writing some pieces for *The National Sun*, but only to help Kalki. Estelle regarded me with deep suspicion. Even so, she allowed me to take her to her favorite restaurant where I would be able to sample New Orleans' fabled Creole cuisine, which you can have.

"Jim's a bastard." This was Estelle's thoughtful analysis of her first husband. We had each polished off a pair of Sazerac cocktails, a local killer. The restaurant was crowded, expensive and bad. I picked at an elaborate dish that had been made with frozen shrimp that tasted of iodine. As of last spring, you put your life at risk if you ate a fish, assuming that you could pay for one.

The waiter brought us a second bottle of California wine. I was eager to get Estelle drunk, to get her to talk. Unfortunately, she could drink me under the table any day of any week. Up to a point, she was forthcoming. My-husband-is-a-bastard was good stuff. But not for me. I was out to serve Kalki as well as the *Sun*. Double agentry had its charms, and dangers. I presented her with mild little questions on the order of: "But you're still on good terms?"

"Why should I be?" Estelle frowned. "One minute I'm the wife. Right? The next minute I'm the ex-wife. No explanation. Things end.

93

That's what he said. Then he took up with that Pannicker girl. I don't think they're legally married. Not that that would bother Jimmy, even though we're both Catholics. At least, I am and he used to be."

"Now," I said, with a confiding smile, and just a trace of skepticism in my voice, "he's god."

"Can you believe it?" A hectic pink muddied Estelle's normally sallow cheeks. I noticed that she had enlarged pores. "I was bowled over when I heard the news. First he gets rid of me. Right? Then I pick up a newspaper and read how he's gone and started a new religion. He's crazy."

I tried to explain to her that the Hindu religion was not exactly new. By the time I had got to the part about Kalki being the avatar, I had lost her attention.

"I suppose," she said, "there's money in it. I mean, you see all those kids in the street with the pamphlets and the paper flowers. Well, they must collect something from somebody. Right? And now those billboards! I couldn't believe it when I drove to work this morning and saw that big sign, showing Jimmy up there, announcing The End. Can you believe it?"

I said that, no, personally I could not accept Kalki's message. But I did feel that he was serious about his religion; and that he really thought that the world was ending.

"You're the one," said Estelle suddenly, "who pays alimony to your ex-husband."

"I feel women ought to. *Some* women," I added, quickly. "Certainly not in your case. Kalki left you. So he owes you a lot. But I left my husband. I was also making more money than he was. And so when he got custody of the children . . ." I stopped the autobiography. "Does Kalki pay you alimony?"

Estelle nodded. I could see that I was not a heroine in her eyes. I had let down the team: "Take 'em to the cleaners" was the perennial cry of the pussycat. But I was not in New Orleans to spread the gospel of equal rights.

"Kalki owns that bird and fish shop, doesn't he?"

For once H.V.W. would have been correct if he had said that a pair of eyes narrowed. Estelle's eyes became "mere" slits. "Dr. Lowell owns it," she said, carefully. "Of course, they're old friends. Jimmy studied with Dr. Lowell at Tulane. Jimmy was premed. Dr. Lowell was his teacher. Now, I should warn you that I'm not going to say anything about Jimmy, one way or the other, except that I think he was a bastard the way he just let me go on for years thinking that we would be living together when he got back from Asia, only he never came back."

"When did you see him the last time?"

"During his last year in the army. We met in Bangkok. R and R. That was 1968. He said as soon as he got discharged, he'd come straight home to New Orleans. This is the best rum cake in town." The rum cake was good. And Estelle's mood began to improve. "He also said he wanted to go on to medical school. But I knew even then that that was all talk. Because he was really into Asia. I mean, he could speak all the languages. I suppose he must have had a lot of girl friends there. Natives. Madame Butterfly stuff. I always thought he was oversexed. Anyway, when he got out of the army, he stayed in Saigon. I said I was ready to join him, though I hate Chinese food. Next thing, he asked for a divorce. Just like that. I *will* say he was generous. He paid for me to go to Mexico. Not long after I got back, he calls me up from Bangkok. He says he's married to this rich girl named Doris Pannicker. He wants me to be happy. He hopes I'll marry again. God, men are rotten! Anyway, I hung up the phone. And took a job."

"At the shop?"

Estelle nodded. There were tears in her eyes. I knew how she felt. "Giles . . . Dr. Lowell, I mean, quit Tulane that year. We'd always been good friends. In fact, Jimmy had been sort of a pet of his. Giles was tired of teaching. Tired of being poor. He loved tropical birds. The fish came later. They were sort of an afterthought, like the shrunken heads. Anyway, he opened the shop, and I went to work for him. He's made a great success. And I like to work." There was not much conviction in that last statement. We finished the wine in silence. At the next table crêpes were burning out of control. A panicky waiter poured brandy on the fire. There was a whoosh of blue flame. Everyone was delighted, and drunk. A tropical town.

"Where does the money come from?"

"Money?" Estelle watched intently as the waiter made us café brûlé. "The shop does real well, if that's what you mean."

"I meant for Kalki."

"God knows. But he can charm the little birds right down from the trees. He's a real con man." Estelle dropped the subject, and I could

95

not get her to take it up again. "You know," she said, suddenly cozy, "between us, I hate birds. I have a thing about them. So I went to a psychiatrist, a friend of Giles . . . of Dr. Lowell. And he told me this story about this woman who went to Dr. Jung, the psychiatrist in Switzerland, and told him how every time she went outside the birds would attack her. So Dr. Jung said, 'Madam, I'm sure that you just think they do. Let's take a walk in my garden and you'll see that this is all in your imagination.' Right? So they walked in Dr. Jung's garden and all the birds attacked her. Well, I'm like that. I mean, they don't attack me but they give me the shivers."

I was feeling a bit drunk by then. The café brûlé was getting to me. "You seem to have chosen the wrong line of work."

"I feel safer when they're in their cages." The first Mrs. Kelly was definitely one for the books. But I needed her. I did my best to draw her out. But it was useless. She appeared to have no real interest in Kalki. They had not met in years. On the other hand, she was obsessed by Lakshmi. She saw her as cashing in. Money meant a lot to Estelle. Also, religion.

"You've got to remember," she said, "that Jimmy was never religious. He never went to Mass. His mother was really upset, because they're very religious, the Irish out by the Irish Channel. My people were Creole. Which does *not* mean part Negro. We're the original settlers, from France, intermarried with Spanish. The Irish came much later. I was at Saint Ursula's convent, you know. Only certain families are allowed to send their daughters there. We were always warned against those Irish boys from the Channel. But I didn't listen."

"Where did you first meet . . . Jimmy?" I was roving reporter; keen, to the point.

"Dance class. We both studied with Eglanova. Here in New Orleans. She's dead now. But her studio's still going strong out on Napoleon Street. She was a prima ballerina with the Ballet Russe de Monte Carlo."

"Dance?" My mind did an H.V.W. reel. "*Ballet* dancing?"

"Oh, yes. Fact, Eglanova always said that Jimmy had the makings of a really great dancer even though he didn't start till he was seventeen, which is late."

"I find it hard to believe. I don't know why."

"I don't know why either. He was very serious about it, too. You see, he had had polio. A light case. But he wanted to build up his legs. That's when he started taking dance class. We both kept going to class while we were at Tulane."

Kalki's uncommonly muscular legs were now explained. Most of the pieces of the jigsaw were now at hand. Ballet. Premed. Roman Catholic marriage to Estelle. Vietnam. Medical corps. Drugs? Civil divorce. Remarriage? Religion. The links of the chain were clattering, but not yet into place.

"There's nothing sissy about ballet nowadays. Jimmy wasn't at all gay, you know." I know, I thought to myself. But then I did not really know. Whoever does? Bisexuality is a strange business. According to the best authorities, there is no such thing as bisexuality except among bisexuals. "He had wonderful elevation. I had a lovely long line. But not much stamina. Jimmy's a strange boy." Dreamily, Estelle slurred already slurred Southern vowels. "Always was, I guess. Not that I had any way of knowing when I was a kid. We were so young. Right? We just drifted along. At Tulane I was prelaw, believe it or not. He was premed. Then he shifted over to chemistry. I thought he'd make a really fine scientist. He had that kind of technical mind. I could see him in a white smock, cooking up things for Du Pont." Estelle sighed, "Wilmington is such a lovely city. I always hoped we'd live there. I really did. I have relatives outside Wilmington, the Jarvises. But then came Vietnam . . ." Estelle looked in need of the proverbial good cry. I needed oxygen. The fumes from the burned crepes were stifling.

"I know what it's like," I said. I played sympathetic girl friend. "When I married Earl Jr. I thought we'd be living in Seattle. He was going to be an engineer with Boeing. I loved Seattle." None of this was true but I wanted to make her feel at ease with me. Sisters in suffering. "But then he went into real estate, in Santa Monica. It wasn't the same."

"No," said Estelle, "it never is." She was beginning to show signs if not of drunkenness, of high-ness. I had let her drink the entire second bottle of wine.

"When," I struck, softly, "did Jimmy get into drugs?"

Estelle sobered up. She took the cigarette that she had just lit and stubbed it out in the remains of the rum cake. She got her handbag off the floor and onto the table. "I don't know anything about drugs, Mrs. Ottinger. I must be going now. Such a nice lunch . . ."

I paid the bill. I maintained an exemplary coolness. "Funny, I thought you did. I mean you know Jason McCloud, and he's with the DEA. You know, the black man with the attaché case."

"I never saw him before." Estelle stood up. "I have to go."

I walked her back to the shop. At the corner of Canal Street we were stopped by a dozen Kalki boys and girls. They wore yellow robes and sandals. They carried books, magazines, white paper lotuses. "Kalki has come," one of them said, nicely. "The end of the world is here. Would you like to be prepared? To purify yourself?" Each of us was given a booklet. And a white paper lotus.

"I average about two of these damned things a day." Estelle threw the pamphlet into an open cellar. But kept the lotus. She was obviously playing the lottery. "I've never read such nonsense. Ever! How a good Catholic boy like Jimmy could end up spouting all this Hindu nonsense is beyond me."

"You don't think he's really god?"

"Are you crazy? Of course not." Estelle's face set, if that's what faces do when the line of the jaw is abruptly squared through a deliberate occlusion of back molars. "On the other hand, I don't think he's crazy. He's up to something. But I don't know what."

"Money?"

"No." Estelle did not expand since any expansion would involve a further discussion of the bird and fish shop. "He's a very radical person. And if he thinks he's right, and if he's figured out all the angles, why, he's capable of anything. You know he's a genius."

"At what?"

"IQ. Scientific capacity. Giles . . . Dr. Lowell says he's unique."

"Do they still see each other?"

Estelle looked me straight in the eye, the way liars are always advised to do. "Never. How could they? Jimmy hasn't been home in years. And Giles never leaves town."

"I thought you told me earlier that he was out of town."

"Out of the office. He'll be back later. I'll tell him you're at the Lafitte Hotel."

In Dauphine Street a second group of Kalki-ites asked us very politely if we would like to go back to their ashram. A guru would tell us about the various ages of man that had led up to the age of Kali, our age, the last age. We would also be shown how to meditate, how to be and not be, how to purify ourselves in order to move on to a higher sphere. As we slipped away from the kids, they waved goodbye to us. They were sweet.

"I don't understand why people are so attracted to Kalki." And I wasn't, not entirely anyway. "All he promises them is The End. And that's not exactly a happy message."

"Well, maybe they're as sick of this as I am!" Estelle was unexpectedly harsh.

"But isn't there always hope . . ."

My Pollyaniad was cut short. "Shit," said Estelle. We were in front of the store. "Thanks for lunch. Give Jimmy my regards. I'll tell Dr. Lowell you want to see him." She went inside.

As I walked back to the hotel, I was more than pleased with myself. Journalists seldom did much more than rewrite what was already known to be news. But I had actually come up with something new; in fact, news. By going to New Orleans, I had been able to meet the unknown first wife and, presently, with luck, I would meet Kalki's old teacher, Giles Lowell.

Why had no one else done what I had done? I tried to find reasons, keeping at bay dark suspicions. For one thing, Kalki had been news for less than a year . . . a year in which he had been obliged to compete for media space with the energy crisis, the drought, recession, unemployment, Reverend Sun Moon, and the blunders of the administration in Washington. Only in the last two weeks had the momentum increased. Between those (thousands?) of young Kalki-ites in the streets and all those billboards, Kalki was now world-famous. Yet of all the world's journalists, I was the only one to have met the two wives, to have. . . .

I was suddenly engulfed by a wave of paranoia. Kalki had deliberately made it easy for me. He had told Estelle to talk to me. He had wanted me to write *her* version of his life. I was being set up. First, by Estelle (but was she really who she said she was?) and then by a mysterious Perfect Master. I was being tested. Why? and for what?

3

WHEN I SAW JASON MCCLOUD SEATED IN THE LOBBY OF THE hotel, I thought for one terrible moment that he was a Perfect Master, posing as a narc. But he proved to be just a narc, and a very jittery one at that. McCloud got to his feet. I said, "Hello." The clerk at the desk gave me a telephone message. I was to ring Bruce Sapersteen in New York. At home.

"I got to see you." McCloud no longer carried an attaché case. I told him to meet me in the bar of the hotel. Then I rang Bruce.

"Hi, Teddy!" Bruce sounded stoned. I could imagine the glowing pinkness of his nose.

"I've been to the bird and fish shop. I'm still trying to interview Dr. Lowell. I've met Kalki's first wife."

"Great! When you hear the blip, start dictating." I heard the blip, and told my story. When I had finished, Bruce came on the line again. "That's good stuff. I don't know how we missed out on the first wife. Lousy research, I guess. Anyway, we're getting a lot of feedback on the stories. The drug connection gets plainer every day."

"But how can you use it?"

"Morgan's trying to work it out with the lawyers. Kalki Enterprises has got a lot of money behind them. But we're getting help from the government, on the sly. Even so, it's tricky!"

"Does Morgan mind my taking the job as Kalki's pilot?" When in doubt, tell the truth. I had written Morgan a letter, to make it official. So far, there had been no answer.

"No. He thinks it's a great idea. We're advertising the next piece as inside stuff from Kalki's personal beautiful pilot, with a picture of you, looking gorgeous, with those big boobs . . ."

"Go to hell, Bruce. I'm a divorced woman."

Sapersteen giggled uncontrollably. I hung up.

McCloud was seated in a corner of the bar, a dark place with a black bartender got up to resemble an ante-bellum old retainer. I decided to risk yet another Sazerac. McCloud was drinking bourbon in great quantities. He spoke in a whisper even though we were the only people in the bar.

"Ms. Ottinger, I feel that you owe the Drug Enforcement Administration an explanation."

That was a startling icebreaker. "For what?"

"Why were you in the New Orleans Tropical Bird and Fish Company?"

"I want to start an aquarium."

"This is not a joke, Ms. Ottinger."

"Let me be the judge of that, Mr. McCloud." I took the offensive. "What were *you* doing there?"

"My job."

"Which is?"

"The detection of drug pushers."

"What was in that attaché case you were carrying? Drugs or payoff money?"

McCloud gave me a look not entirely empty of Weissean bale. "You could be arrested. Right now. By me."

"What charge?"

"Possession of cocaine. In your handbag. Three ounces."

I held the handbag to my chest. "There is no cocaine in this handbag."

"If I *say* there is cocaine," said McCloud in a slow breathy voice, "then there is. And you go to jail. My word against yours."

I was moderately alarmed. Setting up the innocent was a favorite practice of America's numerous secret as well as public police forces. Certain of Los Angeles' finest used always to carry marijuana roaches in their pockets. If they disliked someone, the roach would then be planted in the victim's car or home. The policeman would then say, "Aha! We caught you!" And the innocent would be busted. And he would stay busted because no judge ever publicly doubted a policeman's word. After all, judges can be set up, too. They had a lot of fun, the police in L.A.; elsewhere, too.

I stayed on the offensive. "I know a lot about you." I invented freely. "You are being paid off by Kalki Enterprises. You were with Dr. Lowell today. He gave you money. I can't prove it—yet. But the *Sun* has a half-dozen researchers checking out this story, and you're part of the story. So my advice is lay off. And get a good lawyer." I thought this scene well-played. I reminded myself of Claire Trevor in a Bogart film.

Unfortunately, McCloud had seen the same movie, and saw himself as the black Bogart. "You're getting in over your head, Ms. Ottinger." He still spoke in a heavy whisper. But now he twitched his upper lip. Bogart. "You're right about the bird and fish shop. I've infiltrated it. And I'm in with Dr. Lowell. And I want to stay in with him. I don't want you making a mess. I'm a professional. You're an amateur. We're getting close to an arrest. I don't want you interfering."

"What constitutes interfering, Mr. McCloud?"

"Interviewing Dr. Lowell. Writing about the bird and fish shop in the *Sun.*"

"I would have thought anything that we might write would be helpful to you."

"We have a timetable, Ms. Ottinger. Premature revelation could undo all our work. I'm with White."

I heard this as "I'm white." With blacks the problem of color always danced in my head. "You're what?"

"I'm on special assignment for the White committee." I looked at him, I suppose, blankly. I got an irritable explanation. "Senator Johnson White is chairman of the Senate Narcotics Abuse and Control Committee. They're currently investigating the world drug scene. I've been assigned to Kalki Enterprises. That's why I was in Katmandu. That's why I'm here. In a few weeks there will be a public hearing. Kalki will be called. Senator White doesn't want anybody to break the news before he does."

I assumed McCloud was lying. Whether or not he was working for the White committee was beside the point which was that McCloud was working for McCloud. I was positive that he was on the take from Kalki Enterprises. But I played dumb. And, I think, beautiful. "I didn't realize!" I gave him an awed little woman gaze. "You're *really* important, aren't you?"

McCloud fell, or pretended to fall, which was the same thing for my purposes. I wanted to neutralize him. "Yes, I am," he whispered. I

KALKI *A Novel*

think a "thickly" would be apt. He was getting drunk.

"Do you think you could get me an introduction to Senator White? Off the record? Background briefing, highly-placed-source-on-Capitol-Hill kind of thing?"

"I might," McCloud was now staring at my blouse. Miscegenation was in the air; it hovered like a mushroom cloud between us. I was saved by the bell, literally. A telephone call. I rose. McCloud remained seated. I took his huge black hand in my fairly tiny white ones. "That's my date," I whispered. "You've been an angel." I pursed my lips for an instant; then fled. McCloud did not move. He was smiling.

"This is Dr. Giles Lowell." The voice on the telephone was pleasant, only slightly Southern in accent. "Estelle Kelly said you would like to meet me."

"Oh, very much. I'm working for Kalki, you know."

"Yes, I know. I'm at the shop now. Why don't you come around? Ring the front doorbell three times. I'll let you in."

I said that I would be right over. Just to be on the safe side, I rang Bruce in New York. He screamed, "Hello." It was one of those nights. In the background I could hear the hi-fi blaring Joni Mitchell in her latest phase.

"Listen, Bruce. I'm off to see Dr. Lowell. At the shop."

"Good hunting. Tally ho . . ."

"Shut up. I'm telling you this in case I'm murdered."

"Oh," Bruce sniffed. "You think he's dangerous?"

"The whole thing is dangerous. Life is dangerous. Anyway, I'm off. Also, check out one Jason McCloud, allegedly a narc. He's black. He acts as if he's just been spun off from a TV series that's in trouble. He says he's working for Senator White's committee . . ."

"White's going after Kalki?"

"So he says."

"White's running for president."

"I'm running late." I hung up. I was nervous. There are times when it is a definite drag being a woman. I have never feared rape. Or flying. Or people in general. But I am constantly haunted by the thought of a tall, heavy, male figure. He comes up behind me on a dark street. He doesn't want my treasure. He wants my life. I feel his arm about my neck. I can't see his face. I can't breathe. I'm helpless.

Bourbon Street was at least well-lit, and I walked its length, avoiding the side streets as long as possible, particularly Dauphine Street where the overhanging galleries made an absolute darkness in which lurked, I was certain, innumerable large, heavy, masculine figures, with arms itching to crook themselves about my neck, from the back.

Bourbon Street was not exactly fun for an unescorted woman in an aquamarine dress copied from Halston. Sex was in the air. Also, thudding music from the bars. Everyone looked lurid in the glare of neon lights. At night a single woman was a challenge in that city, on that street. Men stared at me. Some leered. None, thank God, flashed.

I concentrated on my handbag, and filled it with an imaginary revolver which I proceeded to load. Through sheer concentration, I was able to convince even the drunkest John that I was armed, and dangerous. As it turned out, the women were worse than the men. Sex was on their minds—but not with me. I was competition. I was elbowed; kicked. The hookers did not fear the imaginary revolver.

I walked quickly. Avoided as much as possible contact of any kind with anyone. A sailor vomited. A white pulled a knife on a black in a doorway. Everyone laughed at this reversal of the natural order. Junkies drifted by, eyes half-shut, cheeks seeming to rest on air as on a pillow. The Kalki kids did not, wisely, come out at night.

The last two blocks on Dauphine Street were terrifying. Beneath those forbidding galleries, the coffee-scented darkness contained every sort of danger. I walked, trotted, ran the last few yards to the bird and fish shop. It was closed. Through unshuttered windows, lighted fish tanks glowed like fluid opals. I rang the bell three times.

The door opened. Dr. Giles Lowell was tall, thin, bald. He was not, I remember thinking, gratefully, large or heavy or behind me.

When I started to speak, he put a finger to his lips. Then he motioned for me to follow him. On tiptoe we walked between the rows of shimmering fish tanks and shrouded birdcages. Some kind of floral spray had been used to neutralize the harsh odor of the birds. The resulting smell gave me my second headache for the day.

Dr. Lowell unlocked the private door. Stood back to let me pass, in darkness, up the stairs. My heart was pounding. Now he was behind me. But I got to his office without rape, murder, assault. He switched on a light. "Come in, Mrs. Ottinger," He was gracious. "Forgive the stealth and the darkness. But if you so much as switch on a light or say two words in the shop, every one of those damned birds wakes up and it's an hour before you can get them to go to sleep again. Do sit down. I'm Dr. Lowell, of course."

"Of course," I said, not too brightly, taking inventory of the room. There was nothing worth noting. A big desk, a sofa, two chairs, a filing cabinet, a series of watercolors of exotic birds. "Dr. Lowell," I picked up on the title. "Do you still practice medicine?"

"Oh, no. But then I never really practiced. I was just a teacher. Then I became a 'businessman.'" The overhead fluorescent light made the dome of his bald head glimmer blue. "Jim Kelly was a good student, if I may plunge right in. I know you are writing about him. I've read your two pieces in the *Sun.*"

"I don't really write them." I was properly defensive. It had never been my dream to be a nom de plume first for H.V. Weiss and now for B. Sapersteen. Amelia wrote her own books; and poetry, too.

"I quite understand. I have talked to Jimmy—or Kalki—about you. He told me you are to be his personal pilot."

"Yes. But he also wanted me to keep on with the *Sun.* To find out what they . . . know." I was never very good at deceit.

"What they know," Dr. Lowell repeated. He looked uncommonly sinister in the blue light. But then everyone looks sinister in a blue light. "But what really matters is what *you* know, isn't that right?"

I sensed threat. I played Dumb Dora. "I know so little, particularly about the early days."

Dr. Lowell nodded. "I think Jimmy . . . no, let's call him Kalki. He *is* Kalki, after all. Jimmy's real gift was for chemistry. We both realized that during his first year in premed when he developed a completely new hallucinogen from—of all things, apricots."

"A what?"

"A drug." Dr. Lowell mentioned without embarrassment the subject of our midnight visit. "He had a genius . . . well, no, not a genius but a definite flair for improvising drugs that would cause hallucinations. He would make them out of the most unlikely ingredients. But then he went into the army and that was that."

"Did *he* take drugs?"

"That is a delicate question, under the circumstances." Dr. Lowell opened a drawer in his desk. I half-expected him to produce a real version of my imaginary gun. Instead, he produced a bottle of Scotch, and two glasses. "Now, let us have some of the *licensed* drug, the nirvana of Middle America—booze!" He laughed, dismally. There was something depressing about Dr. Lowell; and familiar. He poured us each a glass. "To Kalki!" he said. We touched glasses, and drank.

"Dr. Lowell." I swallowed hard, not used to straight whiskey. Arlene actually gargled with tequila. As a result, her voice had dropped half an octave in less than ten years. "I am aware of the reputation of this shop . . ."

"Finest tropical birds and fish in the world. They come straight from the jungles of the Amazon to your ranch-style house, to your high-rise apartment, to your lonely bed–sitting room." The light from above made his eyes invisible. "We ship anywhere."

"I saw Jason McCloud in Katmandu. I saw him in the shop this afternoon. I met him again this evening. Look. I have a problem. Forget the *Sun.* I don't have to go on with the pieces. But I've signed a contract with Kalki Enterprises. I am supposed to be working for the reincarnation of Vishnu. A bit much, but who knows? Now let me put my cards on the table. If this whole religious thing is just a front for a drug syndicate, what happens to me when Senator White's committee lowers the boom? I'm going to be like the innocent guy in the getaway car who goes to Sing Sing." I was relieved, having come (relatively) clean.

Dr. Lowell shut his invisible eyes. "I see," he said, "your problem. I respect it. Let me try to be helpful. Kalki has no connection with this shop. It is my show entirely. It is true that McCloud is working for the White committee. The committee and Senator White need headlines. I am thought to deal in drugs. I was close to Kalki and we still keep in touch. Ergo, Kalki is not the avatar of the all high but a drug-pusher. For several months McCloud and White have been biding their time. As the publicity for Kalki builds, so will the publicity for their committee hearings. White intends to be the fortieth—or is it the forty-first? president of this great republic. McCloud intends to rise with him. If, of course, McCloud is not a double agent himself."

"Taking money from you? I saw the attaché case." I stuck my neck into the noose. But then the whiskey had made me reckless; and sleepy.

Dr. Lowell took my accusation in his considerable smooth stride. "It is customary for the American businessman to pay off government investigators, no matter how innocent his business. McCloud is quite capable of setting me up."

I nodded. "The cop with the roach," I said.

"I beg your pardon?" Dr. Lowell was getting a bit blurry in the cold light.

"I meant . . ." But I could not for the life of me say what I meant because I had been drugged.

Just as I lost consciousness, I realized that Dr. Lowell was Dr. Ashok.

FIVE

1

Had I been less ill, I might have taken a certain pleasure in Dr. Lowell's old-fashioned sense of melodrama. He had not, as they say, missed a trick. First, I had been drugged by a member of the legendary family of Michael Finn. Second, I had been put to bed in a Scandinavian-style modern bedroom. Third, ominously, I was wearing a black lace nightgown unknown to fashion since the forties, the period of Dr. Lowell's awakening manhood. Had I been raped? Probably. My entire pelvic area was sore. God alone knew what lecherous games Dr. Lowell had played. I wanted to throw up. I felt feverish.

A female voice came to me, as if through a yard of wool. "How do you feel, Mrs. Ottinger?"

"Like death," I replied. I turned and saw a pleasant-looking woman, disguised (?) as a trained nurse.

"I'll tell Dr. Lowell." She left the room. I shut my eyes. I wanted only to sleep. To lose consciousness again. To escape the aches, chills, fevers.

The next thing I knew, Dr. Lowell was sitting beside my bed. He took my pulse. He seemed genuinely concerned with my health.

"I was drugged?" I had difficulty talking. I was also seeing double.

"Yes. I'm afraid I had to. But you've also been ill. Nothing to do with the drug. Believe me. Some form of influenza. I don't know what kind. Something you must've picked up in Nepal."

"From a Legionnaire." I thought this amusing, but he did not. He checked out my reflexes, vision, hearing. He was more reassured than not.

"You're all right," he said. "Thank God. I was scared to death."

"Why was I drugged?"

"I had to get you out of New Orleans. Away from McCloud."

"Out of New Orleans?" I was not really taking any of this in.

"Yes. We're in Washington, D.C. In a suite at the Jefferson Arms, a hotel which belongs to Kalki Enterprises."

"Does the *Sun* know?"

"They know you've been sick." Dr. Lowell produced a hypodermic needle. I let him shoot me up. "You should feel better in a few minutes."

I assumed that he had given me speed. I did not ask. "What about McCloud?"

"He was going to kill you. He is a hit man, working for the Chinese."

I let this nonsense slip by, unacknowledged. "Why am I here?"

Dr. Lowell put away the hypodermic needle. Then he sat back in his chair, and gave me what he no doubt thought was a beguiling smile. "You are a Perfect Master, Mrs. Ottinger. And so am I." Dr. Lowell stared at me, with the yellowy eyes of Dr. Ashok. I shut my own eyes, seeing if not double, doubleness.

"Kalki said I would meet a Perfect Master in New Orleans. He did not tell me that I'd also be drugged, kidnapped . . . raped?" Thus did I take the famed bull by his identifying horns. I know by heart Ms. Brownmiller's book on men, and rape.

"No. You were not raped. Beautiful as you are. May I call you Teddy?"

"Call me anything you like. But what do I call you? Dr. Lowell or Dr. Ashok?"

"My disguise proved penetrable!" Dr. Lowell was undistressed. "So be it. I am Dr. Ashok in Nepal because Dr. Lowell is *persona non grata* in that magical land. Hence, I must travel there in disguise. I am also an agent of the CIA, on a part-time basis. They do not connect me with Dr. Lowell."

"The purveyor of drugs to the Western World."

Lowell ignored the challenge. "From the beginning Kalki wanted us to meet. That is why I was on the plane to New Delhi. He wanted me to observe you. I did. I told him that I thought you were a Perfect Master."

"How," I asked, "can a non-Hindu atheist be a Perfect Master?"

"We are all Hindus, whether we know it or not. That is a fact, like creation. It is also a fact that the one god has three aspects and that the current incarnation of one of those three aspects is Kalki. Dear Teddy, don't frown so! I know it takes some getting used to. When Jimmy told me that he was Kalki . . . that was on his last trip to the States, in 1970, I thought he was mad."

"Can I take notes?" Weak as I was, I felt some obligation to Morgan.

"As your doctor, I must say, no. There will be time enough before the end of time." Lowell thought this sufficiently amusing to punctuate with a laugh. "Like you, I said to Jimmy, 'I'm not a Hindu.' I also told Kalki that he was not a Hindu, either, except by conversion. He said that that was not the point. We are who we are, and we have always been who we are throughout eternity. Sometimes we know. Sometimes we don't. We need enlightenment. That is what the word Buddha means, the one who has been enlightened."

"Then you . . . we are all Buddhas?"

"On the threshold. Except for Kalki, of course. He is god." Lowell said this with all the quiet authority that Michel Foucault would have us associate with the truly mad or sane.

I very much wanted to look at myself in the mirror. "Was he Kalki at Tulane?" My skin felt dry. I tried but failed to see a reflection of myself in the stethoscope on the bedside table.

"He was Kalki. But he didn't know it. Or so he says. I certainly never suspected. He was quite ordinary, outside of his lab work."

"He studied ballet."

"Next to mime, I hate ballet. If there is a hell being prepared for me, it will be an eternity of watching Marcel Marceau alternate with the Bolshoi Ballet." Lowell took a firmer line than I would have. Yet we were not too far apart in our tastes.

"Did you see Kalki before 1970?"

"I used to hear from him. Or about him. From Estelle, a nice girl. I'm sorry for her. So is Kalki. I mean, it's not her fault she was not Lakshmi."

"Kalki might have let her know early on. Women are usually quick to take a hint."

"He didn't know. So how could he tell her? When he realized he was Kalki and that his eternal wife was Lakshmi, he told Estelle. He also asked me to give her a job, which I was happy to do. I invade no privacy when I say that Estelle and I have been very close to one another since I opened the shop."

"Women," I said, from the heart, "have a lousy time in this world."

"Then be glad that it is ending."

"You could at least marry Estelle."

"Too late. The end . . ."

"Sure. Sure. But what about ten years ago? She would have liked that." I was fighting the sisters' battle.

Lowell was losing his suavity. "Estelle is Catholic. I'm not. I've also had a vasectomy. There could be no children. What is the point?"

"If you don't see the point, I can't explain it to you. Men are such shits. Give me a mirror."

Lowell brought me a hand mirror. I was duly depressed. "I look like death. Where's the nearest Elizabeth Arden?"

"You *were* near death, Teddy. If you hadn't been a Perfect Master, you would have died."

"If you hadn't drugged me, I'd never have been sick."

"I swear there was no connection." Lowell wanted very much for me to believe him, but I did not. For some obscure reason, I had been made ill.

For reasons equally obscure, I had been made well again. I had a sudden hot flush, or flash. The drug he had just given me was going into high gear. Suddenly I felt euphoric, and full of energy. "I still don't understand how I happen to be a Perfect Master."

Lowell actually shrugged, something one only hears of in H.V.W. land. But then Dr. Giles Lowell was a melodramatist and so at home in that lurid country. "I don't know, either. Kalki suspected it when he read your book, which I've not got around to yet, I fear. Anyway, I now know for certain that you are one of the Five Perfect Masters.

Don't ask me how I know. I just do. Your trip to New Orleans proved that Kalki was right. That you and I and Geraldine were chosen from the beginning to preside over The End. We have no real choice in the matter. Of us all, only Kalki has the freedom to act, to surprise. But even though he is god, he is obliged—like it or not—to act out the never-ending cycle of birth and death and rebirth. As Vishnu, he is lord of the universe. As Kalki, he is Vishnu temporarily encased in a man's flesh. The Jesus story is just a variation on the Kalki story."

To stimulate circulation, to clear my brain of the drug, I waved my arms in the air. As I did, the left sleeve of the black lace night dress fell back, revealing a blue-black bruise in the crook of my arm. "What's that?"

"One of a series of shots. The first one I gave you was on the plane when you woke up. Remember?"

I was panicky. "What plane?"

"The one from New Orleans to Washington, a private plane belonging to Kalki Enterprises. I'm afraid that's when you took ill. Your temperature went to 104. There were respiratory difficulties . . ."

I was beginning to feel unreal again. "How long have I been here?"

"Six days."

"My God! I've got to get up! I've got to talk to Morgan Davies."

"In time. At the moment you're going to talk to someone a lot more interesting than Mr. Davies. I've made an appointment for you to have breakfast tomorrow morning with Senator Johnson White, at the Mayflower Hotel. I've also spoken to Mr. Davies. He was thrilled about your coming interview with White. Because it all ties in with Kalki, and your pieces for the *Sun.*"

"You've taken quite a lot on yourself, Lowell."

"Giles."

"Giles. Where's my luggage?"

"Everything's here." Lowell got to his feet. "If there's anything you need, just let me know. Or the nurse."

Sitting here in the Cabinet Room at the White House, I still have some difficulty in arranging the pieces of the puzzle. A passage from Jules Renard: "When I notice something ridiculous, I notice it only much later. I do not observe a moment while I am living it. It is only later that I go over every detail of my life." That is what I am doing now, having saved that life. But I must confess that a good deal of what

I observed in Washington and later in New York struck me as surreal. But then it was meant to. Namah Shivayah. To be translated later.

2

THE NEXT MORNING, AS I WALKED DOWN WISCONSIN AVENUE, HAD anyone said that in a year's time I'd be working here at the White House, I would. . . . But, no. This is precisely the kind of hindsight I have been asked to avoid. I will stick only to the facts, as they occurred. My model will be Jules Renard; a man not given to metaphor or to Weissisms. "The romantic," wrote Renard, "looks at a large mirror and believes it to be the sea. The realist looks at the sea and believes it to be a mirror. But the man with a straightforward mind says, in front of the mirror: 'It is a mirror!' and in front of the sea: 'It is the sea.' "

In Washington I was faced with a United States senator who wanted to be the next Republican candidate for president. That is straightforward.

To continue forward in the straightest way possible, I should say right here that I always disliked politicians. They took up too much time on the talk shows, avoiding subjects and otherwise projecting personalities best left unprojected beyond the cozy confines of some small-town Kiwanis club. I was known because I had done something useful. I was a pilot who had broken records. I had risked my life, testing planes. But no politician from the President on down had ever actually done anything tangible. A parasitic trade, I always thought, matching them smile for smile on the tube.

Senator White was already seated at a table in the breakfast room of the Mayflower Hotel. He was alone. Later I was told that this was a great honor, for me. Usually senators (particularly the presidential ones) were surrounded not only by people who wanted something from the government but also by their own staff whose task it was to get, by crook or by hook, their senator's name into the newspapers and his face onto television. This is quite a trick when you consider that no senator actually did anything worth noting. In any case, with a total of one hundred senators, the competition was fierce. To survive, each statesman had to get, at least once a year, thirty to forty seconds on the 6:00 *News,* preferably back to back or, better yet, side by side with Walter Cronkite, the most trusted man in the nation because for each of five nights a week he nicely read the news for a total of seven minutes.

White was a short, thick man with tiny hands and feet, and a very big head. He was about fifty years old. As I approached, he displayed the politician's standard set of white capped teeth: too white, too glossy, too regular, so unlike the artful dental masterpieces that are parcel and part of the California landscape. White dyed his own hair, always a mistake. But then American politicians tended to look like TV anchormen on the cheap; too many corners cut too often. Contact lenses made White's eyes look larger and glassier than Mother Nature had intended. Oh, what a wondrous work is man! wrote a man.

I always thought that Americans would have been better off with a dictatorship somewhat on the order of Indira Gandhi's brief fling. After all, hardly anyone would have noticed or cared, except to applaud the fact that there would have been only one excruciating bore, taking up time on television instead of thousands. I suppose Saint-Exupéry was right. We fliers are not democrats. At thirty thousand feet, the world is an anthill. From outer space the world is a blue-green marble. All in all, I suppose it was a lucky thing that except for Lindbergh (briefly) fliers have stayed away from politics. Of course, Amelia did work in settlement houses, helping the poor. But then she was a saint, in a bad time.

I introduced myself to Senator White. He half-rose from the table; half-blinded me with three thousand white teeth as he thrummed a welcome in the politician's standard (i.e., deep and slightly monotonous) voice. I have noticed . . . no, it was Arlene who pointed out to me the curious fact that whoever is the most popular politician at any given moment is imitated by all the others. I can remember when senators as far afield as California were imitating J.F. Kennedy's Boston accent. During the period that a twice-born redneck from the South was in residence at the White House, a large number of presidential senators affected Southern accents. Senator Johnson White of Michi-

gan and the Harvard Law School had worked out a bumpkin number
that chilled the blood in my veins. "The corned beef hash here is real
good," he said, drawing out the vowels. I shuddered. Ordered coffee.

As we drank our coffee and cased one another, he made it perfectly
clear (through body language) that I could be, if not a president's
mistress, a candidate's lay. I swung my leg as far from his as I could.
Then I switched on my tape recorder. I smiled brightly. If I were a
man, I cannot imagine anything less aphrodisiacal than a woman with
a tape recorder.

"I hear you've just come from New Orleans." This came out dry and
clear. But then White remembered he was just folks and running for
president. "A swell town," he honked, "where they treat you real
good."

"Do they?" I signaled him as best I could that I was not a potential
supporter.

White dropped the fried mush. "I'm a great admirer of Morgan
Davies." This was said with warmth, sincerity; but then everything he
said was warm, sincere. "I think he's done a bang-up job with his
. . . uh, periodicals. I read the *Sun* faithfully. A little far-out politically
for my taste. He's too much in with those eco-freaks, but he's tough
on drugs. And so am I. And I think that you were an inspired choice
to investigate and expose the drug racket for him."

"Not drugs, Senator." I spoke softly. In the opposite booth a half-
dozen professional constituents were staring at us. They had recognized
White. They envied me. "My assignment is to cover Kalki, and the end
of the world."

White gave me a conspirator's smile. "Sure. Sure. I read you, Teddy.
Roger." Thirty seconds over Hanoi was the extent of his cockpit exper-
tise. Politicians always called you by your first name. "Do you realize,
Teddy," and he looked grave, discouraged, the way all the presidents
were obliged to look after talking to their opposite number in the
Kremlin, "that Kalki, and the end of the world, are going to get eleven
and a half minutes on CBS's *60 Minutes* to be aired this Sunday?"
White looked ready to cut his wrists.

"Kalki's a good performer." I was cool. "And the subject has a
certain interest."

Understatement never went over very well with politicians. "Those
billboards!" White looked in pain. "Do you know what it costs to have

twenty thousand billboards across the country *in full color?* Not even Dick Nixon in '71 spent that kind of money."

"I'm told that you think Kalki and Dr. Lowell are in the drug business." I lifted my ball-point; held it over the notebook.

"I thought," said White, "that the whole point to your exposé in the *Sun* was the fact that the New Orleans Tropical Bird and Fish Company is a front for one of the largest drug syndicates in the world. I also thought that my friend Morgan would have told you by now that we expect you to hold off with your revelations until *after* my committee has held its first hearings in New York, and called Kelly or Kalki as a witness, in two weeks' time."

I was disturbed by the reference to Morgan. Had White made some sort of deal with Morgan behind my back? If he had, that would explain why I had not been able to talk directly to Morgan since I left L.A. All messages were passed through the stoned Sapersteen, a faulty conduit if there ever was one.

"Jason McCloud told me about the hearings."

"A dedicated public servant." There was a snap to White's voice. "He is also the only black ever to infiltrate the Hong Kong branch of the Chao Chow. Without him we would never have got the goods on Kelly and Lowell."

"Why?"

That simple question stopped the would-be president. "Why what?" White swiveled around to get a good look at me.

"Why go to the trouble of starting a religious movement if you have already put together a successful drug syndicate?"

"Because, Teddy," White bit hard on the words as they emerged from his wide presidential mouth, *"religion is tax-exempt."*

"Oh." I don't know why one automatically assumes that a candidate for president is stupid. It never occurred to me that Johnson White could have figured out something that I had not. But he had. And it made perfect sense. "Then Kalki's a kind of genius, for having thought this up."

"Or Lowell. We think Lowell is the brains in New Orleans while Kalki's the man in the field. And, of course, the performer on television. Eleven and a half minutes." There were tears in White's eyes as he contemplated the precious minutes of prime time that Kalki had got, and he had not. He sighed. Then he gave the word. "They launder money through their American ashrams. They pretend it comes from foreign contributors. Since any bona fide religion is tax-exempt in the United States, they are home-free. Meanwhile, they are diversifying their very rich portfolio. In the last year they have been buying up choice real estate, growth businesses, warehouses and western North Dakota. Teddy, this thing is an octopus. And you've got to help me. And you've got to help your country. And you've got to help those poor kids who've been hooked on brown sugar, and worse."

Even though the tourists at the table opposite could not hear exactly what was being said, they could detect the patriotic hum to White's voice, as measured and as gooseflesh-making as the opening bars of *The Battle Hymn of the Republic.* I could see that they wanted to applaud.

I shut the notebook. "I can't tell you, Senator, what the *Sun* intends to do. That's between you and Mr. Davies. All I do is collect material. They write it up."

"You can be a big help, Teddy." He lapsed into twice-born redneck lingo. "Help" pronounced as "hepp." "You a goo' lookin' gal. Mighty goo' lookin'." A one-night or rather a one-morning stand was in the air again. U.S. Senators had the reputation of being not only sexually insatiable but impotent. Years ago Arlene had had an affair with a senator from Arizona. She told me all.

"Senator, you're crushing my dress."

White's leg swung away from me. "What," he asked, "were you doing the last few days with Giles Lowell? And how and when did you get to Washington?"

"I think, Senator, that that is for me to know and you to find out."

"Then in due course you will be subpoenaed by the Senate Narcotics Abuse and Control Committee and obliged to testify under oath."

"First Amendment. Must protect my sources." I gave the journalists' creed, in a somewhat sketchy way.

"Supreme Court's decision in this matter still undefined," White rattled the familiar response. "You can be held in contempt of Congress." Then he flashed me a loving twice-born smile. A tear or two of love for me and the whole human race came to his eyes. "But I don't want us to be in an adversary situation, Teddy, because I've got the greatest admiration for you as an aviatrix, and American."

"Thanks." I was vinegar to his oil. "I've got nothing interesting to report on Dr. Lowell. I flew with him in a private plane to Washington.

I've been staying at the Jefferson Arms. Room 437. This is *not* an invitation. The last few days I've been sick with flu and Dr. Lowell acted as my physician. I accept your overall analysis of Kalki Enterprises. I'm pretty certain that they are into drugs. I now understand why they started a religion in order to launder money. Everything is absolutely clear except one thing. Why the end of the world?"

"It's catchy. Everybody in the country's talking about those billboards. Every TV comedian is making jokes about The End. It's like Evel Knievel. On such-and-such a day you're going to shoot yourself out of a cannon. With that kind of announcement, you can build yourself up quite a gate. And then those Lotus Lotteries! Everybody's hooked on them. I almost won five thousand dollars last week. I was just one number off."

"But what happens, Senator, when the end doesn't happen?"

"The guy's had a good run for your money." White saw only the promotional side to Kalki. But then that was his business, too—self-promotion.

"Well, I think Kalki's serious. I think he really believes that the end of the world has arrived. We're running out of energy and food. There are too many people, too much pollution . . ."

I should have been warned by White's earlier reference to eco-freaks. The volcano erupted: "I know. I know. Club of Rome. Ecology. Overpopulation. Oil pollution. Everybody in Michigan poisoned from the PBB in the milk. No fish in the Mediterranean. Elsewhere, high mercury and cadmium count in most of the world's fish. Woman on a diet died from eating too much swordfish. DDT poisoning of the water sources of the First World due to advanced agricultural techniques. Diminished intelligence in the population of the Third World as a result of increased carbon monoxide leading to permanent changes in the weather and the beginning of a new Ice Age while the ozone layer in the stratosphere is being burnt away by the exhaust of jets like the supersonic Concorde. Teddy, all of this is just plain old-fashioned commie horseshit and I'm surprised that a good American and Californian like you would fall for it. Don't you see that's how the commies mean to defeat us? They want to *worry* us. They want us to stop expanding the greatest industrial plant the world has ever seen in order to save these toads and moths and useless varieties of birds and fish from extinction. But, Teddy, *we* are the ones on the brink of extinction if we cut back now and lose the battle for the control of the consumer markets of the world. The choice is a simple one. Between these toads and moths and useless varieties of birds and fish and a society that offers you everything in the electrical appliance line as well as more hours of free TV than any other nation on earth, on top of which we have a superb military machine second to none, not to mention a standard of living that is the envy of every commie and the despair of every Third Worlder. Teddy, you just can't sell out America for a mess of porridge!"

Senator White's command of language was presidential. He also had a coherent world vision. And flawless intelligence input, as H.V.W. would say. Unfortunately, he had missed my point. "I am almost persuaded by your eloquence," I said. "And that's a compliment, because I am an eco-freak. But when I said that the end of the world was at hand, I wasn't just speaking of what everyone knows. I mean, even the American Congress must suspect that everything is running down. No, I meant something much simpler. I meant a real end to the world, thanks to Kalki."

White began to sprinkle hayseed over me. "Honey lamb," he said, "if you think Mistuh Kalki is gonna switch off the human race you got another think comin'. Because," and now the voice was no longer twice-born but that of President White, speaking to his people, "there is no way of ending human life on this planet short of unleashing America's nuclear might against the hordes of international communism—an option which I would never rule out, let me say, as reluctant as I would be to take it, should it fall to me as commander-in-chief to make the fateful decision." The tourists at the next table applauded, quietly. White lowered his voice. "Kelly *can't* end the world. It's not technically possible. Even if he had a dozen neutron bombs, Model B, he couldn't. I know. I've had it checked out with the Pentagon. But the question's academic, because he doesn't even have one bomb. Don't ask how I know, but I know."

I picked up on the phrase "Model B." I had come out against the deployment of the original neutron bomb. Although the N-bomb satisfactorily if painfully kills personnel (as opposed to people) and leaves intact buildings, the neutron bomb's radioactive fallout may last a thousand years in the atmosphere. "Model B? You don't mean there's a new model?"

"I did not say Model B, Teddy." White lied smoothly. "Either you misheard or I misspoke. But that's not the point, which is that the safety of the free world now rests with that li'l . . . little shaver of a neutron bomb that respects property. And those who oppose it are mostly commies and all their fellow travelers at the *Washington Post* and the *New York Times.*" Senator White's mind tended to work in familiar if irrelevant circles. "The Concorde is not only a great aircraft but no proven danger to the environment while the aerosol can is as safe as houses according to disinterested observers in industry. That was room 437 at the Jefferson Arms?" This last was murmured affectionately.

"I'm off to New York," I gave him a radiant smile. "A rain check," I murmured, too. I thought it wise to con him. I was not eager for a subpoena. Or penis. With a flourish, I paid the check. I had been warned by Giles that senators never paid for anything. He thanked me.

As we were leaving, White maneuvered himself so that he would brush against the table opposite us. The fans were thrilled. "We're behind you, Senator," said one. "You gotta be president," said another. "Give 'em hell, Teddy!" said a third.

White's face looked grim. I thought it was because I had been recognized, too. "I still have my fans." I rubbed it in.

"That wasn't for you." White actually succeeded in achieving a Weissean snap. "That guy thought I was Teddy Kennedy. A nation," said Senator Johnson White not so very far under his breath, "of fucking morons."

In front of the hotel, White held my hand for a long time as he said farewell. "You keep in touch, Teddy." The doorman, several passers-by and I were then treated to one final redneck aria. "And you think over what I been tellin' you. 'Cause, Teddy, with your hepp I wanna mekk a country as good and as clean and as compassionate as you and as me and as this great country can be and will be once we have restored it to you and to me and to the people who make up this the greatest nation in the history of the country."

What he said made, of course, no sense. But as of last March that was the way not only the front-running Republican candidate for president was sounding but just about every other politician as well. As entropy increases, energy hemorrhages. Language is affected. Words become mere incantation. When that happens, the end is near, and the cold.

3

I ARRIVED IN NEW YORK TO FIND MYSELF AGAIN IN DEMAND ON
television. My good words for Indira Gandhi had been forgiven if not
forgotten. Everyone wanted to interview the interviewer of Kalki. The
billboards had made a great impression. I had four minutes on *The
Today Show*, six on *Good Morning, America*. I also had lunch with
Morgan Davies in the Oak Room of the Plaza Hotel, a pleasant room
with carved wood paneling as yet unreproduced in Los Angeles.

Morgan had put on weight, which was unbecoming. "The response
is terrific. Kalki is *The* End!" He laughed at what was already a fairly
tired national joke. I gave him the latest news. He was pleased.

"We should get a picture of Mrs. Kelly." Morgan wrote a note on
a piece of paper. "And I like that bit about Kalki being an ex-dancer.
I suppose his old ballet school would have some pictures." He made
another note. "Is he a fag?"

"No, Morgan."

Several times during lunch, the maître d' came to the table and
whispered in Morgan's ear that there was a telephone call. Morgan
would then pick up the telephone beside his chair and discuss whether
or not the President was going to dump the Vice-President before the
next convention. That was the only subject that interested the power
brokers last year. Kalki was just a sideshow.

"Johnson White will get the Republican nomination," said Davies,
hanging up the telephone on a caller who had told him that the
President had at last decided to replace the Vice-President. "But only
if these hearings of his really take off."

"Will they?"

"That depends on you. On Kalki. On the FBI, the CIA,
the DEA, the IRS. Everybody's doing White's work for him. But
even if he's nominated, I don't see him beating the President

unless . . ." Morgan kindly gave me an analysis of the great American political game. Although I was an enthusiastic part of that majority of the electorate who were not apathetic yet never voted because there was no point, I listened politely. Morgan really cared. But then he had no imagination.

When Morgan was finished, I asked about the drug connection. "White told me that you had agreed to hold back until the hearings."

"Did he?" Morgan chuckled. Chuck? Chuck? Chuck? That is not at all the way he sounded. Chuckled is bad onomatopoeia, based on the way English farmers called chickens in the seventeenth century. I just looked the word up in the President's personal dictionary in the Oval Office.

"Senator White won't like that."

"Screw Senator White." Morgan's eyes were those of a cobra contemplating a mongoose. "I can't tell you how much I admire your work, Teddy." He laid it on. He told me that there would definitely be a book. He had arranged everything with Doubleday. They were just waiting for me to sign the contract. The fact that I was Kalki's pilot, telling all, had been a "topnotch selling point," according to Morgan. I thanked him. He suggested that I get in touch with Dr. Lowell, who was in town. "He'll be at the main ashram. That's Fifty-Third Street, just off First Avenue. By the way, we're inclined to think Lowell's the real boss."

"That's what Senator White thinks."

"Johnny," Morgan always called the famous by their nickname, "isn't always wrong, you know." He laughed; then he wheezed (only a neologism could describe the sound, but I am no neologician). "Even so, never trust Johnny. For one thing, he's on the take. From the drug interests."

"Everybody's corrupt." I was not really surprised. Just depressed.

"Well, it's only a rumor. But we're checking it out. The theory is that the White campaign is being financed by the Chao Chow gang in Hong Kong. They want to eliminate Kalki Enterprises. So they're paying Johnny to go after him. Johnny will get his headlines. Kalki and Lowell will go to jail. Johnny will become president. The Chao Chow will regain control of the world drug business. That's the scenario. If it's true. Anyway, we've put an investigator on it. We got this one made. In fact, our only worry is that Kalki will get himself hit *before* the Madison Square Garden rally."

"Can I write the obit?" Oh, we were playing hard ball all right.

Morgan gasped (better word) with amusement. "No. Bruce will write the obit. But we'll run a full-length photo of you in your black leather pilot's jacket, with boots, looking sad and kinky. Bereft pilot . . ."

Lunch ended on that high note. I noticed that Morgan was beginning to develop a certain blueness about the lips, and it occurred to me that the *Sun* might soon be in need of a new editor.

I walked across town to the ashram. I was recognized from the various television programs that I had done. Quite a few people wanted to talk to me about Kalki. If nothing else, he had caught if not fired the imagination of sophisticated New Yorkers. It took me an hour to walk a dozen blocks.

The ashram was three narrow tenement buildings knocked together. The entrance hall was done in beige. Opposite the main door was a life-size color photograph of Kalki; he looked meltingly beautiful. No, I did not want him hit.

Posters announced the rally: KALKI! MADISON SQUARE GARDEN, MARCH 15. *End of the World.* A long table was covered with free pamphlets: "Who Is Kalki?," "After the End," "Before the End." There was a lotus-dispenser in the center of the room. On top of the dispenser was a list of the previous week's lucky numbers. As of that date, more than a million dollars had been distributed in the Lotus Lotteries. Consequently, the Kalki boys and girls no longer had to worry about getting their message across. They were mobbed in the streets. Everyone wanted to draw a lucky lotus.

Male and female receptionists wore fixed Scientological smiles beneath empty e s t-ian eyes. They managed the traffic. Interested people came and went; took pamphlets; asked about classes; bought tickets for the Madison Square Garden rally; collected lotuses. The Muzak was loud with *Sergeant Pepper*.

I presented myself to a large young man with a beard and a broken front tooth. He knew me. He beamed. Or gleamed. "Teddy Ottinger! Pranam! Pranam! What an honor! What a pleasure! I just now caught you on *The A.M. Show.*" He was beside us both with religious ecstasy.

"I'll take you right up. Dr. Lowell's only just arrived. Now you're here! Two Perfect Masters! What joy! I can't wait for The End!" Yes, that is exactly what he said. I was tempted to interview him on the spot. When he spoke of The End, did he see himself dead? Or did he see the sky opening up and a staircase descending? Or did he just think that come April 3 (a date still unrevealed) there would be a change for the good in the human race? I regret that I never really analyzed either in depth or in shallow a typical Kalki-ite as of last year.

I was led through various offices, equipped with all the latest communication devices. Ticker-tape machines extruded tapes in code. Computers added and subtracted. Efficient-looking men and women served the machines quietly, impressively. My guide left me in front of a door on which a brass plate proclaimed PERFECT MASTER.

I knocked; and entered. Giles lay full-length on a sofa, talking on the telephone. When he saw me, he said into the receiver, "Teddy Ottinger, Perfect Master, just walked in the room." There was a pause; then he turned to me. "Lakshmi sends you a special greeting." When Giles had finished talking to Katmandu, he bounded to his feet; he was jittery with energy, excitement. He showed me a proof of the latest poster for Kalki's Madison Square Garden engagement. "Jazzy?"

"Very," I said, and it was. Kalki and The End got top billing. Then four rock groups were listed. I am not into rock. But Giles assured me, "They're all sensational! Out of sight! Eight gold records between them! We'll be selling their disks in the Garden right along with this new platter we've cut of Kalki's end-of-the-world rap, complete with flute and sitar."

I was privileged to observe Giles in yet another metamorphosis. He was now Mr. Show Biz. He paced down and up the room. He talked of box-office receipts. Record sales. TV promos. I almost (almost but not quite) wished that Dr. Ashok was back in town. Meanwhile, aides kept coming and going, showing him bits of paper. "For your approval, Perfect Master."

Finally, Giles told a secretary in the outer office to hold all calls except those from Katmandu. "So how was your lunch with Senator White?"

"He's going to subpoena Kalki. He's going to try to nail you both as traffickers in drugs."

"Poor Johnny. Anything for a headline. When is he holding those hearings?"

"Next week, right after the rally."

Giles frowned. He was no longer Mr. Show Biz. "We'll have to hold him off somehow."

"Until after April 3?"

Giles nodded. "Well, we'll just have to put our thinking caps on. God, you're attractive, Teddy." I was chased once around the room. Fortunately, it was not his heart but his adrenalin that was in the pursuit, and he soon gave it up. He collapsed upon the sofa.

I sat demurely in a straight chair. After a day at Arden's, I looked myself again. The dryness of skin and hair was gone. I felt good. I was now Teddy Ottinger, Glamorous Newshen. "Senator White is convinced that this religious movement is just a front for the drug syndicate."

Giles would have laughed had he not been winded from the chase. "Reverse the sentence and you'll be closer to the truth."

"Drugs are a front for Kalki?"

But Giles clammed up as he always did when Topic A was mentioned. Reluctantly, I moved on to Topic B. "I'm trying to make sense of all this, Giles." I was deeply sincere in manner, a trick I had learned from watching Arlene do television commercials. "Why, if the world is coming to an end on April 3, are you so busy selling tickets, records, making money?"

Giles's fingers combed his few remaining tufts of gray hair. "We— and that means you, too—have a divine mission. We have been put on earth at this time in order to purify people, to help them achieve inner peace and serenity so that when the new cycle begins they can be reborn as Brahmins, thereby restoring the original Golden Age." This nonsense flowed as smoothly as organic honey.

"I hear what you're saying, Giles." I affected an even deeper sincerity. I sounded to myself like a Malibu surfer discussing ways of getting together his/her inner space. "But it still doesn't make any sense."

"Teddy, nothing will ever make any sense if you don't accept the fact that our souls are born and reborn throughout eternity. That's why we are busy selling tickets, records . . ."

"There's also a lot of money in this racket." I replaced sincerity with toughness.

Giles thought this funny. "A lot of money? You ought to see our audit sheets! We're hopelessly in debt. We also have another problem, thanks to Johnny White."

Giles opened a door behind his desk. At a long table in the next room a dozen tired-looking men sat examining ledgers, working hand computers. They looked at us, without pleasure.

"Accountants," he said. "From the Internal Revenue Service. How's it going, Mr. Prager?"

Mr. Prager was a small brown cricket of a man. He sat at the head of the table. "We are making progress, Dr. Lowell. Never fear." The voice was not friendly.

"I just hope you're not too confused, Mr. Prager."

"Quite the contrary, Dr. Lowell."

Giles shut the door. "Prager is the government's number one investigator. Poor bastard. He has met his match. You don't mind if we provide you with security."

It took me a moment to adjust to this Ashokian switch of subject. "A bodyguard?"

Giles nodded. "You won't find them a bother. But they'll be on the job twenty-four hours a day. That's why we've booked you into the Americana Hotel. It's set up for total security."

"Why?"

"McCloud is in town. Better to be safe, dear Teddy, than . . ."

"You have never given a convincing reason why McCloud is after me." I did not add that Giles Lowell had yet to give a convincing explanation of anything. He lied as effortlessly as little birds sing.

"He's after all of us." Giles was suddenly vague. Topic A was again in the air.

"Does he know that you're Dr. Ashok?"

"How could he?" Giles went into his Ashok impersonation. "I am a master of disguise. Remember, dear Madame Ottinger? The narc has no idea that his friendly associate in Nepal Dr. Ashok of the CIA is also his principal quarry in New Orleans Dr. Lowell."

"Then," I said, "McCloud's a lot dumber than he looks."

"That is often the case. Anyway, watch out for him. And now for the good news. Geraldine arrives tomorrow." I was delighted. I had missed her. I had dreamed about her several times. I had not dreamed about Kalki once. What, I wondered, did that mean? Nothing, or something? In dreams begin . . . all things.

Giles gave me an office in the ashram. PERFECT MASTER was on the door. I was introduced to various mandali. I felt an imposter. They were all so thrilled to know me. "It's like a blessing to be able to talk to a Perfect Master," said one starry-eyed girl.

I fled the ashram; paid a call on Bruce Sapersteen at the *Sun* offices. At least no one around there felt that it was a blessing to know me. Curse was more like it.

"I mean, it's a real drag, Teddy, for me to be working my ass off writing those pieces and then you get all the credit." Bruce sniffed angrily. Then he gave me my fan mail. Most of it was from fundamentalist Christians who were praying for me as they stitched their hoods, lit their crosses, planned pogroms.

One letter gave me enormous satisfaction: "I cannot help but say 'well done, Teddy!' Your sentences hit the nail on the head each and every time. You write like I dream. Ever yours, Herman Victor Weiss."

SIX

1

Most Southern Californians disliked New York City. I was with the majority on that one. For one thing, the weather is uniformly depressing except for the fall. Unfortunately, I had never visited the city at that time of year and so I was obliged to take on faith the glories of autumn in New York, as the old song goes, and the thrill of first-nighting. A mysterious phrase. Reference to the seduction of a virgin?

March was cold. Windy. Gray. All blueness had gone out of the sky. Clouds and smog encased Manhattan Island like a celluloid bell. Shreds of newspapers floated on the wind. Everything that could be broken or bent had been broken and bent, at least at eye level. The garbage had not been collected for some weeks. The collectors were striking for money, human dignity. In their place, I would have emigrated.

Despite the weather, the dirt, the discomfort, I was in a splendid mood. I was with Geraldine, and the high mood of the high mountains had, somewhat, returned. She was also staying at the Americana; she, too, had a discreet bodyguard. All in all, I was more pleased than not to be followed at all times by a large black man in a turtleneck sweater, carrying a walkie-talkie. There was a sense of danger in the streets. That is, if you walked, and I always walked. Unlike most Southern Californians, I prefer walking to driving.

Geraldine and I met in the main lobby of the Americana. She was dressed like a young Junior League matron from Connecticut, of the sort you saw only—or at least I saw only—in magazines like *Town & Country*. Although the East Coast and its social arrangements were a mystery to me, I liked to read the gossip, and look at the pictures of weddings, horse shows, gracious living among Hepplewhite consoles and golden retrievers. I was very much aware of the Geraldines, out there in Connecticut.

We embraced. "I *am* glad to see you, Teddy!" She was warmth itself.

I liked the dark green tweed coat that she was wearing. I liked the fact that she smelled slightly of sandalwood, the Kalki smell. I wondered if he had seduced her, too. And if he had, did I care? Yes, I cared. But my motives were confused, to say the least, and it was some time before I was able to sort things out. Meanwhile, we were together. I was in sixth if not seventh heaven, as we breakfasted at the Americana. Our guards sat at different tables, near the door.

"I couldn't take Nepal another minute." Geraldine sounded grim. "Finally, Kalki told me to go. He was very sweet about it. But I felt awfully guilty, leaving him and Lakshmi. You know, we were prisoners in the ashram until Kalki finally made a call to New Delhi, to the Prime Minister. Kalki's really popular in India. Anyway, the Indian Government frightened the Nepalese. And I was allowed to leave the country."

"When are Kalki and Lakshmi coming?"

"As soon as Giles finds a safe place for them here."

I drank frozen orange juice that tasted of chemicals. Last March no American would ever, willingly, squeeze an orange. "Who do you think wants to kill Kalki?" I acted as if I had no theories of my own.

Geraldine sighed. "Rival religious groups. We're getting all the money, or so they say. On the other hand, Giles says we're broke. I don't know. I do know that Kalki is popular everywhere, particularly in Asia. Strange, isn't it? how easily the Hindus accept Vishnu's incarnation as a white American. They also accept the idea of The End. But then it's the end for millions of them, anyway. I mean, half the population is dying of malnutrition."

Geraldine and I strolled down Fifth Avenue. Things were less broken there. In front of the Public Library, we decided to go to Madison Square Garden. Our breath was like smoke in the cold air. Geraldine said, "I want you to meet Professor Jossi, the nuclear physicist. He's a mandalin. He's preparing some special effects for the fifteenth."

We crossed Bryant Park, a small square of green behind the library. Tall bare trees surrounded a shaggy meadow. On benches sat the poor, the derelict. Most were black or Hispanic. Some drank wine out of bottles wrapped in brown paper bags.

We sat for a moment on a bench next to a green bronze statue, streaked with white pigeon droppings. A pale sun tried but failed to burn its way through the brown haze. On the next bench, a white man was shoving a dirty hypodermic needle into a shiny swollen blue and red ankle. Nobody paid any attention.

We watched, beyond horror, the parade of monsters. Drunk, drugged, mad, they staggered past us, talking to themselves. I thought it very apt that on a building opposite us was one of the KALKI, THE END billboards. I could not imagine any of these people wanting to go on.

Geraldine read my mind, which was not hard. "This isn't life," she said.

"No, it's not."

Our two guards looked alarmed. Sitting on a bench in that park, we were perfect targets for . . . the Triad? I tried to find out. "The *Sun* is planning to expose Kalki, as a drug-seller."

"When?" Geraldine was cool.

"After the rally."

"Kalki's ready."

"I wish you'd tell me the truth."

Geraldine managed a small smile. I noticed that the three freckles on the bridge of her nose made a triangle—Golden Triangle? "Look," she said, "what we were, what we are, what we will be are three different things. I *was* up for tenure at M.I.T. I *am* a Perfect Master, sitting in Bryant Park, New York City, with another Perfect Master. After April 3, I *will* be something else again."

A dozen Kalki people had entered the park. They made their way from bench to bench. They gave away pamphlets, cards with the addresses of the different ashrams, paper lotuses. They handled themselves quite well, considering the hazards of that place.

At this point I had accepted the fact that I was not going to be told anything about Topic A until . . . when? The End or after? Although I had got into the habit of talking about the end, I never really took it seriously. At the most, I thought that there would be some sort of television spectacular. Then a number of explanations about a special reprieve for mankind. Or perhaps, cleverest of all, the announcement that the end had already taken place and that we were now all of us, miraculously, purified and living at the start of a new Golden Age.

Who would know the difference? I have often had the sense of having died before. Yet, curiously, I have never had a sense of birth, much less rebirth. In any case, I had figured a number of ways out of the April 3 dilemma and I assumed that Kalki had done the same. Whatever he might or might not be, he was a natural showman.

Geraldine told me about herself and Lakshmi. "Doris and I went to school together, in Washington. First the National Cathedral School. Then American University. We were always very close. I would stay with her one holiday. Then she would stay with me. Even when we went to different colleges, we kept in touch. By telephone. Daily. Sometimes twice a day. She was in Chicago. I was in Boston. Then she married Jim Kelly and moved to Saigon. I really missed those long conversations."

"What on earth did you talk about?" I hate telephones. Keep conversations to the minimum.

"Everything! Her marriage. My career. Her poison ivy. My research. Heisenberg's law. She kept wanting to break it. 'Variations on a Theme of Mendel's,' my doctoral thesis. The telephone kept us from falling apart. Then she married . . ."

"Was it . . . is it a good marriage?"

"On the telephone we decided that there was no such thing as a *good* marriage. That was just before she left Chicago to join Jimmy in Asia. I remember we talked three hours. It was my turn to pay the telephone company."

"Was she happy with him?"

"Well, she was a wife and he was a husband. That's always a problem, isn't it?"

"Why didn't you get married?"

"I wanted children. I can't have any. I am . . . ill-made. So why get married?"

"Good question."

But Geraldine's discontent was plain. "You were lucky," she said, with unexpected envy. "You had motherhood before you went beyond it."

"I am not a good mother." This was true. I felt guilty. I would go to F.A.O. Schwartz. Buy toys.

"But I was happy enough in Boston. Then Doris . . . Lakshmi suddenly appeared. Told me who she was. Who Jimmy was. Who I was."

"Did you believe her?"

Geraldine shook her head. "Of course not. At least not right away. But Lakshmi insisted I come visit them in Katmandu. She was pregnant. She wanted me with her. Then when the child was born, she got typhoid. So did the child. Giles and I saved Lakshmi. The baby died. By then there was no question of my ever leaving her, again. So I was put on the payroll, and given a laboratory. M.I.T. sent me an ultimatum. Either I come back, or lose tenure. I stayed in Katmandu." A cold wind rattled the branches overhead. Geraldine shivered. "We have a marvelous destiny, Teddy. I can't tell you more than that. Because . . . There are," she said, suddenly very hard, *"rats in that ivy."* I looked at the ground cover in back of the statue. Two rats were standing on their hind legs, eyes bright, confident, unblinking. They stared at us until we left the park, in a hurry. Our guards were delighted.

Black prostitutes (ostensibly female) in silver wigs and short skirts lurked in the doorways along Forty-Second Street. "Adult Bookshops" alternated with massage parlors and, worst of all, with Greek restaurants where the smell of frying grease deserved a circle to itself in Dante's hell. Sleazy movie houses advertised porno and murder films, subjects hardly alien to the street people.

"They are all so . . . unlovable." Geraldine's reaction was much like mine. But she had picked a word I'd not have used. "They'll be happy when the age of Kali ends."

"How do you know?" I took a perverse line. "Perhaps they are having a good time."

"I doubt it."

At the corner of Eighth Avenue was another Kalki billboard, advertising the Madison Square Garden rally. Six-foot-high letters proclaimed KALKI. Under a drawing of Kalki on the white horse were the names of the artists who would be appearing with him on March 15. The mixture of show biz and religion was shrewd if disquieting. I thought of the Maharaj-ji in the Houston Astrodome. Of the Pope in Yankee Stadium. Obviously mass delirium was the aim. But to what end? The End?

Geraldine stared fixedly at the sign.

"Are you praying?"

Geraldine shook her head; and laughed. "No. Well, yes. In a way. I was praying that Kalki doesn't fall off that horse and break his neck. He's terrified of horses."

We walked briskly down Eighth Avenue. The pale sun had entirely given up, and the sky was the color of mud. The chill was getting to me.

In front of a place that featured go-go dancers (male), I asked, "What will happen to us on April 3? Are we going to burn up, too?"

"We will go on." This came out very fast.

"As ourselves?"

"Changed, I think. I don't know. I have no recollection of being present at the end of a cycle before. Have you?"

"Of course I don't." The game was beginning to annoy. "I have no recollection of anything except being alive this time around." I stepped aside to let a drug addict stumble past us; his eyes were shut; he was asleep, and walking. "I don't believe we go on."

"We do." If Geraldine was acting, she was more than usually convincing. I had decided that she was in love with Lakshmi. As a result, she was willing to suspend normal belief and help them play at divinity or (was this possible?) she, too, trafficked in drugs. I realized how little I actually knew about my fellow Perfect Masters. I think that if I could have got out then, I would have. I was not amused by Chinese hit men on the prowl. By presidential candidates with subpoenas. By DEA agents with indictments. Unfortunately, I needed the money. I needed the *Sun.* I needed Kalki. I was hooked. But not happy.

The mysterious Madison Square Garden (neither square nor a garden) was familiar from television. Political conventions were held there. Security was tight. Fortunately, our guards were able to vouch for us with their colleagues. We were admitted, only to find that Dr. Lowell had just left.

Geraldine and I entered the auditorium. A half-dozen work lights did no more than illuminate the central area where a number of men were putting the finishing touches to a forty-foot-high pyramid. At the touch of a button the pyramid would open, according to Geraldine; she had helped design the mechanism. On top of the pyramid was the low throne where Kalki would sit.

At the foot of the pyramid a small gray man with a beard was supervising the assemblage of a complicated piece of machinery. Geraldine introduced me to Professor Ludwig Jossi. He had received a Nobel prize for having isolated the smallest (as of that date) manifestation of energy, the quark. He taught at Lausanne. He had been for some years a student of Vedanta. Recently, he had accepted Kalki as the last incarnation of Vishnu. Since Professor Jossi was the first scientist to join Kalki, there had been a good deal of astonished publicity. Certainly, he made a pleasant contrast to all the rock stars who were *into* Kalki. To a man, these performers were absolutely *wired,* as they would say, by or to The End.

Professor Jossi spoke English with an imperfect accent. "I think there will be no bugs. The pictures should be beautiful."

"Exactly when will the atom split?" Geraldine was intense. At that time, any reference to the splitting of an atom tended to unnerve me.

"I shall throw the switch as soon as Kalki gives the exact date for the end of the age of Kali. Then we will be able to observe the actual disintegration of the atom on a specially designed screen just above his head. The colors should be exquisite, and awe-inspiring. Dramatizing for all the world to see, the power of Vishnu to create and to destroy."

I felt ill. If these people were as mad as I was beginning to think that they were, Professor Jossi's machine was not going to disintegrate just one atom. There would be a chain reaction. Dominoes would fall. All earth would be enveloped in nuclear fire. As casually as I could, I asked if there was any danger of a chain reaction.

Professor Jossi did not take the question well. "Certainly not. This is a time of testing, of warning. The people must be given a chance to purify themselves. Later, of course . . ."

Geraldine interrupted him, as if afraid that he might say too much.

"Later Kalki will do what he must do." Suddenly she pointed, to the pyramid behind us. "And here he is!"

Professor Jossi and I both turned, half-expecting to see Kalki. But Geraldine was referring to the top part of a huge Styrofoam statue of Vishnu. Attached to a pulley, the crowned head and upper torso (with four arms) were slowly descending in order to meet the bottom part which was already in place behind the pyramid.

In silence, we watched the two parts come together. The effect in the dim light was ghostly, ghastly. Abruptly, I left Geraldine, and spent the rest of the day shopping for toys at F.A.O. Schwartz.

2

At eight the next morning, the telephone rang. I had a hard time waking up. I was on Valium again. Because of the constant security, the menace of Jason McCloud (if real), of Chinese hit men (if real), the end of the world (if real), my nerves were stretched, as H.V.W. so often observed, taut. "Who is it?" I no longer said hello.

"Geraldine. Kalki's here. We're on the boat. It's called the *Narayana*. We're all waiting for you." She gave me an address on the East River. I said that I would be right over.

I put powdered coffee in a drinking glass, added hot water from the tap; gulped the resulting mess. I am usually a "morning person," but not that day. For one thing I had a Valium hangover. For another, I was aware that I had dreamed a good deal but could not remember a single dream, always a bad sign. I decided to walk to the ship, to clear my head with rich carbon monoxide.

The morning was cold. The sky dark. The spring late. As I walked east along Fifty-Seventh Street, I watched the yellow-robed Kalki disciples go about their business. They were impressive. First, they would approach a well-dressed person of the sort who would normally run a mile to avoid a panhandler for god, any god. Then they would charm him or her. Pamphlets were usually accepted. Paper lotuses were always accepted. Even the prosperous were attracted by the Lotus Lotteries. In fact, the whole country rushed to buy Friday's newspaper which told who had won what.

The *Narayana* turned out to be something on the order of the *Queen Mary*, currently and sadly aground at Long Beach. Since I had never been aboard a large ship, I assumed that the pre-jet ocean liners must have been something like the *Narayana*.

As always, intense security. Armed guards stood on the shore. Armed guards stood on the deck. The immediate neighborhood was crowded with New York police, as well as (presumably) agents in mufti from the thousand and one government spy services. After a long conversation by walkie-talkie with someone inside the ship, I was allowed to go aboard. The gangplank swung dangerously back and forth in the wind.

On the deck, more guards checked me out. Then I was shown into a vast living room or salon. Once inside, there was nothing to remind you that this was a ship. There were chandeliers, marble fireplaces, blue-green tapestries, Samarkand rugs. It was all a bit like San Simeon, William Randolph Hearst's megalo-castle, now a museum.

I sat on the edge of a tapestried chair, somewhat overwhelmed by the *Narayana* (yet another of Vishnu's names: "one who moves upon the waters"). Presently, I was joined by Geraldine, Professor Jossi and a dozen mandali unknown to me.

Geraldine and I hugged one another, as if we had not spent the previous day together. "Kalki's here!" she whispered. "He's on the ship!"

"I know. You told me." I was suddenly curious. "How did he get through customs?" I could see the alleged drug entrepreneur being frisked by narcs; each orifice explored, while all baggage was x-rayed and sniffed at by large Alsatian dogs. Then I imagined the alleged god riding down—is it Wall Street? with tons of ticker-tape and confetti falling from skyscraper windows as he stood in an open car, waving to the crowds the way Lindbergh and Amelia still do in the old newsreels.

"He just sneaked in. The customs people were very cooperative. Nobody wanted any fuss. This boat," she added, "is the third largest yacht in the world. Giles bought it last week for Kalki Enterprises."

"Paid for?" I asked. This was the sort of detail Morgan at the *Sun* would want to know.

Geraldine smiled. "The down payment is all that's necessary, considering . . ." Yes, she really thought that the world had only twenty-one more days to go. Just like Christmas, I thought. I was glad that I had mailed off several interesting toys to the children.

A gong sounded. Then Giles Lowell sidled into the drawing room. He bowed low to all of us, hands together in the Indian greeting. We responded. While we were pranaming, Kalki and Lakshmi made their entrance.

I almost did not recognize Kalki. He wore a mod brown mohair suit. I much preferred him in saffron robes. On the other hand, Lakshmi was ravishing in a St. Laurent copy that must have cost her a fortune at Saks or wherever she had bought it (Russian peasant-style in peacock blue, a color I've always loved but cannot wear because my coloring kills the blue which, in revenge, murders me).

"Shanti!" Kalki made a sign of benediction. He gave me a fraternal embrace and I was, for an instant, made weak by the smell of sandalwood and blondness. Lakshmi did not embrace me, which was just as well: two infusions of so much blondness would have totally unstrung me, even at sea level.

Then Kalki and Lakshmi sat side by side in a loveseat while the rest of us sat in a semicircle around them. Giles remained standing. "I have already made my report to the highest of the high," he announced in a slightly Ashokian voice. "There have been numerous efforts not only to discredit us but to intimidate us. Both here and in Katmandu. Nevertheless, we shall persevere. Just as we shall prevail. Unfortunately, one-third of the tickets for the rally at Madison Square Garden are now in the hands of scalpers who are selling the most desirable seats in Rows A to F for as high as *one thousand dollars apiece!*" We were all pleased to hear this. But Giles was indignant. "*We're* not making the money. The ticket agents are. We may have to take legal action." I thought this slightly inconsistent. After all, if in three weeks' time . . .

Eventually, Giles finished his treasurer's report. We all looked expectantly at Kalki. He was amiable, mild. "I'm glad to see all of you again. I hope you haven't been hassled too much." He was relaxed to the point of ordinariness. He paused; looked at his shoes. For a moment, he seemed to have left us. Then Lakshmi whispered something to him and he returned. The atman (soul) was once again atcha (here).

"In the next few days there will be at least one serious attempt on my life." Kalki might have been discussing the functions of a piece of machinery. "Do not take it seriously." Suddenly he grinned, and crossed his ankles, toes pointed like a dancer. He was most appealing. I had a *frisson* of mountain fever. "I know the future as I know the past. But these eyes are limited." He touched his eyelids as impersonally as if they were a pair of spark plugs. "I can't tell you what will happen in the next few days. I wish I could. I can only see possible combinations. It's like throwing dice. Let's just hope it won't be snake eyes for Jim Kelly because as long as I am located here," he ran his hands down his chest, "I can be killed."

"Oh, no!" This came not from Lakshmi but from Geraldine. A light bulb switched on in my head. Geraldine was in love not only with her best friend but with her best friend's husband, too. I was jealous. But of whom? I suppose I was jealous of all of them. Yet Lakshmi was plainly unattainable, and Kalki was out of the question despite our adventure beside the Nepalese lake. That left Geraldine. Yes, it was Geraldine. Even then. But I was in despair. I had not received any sign of encouragement from her. Worse, if she was in love with Kalki, I had no chance at all. I saw the future as a kind of Turkish harem, with us three girls padding about, wearing bells on our toes as we waited for our lord to come and make his selection for the evening.

"Don't worry." Kalki was soothing. "If I'm obliged to drop Jim Kelly's body, I will take another body and the age of Kali will end right on schedule. Those of you who believe in me, who remain constant despite temptation, will continue into the next cycle, either reborn or as you are." This was the first time that Kalki had explicitly promised some of us personal survival *after* the age of Kali's end.

Now:

What did I really think that cold morning aboard the *Narayana?* To answer honestly (as I have been requested), I must say that I don't know. So much has happened since. I am now all hindsight and cannot honestly report on whatever foresight I might have had. I *think* (I may be wrong but who can prove otherwise?) that I was beginning to accept, in a subliminal way, the idea that there would be no more human race after April 3, except for a few of us, chosen by Kalki. At the same time the conscious part of my brain absolutely ignored the unconscious part. I went right on planning for the future. I had met with an editor at Doubleday's shortly after Kalki's appearance on *60 Minutes*. I had picked the day wisely because Kalki had been a sensation. CBS had racked up a Nielsen rating of 36.3, the highest ever in that particular time slot. The whole country was now aware of Kalki and The End. I do recall that at first the editor was uncertain about the book's value if the world did not end on schedule. Finally, we both agreed that no matter what did or did not happen the story had a lot of appeal. He asked me who should write the book. I said that between B. Sapersteen and H.V. Weiss, I would (believe it or not!) take Weiss as my spectral author. I then made plans to see the children. I let Arlene make Easter reservations for us at the Princess Hotel in Acapulco where Howard Hughes began the cooling process that was to end in the air over Houston. Personally, I would like to die at the controls of a jet. Alone, of course. Of a heart attack. To sum up, I went on planning for the future. But my dreams were uneasy.

Giles again took the floor to burden us with more details. "The IRS audit is now into the second month and they are, I am happy to say, as confused by our finances as I am." Obligatory laughter. Everyone knew that Giles was never confused by anything. Kalki looked remote, atman ready for a take-off.

Then Professor Jossi spoke for the first time. "Be so good, Dr. Lowell, as to explain to me why your tax authorities so stubbornly persevere in the investigation of a religious group which under the laws of your country is entirely exempt from any sort of taxation?" In the age of Kali there was very little that a Swiss—even a nuclear physicist —didn't know about taxes.

"We are a duly organized and officially registered religion. Ergo, we are tax-exempt." Dr. Ashok tended to surface when Giles discussed Hinduism. "But for some mysterious reason the United States Government is morbidly eager to prove that we are—like the dupes of the Reverend Sun Moon—financed by a certain foreign government whose aim is the overthrow of this great republic which is, deservedly, the envy of the earth. What other nation has so many hundreds of thousands of dedicated, cunning secret police in every corner not only of the First, Second and Third Worlds but in every city, town and village of our own beloved United States? What other nation has made itself a world empire not so much through force—or sale—of arms as through the invention of the multinational corporation which owes allegiance, officially, to no nation on earth but, unofficially, is the creation of ruling class United Statesmen or persons? What other nation . . ." Giles was off, and running; and making no sense.

When pressed, Giles liked to pretend that Kalki Enterprises was being persecuted by the American Government because of a supposed Chinese or Cuban or Soviet connection—the foreign power involved depended on who was currently the enemy of the United States as recorded in the press or blurted out on television by one of the President's garrulous employees.

By the time Giles got down to cases, Kalki's atman was plainly roaming around the universe. The blue eyes were open but they did not see. The tenant of Jim Kelly's body was not at home.

"To summarize," Giles was relentless, "we are the victims of the American Government's dislike of any organization that appears to be more attractive to the citizens of the country than the Federal Government, that protean organization with a thousand aspects, including the so-called Mafia which is simply an Italo-American patriotic club masterminded by the Drug Enforcement Administration, our specific enemy."

"Dr. Lowell." Professor Jossi had not been conned. "In Europe I am often asked by the press why Kalki Enterprises is supposed to be engaged in the illicit sale of drugs. I find this question impossible to answer. Tantric rites to one side, Hinduism is opposed to the use of drugs. Am I to assume that this is simply a canard invented by the decadent Judeo-Christian government of your country in order to discredit the one true religion? Or is there the proverbial grain of truth in this allegation? Do enlighten us, Dr. Lowell."

I looked to see if Kalki had been listening. But there was no one behind the face. The atman (Vishnu himself) was no doubt coasting somewhere in the general area of star Arcturus, molding future stars from swirling dust while the quasars sang their songs and black holes opened onto other eternities.

I was curious to hear what Giles would say. I looked at Geraldine. She seemed uneasy. I assumed that she knew the truth, whatever it was, and I was certain that, whatever it was, Giles would not reveal it. With a straight face, he said, "We are not in the drug business, Professor Jossi. It is contrary to the teachings of our lord . . ."

"But, Dr. Lowell," Professor Jossi was a hard-minded man. "According to yesterday's *Neue Zürcher Zeitung* you are the proprietor of something known as the New Orleans Tropical Bird and Fish Company, which is about to be investigated by a Senate committee on the ground that the company is . . ."

". . . engaged in the sale of narcotics." Giles broke in smoothly. "Well, the shop belongs to me. Years ago Kalki was a partner, but I bought him out. You must believe me, my dear Professor Jossi, when I assure you that we deal only in tropical birds and fish. At one time, a very short time and on a small scale, I confess that we bought and sold—illegally, I fear—shrunken human heads from the Amazon Basin. But since that beautiful moment when I entered Perfect Masterhood, I have given orders to our agents in the field to accept no more shrunken heads of people though I have not yet drawn the line at the purchase and resale of shrunken *monkey* heads."

I thought this splendid double-talk. Professor Jossi did not seem convinced but there was nothing he could do about it. He kept looking at Kalki, hoping to be set straight. But Kalki was in farthest space.

Giles shook off the question (he literally wriggled), as he said, "Frankly, in the light of what is due to happen twenty-one days from now, Senate investigations fade to insignificance. Meanwhile, our strategy must be one of delay. At this moment we are threatened by the United States Government in two of its many aspects. First, by the IRS. Second, by the DEA. And . . ."

I made some mischief. "And third by the Triad. A Chinese hit society in the pay of the Chao Chow Society of Hong Kong."

I realized then that all the rumors were true. Lakshmi turned pale. No, that is what H.V.W. would have written automatically, as I just did. Actually she stayed the same color but her mouth dropped open. She turned to Kalki, as though for help. Got none. Turned to Geraldine, who looked angry. I had given a good part of the game away. But the others had no idea what I was talking about. Professor Jossi looked bewildered; and Giles sailed past my interruption with a diversionary bit of information. "I should also mention that the local Roman Catholic hierarchy has gone into an unholy alliance with the Jewish Defense

League. Working together, they will try to disrupt the rally on March 15. As a result, contrary to press reports, in the interest of security, Kalki will *not* appear with a number of Christian and Jewish leaders next Sunday on the *David Susskind Show.* "

There was some discussion of Professor Jossi's nuclear effect. He reported that there would be no technical difficulties.

What did I think? I keep asking myself that question, as I relive those extraordinary days. For one thing, I had decided that if Kalki was mad enough to kill off the human race, he would do so with some sort of nuclear chain reaction. From the first moment that I met Professor Jossi, I had a sense of doom. "Space and time are the domain of the poet. Let him go where he will and do what he pleases: this is the Law." Substitute Kalki for "poet," and Victor Hugo's line would be Kalki's apotheosis. Contemplating Law and poet in the salon of the *Narayana,* I wondered if I could ever comprehend the notion of all human life (except for a few of us?) ending. I gave it up. My mind could not contain the idea. Instead, I lapsed to my usual state; regarded Kalki as a charmer, a crook, a con man, the very essence of sandalwood, blondness.

Suddenly, Kalki was at home again. He yawned. Apologized to us all. Announced that the meeting was over. Asked me if I knew how to ride. When I said, yes, he invited me to ride with him in Central Park. I could borrow a pair of his blue jeans. He also changed to blue jeans; and a yachting cap.

Accompanied by four security guards, we drove to the stables where the white horse from India was in residence. I rented a broken-down hunter. The security guards were assigned guaranteed-to-be-safe ponies. Two guards rode in front of us; two behind. They looked glum.

The day was sharp. Blue fragments accented the sky's usual hazel. My face burned from a cold breeze that smelled of snow. Mid-march was winter. Dust particles in the air were sending the sun's rays back into space. We were scheduled to freeze.

Central Park was brown but pleasant. I found myself thinking of the hills above Burbank where I used to ride with Earl Jr. before marriage put an end to such companionable outings. That was a long time ago.

The bridle path was muddy. My horse shied at every bush; was flatulent. Kalki's white horse was uncommonly beautiful. Unfortunately, Kalki was a nervous rider; he had a heavy rein; did not understand the rhythm of a horse in its paces. Luckily, the horse was good-natured. I did what I could to help them.

Kalki gave no hint of our previous intimacy. "I don't know New York at all," he said. "I came here once. In my senior year at Tulane. But I was too broke to go anywhere except the Radio City Music Hall. Remember the Rockettes?"

"Yes. In fact, I know one. She's retired. She's a friend of Arlene Wagstaff."

"I like your friend Arlene." I could not tell what, if anything, Kalki meant. Did he know? "I remember her from the movies." Kalki pulled his cap over his eyes as a group of schoolgirls rode past us in single file. They did not recognize him. The security guards eyed them suspiciously. So did I. Fortunately, there was not a Chinese in the lot.

Our horses shied as a pair of black criminals chased what looked to be two Hispanic criminals across the bridle path. A knife glinted. Or gleamed. Or shone. As we reined in our horses, the security guards just back of us drew their revolvers. But the criminals had vanished behind a hill. We paused a moment. There was a scream. Then nothing. We rode on.

"They will not be missed." Again, that disconcerting flatness in Kalki's voice; a coldness to match the day.

"But will there be any one left to miss them? Or am I breaking the rules?"

Kalki only smiled. Then he went into a canter. I followed. The security guards did their best to keep up with us. We must have gone a half-mile before Kalki reined in the white horse. Just above the tower of a hotel named the Essex House, a plane threaded the last patch of blue sky like a silver needle.

"I don't think my seat is too bad, do you?" I said nothing. At least he had not fallen off. "We've bought a new *Garuda*. A Boeing 707. Are you checked out in the 707?"

"Yes. But you'll need a trained copilot, a navigator, a . . ."

"I can learn all that."

"When?"

"When I can. Do you like Geraldine?" For the first time Kalki had asked me a personal question. He even seemed interested in my answer.

"Yes. Very much. We have a lot in common."

"I'm glad. She's valuable, too." A funny word, I thought. As if she —and I—were his personal possessions.

I took advantage of Kalki's off-duty mood. "But I can't say that I find Giles entirely . . . straightforward."

"He has the hardest role to play."

"What is that?"

"He must oppose. He must be the other. Study the Vedas." I had been doing my best to get through some of the many thousands of poems, hymns, mantras, anecdotes from prehistory that make up the Hindu holy books. At the ashrams the gurus gave the initiates a crash course in the beginning and the end; unfortunately, they left out the all-important middle.

"I suppose it is the duplicity," I said. "I really thought he was Dr. Ashok."

"You were meant to. Everyone is meant to. If Giles sets foot in Nepal as Giles, he goes to jail."

"Because he is trafficking in drugs?"

"Yes."

Why do we darknesses think that those who are light are necessarily transparent . . . like light itself? From the logbook, a line of Racine: *C'était pendant l'horreur d'une profonde nuit.* I could never make a translation as terrifying as the *sound* of the original. It was during (but, also, hanging . . . no, looming . . . no, threatening) the horror of a dark night. But *profonde* is not just the dark. *Profonde* can also mean the depths of the abyss itself, the universal darkness that buries all. In this context, Kalki's "yes" was somehow more reverberant and chilling than any of his incantations about the end or The End. Dark night was descending now, on two riders in Central Park.

"You, too?"

"Yes." Kalki kept his eyes on the towers of the city. No more denials.

"Why?"

"Money. For the ashrams. The mandali. The books, pamphlets. Where else could we get so much so quickly?"

"I'm shocked," I giggled. Something I never do. I *was* shocked. I was frightened, too.

"Why? We're not exactly secret. Where else *could* the money come from?"

"Disciples. Contributions. The Lotus Lotteries. No, that's not possible. You don't sell the lotuses. I don't know. I mean, I'm not really shocked by this." I was gabbling. "Well, no, I am shocked, I suppose, I mean that Kalki, the avatar of Vishnu and all the rest is phony. That your religious mission is just a front for something so squalid . . ."

"I am Kalki. I am the avatar of Vishnu. I have come to purify. I have come to make an ending. But I am also in the body of Jim Kelly. And he had a history before me. He sold drugs in Saigon. He worked for the Chao Chow of Hong Kong. He had a partnership with his old professor back in New Orleans. When I became manifest, I used what was at hand. I get money as Jim Kelly would get it, by trafficking in drugs. Meanwhile, I have done what I came to do. I have taught. I have warned. I have tried to reach as many people as possible, wearing this man's body."

"You have no moral feeling about drug addiction? I mean, aside from being illegal, it can lead to death, too."

"I am death . . . too.".

As if to make the point, the last remnant of blue sky was obscured by brown clouds. Large flakes of snow fell between us. I was frozen, in every sense.

Kalki turned toward me. The beautiful eyes were as generative of light as ever. "Don't be afraid," he said. "There will be no pain."

"How? What will happen?"

"I shall dream something else. That's all."

"We are your dreams?"

Kalki nodded. He looked happy, as if a student had finally resolved some difficult equation. "I am the mind that contains all things as well as no thing or nothing. I am, and that is all."

"If you're dreaming this, then why did you . . . well, make such a mess of this world. Why allow the age of Kali to exist?"

"I play a game. I must abide by the rules that I make for they make me, too. I cannot tell you more because human speech is insufficient. Just remember, in eternity only my dreams decorate the emptiness."

"You are alone out there, in eternity?"

"In here, out there, these are just phrases. I am. There is nothing else."

I had an inspiration—racial memory? or simply something that I had heard recently and not understood. "Who," I asked, "is Siva?"

Kalki answered me in a voice different from his own, a voice that was deep, harsh, sibilant. "There is no difference between Siva who exists in the form of Vishnu and Vishnu who exists in the form of Siva."

"You are the same but not the same?"

For a moment, we rode in silence. I could not see his eyes but assumed that he was, once again, not at home.

Then he began to chant, "I am the lord of songs, the lord of sacrifices. I am breath. I am spirit. I am the supreme lord. I alone was before all things, and I exist and I shall be. No other transcends me. I am eternal and not eternal, discernible and undiscernible. I am Brahma and I am not Brahma. I am without beginning, middle or end. Know me, and you will not die. There is no other way." The chanting stopped. Kalki turned toward me, the eyes were a blind blue glare. "At the time of the end, I annihilate all worlds. I am Siva the destroyer."

We were riding past something called the Tavern on the Green. I reined in my horse. Alarmed? Yes. Ready for flight? I don't know. But Kalki was now himself again, or at least he was the self that I was most used to. "Did Siva answer you?"

"Oh, yes. An alarming god, isn't he?"

"He is my frown, Teddy. Let's hope I never need to frown. As Vishnu, I only smile. As Vishnu, I am the preserver."

"You don't sound as if you're about to do much preserving on April 3."

"I shall preserve what is best."

Although I did not believe that Kalki was Vishnu, I was now certain that *he* believed it. And so, for all practical purposes, god was again among us. To the extent that this particular god embodied ancient dreams of death and rebirth, he might yet prevail. But in what way?

Nuclear chain reaction. I could think of nothing else. I wondered whether or not to alert the police, the *Sun*, Senator White. But I did nothing. I did not even tell Morgan about Kalki's confession. He would find out anyway. DRUG MESSIAH BUSTED. That would be the *Sun*'s headline. The press was always predictable, if nothing else. But how, I wondered, would they cover world's end?

3

On the morning of March 15 there was a snowstorm. I lay in bed, and watched snowflakes strike against the window. On contact with the heated glass, the snow turned to water.

Arlene rang me. She was an all-out Kalki fan. "I was up at dawn to watch that five-minute special on *Good Morning, America,* I mean, greater love hath no Arlene. Angel, he's out of sight! The End!" Arlene indulged in the national joke, saying The End with a rising inflection. Overnight every comedian in the country had his own way of saying The End. It was a sure-fire laugh-getter. One television comedian always pretended to shoot up whenever Kalki was mentioned. The whole subject was good for a laugh. Yet even early on much of the laughter was uneasy. After all, a great many people had visited the ashrams. Read the pamphlets. Seen Kalki on television. Whether or not they believed in him was not the point. No matter who or what Kalki was, something very odd was happening. Unfortunately, there was almost no serious analysis of the Kalki phenomenon in the press. As of March 15, the hot subject was whether or not the President would replace the Vice-President. The putative end of human life was a non-subject.

"Now," said Arlene. "Give with some inside info. What's he going to do? What's he cooked up?"

"I don't know," I was vague. "Just a sermon, I guess." My blood still turned to ice at the thought of what he had told me in Central Park. A few comments like that on national television and there would be total panic.

"You're an old meanie. You know and you won't tell me. Well, you tell him that I think he's a pussycat, and really groovy." Arlene was addicted to the slang of her youth. "A solid sender!" she added, nicely dating herself to World War II during which she entertained the troops, and I was born.

"He told me that he liked you, too."

Arlene was thrilled. "We have the same body waves, you know. I've read his chart. We complement each other. So you tell him that I'm giving a Kalki party tonight and that we're all going to sit around and watch him on the tube because he's about the biggest thing that's hit the Hollywood Hills since what's-his-name walked on the moon."

Arlene was not far off. Not only the whole United States but that fortunate part of the world which had access to Telstar tuned in to watch Kalki proclaim (live from Madison Square Garden) the end of the age of Kali.

Madison Square Garden itself had been in a state of siege all day. Every entrance was guarded by mounted police while the streets leading to the Garden were jammed. In Eighth Avenue alone there were an estimated fifty thousand people, waiting for a glimpse of Kalki. It took me (and my bodyguard) an hour to penetrate the Garden, to get to Giles's command post overlooking Eighth Avenue.

On arrival, I was told by a harassed secretary (eight telephones never stopped ringing) that Kalki had not yet arrived but that Giles was giving a briefing in the pressroom.

As I looked down at the crowd in the avenue, I remembered something my father had told me about Amelia Earhart. He had taken her to a football game at USC. Amelia was not a fan. My father was. At the most exciting moment in the game, when someone had made a touchdown and everyone was on his feet, yelling, cheering, booing, Amelia asked, "What color is a crowd?"

The pressroom at the Garden was just back of the pyramid on which Kalki would sit. Between pressroom and pyramid stood the colossal blue Styrofoam statue of Vishnu, four arms outstretched, face scowling beneath a tall crown.

Giles was seated on a desk. At least a hundred journalists were crowded into the room. Overhead fluorescent lights turned us all a Vishnu blue. Everyone talked at once. Finally, one journalist was heard: "Is it true that Mr. Kelly, who calls himself Kalki, has never actually changed his name legally to Kalki. Do you care to comment on that?"

This was par for the course. Giles was in his element. But then he was a natural (which is to say spontaneous) liar. He answered at irrelevant length.

"Have you any comment," announced a tall black lady from *The Village Voice*, "on Senator Johnson White's committee and its alleged intention to investigate Kalki Enterprises and their alleged connection with the trafficking of drugs in Asia and elsewhere around the world?"

Suddenly that crowded smoky room was so quiet that I could hear the humming of the air conditioning.

Giles was superb. "Like all good Americans, we at Kalki Enterprises are indebted to Johnson White, and to his committee's hard-hitting investigations. If ever there was a great American it is Johnson White and, for what it is worth, we at Kalki Enterprises applaud his efforts."

This had the effect intended. Everyone was confused.

"Senator White says that next week he's going to call Mr. Kalki, as a witness." The black lady persisted. "Will Mr. Kalki be supportive?"

"Hopefully, Kalki is supportive of all of us all of the time and for all time." Giles was launched on what sounded to be a major aria. Unfortunately, the other journalists were now coming to life.

"Has he been subpoenaed?" Asked one.

"No."

"What is the capitalization of Kalki Enterprises?" Asked another.

"You must ask the Internal Revenue Service. For some weeks their top accountants have been examining our books. Off the record," Giles was back in stride, "they are not going to finish their work before the end of the world."

Giles laughed loudly, and alone. The press did not know how to react. Bruce Sapersteen was suddenly at my side. "Hi, Teddy," he sniffed. Then he asked Giles, "Just when will the world end?"

Giles's response was coy. "This evening Kalki will speak to the city, to the world, and to the cosmos beyond. He has told me that he will give us the date then."

Bruce and I left the pressroom. The houselights in the auditorium were on. Ushers were roaming the aisles, preparing for the arrival of the audience. The television crews were in their places just opposite the pyramid. Guards were everywhere. In front of the pyramid a stage had been set up for the rock stars. Technicians were adjusting microphones. The towering statue of Vishnu was as alarming as ever. Bruce asked me to explain the statue to him. He seemed less stoned than usual.

"Well, one hand is holding a club and another hand is holding the sacred lotus . . ."

"While the other two are picking the pockets of the faithful. You know, Teddy, I think you're a closet convert. So does Morgan."

"You're both wrong. Christ Scientist is my shepherd, and general practitioner."

"Are you making it with Kalki?" Bruce had modeled himself on one of the two young journalists who had investigated Watergate, not the Robert Redford one in the film, alas; the other one. I found Bruce's impersonation highly resistible, and told him so, using short brutal Anglo-Saxon words.

"Well, I was just curious. I mean, you don't have to bite my head off. Here. Let me buy you some coffee."

A vendor sold him two containers of coffee. Then we sat side by side in the front row, looking up at stage, pyramid, statue.

"Those arms move?" Bruce was plainly freaked out by the statue.

"I hope not."

"Did you know that the de Laurentiis King Kong was mostly a guy in an ape suit? They never did get a monster that really worked." Bruce was always full of information, most of it depressing.

"I haven't seen a movie since *Elvira Madigan,*" I lied. But I did love *Elvira Madigan.* But then I am romantic.

"There's a rumor that your boy is going to be arrested tonight." Bruce sniffed, a happy sound.

"He's not *my* boy. Who's going to arrest him? And why?"

"The narcs."

"McCloud's an idiot." My educated guess graduated with honors.

"McCloud's a pretty savvy guy." Bruce often talked like a running character in a minor TV crime series.

"So who's he working for? He's a double, maybe triple agent." I could talk television, too. But then what American could not at the end of the age of Kali? Each day the average American watched seven not necessarily consecutive hours of television. Periodically, there would be a widely published report to the effect that thanks to all this TV-viewing, Americans now knew more about wildlife, detergents, foreign countries, and electrical appliances than ever before.

"McCloud's working for White," said Bruce.

"He's also working for Kalki." I wanted to see how Bruce would react to that one.

But Bruce was one up on me. "I know. He's also in with the Chao Chow. And with the Triad."

For the first time in our acquaintance Bruce had managed to interest me. I wanted to ask him more. But the audience had started to arrive and, in the confusion, we were separated.

Just back of Vishnu's head was the Green Room. Here a number of the mandali were gathered. A window of one-way glass looked out onto the auditorium. We could see the audience but they could not see us. On the wall opposite the window a row of TV monitors showed us, variously, the interior of the Garden, the street outside, a rerun of *I Love Lucy*, a panel program . . . everything that was being shown on network television as well as whatever the cameras inside and outside the Garden were picking up.

Geraldine wore a jade-green sari. Impulsively, she kissed me. Lakshmi did not. But her greeting was affectionate. Professor Jossi looked pleased with himself. Apparently, the atom would split in an orderly way.

"Kalki's arriving by helicopter." Geraldine was as excited as a child at the circus. I fell, once again, in love. "He'll land on the roof."

Giles came to us straight from the press conference. He was more than usually manic. He waved a telegram at us. "The President hopes that the course of world peace and understanding will be advanced by what happens here tonight!" Everyone applauded.

"Now," said Lakshmi, "he will be thrice-born."

Giles went off into a corner where he communed with a walkie-talkie. The rest of us looked at the television monitors. Everyone preferred to watch the doings in the auditorium on television rather than directly through the window. This was a commonplace in that era: events were only real if experienced at second hand, preferably through the medium of the camera.

I told Geraldine what Bruce had said. "I don't think people would like that." Geraldine was unexpectedly mild. "After all, you don't arrest god."

"They arrested Jesus Christ."

"Don't worry, Teddy. This is the homestretch!"

Professor Jossi had much the same message. He addressed the two of us as if we were in one of his classes, not the advanced one. "There will be a clear and unusual picture of the atom or, to be exact, the atom's shadow or mandala or *effect*, as it explodes, producing some quite vivid and unusual colors within the tiny spectrum that the human eye can comprehend as opposed to all those radiant colors which our eyes may not see until we have attained Vaikuntha."

"I hope, Professor Jossi," I spelled it out, "that there is no risk of a chain reaction."

"There will be," said Professor Jossi, spelling it out, too, "no errors of any kind."

I found this ambiguous; hence, ominous. "Because," I said, "if there should be a nuclear chain reaction the earth will not be habitable for centuries."

"You confuse two things." Professor Jossi raised his right hand. Thumb and forefinger came together, as if he were holding chalk. "One, you seem to think that I might make an error. Let me put at ease your mind. There will be no error. All around the earth, thanks to television, the audience will see a unique atomic display, symbolizing the power of Vishnu, the sole originator of that primal explosion which launched the knowable universe. On the other hand, your analysis of what would result if an atomic chain reaction were to be set off is *not* accurate. Depending on the sort of fissionable material used, the reaction might kill certain living things whilst sparing others . . ."

Professor Jossi was interrupted by the sound of Kalki's helicopter which came, needless to say, not from overhead (the room was sound-proofed) but from one of the monitors which showed the helicopter, hovering over Eighth Avenue.

Then there were shots of the roof of Madison Square Garden where television units were waiting to record Kalki's arrival. Most of the press corps was also on hand. There was a shot of the crowds in Eighth Avenue, looking up at the helicopter from which, suddenly, thousands of paper lotus flowers were released, to the crowd's delight. Like a swarm of white butterflies, the lotuses circled slowly in the icy evening air.

We watched the landing of the helicopter. The helicopter door opened. Kalki stepped into the television lights. So harsh was the glare that the saffron robe looked white. In one hand, Kalki held a lotus. As

Giles hurried forward to greet him (and get into the picture), an announcer's voice kindly told us what we could see for ourselves. "Kalki has left the helicopter. He is crossing the roof of Madison Square Garden. He is being mobbed by his fans. There's also a mob scene outside."

The scene shifted to Eighth Avenue where enthusiasts were chanting, "Kal-ki, Kal-ki!" The announcer told us that the people were chanting "Kal-ki."

I turned from the network monitor to an interior monitor which showed the backstage of the Garden. The corridors were jammed with security men and police; deafening was what H.V.W. would call the din from the rock stars' dressing rooms where electric guitars whined, drums rattled, sitars plunked; and marijuana made the air a tender blue. Over the ear-splitting noise, someone could be heard screaming "Shanti!" Even the camera that moved shakily through the backstage area seemed stoned.

Geraldine and I looked at all the monitors. Public television was doing the entire program from beginning to end. The networks were doing bits and pieces, and the usual reruns.

We settled in front of a monitor which displayed a solemn analyst who wondered how Kalki had been able to fill the Garden with people who had paid as high as three thousand dollars for a single ticket on the black market. Apparently, nothing like this had happened since the time of the Beatles, the spiritual high noon of the twentieth century.

The Solemnity then did his best to appear serious. Gravely, he told us that "The phenomenon which is known as Kalki is not something new in American history." (I paraphrase from a faulty memory.) "In the nineteenth century there were a number of end-of-the-world Christian movements. Today, of course, we have our Seventh-Day Adventists and Jehovah's Witnesses. But, to date, not even the North Hollywood First Assembly of God has had quite the attraction for the public that this young man from New Orleans has had. By calling himself Kalki and claiming that he is Vishnu born for the last time, the young man from New Orleans has obviously touched a nerve. Certainly he has successfully exploited that fascination with Eastern mysticism in recent years which led, not so long ago, to the election as governor of California of a Zen Buddhist who slept on the floor."

153

I looked through the window of the auditorium. Thousands and thousands of people were still crowding the aisles. Gray-pink, Amelia, is the color of a crowd.

I wanted to go down into the auditorium, but for some reason Geraldine was fascinated by the talking head on the monitor. So we listened to: "But there is something deeper at work here than just a fad like sleeping on the floor. Something deeper and, perhaps, alarming. Although Kalki has announced that the end of the world is at hand, something that does not, at the moment, seem very likely." We were favored with a little smile to show that the Solemnity was not only a kindly and tolerant person but also a practical one, and not about to be conned. "Nevertheless, it is significant that so many people have responded to Kalki's message of non-hope."

"You will be reborn," said Geraldine to the TV set.

"Is that a good thing?" I asked.

Geraldine did not answer. The Solemnity did. "Where then have we failed as parents, teachers, opinion-makers?" The color was now out of sync. A modest smile hung from acid-green lips. *"How* have we failed those young people who today follow Kalki? Young people who accept the obliteration of this world, of this great nation even, as something matter-of-fact, and not to be mourned? There are no easy answers . . ."

"Only easy questions." Geraldine finally turned away from the monitor.

We entered the auditorium from the pressroom which was just back of Vishnu's left leg. As usual, our security men (likable, rather talkative men) got us past their colleagues. We stepped into the blazing lights that flooded the pyramid from every side. A rock band deafened us.

Holding hands, we tried to find a place from which to observe Kalki's entrance. Just beneath the banks of television cameras, there was an empty square yard of space. We settled it.

Gradually our eyes grew accustomed to the lights. We could now see the blue head of Vishnu, hovering over all like a face in a dream. Then the rock band lowered its decibel rate and I could hear, once again, the beating of my own heart.

Kalki appeared atop the pyramid. He seemed made of yellow fire. The whole auditorium rocked with: "Kal-ki!" as in unison everyone chanted those two magical syllables.

Geraldine clutched my arm and said something, which I could not hear.

For a moment Kalki stood, not moving. Then he made the pranam sign and sat cross-legged on the throne. Suddenly there was not silence but stillness all around us.

When Kalki's voice came, it was soft, serene, seductive—and marvelously amplified. "I am the highest of the high." As that first sentence hummed upon the air, Vishnu's face was lit in such a way that for an awful instant, the statue appeared to smile. The audience gasped; so did I.

"When there was nothing, I took three steps. In space. In air. In earth. In space, I am the sun. In air, the lightning. In earth, the fire. I was the beginning. I will be the end. I am Kalki, the ultimate avatar of Vishnu."

I have yet to see the cassette of Kalki's Madison Square Garden performance (we don't seem to have one here at the White House) but I doubt if there was ever anything like it in the history of entertainment. Obviously I cannot speak with any authority about the history of religion. But I will say that Kalki achieved his effects without tricks, magical or otherwise. He relied on nothing but that not quite New Orleans voice with which he spun his curious web around the world.

As Kalki described the creation of the universe, according to the Hindu cosmogony, he used enough terms from contemporary science to sound if not entirely plausible, familiar. In describing the cycles of creation, he explained how nothing ever ends. How the dust that caught fire to make the sun was the same dust that makes up each human being. How all things are interchangeable. How nothing is ever lost or can be lost. How we came together through birth in one arrangement and how at death our matter is reassembled as something else. Meanwhile, the soul continues in new incarnations until the ultimate sleep or apotheosis, until nirvana or Vaikuntha.

Kalki then described how the world is divided into ages. How each age is introduced and ended by a time of twilight. How we were now at the end of the final twilight of the last of the four ages of man, the age of iron or Kali. How with each age since the original Golden Age, all things human have lost energy. How the god Vishnu came to us nine times since the first creation. How Vishnu tried to teach men the way to enlightenment, but his way was never taken by more than a few.

Now Vishnu was among us for the tenth and last time.

"Since the beginning, I have taught. Since the beginning, only a few have listened. Throughout eternity man and god have been in necessary conflict, as are all the other elements of creation, as are all the elements of matter when my will breaks the atom." Thus Kalki prepared the audience for Professor Jossi's special effects.

With some effort, I forced myself not to look at the small golden figure on the throne. I wanted to see how the people in the audience were reacting. They were transfixed, mesmerized. When I say that Kalki achieved his effects entirely with his voice, I exaggerate. The audience had been conditioned in advance by the rock bands, by psychedelic lighting, by the scent of incense burning in braziers at each corner of the pyramid.

Enchanted as I was by Kalki's performance, my mind was nervously preoccupied with Professor Jossi's fireworks. I looked about, trying to find him. I did not see Jossi. But I did see Jason McCloud just as he stepped from behind Vishnu's statue.

McCloud was clutching what looked to be the same attaché case that I had seen him with in New Orleans. He appeared nervous. I remember wondering whether or not he had come to arrest Kalki. I was about to draw Geraldine's attention to McCloud when Kalki sprang from a sitting to a standing position.

"I am Vishnu!" Kalki's voice rang through the auditorium. "I end but cannot end. I die but forever live. Have faith, and you will be reborn!"

Then Kalki began to chant something perfectly incomprehensible to me but not to Geraldine and to the other mandali. He was reciting the Sanskrit hymn in celebration of the end. Yes, The End.

"My God!" Geraldine gave a cry.

As Kalki chanted, he pointed to the sky or, more specifically, to Jossi's screen which was now pulsing with light. Everyone looked up at the screen. Except Kalki. He had vanished into the pyramid. Most people were not aware that he was gone until the pyramid began, slowly, to open, revealing Kalki astride the white horse.

There was no one in that audience who did not know that when Kalki mounted the white horse the world was supposed to end. Waves of emotion—not to mention sound—flooded the auditorium. There was horror. There was . . . expectation? Hard to say. Things happened too quickly. Geraldine dropped to her knees. Covered her face with her hands. I did the same.

Kalki rode toward us, brandishing a jeweled sword. The voice was strident and unfamiliar. "Those who are with me even to the end and beyond will be with me in Vaikuntha!"

Then all creation exploded. Waves of sound engulfed and deafened me. Yet I had one fraction of a second in which to congratulate myself on having guessed correctly the way that the world would end.

At Kalki's order, Jossi had set off an atomic chain reaction. Earth was now aflame, and dead. I took a bitter joy in having been right.

· But once the initial blast had spent itself in waves of sound, the world was still intact. So was I. So was Geraldine. So was the statue of Vishnu. So was the screen on which could be seen particles of the broken atom, like comets gone beserk.

Nothing on earth had been affected except the rider and the white horse. They had been disintegrated. Blood was everywhere. I was the first to scream.

SEVEN

1

THE MURDER ON TELEVISION WAS THE MOST DRAMATIC EVENT IN THE history of that medium. The Kennedy brothers and Martin Luther King had been killed off camera. Although Oswald had been satisfactorily murdered on camera, he was not at the time a star, or even a featured player. On the other hand, Kalki was already god to millions of people. To those other millions who rejected him as god, he was undeniably that most eminent of all creatures in the last days of the age of Kali, a superstar.

I have surprisingly few memories of those traumatic days just after the murder in Madison Square Garden. For some reason, I vividly recall the debate in Congress as to whether or not the country's flags should be flown at half-mast. Finally, each community was given its own option. The Mayor of New York refused to allow the flag at City Hall to be flown at half-mast, out of respect for the city's numerous Roman Catholic and Jewish voters. Two daring Kalki-ites promptly shinnied up the flagpole and lowered the flag. A photograph of this event appeared on the front page of the New York *Daily News*. Yet one word is worth a thousand pictures. Particularly if it is "no."

What else? The explosion that disintegrated horse and rider was immediately blamed on Professor Jossi and his atom-smasher. Jossi met with the press. He filled an entire blackboard with diagrams, proving that his machine could not have done the slightest harm to anyone. This explanation was accepted because Jossi's demonstration in applied physics was not understood. I confess (now) that at first I, too, blamed him. But we were all of us wrong.

Sulkily, Professor Jossi withdrew to Lausanne. Final words: "This man Kelly was not the true avatar of Vishnu. I was gulled." Because of Jossi's accent, the press thought he said, "I was guilty." There was more confusion when that was printed.

I have now forgotten at what point we all became convinced that Jason McCloud was the murderer. Fairly soon, I should think. Giles assured us that McCloud had been acting on orders not from the Drug Enforcement Administration but from the Chao Chow Society, his principal employer. McCloud was a triple agent. As a bona fide agent for the DEA he had infiltrated Kalki Enterprises and Giles had been obliged to pay him a "consultancy fee." McCloud had also infiltrated the Chao Chow Society of Hong Kong. When McCloud learned that they had taken out a contract on Kalki's life with the Triad, he convinced them to let him do the job. They were delighted. Who would dare accuse an American narc of such a highly visible murder? To this day, no one knows just how McCloud set off his bomb, but we know that he did. At no point was McCloud suspected by the newspapers where rife was speculation.

How did I take these events? I was stunned. Kept out of sight for twenty-four hours. Watched television in my room at the Americana. Every hour on the hour, there was a gruesome rerun, in slow motion, of rider and horse coming apart in vivid color. I could not stop watching this horror. I drank heavily. Took no calls except from Arlene, who was as distraught as I, and drunker.

Two days after the murder, Giles gave a press conference aboard the *Narayana*. Geraldine was on hand. Lakshmi was under sedation in another part of the ship. I wore a black dress. I had had my hair done that morning. Did not mind too much the photographers. I did mind Bruce, who squeezed beside me on a sofa while the cameras were being set up, lights adjusted.

"He did it." Bruce pointed a grubby finger at Giles.

"Why?"

"To get control of the Mob. It's his now."

"No." I will confess to this record that I had had a suspicion or two that Giles *might* have wanted Kalki out of the way. Suspicions that were soon dispelled. For one thing, Giles had no real motive. After all, he and Kalki had been equal partners in the drug syndicate. They needed one another. Giles had nothing to gain by Kalki's death; and a good deal to lose. In the hot glare of the television lights, Giles looked remarkably unhealthy, even for him. I also noticed that Geraldine's eyes were red. Yes, she had been in love with Kalki, I decided. Had I? In a way. And what else is there when it comes to love but a way to be in or out of it? including no way.

"You seem awfully certain." Bruce gave me his shrewd investigative-journalist stare. I gave him my bland journalist-of-record gaze.

"Yes," I said. "I am."

"Then who did it?"

"Another religion. The U.S. Government. Does it matter?" I was offhand.

"Does it matter?" Bruce looked as if a door had opened in my forehead and a little bird had come out. "If you think that the Warren Commission spent a lot of time on who killed J.F.K., it's nothing compared to what Congress will do with this murder. White's already hit town with half his committee. You don't have a Quaalude, do you?" Bruce was looking a bit wired.

Quaalude was a depressant, popular in show-biz circles at the end of the age of Kali.

"No," I said, happy to be able to refuse him succor. "You'll just have to shake a bit."

Giles stood up on a chair. "I have," he announced in a strained voice, "a statement to make." The salon was quiet, except for the hum of the cameras. Giles began to read from a piece of paper. "Kalki lives." Giles paused. Definitely? Yes, I suppose so. The immediate reaction was amazement. Then there were a number of snickers. Media personages were not precisely amiable.

Giles's annoyance was plain. Anger gave urgency to his voice. "Kalki lives," he repeated. "Vishnu lives. All that died in Madison Square Garden was one of the four billion human bodies currently crowding the planet. As predicted, Kalki was obliged to discard one of those bodies. Presently, Kalki will inhabit a new body. He will return to us and, as predicted, he will end the age of Kali on April 3."

The boldness of these statements produced, first, a deep silence. Then someone gave a nervous laugh. Bruce bit his knuckles. Withdrawal symptoms?

Giles stared straight into the recording camera; he seemed at ease now, relaxed. The television camera often has that effect.

Finally, a journalist asked the obvious if slightly deranged under the circumstances question. "Where is he now, Dr. Lowell?"

"Kalki is Vishnu. Vishnu is the universe. Therefore Kalki is everywhere and nowhere." I groaned to myself. This rigmarole always depressed me. Others, too.

"I meant, Dr. Lowell," said the inquiring reporter, "where exactly is this spirit that you say is going to reinhabit some other body between now and April 3?"

"I've just told you." There was a definite snap in Giles's voice. "The spirit is everywhere."

"In that case," a lady asked, "could you tell us, then, where the body is that he is going to occupy? And who does it belong to now?"

This struck me as a good question.

"I don't know." Giles was curt.

"Then could you maybe explain to us what will happen to the present tenant of the body when Kalki takes over?" The questioner was a syndicated columnist, known for his unready wit. Everyone laughed, except Geraldine who looked furious, red hair bristling. Red hair always bristles in Weiss-land.

"Since Vishnu is already present in that body, as he is present in me and in you and in all things, there should be no dislocation." When Giles became unusually precise, it was a sure sign that he was getting angry.

"*Why* did Kalki leave the old body?"

"Because, dear lady," Giles was now pouring out his special organic honey with unstudied ease, "a person or persons unknown saw fit to throw an as yet unidentified explosive at the old body, totally disintegrating it. The god Vishnu, of course, continues to exist in the various bits of the old body that were so criminally and so savagely scattered around Madison Square Garden. Presently, he will either reassemble those fragments and appear amongst us as he was or he will select an altogether new body in which to reappear. We shall just have to wait, and see."

"This is all very fanciful, Dr. Lowell," said a tough Barbara Walters type. "But what I don't understand is why Kalki or Vishnu or whoever would allow somebody to blow him up like that, anyway."

"Karma, dear lady. Fate. Destiny. It was meant to be and so it was."

"So Kalki *knew* he was going to be blown up on the TV?"

"Vishnu knows what was, what is and what will be."

"But did Kalki tell you in advance that he expected to be blown up on the TV?"

"Yes, he did. He predicted everything."

This had the desired effect. News was now being made. Everyone shouted at once. When did Kalki know? What did he say? Bruce's voice was the loudest; and he was heard by all when he asked, "Did Kalki tell you *why* he was going to let this happen to him?"

"I am so glad, dear Mr. Sapersteen, that you should be the one to ask me that." Glowing with sweat from the TV lights, Giles looked almost healthy. Everyone leaned forward to hear what he would say. "To begin with," he began, "we are all of us involved in a most intricate ceremony. Think of the end of this cycle of creation as a sort of dance. Indeed, there is a legend that the end will come when Siva begins the Tandava Dance, or dance of eternity. For Siva is also known to the gods as Nataraja, the king of dance."

"How do you spell Siva? And who is he or she?" The man from the Associated Press was required to get straight what news there was. The rest of the print media dealt mostly in opinion.

Giles spelled Siva. He also explained that Siva was one of the three aspects of the single god. For some reason, the Christians in the salon found this difficult to understand even though their own religion involved an equally tripartite or trilateral god. Mary Baker Eddy, bless her, never went in for this kind of nonsense. It was enough that she herself had three names.

"So let me return, if I may, to the image of the dance." Giles was in full stride or gallop now. "Kalki appears. Makes a gesture. Disappears. Reappears. Is transformed. Moves to left, to right. All the while we watch him. All the while *he* watches us. Because he is testing us."

"For what?" asked Bruce.

"For our faith. Now I must give you a most solemn warning. Those who believe that Kalki ceased to exist in Madison Square Garden are doomed never to achieve nirvana. Those who have faith in Kalki's return will know paradise, and soon."

Giles had a lot of guts, if nothing else. To unreel that sort of line to the press was asking for it. And there was a lot of *it*. The black lady from *The Village Voice* spoke, "You said a while back that April 3 is the new date for the end of the world, is that right?" Journalists always liked to answer the question that they have asked on the ground that it might turn an essentially one-way street into a thoroughfare. As Giles reaffirmed the date, I motioned to Geraldine. We left together, unnoticed by the crowd. They reminded me of a pack of wolves . . . of the sort that Arlene so much enjoyed rooting for in those television documentaries. Giles was plainly wolves' dinner.

Geraldine and I walked back to the Americana Hotel. She was tense, guarded. She agreed with me that McCloud was the murderer. "But he's safe. They'll never catch him . . . in time."

On Lexington Avenue we watched a group of Kalki boys and girls. They offered their literature, as politely as always. But no one took the pamphlets. Even the white paper lotuses were refused. The mood had changed overnight.

"It's all over," said Geraldine. She seemed sad.

"Isn't Kalki returning?" I probed.

"Yes." Geraldine was brisk. "But even so, this phase is over." Geraldine made a funny sort of pushing-to-one-side gesture. "They're all excluded now."

"Who's excluded?"

"Everyone on earth except . . ." Geraldine stopped. She did not look at me. We crossed Park Avenue. The wind was cold; from the northwest.

"Except the mandali?" I asked.

"Except the ones who believe."

"And you're doubtful about me?"

"I don't know. Everyone seems to have given up." For a moment we lingered in the bare garden of the Lever Building. Geraldine told me that most of the devoted mandali had defected. Some had been frightened. They had thought that whoever had murdered Kalki might want to make a clean sweep of his followers. Some feared that the

American Government might find it irresistible to behave illegally and arrest or deport them. Some had just lost faith. "It's really only us now. Lakshmi and Giles and me and . . ."

"Well," I said quickly, "I'm still available. I mean, I'm still under contract, am I not?"

What did I believe as of March 18? I must be absolutely honest. I thought that Kalki was doornail dead. But I assumed that Giles would come up with some sort of substitute. Yet even if he did, the game was over. April 3 would come and go. Meanwhile, I was eager for Kalki Enterprises to honor my contract as a pilot because it now looked as if my book with Doubleday might fall through in the same way that the pieces for *The National Sun* had fallen through because, as Bruce had said as I was leaving the press conference, "I'll be writing the wrap-up piece on Kalki alone."

"Thanks, pal," I said. I never saw Bruce Sapersteen again. All in all, a plus.

Geraldine was grateful for my display if not of loyalty, of solidarity. When I asked about Lakshmi, Geraldine said, "No one has seen her, except Giles."

"But she must have known." I played along. "I mean, if Kalki predicted this would happen . . ."

"It's still a shock," said Geraldine, matter-of-fact as always. I could not fathom her. Or any of them. I was genuinely sad that the beautiful construct of flesh that had been J.J. Kelly was no longer in its original blond arrangement.

There were a number of messages for me at the hotel. One was from Senator Johnson White. He wanted to meet me the following day, at my convenience. He was at the Plaza Hotel.

I turned on the television in my room. In time to watch Arlene do the Jedda Coffee commercial. I never tire of her. After being soothed by Arlene, I was promptly disturbed by a special news report on the murder of the Hindu messiah from New Orleans at Madison Square Garden. First there was the by now obligatory bit of film showing the disintegration of horse and rider. Then an actor playing the part of a journalist looked into the camera and said, "The murder is thought to be the work either of a rival religious group or of a rival narcotics ring. A spokesman for the Reverend Sun Moon denies any complicity in the murder and quotes the Korean messiah as saying how sorry he is to hear of the death of the Hindu messiah from New Orleans, James J. Kelly, known to his many fans all over the world as Kalki. Various Mafia capos all around the country have denied any knowledge of the murder of what many believed was a leading trafficker in drugs." The drug connection was now entirely in the open.

Then Jason McCloud's round black face filled the screen. He stood between a large American flag and a globe of the world. He seemed a bit incoherent. "That's true, Jim." He spoke to an invisible questioner. "I mean Bill. The Drug Enforcement Administration is. Absolutely."

"That's for sure, Mr. McCloud?"

"For sure, Bill. I *could* say, no way. But I won't. I *will* say that Kalki Enterprises are under investigation, and now that the mastermind himself has been removed from the scene by a rival gang, we will be able, I am sure, to somehow nail once and for all this dread octopus whose tentacles extend from the poppy fields of Turkey to the playgrounds of Buffalo and Fort Lauderdale."

"I think that all of we Americans feel a lot safer knowing that Jason McCloud is on the job."

I decided that Geraldine was right. McCloud was safe. Between the flag and the globe, he was invulnerable.

The next image on the screen must have been recorded only minutes before. There was Giles. He was coming down the gangplank of the *Narayana*. Suddenly a man stepped in front of him. Giles looked startled. The man handed him an envelope. According to a voice-over: "Dr. Giles Lowell is now being subpoenaed by the Senate Drug and Narcotics Abuse Committee."

The camera came in for a close shot of Giles. He showed his teeth, like a tiger at bay; no, worse, a tiger at sea. "The committee will be meeting in New York City this week . . ."

2

Senator White was installed in a corner suite at the Plaza Hotel. From tall windows, there was a fine view of Central Park. Although flowers from admirers decorated every table of the sitting room, I looked in vain for the symbolic poppy.

In shirt sleeves, the Senator was talking on the telephone. A male secretary motioned for me to sit down. I stood. The Senator concluded his conversation. I was given a brilliant fortieth or maybe forty-first President of the United States smile. "Sit down, Teddy. Get a load off those pretty feet. I've just about cracked the largest drug ring in the world. I'll see you later, Teddy," he said, not to me but to the secretary. Same name. "In a few minutes we will be joined by an agent from the CIA. *Who has the goods.*" White punched a tiny fist into a tiny hand, making a small sound.

"You wanted to see me, Senator."

"Yes." White put on his solemn State of the Union face. He looked historic. Mount Rushmore in rosy soap. "As a good American, Teddy, than which you are—and I can always tell—no other, I want you to testify before my committee on April 4. Naturally, you'll want to be briefed on exactly what to say which is why I have proposed this little get-together with me and the man from the CIA. But first, Teddy, what do *you* think happened at Madison Square Garden?"

Under the circumstances, I thought this an odd question. So I gave him an odd answer. "Well, for one thing, Kalki filled the Garden. And you said he wouldn't."

"There was a lot of paper." White lapsed into show business lingo. "Paper" meant those free tickets that are given out in order to make it look as if there is a full house.

"There was no paper. The house," I show-bizzed, too, "went clean."

"Be that," said White snippily, "as it may. What exactly happened at the end?"

"Kalki was murdered." I decided to follow the party or Giles Lowell line. "As he expected to be."

"So that's the story, is it?"

"That's what happened."

"Did Kalki ever tell *you* that he expected to be murdered?"

"In a way, yes." Since I was in the dark, I saw no reason not to share my darkness with White. It was unlikely that he knew anything I did not.

White scratched his head in such a way that the cowlick in the back stood straight up. He looked a country slicker. "Well, now I'm just a boy from up the creek a ways, and what I don't . . . dohn unnerstan is jest who in tarnation lobbed that big ole bomb at Jim Kelly and his real nice white horse."

I gritted my teeth. White's voice was like a plate of cold okra. I hate okra of any kind. I answered noncommittally. "The FBI are supposed to be investigating."

"They're hopeless." White dropped the accent. "They aren't even sure what kind of explosive was used. Or where it came from. Or who threw it, assuming it was not already in place, with a timer attached. Anyhoo, that ain't no concern of us'n." Into a frying pan filled with lard went the okra. "Now, ole buddy. I got me a theory. And it is this. Dr. Giles Lowell set that bomb."

"Why?"

" 'Cause he wants to take over the Mob."

"I don't buy that, Senator!"

"Well, I'm a-peddlin', ole buddy."

I broke down. I swept frying pan and okra to the ground, metaphorically speaking. "Please, Senator. Don't talk Southern to me. I mean, it's bad enough listening to the President and his wife and his brothers and his sisters and his sons and their wives and his aides and his mother without having you, the white hope of the Republican party and I pray our next president, coming on like Li'l Abner when what this country of ours needs is Honest Abe." I laid it on.

White surrendered. He flashed a winner's smile. "Lordy!" he said. Then he stopped himself in time. "I guess it's contagious, that truly awful accent we hear morning, noon and night in Washington. Anyways . . . I mean, anyway, Teddy, I always knew you would end up in my corner if only because fiscal responsibility is my watchword." Politicians did not talk so much as respond to buttons pushed. Somehow or other, one of us had pressed "fiscal responsibility." Or was it "watchword"? With some effort, we got ourselves back on track, and I helped White push the Kalki button.

"Teddy," he was grave, "I want you to testify that during the period of your employment as Kalki's personal pilot, he told you on more than one occasion that, a, he was the actual head of this great narcotics ring and, b, that he feared Dr. Lowell would knock him off and take his place."

"Senator, you're asking me to commit perjury before a Senate committee."

"I'm asking you, Teddy, to tell the truth, and nothing but the truth." White's contact lenses reflected, disagreeably, my anxious face.

"The truth is," I said, "Kalki never said either a or b to me."

"I think, Teddy, that you are showing signs of being an uncooperative witness." Capped teeth were bared. "And I think you know what happens to uncooperative witnesses who are in contempt of Congress."

I was ready to kick that one around. But we were interrupted by Teddy, the secretary, who poked his head in the doorway and announced, "He's here."

In retrospect, where I seem now to be in happy residence, I am not as surprised as I was then to see Dr. Ashok. Although I never found Giles's Dr. Ashok number as convincing as Dr. Ashok's Dr. Lowell routine, I had to admit that he was in good form that day with Senator White. But then he had to be. As Giles Lowell, he had been subpoenaed. With the greatest of ease, he could have ended up in the clink. It took a lot of guts to enter the lion's den, beard in hand, as it were. I remember wondering whether or not White knew that Dr. Ashok was Dr. Lowell. After all, Morgan had hinted that White might be involved with Kalki Enterprises. The hallmark of the age of Kali was not good government.

"My dear Senator! What a pleasure! And dear Madame Ottinger, my Katmandu 'pal'! Put it there!" Golden eyes and teeth shining, Dr. Ashok gave me a fragile brown hand to shake. He even smelled of curry powder. A true artist.

"Dr. Ashok, we need your counsel," said White, putting his tiny feet on the coffee table.

"I am yours to command, like the genie in the lamp. Simply rub, oh Aladdin! And you will get your wish." I always thought that Giles tended to overdo Dr. Ashok in a way that Dr. Ashok never overdid Dr. Lowell. But if White was not in cahoots with Giles, he was plainly taken in.

"What are they saying at CIA headquarters?"

"Langley is more than usually confused." Dr. Ashok patted my knee. I moved my chair away.

"Dr. Ashok, I may as well jump in with both feet," said White, adjusting a contact lens. "In the course of my committee hearings I am going to expose the murderer of Kalki. In order for me to do this, I must hold off the CIA, the FBI, New York's finest . . . in short, anyone who might solve that murder before I do. So, Dr. Ashok, can you keep the lid on at Langley?"

"Dear Senator White, you have, I fear, overestimated my humble intelligence. Before I can begin to keep a lid of any sort in its appointed place, I must know—oh, superb simile or even metaphor!—what precisely do you have in your pot?"

"Kalki's murderer is in my pot."

"His name, dear Senator White?"

"Giles Lowell, M.D."

Dr. Ashok rose, quietly, to greatness. "I take it, then, that you have in your possession absolute proof that the unsavory Dr. Lowell murdered his partner in crime?"

"I have the proof."

"In what form?"

"That is for my committee to decide. I am making a joke, of course," he added seriously. "But since we know in advance the murderer's identity, we should have no problem in constructing the case against him. Particularly with your help, Dr. Ashok. Yours, too, Teddy . . ."

"No dice!" I had decided that this was a matter best left unminced. "I don't hold any brief for Dr. Lowell, but . . ."

"A truly evil man." Dr. Ashok spoke with absolute conviction.

I was deflected by this aside. "I assume," I said, really curious, "that you would know."

"Indeed I do! After all, I have been on the trail of Giles Lowell lo!

these many moons. I have followed his spoor from New Orleans to New Delhi to New York. And I mean to have his head. Do you hear me?" Dr. Ashok added decibels to his voice as he repeated, *"I mean to have his head!"*

"So do I, Doc." White took refuge in bumpkinhood. He teased the cowlick into a haystack. " 'Cause he's a bad'un and that's a fact. Even so, we gotta figure out jest how he got that bomb into the Garden, and where he had it hid. Our guess is that it was inside of that heathen idol."

"You are referring to Vishnu *the* god, who is holy to me, Senator." There was gentle Weissean reproof in Dr. Ashok's voice.

"Sorry about that, Doc. I guess you know that I'm as great a believer in religious tolerance as the next senator and I respect every man's god, blue or not. Now then, fellas, let's put our thinking caps on and try to figure out *how* Dr. Lowell managed to set off that bomb . . ."

"Don't you think you first ought to figure out why?" I asked.

"With Kalki out of the way, Dr. Lowell would control the largest narcotics ring in the world. Right, Dr. Ashok?"

"Right, Senator White." Dr. Ashok poured his characteristic honey over the statesman. "Also, we must never rule out the mysterious passions that govern men. We have only to recall the Bawd of Arden's greatest work of art in which the envious Agnello destroyed his admirable superior Dago, a man whose very name was a watchword for loyalty and integrity in the Vespasian Army. I see Dr. Lowell as Agnello and poor, yes, poor, weak, loving, loyal Kalki as Dago, destroyed with a kiss."

White nodded, as if this speech made sense. I always found it odd that although Dr. Ashok suffered from metaphasis, Giles did not. But then Giles did not go in for quotations.

Dr. Ashok turned to White. "I shall do my best to defuze Langley. Meanwhile, I am certain that Madame Ottinger will tell your committee how, on more than one occasion, Kalki told her that he feared Dr. Lowell would one day kill him."

"But . . ." I started. Then stopped. After all, Dr. Lowell as Dr. Ashok or Dr. Ashok as Dr. Lowell was in charge. This was his show, not mine.

"Agreed?" Dr. Ashok gave me a yellowy smile.

I said nothing.

"Good girl!" White was pleased. "I've already prepared your statement to be made under oath." He indicated a folder on the coffee table.

"You can take it away with you. Read it, if you like. Then sign it in the presence of a notary public, and return to me."

I took a long leap in the dark. "What about Jason McCloud?"

White was suddenly tense. "What about him?"

"I think he was in on it. I was watching him just before the bomb went off. He was scared to death."

"But, my dear Madame Ottinger, what would *his* motive be?" Dr. Ashok was silken. "The Drug Enforcement Administration has only one objective, and I believe that Senator White, unofficially at least, will bear me out. The single, nay, unique objective of the DEA is the *increased* sale of every kind of drug all over the world."

"Quite true." White was equally to the point. "Without enterprises like Kalki's, the DEA would wither away, as would my committee on Narcotics Abuse and Control with its very rich funding by the Congress. McCloud had absolutely no motive for killing Kalki."

"He was on Dr. Lowell's payroll when he was in New Orleans."

"Dear Madame Ottinger." Dr. Ashok laughed, as if someone had described to him what laughter was but then forgotten to give him an actual demonstration. "Of course McCloud was on Dr. Lowell's payroll. After all, McCloud is a narc. But doesn't that fact prove that he would *not* kill Kalki? Geese that lay golden eggs are sacred to those who lust for gilded omelets."

I let it go. I realized that I was in the presence of two great Americans contemplating crimes against the state. The secretary gave Senator White a thin folder. "Tonight's speech, Senator. In favor of Right to Life."

I don't know why this one straw among so many should have proved to be the terminal one that broke the Bactrian back. "Senator White, are you *against* abortion?"

"Teddy." White was now standing up; tiny feet wide apart. "Abortion is murder," he said slowly and seriously. "In the first degree."

Dr. Ashok agreed, with sycophantish gusto. "We Hindus believe that with the meeting of sperm and ovum, karma begins and the dharma is off and, how you say? running."

"Look here, White, the world is dying from too many people." I gave him close to twenty minutes of my overpopulation rap. But just as I got to the cruncher: how world population will double in thirty-two years, White interrupted me. He was very good at interrupting. But then most of his adult life had been spent on television, evading issues and interrupting those with something to say.

"That's simply not true, Teddy. You have been duped by the sort of big lie that the communists want us to believe so that we will dwindle in numbers while they and their kind, in the Third World especially, increase and multiply and like the bay tree flourish. There is, Teddy, more than enough food and natural resources on this hospitable planet for a hundred billion people, but the big question is who can best exploit and distribute those goodies? The free enterprise system which has made this nation great? or the slave world of the commies that does not even have the technical know-how to put color television into orbit?"

"That's not the point." I should have known by then that it was a waste of time to argue with a senator who was getting set to become the next or the next-but-one president of the United States. But I persevered: "The problem is that people are starving right here in the U.S.A. and there aren't enough jobs, or food!"

"Jobs! There are more jobs, let me tell you, than there are willing persons to fill those jobs. Mrs. Johnson White is a homemaker that any nation would be proud of, but can she get a cleaning woman or person for less than three dollars and fifty cents an hour to help her home-make? No, she can't, and even when one of those shiftless types does say that she'll come to work, she doesn't show, even with the carfare paid up front. And then who cuts the lawn? Who?" By then Senator White was beginning to look as if he might have a stroke. Fortunately, Dr. Ashok was a master of the soothing arts. He intervened. He was understanding. He was helpful. He would do anything, *any*thing to help a great American. Particularly *this* great American. He would also vouch for me. I, too, was a great American. We shook hands all around.

As Giles and I walked down Seventh Avenue, I said, "I didn't know you were still doing your Dr. Ashok routine."

"I have no choice." Giles went right on sounding like Dr. Ashok. The winds of March were cold, and full of torn newspapers and dust. "I'm obliged to keep the better part of one foot in the enemy camp."

"But who's the enemy, Giles? I've never been able to figure that one out."

Giles gave me a sidelong Ashokian glance. "You are a sly-boots, Teddy! But then still waters run deep. Except, of course, to be precise, still waters don't run at all. I have never ceased to be Dr. Ashok, on special assignment with the CIA. At the moment, it is wise for Dr. Ashok to surface and Dr. Lowell to submerge. I have . . . Giles Lowell has no desire to testify before the White committee, particularly now that we know just how poor Giles is being set up as a patsy by Johnny White."

We paused as an elderly white man with a baseball bat chased a young black man out of an Adult Book Store. As the colorful pair vanished into a side street, I said to Giles, "Now that you're the head of Kalki Enterprises, I want you to know that I'm willing to honor my contract if, of course, it has not been abrogated by events." I was relieved to get this said. I had not yet paid the March alimony to Earl Jr., and I did not want to have to go to Arlene for money.

"My dear Teddy, you are employed, as agreed, until April 3." Giles reached into Dr. Ashok's pocket and took out a checkbook. Standing in front of the dirty window of an Orange Julius shop, he wrote me out a check for two months' salary.

"Thanks." I put the check in my pocket. "And after April 3?"

"*Before* that day, Kalki will have returned. *On* that day the age of Kali will end. Look! A *kosher* hot dog! I cannot resist." We ate garlicky hot dogs at a dirty counter.

"What form is Kalki going to take?"

"His own. What else? Attended by the Perfect Masters, he will . . . what is your American phrase? do most beautifully and terribly and finally his thing."

"Then they," I pointed at the people coming and going, "will all die."

"Peaceful thought, isn't it? No more pollution. No more hideous cities, slums, people. No more television. Yes, Teddy, Walter Cronkite, *The Hollywood Squares*, *The Gong Show*, all will be as one with Nineveh and Tyre."

"I find it impossible to . . ." I was going to say believe but shifted to "conceive. It's so brutal. I mean, think of all the children." I thought of my two children. I had a pang of guilt for having seen so little of them; for having thought so little of them. Beyond Motherhood had proved, psychically if not financially, to be really beyond.

"But they are all going to die anyway. Just think! Every bright-faced child on earth is scheduled to die sooner or later, of cancer, Legion-

naire's disease, swine flu, whatever. But when Kalki raises high his
sword, they will . . ."

"What?"

"They will cease to be." A non-answer.

I wiped bright yellow mustard off my fingers with a tiny paper
napkin, and wondered if Giles had been responsible for Kalki's death.
I thought him capable of anything. Did I believe that Kalki would
return? No. At the most, I expected Giles to announce that Vishnu had
suddenly occupied *his* body, and that now *he* was the avatar.

"Death," said Dr. Ashok, as we went east along Forty-Second Street,
"is as much a dream as life. Unfortunately, the human brain cannot
comprehend death because of death's lack of symmetry, and symmetry
is all-important to us since we think with *two* lobes of a single brain.
We breathe air through *two* nostrils into *two* lungs whilst looking at
and listening to the world outside through *two* eyes, *two* ears. Since we
are obliged to pair all things, death seems to us to be all wrong because
it is the ultimate *im*balance. Once the see has sawed, there is no seesaw.
So, where do we go from there? We don't go. We stay. What really
matters is that as the matter of each of us ceases to exist in its present
form, it reassembles in yet another form. Naturally, there can be no loss
of anything in a constant nature. But there is rearrangement. Once you
have given up to death your own sweet self—a yummy treat for Yama
—you will be rearranged. You will reappear, as a king or a turnip; as
a poet or a melon; as a camel or a star. But no matter what your new
arrangement, the unifying spirit—call me, I mean it, Vishnu—ani-
mates all things at all times, and all things are constantly in flux,
coming, going, rearranging. Ah, dear Teddy, have you not always
known, deep inside you, that over the millennia you have died not once
but a thousand million billion trillion times? Starting with the big bang
which is still within your body, a body that contains at this very instant
all the elements that make up not only the universe but each of your
previous incarnations as amoeba, fish, gibbonous ape . . . a whole
crackling chain of creation at whose present but nowhere near to final
end stands or rather strolls the beauteous Teddy Ottinger as together
we approach the southwest corner of Grand Central Station where the
early edition of the *New York Post* has just arrived and I can see from
the headline that the vivacious proprietor from the Antipodes is very
much in the saddle."

that the vivacious proprietor from the Antipodes is very much in the saddle."

WAR FOR KALKI DRUG EMPIRE was the headline.

"I see the large black hand of Jason McCloud at work," Giles began to drop his Dr. Ashok mannerisms.

"But McCloud works for you, doesn't he?"

"He shakes me down from time to time."

"I believe that he killed Kalki. I know Dr. Ashok disagrees. But what do *you* think, Giles?

"Ah, Teddy, there are more things in heaven and on earth than there are anywhere else. Besides, the fault, dear beauty, is not within our sleeves but in our scars that we are ring-a-lings." Metaphasis metastasized.

Security at the *Narayana* was almost as tight as it had been before the murder in Madison Square Garden. In addition to the ship's own guards, a number of plainclothesmen lurked about the dock, spying. There were times when it seemed that the principal function of the American Government in the age of Kali was to spy on its citizens.

Lakshmi and Geraldine were in the main salon, getting drunk on Bloody Marys. I was about to advise them on the dangers of drink in the middle of the day. But I lost heart. They had been through a lot.

"Teddy!" Geraldine appeared genuinely happy to see me.

So was Lakshmi. "I knew you'd be loyal." She embraced me.

"Teddy Ottinger is a *radiant* Perfect Master, and an inspiration to the rest of us." With that testimonial, Giles took off his white wig, poured vodka on a cocktail napkin and rubbed the make-up from his face. Then, restored to Lowelldom, he announced, "It is time."

"Yes," said Lakshmi. She was a bit unsteady on her feet. Geraldine took her arm. In their flowing saris the girls swayed, as if in a summer wind. They looked happy, and I wondered why. The vodka?

Kalki entered the salon. The others fell flat on their faces. Not wanting to let down the team, I did the same. I had decided that I was caught in a dream. There was no other way of explaining the figure in the doorway. Or, put another way, if this was not a dream, it was a ghost; and I did not believe in ghosts.

"Namah Shivaya!" The three chanted in unison five syllables that meant nothing to me.

Kalki came toward us. Face like a mask of hammered gold. Voice purest bronze. "I am Siva," said the voice. "The destroyer."

"Namah Shivaya," chanted the others.

Namah Shivaya is Sanskrit for "I bow to Siva."

3

As Siva, the annihilator of worlds, Kalki was quite unlike his earlier self. The blondness had congealed. He was ice-cold. I thought of glaciers, sliding south.

Kalki sat down. I did not. I just stared at him, mouth no doubt ajar. Do I wake or sleep? I asked myself. I recall thinking that if this was really a dream, the details had been nicely laid on. Dream-scenes usually lack proper ceilings or convincing vistas through open windows. But there was a ceiling to the room. And the skyline of New York harbor could be seen through open windows. If this was a dream, it had been meticulously constructed.

Kalki looked up at me. The eyes were his eyes, no doubt of that. But now they were sapphire-hard. "You are with me." This was a statement.

I mumbled something idiotic, to the effect that our contract had never lapsed.

"You'll be doing some flying soon." Kalki made a second statement. I was now certain that I was awake. And was more than ever confused. As usual, Giles was the explainer. "Dear Teddy, I can see that you are puzzled."

"Poor thing!" Lakshmi was compassionate. "Tell her what happened, Giles."

"Gladly!" Giles was in his element, a substance identical with hyper-hyperbole. "On the evening of March 15 there existed two versions of James J. Kelly's handsome body. One was, alas, destroyed by the villainous McCloud, hit man, narc, political dreamer. Happily, we still retain our precious reserve model, and there he sits."

Giles always knew how to annoy me. Even at world's end, he was able to get a rise out of me. I rose, to object. "You can't have two copies of the same person."

"The images of Vishnu are endless," began Giles. I headed him off at the Weissean pass with Ottingerian logic. "Check one of two, Giles. Either this is Kalki and someone else was killed. Or Kalki was killed and this is someone else."

"Check one, Teddy." Geraldine was pleased with my sharpness.

Lakshmi smiled her special queen of heaven smile. "This is really and truly *our* Kalki. The original. Safe and sound."

"Then who was killed?" I asked.

"A double," said Geraldine. "You see, we've known all along that someone, probably McCloud, would try to kill Kalki . . ."

"You knew all along?" I was surprised. Kalki had only spoken of a *possible* attempt on his life.

Geraldine nodded. "Four of the Five Perfect Masters knew."

"So why didn't you tell the fifth?"

"You were being tested, dear Teddy." Giles produced a twinkle. "In the crucible, as it were, and with flying colors you have passed, to mix gorgeously a metaphor."

"So who was killed?"

"An actor named Rod Spenser."

"By McCloud?"

"Yes." Giles did not, for once, so much as produce a bush that he could beat about.

"The actor at Madison Square Garden, did he know what might happen to him?"

"We are not cruel, dear Teddy, only inexorable." But Giles did not sound as impressive as the words warranted. I turned to Kalki. But he was no longer with us. The blue eyes were out of focus. I wondered, suddenly, if this Kalki was really the original. Might he not be a double, too? I was still astride a nightmare, cantering toward terror.

Lakshmi said, "Rod Spenser looked a lot like Kalki. He was also a good rider, which Kalki isn't. And since he'd been out of work for almost a year . . ."

"You saw him in Arthur Penn's *Missouri Breaks*. He played a cowboy, just a small part." Geraldine was a movie buff. I am not. "He photographed well but he wasn't very talented."

"But didn't he have a family? And won't they or his friends or his agent know that he's missing? And then won't someone figure out that *he* was the one who was killed and not Kalki?"

"Dear Teddy, don't be such a worrywart!" Giles was teasing, which always made me nervous.

But Lakshmi was soothing, and to the point. "In ten days it will be April 3, when all of Rod Spenser's family, friends, associates will join him in . . . the next phase."

"And you will see it all, Teddy." Geraldine sounded excited. "The Five Perfect Masters will preside at The End."

"Who are the other two Perfect Masters?" I had never thought to ask. But then I had never taken any of them seriously until the actor on the white horse was killed. For me that was the turning point. I was now able to see beneath the familiar flesh of everyone alive the hard essential bone. I was frightened.

"One of the other two Perfect Masters was Professor Jossi." Giles sounded genuinely sad. "During our time of testing, he failed us. So did the fifth Perfect Master. Someone you did not know. Poor devils, they have now forfeited perfection and paradise. But since there must always be five of us in order to create spiritual harmony on this earth, Kalki and Lakshmi have condescended to act as Perfect Masters. So that, dear Teddy, is the ball game." Giles was uncommonly pleased with himself.

"So what," I asked, "are we to do?"

"Fly." Kalki had returned to his body. He turned to me, and for the first time he resembled his pre-Siva self. And I was now certain that the man I was talking to was really Kalki and not a double. I was relieved. A succession of Kalkis would have been intolerable. "You will fly the *Garuda* around the world at the equator. Then you will fly the *Garuda* around the world over the two poles. You will be my messenger."

"What is the message?"

"The fact of the flight."

"An itinerary is being prepared." Giles sounded businesslike. "You will have a full 707 crew . . ."

As I was about to ask when I was to leave, Arlene Wagstaff entered the salon. She was made up for television, and sober as a judge.

Kalki rose to greet Arlene. When she saw him, she gave a funny little gasp, not unlike the one she did so effectively in her nasal decongestant commercial. "Sweet Jesus, you're not dead! Oh, but I knew it all along! I mean, that was a special-effects trick back there in the Garden, wasn't it? Sure it was. You were putting us on. For the ratings. They went through the roof, too! Well, let me tell you, I am absolutely and totally your greatest fan. Teddy, didn't I always say Kalki is a pussycat? In fact, not since Monsignor Sheen was dropped by network television have I . . ."

Kalki had taken both of her hands in his. He radiated pre-Siva charm. "I'm *your* admirer, Arlene. But then so is everyone else. I'm glad you could come."

Arlene gave me a quick peck; and a slow explanation. "Angel, I was flabbergasted when I got this call from my agent, saying would I sky in to Gotham and tape an interview about Kalki because the Kalki people wanted somebody the public loves and trusts, like me. My God, I'm thirsty. But no drinkee before telly, that's my cardinal rule. Anyway, I said, what's there to say? Wasn't Kalki blown to bits before our very eyes on prime-time? Who are you trying to kid? Not that I really believed anything *serious* had happened to you!" Arlene put her arm through Kalki's. "He's cuter in person!" She winked at me. She turned to Kalki. "It was a special effect, wasn't it? Like in *Towering Inferno?*"

Kalki smiled; said nothing.

Arlene continued: "Anyway, the William Morris office said, Arlene, we don't know what this is all about but whatever it is it's a firm offer. It's also very hush-hush. Dr. Lowell wants you to do a special show, guaranteed to hit a top Nielsen, maybe even in the high forties. Well, I tried to call you, Teddy, but no dice. Anyway, since part of the contract was my telling nobody, I told nobody and here I am. You look good enough to eat, Kalki, if you don't mind my saying so."

"You are thinking of Jesus Christ, dear Miss Wagstaff. He is periodically eaten by his followers in the course of something called Communion." Giles smoothly started to unwind the overwound Arlene. "But Vishnu is never eaten. After all, how can one take a bite out of the sun? Now then, I see that you are all made up and ready to go." Giles indicated the beaded eyelashes that Arlene only wore in such sophisticated spots as Oil of Olay where she looked like Theda Bara. "And so are we."

"What's happening?" I asked Geraldine, in a low voice. But not so low that Arlene's sharp ears did not detect a special relationship. Arlene tried hard not to frown. And failed. Yet we had never been exclusive, she and I. But jealousy is irrational. Arlene was aware that there was something between Geraldine and me. But though she was not pleased, she was a professional; and duty came first.

"This way," said Kalki. He put an arm around Arlene's waist. She was ecstatic.

Geraldine answered me, "What is happening is now happening. Kalki is going to make a tape for television with your friend."

Together we went down a long corridor. Deep inside the ship a stateroom had been converted to a television studio. Technical crew and director were already on hand.

Kalki sat cross-legged on a dais. Arlene sat in a chair beside him. Kalki whispered instructions to her. Arlene moistened her lips. She was a quick study. At a gesture from Kalki, the taping began.

Arlene looked at Kalki, with true and unfeigned adoration. It was clever of whoever it was (Giles?) to select Arlene as an interviewer. Aside from being my friend, she plainly adored Kalki. She was, also, the greatest pitchperson on television.

"Kalki. You . . . have . . . returned . . . from the dead!" Arlene's voice was reverent.

"I am eternal." Kalki glittered like those Northern lights you can see at forty thousand feet, flaring on the Arctic horizon. "I cannot die. I alone was before all things. I alone shall always be."

"That's very interesting." Gamely, Arlene gave the conversational ball a push. "Were you surprised at what happened to you the other night in Madison Square Garden?"

"I know all things that have been, that are, that will be. I knew that I would drop one human body and take up another. This one that you see."

"Which looks very nice to me from where I am sitting." Arlene gave him her contented, maternal glance, the one that she had brought to perfection in that commercial where the preferred detergent cleans in one second flat the children's muddy clothes. "Now then, Kalki, what you've done by . . . well, coming back from the dead, is something of a miracle to us civilians, both in and out of show business."

"I was never dead."

"Yes," said Arlene, not listening. "I know. But now that you have come back to us like this, what are your immediate plans, if I may ask?"

"I am Siva."

Arlene had not been briefed on Siva. I could tell that she was thrown. But she covered up expertly. She had been doing this sort of thing for half a century. "That's interesting. About your being . . . uh, Siva. Could you tell our audience a little bit about who Siva is? And who you are, really? Like where you were born, originally?"

But Kalki was now in full flow. He described Siva as he had described him to me that day in Central Park. Then he announced that at noon, Eastern Standard Time, April 3, Siva would begin the dance of eternity and all human life would end. As usual, Kalki was his most effective when he was most matter-of-fact.

"That is not really a very upbeat sort of message." Arlene rallied, as best she could.

"But death . . . Yama, as we call it . . . is peace, and peace is the ultimate blessing."

"But what about a message of hope for all of your many fans out there. For those of us who were rooting for you at Madison Square Garden and who are all pleased as punch that you weren't really killed but are back in the saddle again as . . . uh, Siva."

"A message of hope?" Kalki smiled a most boyish and un-Siva smile. "All right. People of the world, enjoy yourselves. Don't worry about the future. There will be no future. Delight in this world. Delight in each day. Delight in one another. Those of you who believe in me will continue forever, but in different forms.

"So take this earth. It is yours. Everything is yours. Until I begin the dance of eternity, and all the stars go out."

EIGHT

1

SINCE THE NETWORKS REFUSED TO TELECAST THE KALKI–ARLENE Wagstaff interview, Giles was obliged to buy thirty minutes of prime-time television. Although the networks decided, in their solemn jargon, "to pass" on the interview, they were eager to interview Kalki whose return, predictably, had caused a sensation. Sample headline (New York *Daily News*): KALKI BACK FROM DEAD. Under this: "Hoax suspected: Garden Murder Done with Mirrors?"

"Teddy, we want you back on board again!" It was Morgan Davies. He was shameless. I had been dropped after Madison Square Garden. Now I was to be picked up again.

I told Morgan that the ship had sailed. "Anyway, you don't need me. You have Bruce Sapersteen."

Morgan started to wheeze, and beg. I took pleasure in hanging up on him. I no longer needed the *Sun*. Only that morning Doubleday had told Herman Victor Weiss that once again his highly honed sentences were to be deployed in my behalf.

These conversations took place the day after the taping in the sitting room of Arlene's suite at the Regency Hotel, where I had spent the night. The evening before, the 6:00 *News* had reported that Kalki was alive and that Arlene would interview him. Arlene's telephone never stopped ringing.

I mixed the margaritas. Listened to Arlene talk simultaneously to me and into the telephone. "Who? Stan Kamen?" She put one hand over the receiver. "The William Morris office! He's the biggie!" Took her hand away. "Stan, baby! A series? Norman Lear? Well, not if Ross Hunter comes through with that co-production deal on *The Amelia Earhart Story,* starring Teddy Ottinger. The property's hot, Stan. Really hot." While Arlene dealed and wheeled, I twirled the knob of the television set. At regular intervals there were still pictures of Kalki talking to Arlene. A voice-over gave the time of the telecast.

"That one picture," said Arlene, putting down the receiver, "is worth one million dollars to me in this fiscal year alone!"

"What did you think of Kalki?"

"A liv-ing doll." She spaced out the words. "But was I nervous! I mean he's got such balls. Such star quality. You can take your Alan Ladd—the father, I mean, not the son who is a doll and chief of production over at Fox where I expect a firm offer before the end of the week on the new Henry Hathaway flick—you can take all those macho stars and throw them out the window, because Kalki's got *it!*"

"On the other hand, if Kalki's right, there won't be any Henry Hathaway or Twentieth Century–Fox next week."

"Teddy," said Arlene, missing the point, "I have been reading about and listening to this end-of-Hollywood bushwah for thirty or twenty years, and I'm here to tell you that entertainment is here to stay! So you don't have L.B. Mayer and block-booking any more. So what? You have the big movies for ABC. You have the mini-series for NBC. You have . . ."

Although Arlene had conducted the most important interview in the history of television, she had not understood a word that Kalki had said. She was like most people. World's end was too much to cope with. Far easier to think of Kalki as just another TV superstar who was about to score an incredibly high Nielsen rating.

2

THE DAY OF THE TELECAST SENATOR WHITE ARRIVED IN NEW YORK, subcommittee in tow. From his quarters at the Waldorf-Astoria, White announced, "Special hearings will be held here in New York, a great city that can always depend upon my support, financially and otherwise, in the exciting years to come. Working together for fiscal responsibility, we can and we will put the Big back into the Big Apple. In the next few days my committee will be investigating the alleged connection between a certain alleged religious movement and an international drug ring. Our first witness will be James J. Kelly, also known as Kalki." Senator White was able to get this message (and himself) onto the 6:00 *News*.

Although White made the next day's headlines, he was upstaged. The subpoena that had been prepared for Kalki was not served because Kalki had disappeared. The *Narayana* was searched from top to stern. Kalki was gone. In fact, all the Perfect Masters had vanished except for me. Luckily, the committee did not know that I was a Perfect Master. Nevertheless, as Kalki's pilot, I was questioned by an investigator who found it hard to believe that I had no idea where anyone was. The committee was fit to be tied.

Senator White ordered the police of New York City to conduct a manhunt for Kalki. The Police Commissioner refused to do anything on the ground that this was a federal, not a local matter. In any case, there was very little that the police could do as they were all out on strike not only for an increase in their pensions but for added human dignity.

During this confusion, I said goodbye to Arlene. She headed back to Los Angeles. *The Amelia Earhart Story* starring Teddy Ottinger was, she declared, "absolutely in the bag." I hoped so. Privately, I was not optimistic. That project had always been doomed . . . like Amelia herself.

I rang Earl Jr. "About time you called, Teddy. The children keep asking when is Mummy coming to visit us. Of course, Lenore is wonderful with them. Her hair is mostly grown back. But she has no strength, Teddy, none at all. The chemotherapy has left her limp as a rag. It's also a pretty terrible burden, having to undergo all that therapy while acting as a mother to two wonderful kids."

"The alimony check for March is in the mail," I said.

Down cooled Earl Jr. "I see where this messiah of yours didn't really get killed on the TV."

"He did," I said, not wanting to get into that subject, "and he didn't."

"Uh-huh." Earl Jr. was disagreeable. "So what's going to happen on April 3? Has he got an encore?"

"Watch tonight."

The telecast (paid for by Kalki Enterprises) rang up a Nielsen rating of 46.7. This is the sort of rating that the Super Bowl gets. Or so the experts said. I still have no idea what sport it was that they played in the Super Bowl. My editor at Doubleday said that if the program had not been prerecorded, the ratings might have been the highest in history, because everyone would be watching in order to see whether or not Kalki got himself killed again. As it was, people were eager to see if this Kalki was the same as the one that they saw killed at the Garden. If not, was the new Kalki a convincing double? On the order of that perennial phenomenon of those years, the new Nixon.

The next day it was generally agreed that what had been revealed was indeed the original Kalki, which led to a good deal of wild speculation. Many pundits thought that the Kalki-Wagstaff interview had been taped *before* Madison Square Garden. Others thought that the murder at the Garden had been no murder at all but some sort of stunt, to increase interest in Kalki. White's subpoena did not exactly diminish interest in Kalki.

I watched the program alone in my room at the Americana. Kalki was brilliant. Arlene was expert. The instant the show was off the air, the telephone began to ring.

The first caller was Giles, pretending to be Dr. Ashok. *"They* have gone underground," he said. "But we shall find them, dear Madame Ottinger, never fear! We shall bring them to earth. The foot's agame, as your Bard of Auden would say. I shall meet you just outside the men's room at Grand Central Station tomorrow noon, with instructions. This telephone line has been bugged. But only by the CIA. Therefore, whatever you say to me you can regard as privileged."

Arlene rang next. She was thrilled with her performance. Ross Hunter was prepared to co-produce *The Amelia Earhart Story.* With me. Or so he said. The next call was from Jason McCloud. "Where," he said in his loud toneless voice, "is Kalki?"

"I have no idea." Which was the truth.

"Senator White's just this minute signed a subpoena. And you know what? It's got your name on it, Ms. Ottinger. You will be served tomorrow. Then on Wednesday morning, at eleven o'clock, you will go before the subcommittee, at the Waldorf-Astoria. We will be meeting in the Mermaid Room." McCloud hung up. I remember thinking that he was very bold indeed.

Dr. Ashok and I met as planned at Grand Central Station. Dr. Ashok carried a brief case. I noticed that not only was the wig on straight, but the performance was less surreal than usual. In fact, he was nervous.

"Have you been served yet?" Dr. Ashok had not been joking about my telephone line being bugged.

"Not yet."

"Good. Don't go back to the hotel. You can pick up what clothes you need right now. Then go to Kennedy Airport. The *Garuda* is ready for take-off. The crew is on stand-by. The cargo is aboard. And here is your flight plan."

I took the brief case. "Where is Kalki?"

"Out of sight if not out of mind or as the Bawd of . . ."

I cut him short. "What," I asked, "is the cargo?"

"Read your instructions."

A well-dressed black man entered a telephone booth just back of us, and began to urinate. Drunk, he had thought that he had already made it to the men's room. No one paid the slightest attention to him. Dr. Ashok and I moved out of range.

"Your trip is essentially a gesture, a symbol of Vishnu's power." Neither Dr. Ashok nor I could keep from staring at the telephone booth from which came the sound of water, rather like that made by

Niagara Falls in Arlene's Sada Soda Water commercial. A slow flood
began to spread out onto the cement floor.

"Your flight plan divides the planet into quadrants. You will go once
around the world at the two poles. En route, the plane will, at specified
intervals, drop its cargo . . ."

"Of what?

"Lotuses. The symbol of immortality. Of Vishnu, the all-pervading.
Of Siva, and his love."

"That's quite a lot of lotuses."

"Seventy million. There is going to be a super-lottery. Thousands
and thousands of winners of jumbo cash prizes or, as the author of the
Old Testament's Adverbs so wisely said, 'He that maketh waste to be
rich shall be innocent.' No matter. The crew knows what to do. All you
will have to do is fly the aircraft. Of course, you may want to speak to
the curious at the different fueling stops. So I've prepared several little
speeches, just in case."

"When do I get back?" I could imagine the sort of speeches Giles
had prepared; and vowed to make only my own.

"You will return April 2. You will join us aboard the *Narayana,*
which will be anchored off the Battery in downtown Manhattan. All
instructions are here." Dr. Ashok indicated the brief case in my hand.
"Go to it, Teddy Ottinger, Test Pilot and Perfect Master!"

The occupant of the telephone booth had gone to sleep, standing
up.

The new *Garuda* was ready for take-off. The crew was first-rate. My
instructions were surprisingly intelligent. Giles had figured out exactly
when and where I would need to put down for refueling and maintenance. As a result, the flight went off without a hitch.

I felt like Amelia; particularly on the trip that followed the line of
the equator. I was only sorry that Lae was not part of the flight plan.
I would like to have seen the last airstrip she ever saw.

Wherever I did put down, I was met by the press. The Australian
press was unusually aggressive. Apparently, they had once been able to
drive Frank Sinatra out of Australia. This feat had made them over-
confident.

I was mobbed at the Sydney airport. I did my best to appear serene.

"What's this lotus dingus you're promoting?" asked one of them.

"We're not promoting anything." I handed out white paper lotuses.

I also told them about the Lotus Lotteries. And the cash prizes. The press found the whole thing difficult to absorb. Meanwhile, a dozen cameras recorded this exchange.

"You mean you're *not* selling these lotuses?"

"We simply let them fall upon the air. They are the symbol of . . ." I had worked out rather a pretty speech. But no one wanted to hear it that afternoon in Sydney. A journalist from Melbourne asked, "So what *are* you selling on this trip?"

"Nothing."

"So what are you doing?" The man from Melbourne was persistent. He had a hearing aid in his left ear. "Besides dropping paper flowers all over the map."

"Kalki is making one final gesture. He wants you to contemplate eternity before the end . . ."

There was rude laughter. "And the end is due to take place April 3?"

"Yes." I smiled sweetly. "At noon. Eastern Standard Time."

More rude laughter. I turned my back on the lot of them. Conferred with the maintenance crew. But the journalists would not let up. One asked, "Will it be like *On the Beach?*" A reference to an end-of-the-world movie made years ago in Australia, starring Ava Gardner. When the local press had asked Gardner why the picture was being made in Australia, she had replied, "Well, it's about the end of the world and, God knows, this place is the absolute end." The press tried but failed to drive her out. She was obviously a good deal tougher than her ex-husband Mr. Sinatra.

Finally, bored by dull questions, I gave them selected arias from Giles's richest and most flowery speech. Ending with "The lotus is the symbol of the creator of the universe, a reminder of man's oneness with the spirit of the cosmos. Believe in Brahma, Vishnu and Siva, and you will achieve heaven."

They were not buying this line in Sydney. They got personal. Finally, when asked if it was true that I was a lesbian, I belted the reporter from the *Bulletin.* This made for entertaining television, though not exactly suitable for the family hour.

Elsewhere, I was well received. For one thing, Kalki's television interview with Arlene had been shown in every country that had television. People were fascinated by him. Did they believe in The

End? I don't think so. Did I? No, not really. I was, obviously, curious to see how he was going to explain the approaching Non-End.

At least once a day I talked by radio to Giles aboard the *Narayana*. "You're doing a bang-up job, Teddy. We're getting the wildest press coverage. So just keep those lotuses floating through the air, like millions of kisses from the all-loving Siva."

Finally, right on schedule, I landed the *Garuda* at Kennedy Airport. I was exhausted. Overnight bag and logbook in hand, I got into a waiting limousine. And went straight to sleep. I was awakened by Geraldine's excited embrace. "Teddy!" she cried. "You're a hero!"

"What for?" Groggily, I got out of the car. We were at the Battery, a sort of park in downtown Manhattan, with a view of the bay. Some distance from shore, the *Narayana* rode at anchor. Because of a recent oil spill, the waters of the bay were a thick gumbo in which dead birds floated alongside dead fish. We tried not to breathe too deeply as we climbed into the *Narayana*'s launch.

Geraldine kept telling me how delighted they all were. "Giles was terrified something would go wrong. But Kalki said, 'Teddy Ottinger is the best,' and you are!"

With our arrival in the main salon, the Five Perfect Masters were at last united. I was embraced by each in turn. Giles was beside himself (but that self, thank God, was Giles and not Dr. Ashok). "You did not fail me, dearest Teddy. Others may have had their doubts about you, but not I."

Kalki put his arm around my shoulders. "You have been my fourth arm," he said, with a smile, "the one that holds the lotus. You did a swell job."

Lakshmi pointed to a map of the world on an easel. "You see?" she said. "We kept careful track of you." The *Garuda*'s flight plan made a cross on the map. Each refueling stop was starred. Someone had also written in each day's wind direction and velocity.

"The lotuses are now in every part of the earth, including the two poles." Giles tapped the cross at the map's center. "All in all, a superb exercise in logistics for which our two scientists, Geraldine and Lakshmi, are to be commended, as well as you, dearest Teddy, the sole executor of the master plan."

"The lotus," said Kalki, "is for all men now."

3

THAT NIGHT WE ALL HAD DINNER ABOARD THE *NARAYANA*, EXCEPT for Kalki. He would not be seen again, I was told, until noon the next day.

My mood? Exhausted. I went to sleep in a hot bath and did not wake up until the water turned cold. Shivering, I rubbed myself hard with a bath towel. Noting the large blue K monogram, I again marveled at the money that was being spent. My two trips around the world must have cost a quarter of a million dollars. I also recall thinking that if nothing happened the next day, Kalki would never be able to recoup financially. As I dressed (black velvet: a chilly night in April), I wondered if he might not be planning to hold up the world. Something on the order of: If you don't pay me X millions of dollars, I will set off a cobalt bomb in Grand Central Station.

Geraldine was alone in the salon. She looked lovely . . . in red! That took courage, I thought, and a degree of good luck to pull off. Redheads are usually washed out by all strong colors excepting the complementary green. In a low voice she warned me not to discuss anything to do with the next day's activities because "The waiters are all agents."

Geraldine made Bloody Marys for two. I prefer plain vodka but have never told her. Reticences between people are often strange. I asked her what Kalki was planning for the next day. Geraldine said, "Dance."

"I hope he's been doing his barre work. But then after he dances . . ."

Geraldine put a finger to her lips. "The rooms are bugged," she said. She was maddening. With a secret smile, she turned on the television. The news was about to go on.

I drained my glass. I was drunk. Fatigue, jet lag, vodka, together did their merry work. I was hectoring. (Why no verb from Achilles?) "Well, then *where* will he dance?"

"On a barge, off the Battery. There's going to be *live* television coverage."

For some reason this last detail struck me as unnaturally funny. Loonlike, I laughed. And laughed alone. Geraldine looked at me the way that I used to look at Arlene when drink had turned her head in a wrong direction. Fortunately, the appearance of Walter Cronkite had if not a sobering, a solemnizing effect.

The news that Cronkite thoughtfully read for us was pretty much par for the course at the end of the age of Kali. Energy was in short supply. Arab oil was going up in price. A new ice age had just been predicted by all those scientists who had not predicted a new inferno due to the so-called "greenhouse effect" due to increased man-made fumes in the atmosphere due to all the due to's that had together made a man-made chain or noose about the human race's neck. There was famine. There was a mysterious new epidemic rampaging around the world. There was an announcement from the President that he had every confidence (he himself spoke to us with deep sincerity) that the Vice-President would be his running mate which meant, of course, that the Vice-President would *not* be his running mate.

Finally, there was a small smile on Walter Cronkite's face as he read: "Tomorrow the Hindu messiah from New Orleans, James J. Kelly, sometimes known as Kalki or Vishnu or Siva, will appear at noon Eastern Standard Time on a barge in the Hudson River just off the Battery in downtown Manhattan and, as the god Siva, Mr. Kelly will begin what he calls 'the dance of eternity.' According to the ancient Hindus, when Siva does this dance all worlds will be annihilated. So the big question is this: is Jim Kelly of New Orleans really the god Siva? If he is, then tomorrow is the end of the world."

Walter Cronkite allowed one eyebrow to lift. Had it not lifted, there would have been a national panic. The Dow Jones would have dropped through the floor. "And that's the way it is, Monday, April 2 . . . "

Dinner was peccably served by two waiters. But then it is not easy to deal plates and serve food while listening eagerly to every word being said. I narrowly avoided a lapful of petite marmite as one bemused agent's ladle missed the soup plate.

Giles gave a lecture on food. "We are being slowly poisoned to death." He listed the poisons, as we ate without pleasure the poisons named. Each of us knew by heart the cadmium-mercury litany. Then, together, we mourned what dedicated horticulturalists had done to the American tomato, a vegetable fit for shipping but not for eating.

Lakshmi raised her wineglass. "To organic food!" We toasted organic food. "There will be nothing else," she said, "in our future."

The two waiters exchanged wide-eyed glances. "Our future" was a key phrase.

Shortly after dinner, we were joined by Jason McCloud; he was accompanied by Owen Prager, the chief of the Internal Revenue Service squad that had been investigating Kalki Enterprises. Mr. Prager reminded me that we had met at the ashram. He was a courteous little man.

"We're here to see Kalki," said McCloud, making himself more than at home in the salon. Giles served Jason Scotch.

Prager asked for Sanka. "I have an ulcer," he said. "I not only give ulcers, I also," he laughed softly through his nose, not a good sound, "get ulcers!" His little joke. We left it where it belonged, in Lilliput.

Giles was all oil, and extremest unction. "I'm afraid that Kalki has withdrawn for the evening."

"As have I," said Lakshmi.

"And I," said Geraldine. And they both swept from the room. I remained. I was curious.

"We're on government business, Lowell." McCloud's constitution must have been uncommonly strong. He drank glass after glass of Scotch, and did not get drunk. But then his normal manner was abrupt, nonserial, boorish.

Prager was polite, and of course abstemious. "We have finished our audit of Kalki Enterprises, Dr. Lowell. And I think it only fair to tell you that your corporation owes the government, in back taxes, something in the very expensive neighborhood of four million dollars. I have the exact figures in my brief case."

"But the big casino," said McCloud, "is that you, personally, are also guilty of fraud."

"Now, now, Mr. McCloud. Let's not get ahead of ourselves." Prager was stern. Admonishing. "We at the IRS never assume that anyone is innocent until he is proved guilty. That is the American way." Prager looked pleased as punch with his little speech.

Giles coolly monished right back. "Naturally, I will consult my lawyer." I remember wondering why he was not more upset. If anything, he seemed amused.

"You will be arrested tomorrow," said McCloud, "by the New York Police."

Giles was rummaging through a handsome eighteenth-century secretary. "I believe," he said, "that the police are still on strike."

"The strike was settled this afternoon." McCloud stared at Giles through the amber liquid in his glass. *La vie en whisky.* I've always regretted that I was never able to see and hear Edith Piaf in person. I owned most of her records once. Earl Jr. got them at the time of the settlement. Yet he only liked *country* music, as sung by urban Americans of the sixties. I hate Bob Dylan.

"No public employee or servant has the right," said Prager suddenly, "to strike against the state. That principle was laid down by Calvin Coolidge when he was governor of Massachusetts and it is a precept whose denial, Dr. Lowell, spells social anarchy!" Prager spoke with conviction.

"You don't need to tell *me* that, Mr. Prager." Giles removed a brief case from the secretary. "I completely agree." Giles gave McCloud the brief case. "These are the papers that you asked for."

"They better," said McCloud, "all be there." I was astonished at the brazenness of the payoff.

I looked at Prager. Surely, he must have guessed at the meaning of this transaction. But he was busy with his own brief case. "I would like, if I may," he said, "to go over with you the high points of our audit."

"By all means." Giles sat down; looked alert.

"We think, speaking purely from a criminal point of view, that your management of the affairs of Kalki Enterprises has been superb."

"Thank you, Mr. Prager."

"You're welcome and—hats off to you, sir! You make the Mafia seem nice-nelly. I should also tell you that because of your flair for bookkeeping, our agents have put in close to twenty thousand man-hours on this project."

"Twenty thousand!" McCloud whistled. "What's your annual budget, Prager? I mean the *actual* budget of the IRS."

As the two bureaucrats compared budgets, I lost my second wind.

There was no third. I excused myself. The government agents were polite.

"Good night, dear Teddy," said Giles, tenderly. "Sweet dreams. We shall meet at breakfast." I remember thinking that, under the circumstances, he was tempting fate.

Fate, tempted, duly struck. Shortly before dawn, the police came aboard ship. Giles was arrested. I slept through whatever commotion there was. By the time I was up, Giles was gone and the decks were crowded with New York's finest.

The morning was bright but cold. Snow had been predicted. Wind north-northwest. Lakshmi was on deck, wearing a heavy winter coat over her sari. Geraldine had exchanged sari for a practical tweed suit from Peck & Peck. I joined them at the railing of the ship's prow. Together we looked down at the floating platform on which Kalki would do his dance. Just opposite us, the ubiquitous television crews had placed their cameras on a tugboat.

I thought of the director from Katmandu. Red, white and blue sneakers. Blond hair. Glasses. Red hands. I had a sudden spasm of lust, no doubt brought on by the hysteria of the occasion.

Lakshmi was nervous. I asked why. "They're trying to arrest Kalki," she said.

"That's a good reason. Where is he?"

"Hidden," said Geraldine. In the cold April light her three freckles looked like miniature copper pennies.

"But then he will have to come on deck at noon," I said.

Lakshmi nodded. "That's the problem."

The police were still searching the ship. They were everywhere. They seemed to be having a wonderful time. I can't think why. They laughed, made jokes, waved at the television cameras on the tugboat. Although they were very much aware of us, none came near . . . except McCloud. He stalked across the deck like the monster in a low-budget *Frankenstein*. He was still high from the night before. Except that this particular morning was, for him, an extension of the night before because he had never slept. He had spent the night talking to Giles. After the arrest, McCloud had eaten a hearty breakfast, and continued drinking.

"Good morning, ladies." McCloud was courtly. We greeted him

coldly. "Sorry about our friend Giles. But just as soon as he posts bail, he'll be out."

"Where are they holding him?" asked Geraldine.

"First Precinct. That's 16 Ericsson Place. Two blocks south of Canal. We'll have him back with us by tomorrow at the latest."

"That's late," said Lakshmi.

"What was the charge?" I asked.

McCloud rattled off a series of crimes that were, in number if not in magnitude, presidential. The chief crime was trafficking in narcotics. "Sorry about this," McCloud added. He looked almost guilty. After all, triple agent or not, he had been an employee of Giles for a long time.

"The least," said Geraldine, with some anger, "you could have done was to wait until noon."

"Well, there's been all this pressure on me." McCloud sounded vague. "Senator White, you know. Noon," he repeated. He blinked. Remembered what was afoot. "Hey, what's going to happen?"

"Siva will dance," said Lakshmi.

"But not," I said, "if he's arrested."

"Jason," Lakshmi took McCloud by his right arm, "you've got to talk to the police. You must explain to them that no one must come near Kalki until after the dance."

"Well," said McCloud. And stopped. And thought. Then, "I don't know if I can. You see, the warrants have already been sworn . . ."

"People are often given an hour's grace," I invented. "To put their affairs in order. Say goodbye to loved ones . . ."

"But these charges are pretty serious."

I had a lucky inspiration. But then when dealing with a triple agent, one is triply armed. "I know for a fact," I said, speaking slowly, as to a child, "that my friend—and yours, too—Senator Johnson White is going to be very, very upset when he finds out that Kalki has been arrested *before* his hearing tomorrow."

McCloud looked ill. I had scored. "I know," he said, dismally.

Lakshmi scored, too. "Dearest Jason, you are such a friend of ours. And you've been so close to us for so many‾years! I'm sure you don't want anything unpleasant to happen to your associates."

"I am not," said McCloud, "an associate." It was plain that prison doors had begun to open in that treacherous mind.

"No matter what you are," said Geraldine, "you can certainly convince the police to hold off for at least a day. If you do, you will make Senator White happy. And you will make Kalki happy."

Without a word, McCloud left us. We could see him on the ship's bridge, talking to several high-ranking policemen.

"Will he hold them off?" I asked.

"If he doesn't, he goes to jail," said Geraldine. "We've paid him off for years. And we've got the proof."

Lakshmi was uncharacteristically grim. "And some of the proof was given him last night by Giles."

"The brief case?" I asked.

"Yes," said Lakshmi. "It was the payoff for what he did at Madison Square Garden."

I was, momentarily, floored or decked. But before I could speak, the noon siren went off. There was silence aboard ship. Then music played over the public-address system . . . sitars, flutes, horns; and Kalki appeared on deck.

Except for a tiger's skin at the waist, Kalki was nude; his torso had been smeared with ashes; his neck had been painted blue. What looked to be miniature human skulls hung about his neck. Three writhing snakes were tangled in his hair. He carried a small drum.

I have no idea whether or not McCloud had persuaded the police to postpone the arrest. I do know that one look at that glittering figure and everyone fell silent. There were no more jokes, no laughter. No one made a move to stop Kalki . . . to stop Siva, as he walked toward the bow of the ship.

When Siva passed the three of us, we bowed and said, "Namah Shivaya." We were neither heard nor seen.

Siva descended the ladder to the floating platform. A circling plane released a cloud of white paper lotuses. For an instant, the April sun was completely obscured. Then there was confusion as the police scrambled to pick up the paper lotuses.

Siva struck the drum with his right hand. Unnoticed by the lotus-collectors on deck, the dance of eternity began.

As Siva twisted and turned, leapt and whirled, the age of Kali came to its predicted end.

NINE

1

PASCAL: *"Le dernier acte est sanglant, quelque belle que soit la comédie en tout le reste."* I had better translate that. After all, I am the last person on earth who knows French. "The last act is bloody, no matter how charming the rest of the play." I leave to future historians all of the earlier acts, charming or not. I must now do the best I can to describe the last act, and its bloodiness.

When the dance of eternity ended, the age of Kali ended. Four billion or so men, women, children died. Not all at once. Some may have survived for as long as a week. We shall never know for certain. In most cases, death was swift—a matter of seconds, minutes, a mercifully unconscious hour.

How did this happen? Let me go step by step. This is the dangerous part of my narrative. A false step and . . . no history.

First things first. Practical matters. We did not find Giles until late afternoon. He had been locked up in a back room of the 1st Precinct station house. We searched. We shouted. He shouted, too; faintly.

We were obliged to break locks. To jimmy open doors. All this in the disturbing presence of dead policemen slumped over desks or fallen to the floor. One fat sergeant embraced a water cooler. Behind bars, we could see the prisoners as they sat or lay on their bunks. Many looked to be alive. None of the faces betrayed any sign of pain. Some looked surprised. But then death had made no appointment. In most cases, the eyes were open; and seemed still to see.

As the door to Giles's cell swung open, he shouted, "We've won!" Giles embraced each of us. Then he kissed Kalki's hand, murmuring, "Namah Shivayah."

Giles looked haggard. He was full of complaints. "Do you realize that they didn't even give me time to shave." He rubbed the stubble on his narrow cheeks. "Fascists. No, really. They are. And you know that I never use that word lightly." Giles carefully combed his fringe of hair. "They wouldn't let me bring so much as a toothbrush. But," he turned to Kalki, "they did let me watch you on television. I saw you dance, Lord."

How did Kalki respond? Not at all. Other than an air of mission accomplished, he seemed perfectly unimpressed by what he had done. But Lakshmi and Geraldine were subdued, awed. Later Geraldine said that all she could think of at the time was Robert Oppenheimer's description of the detonation of the first atomic bomb at Los Alamos. As the atom broke and the light flared and the mushroom cloud raped the sky, Oppenheimer wrote that no words could express his horror except the Hindu text: "I am Siva, the Destroyer of Worlds." In a way, Oppenheimer was prescient. Myself? Trapped in a dream, I expected any minute to wake up because I could not comprehend the unthinkable that Kalki, alone of all men, had thought.

Later, I was to wake up. When I did, I found that I had blotted out much that would have been unbearable. There are mostly blank pages in my mental album marked The End.

But I recall the rescue of Giles. I recall, vividly, the drive uptown from the police station. Kalki was at the wheel of a Call-a-Ride limousine that he had commandeered in Battery Park. I sat beside him in the front seat. The others were in back. I don't know why Lakshmi didn't sit beside her husband; or why I did.

Everywhere, stalled cars, buses, trucks. Many of the drivers had died at the wheel. Out of control, cars had crashed into one another, driven up onto sidewalks, into glass showrooms. Since the city's traffic had stopped during the noon rush hour, Fifth Avenue was an obstacle course that Kalki managed, skillfully, to navigate.

None of us talked. Even the manic Giles was overwhelmed. While driving, walking, talking, eating, four billion or so bodies had been unceremoniously dropped by their owners. They had fallen to earth in the most extraordinary attitudes. As we drove, nothing moved except the paper lotuses. Whenever the wind blew, they floated through the air, down silent streets.

On the drive uptown, only Kalki took for granted the sights that we saw, the sounds that we did not hear. The traffic lights continued to blink for an hour or so. Kalki went through green lights and through red. I was conscious of his body next to mine. The sweat from the dance had dried. I noted in addition to familiar sandalwood and blondness, an acrid odor totally unlike Kalki . . . Siva?

We parked in front of the Sherry-Netherland Hotel, across Fifth Avenue from the Plaza Hotel. I wondered if Senator White was still in his corner suite.

As we got out of the limousine, smoke began to curl languorously from the main door of the Plaza, gray and black stripes of smoke. From one end of the city to the other, untended kitchens had caught fire. But the fires did little damage, thanks to a series of torrential rainstorms.

Kalki suggested that we take rooms on the third floor because "when the electricity goes off, the elevators won't run and who wants to walk up and down twenty flights of steps a day?" I did not mention that I would have been happy to put a thousand stairs between me and those decomposing bodies. But I joined the others on the third floor. During the three months that we lived in the Sherry-Netherland, I used up a thousand aerosol cans of floral spray. Whenever I went outside, I wore a gas mask, courtesy New York City Fire Department.

In April we left the city only once. Lakshmi wanted to free the animals in the various zoos. So I flew her and Geraldine from city to city; helped them open the cages; let all the animals go, even the predators. Reptiles, too . . . except the poisonous ones. Geraldine was firm, and reluctantly Lakshmi gave way.

I was spaced out. The zoos. The hungry frightened animals. The smoldering fires. The pervading smell of smoke, of putrefying flesh. The flies. The silence.

Except for that one trip, we seldom left the hotel, much less New

York City. Obviously we were waiting. But I did not ask for what. I asked no questions at all those first weeks. I did what I was told to do. Took Valium. Was a blank.

At night, we ate communally. Giles was a good cook. Lakshmi helped him in the kitchen while Geraldine set the table. No one cleaned up. All the dishes in the world were now available to us.

We took turns "shopping." Fresh fruit and vegetables went bad almost immediately, but there was every sort of tinned or bottled or preserved food. We lived on ham, sausage, bacon. From time to time one of us would drive out to Long Island and pick fresh vegetables. If I had had any choice in the matter, I would have stayed in the countryside, where I was able to take off the gas mask and breathe fresh air. But I had no choice.

What happened?

I had not a clue until our first dinner party at the Sherry-Netherland. This must have been a week after The End. I remember how taken aback I was when Lakshmi proposed "a dinner party." She was festive. I was not. But then I was completely narcotized. I no longer dreamt at night. Nor, properly speaking, was I ever awake. Not only did I not understand what had happened, I was by no means certain that it had happened. I did not rule out the possibility of a long and elaborate nightmare.

Yet I got up each morning. Did whatever had to be done. Then I made the rounds of nearby apartments and private houses, freeing trapped pets. But after the third week, there was no point to that.

Each time I went to Long Island, I freed dairy cows, chickens, pigs, ducks . . . whatever I could. I don't suppose any of them survived the winter but my conscience was clear . . . clearer. The second day, Kalki and Giles had got a pickup truck and drove out to New Jersey where they liberated a cow and took her back to Central Park. Kalki milked the cow every day. But the milk was disappointingly thin. I preferred condensed milk. So did Giles. He made a splendid beef Stroganoff with condensed milk to celebrate our (victory?) dinner.

Lakshmi set the table. I lit candles. Giles kept promising to go to the main office of Con Edison and figure out how to light our section of the city with whatever fuel was still in the pipeline. But he never got around to it.

I lit the candles. Geraldine arranged the fresh lotuses that I had found in a Madison Avenue florist's shop. Giles cooked at a gas stove in Kalki and Lakshmi's "Imperial Suite." Giles and Geraldine had each taken a suite. Masochistically, I had chosen a single, rather uncomfortable room in the back. Saving money?

Indian costume had been abandoned. Lakshmi and Geraldine were both elegantly turned out. The result of hours spent across the street at Bergdorf Goodman's. Eventually, out of need, I made a visit to Saks where I hurriedly assembled a number of unattractive odds and ends. Why unattractive? I don't know. I suppose that I didn't want to take advantage of our situation on the ground that, *un*taken advantage of, whatever that situation was it might be tempted to go away. Everyone now ate meat. I noted all this without comment. I assumed that whenever they wanted me to know the new rules to whatever game they were playing, they would tell me.

Kalki mixed Sazeracs. Somehow he had got the impression that I liked them when I was in New Orleans. I had not. Do not. Despite or because of the Valium and the Sazeracs, I was, if not festive, at least more at ease than I had been since The End. The others were in their very own seventh heaven. Kalki wore a denim suit; a flowing tie. Geraldine and Lakshmi were in evening gowns. Giles had found a tuxedo for himself, a size too large.

Sitting beneath chandeliers fitted out with real candles (my contribution), observing our reflections in tall gold mirrors and drinking potent Sazeracs, I had a sense of lunatic well-being. Was glad that I was not one of the billions outside that suite, rapidly approaching maximum entropy.

We talked of clothes. Yes, clothes. Even Kalki had opinions. I listened. Narrowed my eyes so that the others became flickering amber blurs in the candlelight. For a moment, I had a sense that we had slipped, somehow, back into another century. The eighteenth. Soon Mozart would play. Voltaire would talk. I would practice my French, and never once dream of the twentieth century, the last century . . . the horrors.

We talked of food. Of travel. Kalki turned to me. I saw him through half-shut eyes. A blue-gold blur. "You'll be traveling soon," he said.

"Where?" I asked. "When?"

"June. July. As soon as the streets are a bit cleaner." That was putting it nicely, I thought.

"To Europe," said Geraldine. "And I'm coming, too. My first trip."

"I'll be joining you, too," said Giles. "Europe. Africa. Asia. Wherever the kiss of Siva was bestowed."

"Yes." I let the monosyllable drop like a stone into their conspiratorial chatter. They stopped talking. Looked at one another. I could tell that I had been discussed at length. Should Teddy know or not?

It was Geraldine who inducted me, finally, into Perfect Masterhood. "We've been unfair," she said to the others as well as to me.

"Yes." I let the monosyllable drop a second time. I felt more than usually unreal.

Lakshmi seemed truly concerned. "But Teddy knows what happened."

"I don't think so." Giles looked at Kalki who was looking at me. Kalki's expression was what was known to certain writers no longer with us as quizzical (origin, according to the *OED*, "obscure").

"Well," said Geraldine, somewhat unexpectedly, "*you* did it, Teddy."

"I did what?" I looked at Kalki. He gave me a friendly smile. Blondness unfurled in the golden light like a medieval flag.

But Kalki did not speak. It was Giles who proclaimed, "You, Teddy Ottinger, delivered the kiss of Siva to the world."

I looked into the mirror opposite to see if my face was suitably blank. The mirror reported not blankness but anxiety. "How?" I asked; but knew the answer.

"The lotuses," said Geraldine. "You dropped more than seventy million. They did the job."

Giles stood up. Crossed to the dining room. Paused. He was torn between two passions: cooking and explaining. "Those paper flowers," said Giles, "had been saturated with bacteria that are instantly fatal to human beings as well as to certain but not all of our monkey cousins. Other mammals, fowl and saurians are unaffected by this bacterium or plague or kiss of Siva which is known to your friendly neighborhood pathologist as *Yersinia entercolitica.*" Giles sniffed. The odor of beef Stroganoff was in the air. It was ready. Giles raced through his lecture. "Ordinary or garden variety *Yersinia* is deadly but not invariably so. It is also not instant, not total. During the Vietnam war the American army's clandestine chemical warfare division was able to isolate a peculiarly virulent strain capable of ending all human life on earth. This discovery was not only an enormous feather in the cap of the American army's clandestine chemical warfare unit but a triumph for the man who actually developed it, Sergeant J.J. Kelly." Giles bolted into the kitchen.

Lakshmi put her hand on Kalki's. "That's how he got the Distinguished Service Medal." She looked proud. "In fact, Jimmy was the only noncommissioned officer in all of chemical warfare to get such a high decoration." This was, by the way, the first time that Lakshmi ever called Kalki Jimmy in our presence.

"The research was fascinating." Kalki was suddenly alert. We all were. But then the one (the only?) thing that the five of us had in common was a fascination with the technical, the theoretical, the empirical. It is no accident that we are who we are.

"Just outside Saigon," said Kalki, "the army had this dream setup. A first-rate lab. First-rate personnel. Naturally, the whole thing was top-secret because our army wasn't supposed to be into bacteriological warfare but of course we were. Anyway, in less than six months, I was able to isolate my own mega-variation of *Yersinia.*"

I had a picture of Kalki wandering about the world with a bottle full of deadly poison. I hung my picture for them.

Kalki was amused. "No. I didn't keep the original strain. I didn't have to. Since I already knew the process of isolation, I re-created the bacteria in Katmandu."

"We didn't need much," said Lakshmi. "Six ounces was all."

"Six grams," Kalki corrected her. "But that was easy. The tricky part was, first, achieving the right dilution. Then the impregnation of the paper lotuses. That was a real headache. I had to do most of it myself in a lab on the *Narayana.* Giles did what he could. But he's not very good with his hands."

Geraldine made a gesture, as if to bestow on me a medal or a rose. "But the greatest problem was delivery. You handled that, Teddy. Without knowing it, of course."

"None of this would have been possible without you, Teddy." Lakshmi was, gravely, loving. I was, simply, insane. "If every part of the world did not receive, simultaneously, the blessing of Siva, the age of Kali would not have ended all at once but gradually."

"That was the toughest part of all," said Kalki. "The instant that the mega-variation of *Yersinia* becomes operative, it is immediately fatal, as we've seen. But if different people are exposed at different times, there is always a chance that an immunity might begin for those exposed last. So my main problem was finding a way to keep the bacteria dormant between your delivery of the lotuses and April 3. I solved this problem by staggering the intensity of each dose . . ."

Giles announced dinner.

Kalki sat at one end of the table with Lakshmi on his right and Geraldine on his left. I sat on Geraldine's left. Giles sat on Lakshmi's right. I give the *placement* (no French: I mean the seating arrangement) because that is the way we always sit at meals, and so must be depicted for all eternity. Namah Shivaya.

Everyone agreed that the dinner was excellent. Dutifully, I chewed. Swallowed. Tasted nothing. But I did drink champagne. A great deal of champagne.

"And so, finally, my dear Teddy, it was you and the *Garuda* and the prevailing winds that made all our dreams come true." Giles was teary-eyed.

"Why?" I was back to monosyllables. The others looked blank. I elaborated. "Why aren't we dead, too?"

Geraldine turned to Giles. "Doesn't she know?"

Giles shook his head like Dr. Ashok, head lolling disagreeably like a baby's, neck too weak to support Mother Nature's grotesquely swollen cortex. "No. On the excellent ground that, for security's sake, mum was for quite some time the *mot juste*. But now, dear Teddy, it is safe for you to know that we are, each of us, totally immune to the ravages of *Yersinia.*"

"We've all been immunized." Geraldine seemed angry at Giles for not having told me. "Through inoculation."

I surfaced. "I was never inoculated."

"But you were, dear Teddy. In New Orleans. By me. Think back. You have just regained consciousness in a bedroom of the Jefferson Arms, a stone's throw from the Watergate complex. You notice a bruise in the crook of your left arm. You ask me, what is that? I say, I injected you with a sedative. Well, that was not a sedative but the anti-*Yersinia* toxin to which you had, I must now confess, a nearly fatal reaction. For two days you were so ill that I feared we might, dread thought, lose you. But happily, you pulled through and . . . ergo, you are here."

"We're so glad!" In the uneven candlelight, Lakshmi looked more than ever like some ancient love goddess come to life. But then when she congratulated me upon being one of the five people left alive on earth, I had a sense of drowning; heard my own subaqueous voice ask why she was so certain that there were no other survivors; tried not to hear (but heard) my question answered.

"We're almost certain." Gile's head stopped its unpleasant lolling. "But almost is never good enough. To make doubly certain, I go each day to the main studio of NBC in Rockefeller Center. I monitor the world for radio signals. To date, there are none. For the first time since Marconi, the four winds bear not a single human message."

"How quickly," murmured Lakshmi, her eyes on Kalki, "the Golden Age began."

"And how quickly," said Geraldine, "the age of Kali ended."

"I am dreaming," said Kalki, looking straight at me. "I am dreaming a new world, and we are the only people in it."

"For now," said Lakshmi.

I think I must have sunk to the sea floor then. No further memory, of that night.

2

LAST JULY THE WEATHER WAS UNCOMMONLY GOOD IN NEW YORK. By good, I mean traditional. There were no freak storms. The climatic anomalies of the last decade seemed to have stopped. Has the Ice Age (or Greenhouse Age) gone into reverse now that man-made fumes have ceased to pollute the air? Too soon to answer. But skies are bright now, and the weather of the northern hemisphere appears to be changing for the better. For *whose* better? A question hard to answer. I am studying meteorology.

During June and July, I trained Geraldine and Giles in the mysteries of the DC-10. Although they were quick to learn, I was uneasy at the idea of flying around the world with two nonprofessional crewmen. But I had not taken into account that without air traffic, take-offs and landings are no problem. For obvious reasons, I take off and land only in the daytime. Most of the time I fly manually. With a map on my knees. The way Amelia flew.

One curious thing: whenever I make an approach for a landing, I still switch on my radio and wait for instructions that do not come.

Kalki drove us to the airport. By now we were used to the stalled cars and to the heaps of clothes containing what we refer to, neutrally, as "remains." By the third month the remains were no longer corrupt, and white bone was beginning to show. I can . . . word, Weiss! *relate* to bone better than to abandoned flesh. But then one can get used to anything, even the horror of a profound night, silence.

I confess to one morbid moment. Sometime toward the end of June, I forced myself to wander through the rooms of the Sherry-Netherland and look at what was left of so many people. Most were seated in front of the television. They had been watching Kalki. (Giles estimated that Kalki's last Nielsen rating was a 49.0. An all-time high. Trust Giles to care.) Occasionally I would open wallets. Examine credit cards. I don't know why. Perhaps I was looking for someone that I knew. The way one does—did—at a party given by strangers. But I knew none of the guests except for Ralph J. Damon. He had been a vice-president at Lockheed. I had met him twice. At airshows. He had been dull. For some reason, he was on the floor of a closet.

In high spirits, Kalki raced through streets, zigzagged around stalled cars. Lakshmi was furious. But he was like a child, with a toy.

To my surprise, we got to the airport without a single accident. I directed Kalki to the Swissair DC-10 that I had been using.

Eerie sensation, always, to drive down the center of a runway, with planes to left and right, in various stages of loading and unloading. Several had crashed on landing or on take-off; their pilots terminated in mid-procedure.

Lakshmi kissed each of us goodbye. Kalki shook hands. "Contact us every day," he said. "Use the box." Lakshmi and I had put together a special communication device, part telephone (the international telephone cable was still operative) and part radio.

"Tomorrow we're moving to the St. Regis." Lakshmi was firm. She had never liked the Sherry-Netherland. Although Kalki had opposed the move, Lakshmi got her way.

"She wants to be closer to Elizabeth Arden's," Kalki grinned. "Not to mention Saks."

"Well, you'll still be within shooting distance of what's left of the old Abercrombie & Fitch."

Since The End, Kalki had assembled an enormous gun collection. Lakshmi was not pleased. Guns made her nervous. She could not understand why he so much enjoyed target practice in Central Park. Fortunately, they had both agreed that he was not to shoot any living creature. Birds, squirrels, rabbits were out of bounds. Because, as Lakshmi said, "It's their world now."

"Anyway," said Kalki, "the telephone number's the same wherever we move to." Everyone thought this was funny. At least, everyone laughed.

We boarded the plane. I took off. Kalki and Lakshmi waved to us. I know that both Kalki and Lakshmi had wanted to come with us. But could not. Should we all crash, the human race would be at an end. As it was, three-fifths of the world's population was aboard the DC-10.

I was nervous, flying the Atlantic with an inexperienced crew. But luck was with us. Weather was good on the route. Visibility was excellent when we landed at Paris.

I am slow to react . . . emotionally, that is. I had lived entirely on the surface since The End. Kept busy. Scarcely thought at all. Felt nothing. Nothing at all. Did not allow myself to feel. Did not take so much as a single stroll down memory lane. Could not bear what I was bound to find in that lane: white bone. Briefly, at the Sherry-Netherland, I had considered suicide. But what was the point to that? It is the nature of life to live. And I was alive. I had no problem coming to terms with my role in The End. Since I had not known what I was doing, I was not guilty of mass murder. As for Kalki and the others . . . How is one to judge the judge who is also the executioner?

In Paris I started to react . . . emotionally. To think. To feel. Even to remember. Almost immediately, I started to come unstuck.

But first, I will describe, step by step, what we did, as if I were the author of *Locus solus*. (After me, will anyone ever read French?)

Near the runway, I found a brand-new Peugeot. Empty, thank God. And locked. I got the door open. We have all become expert at picking locks. I lifted the hood. Crossed wires. Started the car. Let Giles take the wheel.

"I've been here before," he said. "A marvelous city! I know every inch."

Two hours later, we were in Versailles. Giles was full of apologies. I took over. Drove to the nearest bookstore; picked the lock (in Paris, The End had come at six in the evening); acquired a Guide Michelin and a map of Paris. For some reason there had been fewer fires in Versailles and Paris than in New York.

I was glad to be busy. To be using my hands. To *not* think. But this mood did not last long. In fact, it ended as I was driving across the Pont Neuf and saw before me the vivid green gardens of the Tuileries in full summer leaf. I began to shake. Fortunately, Giles and Geraldine were looking at the palace of the Louvre, which Giles correctly identified.

I stopped the Peugeot in front of the gilded statue of Joan of Arc at the corner of the Rue de Rivoli. As we got out of the car, I was overwhelmed by the perfume. Without the carbon monoxide of a million cars, the air of Paris was like that of a huge garden. We were all ravished. We breathed deeply. Then Giles started to sneeze. "Rose fever," he said; and kept on sneezing until we were again airborne. But not even Giles and his sneezing could spoil for me the beauty of a city that I had dreamed of since childhood.

Arm in arm, Geraldine and I walked in the gardens of the Tuileries. Although the flower beds were scraggly and needed weeding, roses bloomed as if there were still attentive gardeners on earth, ready to prune and weed, maintain. Giles left us in the gardens. He wanted to get cigars at Dunhill's.

We were quite happy without him. We picked roses. Then we sat on a bench and looked up the Champs Élysées toward the Arc de Triomphe. The air was lambent. The vista plangent. Whatever those adjectives actually mean, I mean them to mean uncommonly lovely despite the debris. We see but we do not acknowledge rusted automobiles, torn clothing, pale bone.

"It's as beautiful as I thought," said Geraldine.

"Yes," I said. And I told her everything. How I had postponed visiting Paris until I was in love. Unfortunately, love and Paris had never coincided. Now it was too late for Paris, if not love. I burst into ignominious tears. Of self-pity.

Geraldine was tender, loving. I think she wept, too. I know that we held each other for a long time, and only parted when we heard a sneeze from the nearby arcade of the Rue de Rivoli.

"I propose we stay at the Ritz," Giles's cigar smoke made circles in the rose-scented air. "It's just around the corner. And, of course, everyone stays there." This struck him as amusing. I was not so struck. "It's also close to all the shops, museums . . ."

Prattling, Giles led us into the Place Vendôme.

Prattling, Giles escorted us past the remains of the chasseur at the door to the Ritz, and into the lobby. I thought of Proust. Of Albertine.

Prattling, Giles led us into the bar. "The most exclusive bar in Europe, girls!" He showed us at which table he had first seen Hemingway, Dietrich, the Windsors.

I did my best to blot out the past, and for a while my best was good enough. Giles made us martinis, while Geraldine found some stale potato chips and almonds in the pantry. I cleared a corner table. The bar had been crowded. It had been six o'clock: and *tout Paris* was having an apéritif. Then I remembered that *cinq à sept* was the time when Parisians made love and Americans got drunk. I checked passports, cards of identity; saw that I was right. Nearly all of the last customers in the Ritz bar at six o'clock on April 3 had been foreigners.

As I thought of the French who had been making love when The End came, I started to go over the edge again. I was saved by gin, without ice. The electricity was forever off in the city of light. Even so, I was grateful for the drink. Grateful, even for Giles. He had no imagination. Geraldine did. She knew what I was going through. She kept giving me anxious glances.

"I could never afford the Ritz when I was young." Giles's mood was mellow. "That was right after the Second War. And just before I went to medical school. I came to Paris in the summer of '48. I used to stand over there at the end of the bar and drink Perrier and watch all the glamorous people. It's a pity you girls missed those days."

"Well," I said, "better too late than never." This sounded more savage than I intended.

"The past," said Giles, dropping the prattle, "is an illusion. A painted backdrop. Nothing more."

"These are not illusory things," I said, touching the Baccarat shaker on the table. The table. The glass.

Geraldine changed the subject. "Let's see if the water still works in the bathrooms. If it doesn't, I'm going to take a bath in the Seine."

Fortunately, there was enough water in the taps for a cold shower apiece. Afterwards, we assembled candles to light our rooms. Each of us always carried a flashlight. The logistics of survival in a dead world are complex and, thank God, distracting.

Giles insisted that we go to Maxim's. As we crossed the Place de la Concorde, I realized that there is no city as beautiful as Paris, even in death.

It was sundown when we got to Maxim's. There was just enough natural light to illuminate the Belle Époque dining room. Although Giles wanted to make us dinner in the famous kitchen with whatever happened still to be at hand, Geraldine and I insisted on going somewhere else. The dusty glamour was like that of Tutankhamen's tomb.

In the Place de la Madeleine we studied the Guide Michelin. The setting sun had turned all things to rose. *La vie en rose, enfin.* We picked a one-star restaurant on the Ile St. Louis; it was famous for game and, as Giles reminded us, game keeps without refrigeration. The restaurant was small, charming. The tables had all been set for diners who had never dined. Dead flowers in vases were the only hint that something had happened.

Giles made us a splendid dinner of pheasant; of the contents of tins, glass jars. The three of us drank a half-dozen bottles of burgundy. Admired the view of Notre Dame in the moonlight. Watched the gray-silver river flow beneath us. During coffee, an empty barge glided by.

What did we talk about? I don't recall, which means that we kept the past at bay. Except for Jason McCloud. Somehow his name was mentioned. Despite his triple agentry, he had served Kalki well. He had killed the actor at Madison Square Garden not for the Chao Chow Society but for Kalki. And Giles had paid him off that last day aboard the *Narayana.* Why, I asked, had Kalki wanted people to think that he had been murdered?

"Because," Giles lighted a long Cuban cigar (how long will they keep?), "if Kalki was not thought to be dead at that time, he was in danger of really being killed by the Chao Chow. Also, Johnny White was closing in on him . . ."

"But most important," said Geraldine, aware that I was not taking any of this too well, "there had to be one final test. Those who thought that Kalki would not return were lost."

"Those who did were lost, too."

"No," said Geraldine. She sounded positive. I think she believed what she said. "They will return. In other forms . . ."

I let the matter rest. This was not my favorite topic. Giles intervened. "A moonlit drive," he proposed, "from one end of Paris to the other!"

We drove, drunkenly, through empty streets. The moon was waxing. The sky was clear and full of stars. The air . . . roses. The silence awful. In the moonlight the dome of the Invalides looked like a skull with a hypodermic needle on its top.

At the hotel Giles proposed that I join him for a nightcap. I am reasonably certain that he raped me in New Orleans. I am also reasonably certain that there will never be a *conscious* rematch. I said good night to him; and donned a nightcap with Geraldine. By candlelight, we drank warm champagne. Through the window the column to Napoleon made its unmistakable point.

I said how depressed I had been. Confessed to horror at what had happened. Geraldine was warm, helpful. She was also hard as (or is it tough, ghost of H.V.W.?) nails.

"Look at it this way," she said when I had finally stopped. "They had a wonderful end. Quick, painless. And, best of all, there's nothing human left on earth to mourn them."

"Except us."

"We're not really human."

"I feel very human."

"No, you are a Perfect Master."

"I don't know what a Perfect Master is." I can be harsh, too. "I don't know who Kalki is. Beyond being a mass murderer . . ."

Geraldine was on her feet. Furious. "Don't say that! He is not, because . . . he *is*. That's all. This was ordained from the beginning of time. He came to make an end. And he did."

"He made an end." I agreed.

"And a beginning."

I was by no means certain that Kalki had been ordained from the beginning to make either an end or a beginning but I was positive that from the beginning of time Geraldine and I were intended to be the perfect match. I was Lilith to her Eve. And we promptly made a corner of the garden of Eden all our own. That night we made love for the first time.

Later, we slept. Toward morning, I waked up. Realized for the first time what had happened. Realized that I had been in a catatonic state since April. Wondered if I would go mad or, worse, had gone mad and did not know it.

I thought for the first time of Arlene. I started to shudder. Reminded myself that she would have died soon, and painfully. Leukemia's remission is nothing compared to the inexorable mission itself. All in all, Arlene had been lucky. She had been spared the terminal ward at Cedars-Sinai. Even so, I was shattered.

I was also delighted to be alive. To be with Geraldine . . . who had never had a love affair before. She had been too frightened to experiment with women; too inhibited to experiment with men. Or was it the other way around? Anyway, she had been waiting for me all her life. And I for her.

The next day, while Giles monitored radios, Geraldine and I went sightseeing. At Sainte Chapelle, the floor-to-ceiling stained-glass windows turned the interior to fire, thus matching our mood. We made love in a secret corner where Louis XI heard Mass. When I held her . . . but *tout le reste est littérature.* Verlaine.

Next stop: the Cathedral of Notre Dame. In the silent gray nave, I asked her why I had been chosen for survival. When she began the usual song and dance about Perfect Masterhood, I brought her to a halt with: "That's not the reason."

Geraldine climbed into the bishop's throne. "Kalki needed a pilot," she said.

We were making progress. "Yes. I figured that one out in Katmandu." Light from the rose windows dappled the floor. The stillness, for once, was suitable. "But the world is—or was—full of pilots."

Geraldine looked at me for a long time. Studied my face as if it were a barometer . . . falling? I have no idea what she wanted to see that she had not already seen before. Then came the first question: "What is the one thing that you and I and Giles have in common?"

"We are Perfect Masters."

"What else?"

I thought hard, and thought of nothing. But should have guessed.

Geraldine spelled it out for me. "I cannot have children. Giles has had a vasectomy. You went, as we all know, beyond motherhood when your tubes were cauterized."

I cannot think why I was so slow to get the point since, subliminally, I must have known it from the beginning.

Geraldine asked the second question: "What do Kalki and Lakshmi have in common?"

"They are able to have children." The point was taken. I stared at the lozenges (always lozenges . . . why not diamonds?) of light upon the floor. I thought of nothing.

"Just before we left, Giles examined Lakshmi. She's pregnant."

The enormity of what Kalki had done was more than matched by what he now intended to do. I completed the catechism. "He intends to be the father of the new human race."

"Yes," Geraldine looked happy. "And Lakshmi will be the mother. And we will be the teachers."

"But is it possible? Genetically? And . . ." I could not, entirely, take it in. I tried to remember old biology courses in college. Mendel's law. More to the point, the law of averages. "What happens if the children are all girls. Or all boys? That's quite a risk."

"There's no risk. After all, I'm a pretty good geneticist."

Geraldine the geneticist and biologist. Lakshmi the physicist, and mother. Giles the doctor of medicine. T.H.O., test pilot and engineer. Kalki, destroyer . . . and now creator. We had indeed been chosen.

"You can predetermine the sex of the children?"

"Yes. I can also reduce the dangers of inbreeding. We've worked it out very carefully. The first child will be a girl. She's insurance in case something, God forbid, should happen to Lakshmi. But if Lakshmi were to die, in fourteen years or so, Kalki would be able to reproduce with his own daughter. But that's only if worse comes to worst. If everything works out as planned, during the next twelve years Kalki and Lakshmi will produce three boys and six girls. Those nine will then repopulate the world. I think it's awesome, Teddy."

I demonstrated awe by just staring at her while, mentally, trying to figure out how long it would take for three males and six females to produce a million people. Later, I worked it out with a slide rule: a bit less than two centuries.

Geraldine climbed off the bishop's throne. "Biologically, they are a perfect match."

"But perfect matches can produce perfect monsters."

"That's my job. To control the genetic programming. The last few years there have been all sorts of breakthroughs . . ." Impulsively, Geraldine kissed me. "Aren't we the luckiest people that ever lived! To be the teachers of a new human race."

There was no answer to that one. We made our way back to the Louvre through quiet streets. Dogs and cats looked at us curiously; also, a bit wildly. They had quickly grown used to a world without people. Toward the end of our trip around the world, Giles insisted that we carry guns. "Rabies," he said. "There is bound to be an epidemic now that no one is immunizing the animals." But that day in Paris no dog or cat came near us.

As we entered the Louvre, I asked Geraldine if she really thought that Kalki was god.

"Yes." She was straightforward; looked me in the eye.

"You've never doubted him?"

"No."

"I find that hard to believe."

Geraldine indicated the silent gardens of the Tuileries, the silent Champs Élysées beyond. "Kalki made all this stop. What more proof do you need?"

"Sergeant J.J. Kelly of the Army Medical Corps could also have done it."

"No," said Geraldine. "This is the work of Vishnu. And no one else."

I believed Geraldine. That is, I believed that she truly thinks that Kalki is god, and so religious faith combined with a pure passion for the science of genetics made it possible for her to help make an ending of a human race that had been found wanting. I chose not to judge. But then, in Paris, I was beyond judgment.

Good and evil cease to have meaning if there is no human scale in which to weigh such entirely human qualities.

3

Our last day in Paris was spent "shopping," as Geraldine called it, or "looting," as Giles put it. Illegality always excited Giles. But then there is nothing illegal about taking what belongs to no one.

Geraldine and I made the rounds of the famous dressmakers. We collected for Lakshmi as well as for ourselves. I must admit, guiltily, that I enjoyed myself. I was in Paris. I was in love. I was also nearly killed when I dynamited the safe at Cartier's. I had miscalculated the amount of explosive needed. Luckily, I escaped with only a black eye.

The contents of the safe at Cartier's was well worth a black eye. I have never cared for jewelry. I suppose that was because I thought that jewelry was, somehow, giving in to the enemy that I had left behind when I went beyond. But now I am hooked. So is Geraldine.

I assembled a set of star rubies. Each stone was the size of a pheasant's egg. Geraldine appropriated the Empress Josephine's emerald necklace, a breath-taking creation. We also took several ropes of gray, pink and white pearls for Lakshmi. "She can wear them," said Geraldine, who was surprisingly knowledgeable about jewelry. But then she had come not from San Diego but from the pages of *Town & Country*. "She has the right sort of skin. Pearls have to breathe or they die. Some people have the right skin. Some don't. I don't. Once a set of Teclas committed suicide on my neck."

While Geraldine and I were shopping, Giles had got himself a truck, and backed it up to the main door of the Louvre. With some help from us, he assembled a marvelous collection of paintings, including the *Mona Lisa.* "A picture I've always hated," said Giles, "but it'll look nice in the powder room. What they call a conversation piece." I made my own selection of pictures at the nearby Jeu de Paume. I took the best of Bonnard, Cézanne, Manet.

If it had not been for Geraldine, I would have killed myself last July in Paris. But then if it had not been for Geraldine, I might never have waked up to what had happened.

We talked daily with Kalki and Lakshmi. They had moved to the St. Regis. They were debating whether or not to go south for the winter. Kalki wanted to settle in New Orleans but Lakshmi was opposed. "We'll wait till you get back," she said, "and then we can take a vote on it. Anyway, I'm sure nobody wants to live through a winter in New York."

In all the five continents that we visited, there was no sign of human life.

As one city blurred into the next, I remember mostly airports. And stalled cars. And the cows in Calcutta. The cows had now taken over the city. They slept in the middle of the streets. Chewed grass in the downtown park. I thought it odd that they wanted to stay in the city when the whole countryside was theirs to roam around in. No doubt, they, too, are victims of habit.

A tribe of bad-tempered monkeys had taken up residence in the Calcutta air terminal. They seemed not at all pleased to see us. Obviously they had duly registered the fact that their old enemy and cousin *Homo sapiens* had mysteriously died out; and if they thought at all, they could not help but be pleased that (except for us) they are the sole quasi-reasoning primates in the world. According to Geraldine, their cortices are almost identical to ours. Had they evolved a larynx, they would have been able to speak.

On impulse, I stole two baby monkeys. I must have been out of my mind. I hated motherhood. Now I am bringing up Jack and Jill (Geraldine named them). There is no satisfactory way of deciphering our genetic programming. Apparently motherhood was so built into my DNA that although it could be rooted out physically, it has remained forever on file psychically.

In Hong Kong we collected jade. There were squabbles, mostly with Giles. Who had seen what piece of Imperial Jade first? He was unusually acquisitive. An anal personality, according to Geraldine. I could tell that she disliked him. Yet she never, directly, criticized him. When I told her that I thought that Giles had raped me in New Orleans, she was doubtful. "I don't think he would have had the time," she said. "After all, while you were unconscious, he had to examine you gynecologically, to make sure that you were really sterile."

That explained the soreness in the pelvic region. I was properly chilled. Had I proved to be fertile, I would not have been immunized. Rape seemed, suddenly, trivial.

In Hong Kong we noticed what turned out to be a world phenomenon. After millennia of keeping a low profile, the rats had taken to the streets. They were bold. Dangerous, too. But Mother Nature can always be relied upon to strike a bloody balance. In a very short time cats and dogs were joined by carnivorous birds and the rat population declined.

With a movie camera acquired in Stuttgart, Geraldine shot miles of film. Mostly of cats and dogs eating rats. As a scientist, she was thrilled. "We're going to be able to see just how nature maintains population balances. We're also the first human beings ever to be able to observe how other species behave without the dislocation of man's presence."

"Poor Claude Lévi-Strauss," I said. "I'm sure he'd give his right arm to be with us now." I am not sure that Geraldine found this funny.

In Sydney, domestic animals roamed the streets. Chickens were everywhere. As a result, those predators that enjoyed chicken were also in evidence. Cattle grazed in front of the Opera House. Geraldine filmed. Made notes. Giles collected, and collected. I flew the plane.

The sky over Los Angeles was the color of a perfect aquamarine. No more smog. No more anything. I did not want to stay overnight. But Giles insisted. He also wanted to visit the Polo Bar in the Beverly Hills Hotel. For old times' sake. Unwillingly, I went along.

As we entered the hotel, I thought of Morgan Davies. Of Arlene. Of Earl Jr. and the children. I was starting to come unstuck again. Then Geraldine took my arm. I rallied, somewhat. In a sense, the very completeness of The End made the situation bearable. You cannot mourn everyone. Only someone.

Giles mixed us bullshots. They were delicious. For some reason, the electricity was still on in Beverly Hills, and there was ice. Since The End had come at nine in the morning, Pacific Time, the bar area was empty of customers. But the nearby dining room and patio were filled with the remains of those who had been having breakfast while making deals, reading the trade papers, planning television mini-series that will never, now, be made.

That night we were shocked by what, at first, we took to be the return or revival of the human population. Streetlamps and garden lights went on. From Beverly Hills to Brentwood, there was a blaze of light. But then we realized that all those lights had gone on automatically. Meanwhile, at prescribed intervals, sprinklers continued to wet what had once been lawns but now were tall green jungles.

From the Bistro restaurant, we rang Kalki and Lakshmi in Washington, D.C. "We're in the White House," said Lakshmi; she sounded excited. "We're living here. It's wonderful."

"And convenient," said Kalki.

"And comfortable," said Lakshmi. "You'll love it."

"It's also got the best security," said Kalki. I was about to ask him what he meant by that when the connection broke.

We spent the night at the Beverly Wilshire Hotel. I had a crying jag. Geraldine was a blessing.

The next morning we drove to the airport; and noted yet another phenomenon. Hollywood had been taken over by tropical birds, to the delight of Giles. "There must have been a hurricane," he said. "There's no other explanation. They were blown here from . . . Look! There's a *Conurus patagonus!* That's very rare." Giles was at the wheel.

"Keep your eye on the road," said Geraldine, a nervous passenger at best, and driving is always hazardous now because the streets of the world resemble used-car lots, junkyards.

"You must miss your shop," I said to Giles, wanting to make him suffer.

"Yes," he said, "I do. And I kick myself that I didn't go with you when you made the rounds of the zoos. I could've gone back to New Orleans and saved my birds. Poor things." Then he added, "Poor Estelle."

Geraldine and I exchanged a glance. Giles obviously had his gentler side.

I was glad to leave Los Angeles, and all those bright birds; dark memories.

On the afternoon of July 30, we drove up to the main gate of the White House. Kalki and Lakshmi came toward us, hand in hand like newlyweds. We were greeted as warmly as the day, which was sweltering. Washington is as tropical a city as New Orleans.

"What are we going to do without air conditioning?" Giles hates the heat almost as much as I do.

"We have air conditioning," said Lakshmi. In a water-green sari, she resembled her Katmandu self.

But Kalki was post-Katmandu (Vaikuntha?); he wore shorts, and a polo shirt. "There's a backup generator in the White House," he said. "So we've got all the electricity we need. I also checked out the light company. If we want to, there's enough fuel on hand to light up this section of town for . . ."

Kalki was interrupted by a loud roar from the other side of Pennsylvania Avenue. We turned. At the edge of Lafayette Park, a pair of lions stared at us, curiously.

"From the zoo," said Kalki sourly. "Thanks to Lakshmi."

"They're perfectly harmless," she said.

"Don't bet on it." Kalki suggested that we all carry guns. "Just in case."

"We do," said Giles. One of the first movies that I ever saw was *Annie Get Your Gun.* Now Teddy has got her gun, too. I have always hated violence. Killing. Well.

Lakshmi has a passion for all animals, including the two monkeys that I had brought back from India. She kissed them both. Reminded them of their ancient alliance with Rama in his war with the demon-king. The babies looked a bit stunned. But they approve of her.

Unlike Kalki, Lakshmi is not afraid of the lions and other predators who wander about the city. "They won't attack unless they're frightened or hungry. And they're never hungry now. Besides, they like us. I mean, they're used to having people look after them. That's why they want to be near us. Until it gets cold. Then they'll go south. Don't worry, Giles." Lakshmi could see that Giles was not an animal lover. "They can't get inside the gate."

Our first night in the White House was . . . what? memorable. And comfortable. We had electric light; also, fresh milk, butter, eggs, vegetables, fruit. "Everything we eat," said Kalki, "is grown right here on the White House grounds." Lakshmi had cooked us a fine dinner which we ate in the State Dining Room.

When I remarked upon how spotless the mansion was, Kalki took full credit. "I've never worked so hard," he said. "You remember all that talk about how the President had cut back on the White House staff? Well, you've never seen so many remains . . ."

"Now, Jimmy, we don't really know which ones were on the White House staff and which ones were tourists, because April 3 was a tourist day." Lakshmi had liked the last president. But then, of us all, she was the only one who was politically minded, the result of having been brought up in the house of a Washington lobbyist.

"Anyway, we cleaned it all up and here we are!" Kalki was entirely happy at the head of the table. Back of Kalki's chair was a fireplace beneath whose mantel had been inscribed a quotation from John Adams, expressing the hope that only Good Men should Live in this House. More than once, lately, irony has entered my soul like a rusty nail.

Kalki told us about the last meeting of the National Security Council. "There they all were, sitting around that big table in the Cabinet Room. The President, the generals, the head of the CIA. I even found my old boss from Chemical Warfare. He had a long memo on biological warfare which he never did get around to reading. But *I* read it. Scary stuff. A super nerve gas. Ten new bacteria. Really out of sight, some of them. You've got to hand it to Chemical Warfare. They've come a long way since my mega-*Yersinia.*"

"Tell Teddy about the latest neutron bomb." I had mentioned to Lakshmi Senator White's slip about the model B. "It's called the n-C. And it's really horrifying."

Kalki nodded. "I've got the plans. Not that I can make head or tail of them. That's not really my department. Maybe you can," he said to me. "But I know from the transcript of the meeting what the n-C can do. Apparently, everything within the immediate impact area would be exposed to ten thousand rads. That's about as lethal as you can get. Then there will be fallout. But every time the President would ask just how bad the fallout was, the generals would change the subject. The answer is in another memo that didn't get read. The radioactivity would be active for no less than a thousand years. So if enough n-Cs were deployed all at once, the whole earth would be contaminated and nothing could live."

"Are you so certain?" Unlike the rest of us, Geraldine had always liked the idea of the neutron bomb. She had persuaded herself that it was as safe as the Pentagon claimed. In some ways, she is very innocent. "I mean, how can you be so sure that there will ever be enough n-Cs deployed at any given moment to have that effect?"

"Because," said Lakshmi, "they were getting ready to try it out. They were waiting for the next 'trouble-spot.' Probably in Africa."

Geraldine persisted. "If a half-dozen were used only as a deterrent, the fallout would be minimal."

"There would be a lot more than a half-dozen used," said Lakshmi, grimly. "The Russians had developed their own variation of the n-C. They were also waiting to try it out. According to the CIA they were looking forward to a confrontation with us, in Africa."

Kalki smiled. "You know, I think we've all given the CIA a bad rap. They had the good sense to be scared to death of the n-C. They advised against using it. But the Pentagon was gung-ho. And the President was positive that the Russians would back down, the way they did over Cuba. And when they did, he would have been a hero, and reelected in a landslide."

"But," said Lakshmi, "if the CIA was right, the Russians were not going to back down." She shuddered. "It was a near miss."

Giles was solemn. "Vishnu came, as foretold, and saved us for the next cycle."

Noah's Ark, I thought to myself. We are adrift in Noah's Ark, and still the rain comes down.

The main course was fish, caught by Kalki in the nearby Potomac River.

"We have fish every day," said Lakshmi, "because Kalki can't bear to kill any of the animals, not even a chicken."

"Then I, my dear Kalki, will be not only your doctor and Perfect Master, but White House butcher." As Giles is as good a butcher as he is a cook, we always eat well when he is in charge of the White House kitchen.

After dinner Lakshmi led us into the Red Room. Here we produced our presents. Lakshmi was delighted with her pearls. Kalki was pleased with an elaborate Chinese clock which Giles had found in Tokyo, at the Emperor's palace. The clock not only told what time it was everywhere in the world but also recorded the positions of the moon and stars.

We drank too much champagne, and made jokes about the last president's alleged austerity, dryness.

Kalki had been reading the President's private correspondence. Apparently Morgan Davies had been right after all: the Vice-President was going to be dropped. In favor of (Kalki suspects but does not know for certain) Teddy Kennedy. We discussed Kennedy's political future until Geraldine laughed and said, "All that's over." And so it is. Was? I find this hard to get used to. How is that for understatement?

Giles looked at Lakshmi. "How is my patient?"

Lakshmi smiled. "Never better, or fatter. I crave seedless grapes. But there aren't any."

"When is the baby due?" I asked.

"In December," said Kalki. Solemnly, we drank to the new human race.

Kalki and Lakshmi then escorted us to the surprisingly small living quarters on the second floor where Giles was assigned the Lincoln Bedroom. I should note here that in Paris Geraldine and I had decided that we would be entirely open about our relationship. We were. And we are. The others have taken it well, I think. Certainly, Lakshmi seems to approve, while Kalki is benign. Giles . . . ? He is deep. He appears to be entirely . . . what was the Weissean word? supportive of everyone. Except the monkeys. He has a neurotic horror of monkeys, and we do our best to keep Jack and Jill away from him.

That first night in the White House, Geraldine and I slept together in the Queen's Bedroom. Slept soundly in spite of Jack and Jill, whimpering in the bathroom; in spite of the yelping of a pack of wolves that likes to patrol Pennsylvania Avenue whenever the moon is full.

TEN

1

ALTHOUGH THE WHITE HOUSE REMAINED OUR HEADQUARTERS, WE decided that it was much too small a place for five people and a pair of lively young monkeys.

Giles moved across Pennsylvania Avenue to Blair House, a building used by official guests to the United States in the old days. "The old days" is the way we describe life before The End.

Geraldine and I also moved across Pennsylvania Avenue, to the Hay-Adams Hotel. We have a fine view of Lafayette Park, which is full of wildlife. I have taken up bird-watching, a childhood hobby.

In August Geraldine set up a laboratory on the third floor of the hotel. We looted the city for special equipment, and she was able to find pretty much what she needed. Every day, all day, she works with eggs, chicken embryos. . . . I assume that she is making genetic alterations. But the correlative of a chicken with a human being seems to me to be tenuous. She seldom discusses her work.

My own days are busy. Mornings I go to the White House. I help Kalki and Giles with the livestock. There are two young milk cows (older cows are all dead: no one to milk them). Giles has built a chicken

coop in the rose garden. A herd of sheep are beginning to make some
progress with the shaggy White House lawn. I weed vegetables. Tried
but failed to learn how to milk a cow. But then I've never been able
to contemplate a cow without going into a deep depression, of the
postnatal sort. I suppose that my reaction is somehow related to the
idea of motherhood. I hated my own lactation.

Lakshmi makes bread for all of us. The flour is getting moldy. Giles
thinks that the wheat in Virginia should be ready in a few weeks. But
none of us knows how to harvest it. I have been studying books on
agriculture. Lakshmi says that close to Silver Spring, Maryland, there
is an old-fashioned mill, run by water from a stream. She thinks that
the mill must still be functioning. If so, we can have water-ground meal.
There is a lot of work to do, just to keep going, day by day. Ah, day
by day.

I get back to the Hay-Adams in time for lunch with Geraldine. I
prepare the food. She cooks. Evenings we usually dine at the White
House. Giles takes chefdom seriously. We talk a lot about food. There
is not much else, after all.

2

LAST SUMMER, DURING THE DAYTIME, WE ALL WORE BATHING SUITS.
I felt odd, maintenancing aircraft in a bikini. But the heat was crushing.
At night, we dressed up.

Geraldine and Lakshmi went into a friendly competition. Each night
they revealed new evening dresses; not to mention tiaras, necklaces,
earrings, bracelets. Beneath the crystal chandeliers in the East Room,
the girls shone. I was demure. I usually wore black, or white. Only on
rare occasions did I wear the star rubies. Although Kalki and Giles
enjoyed the fashion parade, they themselves seldom dressed in anything
but slacks, shirts.

Late in August, at the end of dinner, just before we went down to the projection room to see a film, Lakshmi suddenly said, "You know, I'm a native of Washington and I've never been to Mount Vernon. Who wants to go?" George Washington is often on our minds. Wherever you look in the White House, there he is: a painting, a relic.

Since none of us had ever visited Mount Vernon, Kalki proposed an outing. Lakshmi and Geraldine would prepare a picnic. Giles was commissioned to find a boat. I would be skipper. My mastery of machinery puts me forever in the cockpit, at the helm, wheel.

On a hot windless morning we left from a dock near the White House. I was at the wheel. Having no map, I headed upriver toward Great Falls instead of downriver to Mount Vernon. But it made no difference. All that mattered was the normality of a day's outing.

In nothing but a pair of frayed trunks, Kalki looked uncommonly boyish; blondness smeared with oil. Geraldine wore a floppy straw hat, and a mu-mu. Deathly afraid of skin cancer, she hurries to Giles every time she thinks that a freckle has gone awry.

Lakshmi lay on an air-filled mattress in the stern. "So peaceful," she murmured. Then she crossed her arms over the belly that now contains the future of the human race, and slept a deep sleep, for two.

Giles and Geraldine played backgammon. I could not believe it. Although we were passing close to the beautiful wild green shore of Virginia, they did not look up once from their game. Landscape does not exist for either of them.

Kalki joined me at the wheel. Fortunately, he is a nature-lover. He has also taken up bird-watching, and we compare notes at the end of each week . . . each week! We still govern our days by clocks and calendars, just as if there was still such a thing as historic time.

"Look how clean the water's getting!" Kalki pointed to starboard. The water was muddy; but unpolluted.

"The water's better every day." This was true. What had been until recently an open sewer was now reverting to what it had once been, an abundance of pure water and a spawning ground for fish.

In a voice too low for the others to hear, Kalki asked, "Do you find it lonely?" Considering the source, the question was startling.

I answered honestly. "Yes."

"So do I." Again considering the source (Vishnu the creator in terminal tandem with Siva the destroyer), I was taken aback quite a distance. Without the illusion of Kalki's godhead, we were all of us . . . lost? No, worse: instruments of a force beyond evil.

I looked at Kalki. He was staring at a high green-covered cliff that rose perpendicular from the muddy water. When he spoke, the voice was sad. No, pensive. "I'm human, too," he said. "That's the hard part. I sometimes think that this body of mine is a sort of anchor." He looked at the river; found a simile. "Dragging in mud. I miss all sorts of people. And I ought not to. The best will go on into the next cycle. So why be sorry? Particularly, when I am the creator. The one who preserves. Yet there are times when I feel . . ." Again his eyes strayed to the soft swirling of the river. ". . . drifting."

"I miss Arlene," I spoke in a low voice. I did not want Geraldine to hear.

Kalki did not hear me, either. "But then it's only Kelly who drifts. Not I. You must miss your kids."

Fortunately, I had long since dealt with that problem, emotionally as well as intellectually. If I had lost them, suddenly, in a car accident, I would have been shattered because they would have been deprived of what was their due, a full life in the world. But when the world died, too, I had a sense not so much of loss, as of an eraser going across a blackboard, of one game being supplanted by another, of a certain time forever stopping.

Kalki understood me. Up to a point. For the first time that day he looked at me: blue eyes pale in the dull August light. "Since the radioactivity from those neutron bombs would have made the planet uninhabitable for thousands of years, I was obliged to intervene. Just in time. So as Siva, I am most truly Brahma. I destroy in order to create. And to preserve. I have now begun the next cycle and all is well. Except," he looked away, "I am also human. And there are times when the brain of Jim Kelly cannot begin to understand the use to which I have put it. I don't think he tries to understand any more. But," and Kalki frowned. "Sometimes the whispers in my head tell me that symmetry may require the absolute end of this race in time. Strange, isn't it? Siva whispers, annihilate man. Vishnu whispers, preserve. Brahma whispers, begin a new cycle. Is there any beer?"

"Coors," I said. The only beer Kalki liked. "It's in the cooler." Kalki went for beer.

I steered the boat beneath a bridge. As I did, Giles looked up from the backgammon board. "My dear Teddy, we are now passing beneath historic Chain Bridge. That means you are going in exactly the wrong direction. Mount Vernon is downriver."

Lakshmi opened her eyes. "It's my fault," she apologized. "I'm the Washingtonian. I should have told you." With that, she went back to sleep. I turned the boat about. The heat was oppressive. Even on the river, there was no breeze. I noted that the barometer was falling. We were due for a storm. From the southwest.

Giles and Geraldine continued their game. Kalki drank beer, and looked at the scenery, and seemed at peace.

Just off the Virginia shore, a large rock broke the muddy water like a miniature Italy. On the rock's smooth surface lay, intertwined and intermingled, two skeletons. Male and female? Male and male? Female and female? There were no identifying clothes. They had been nude. Had they been making love, I wondered, when life ended?

Tired and sweaty, we docked at Mount Vernon. Except for Lakshmi, we all dove in the warm water. Swam among weeds. Walked on the slithery mud bottom. Made nervous jokes about poisonous snakes. Copperheads frequent the Potomac River. But we saw none that day.

Like tourists, we toured the mansion. We stared at the old furniture, and paintings; at the glass cases that contained swords, gloves, stockings, hats, shirts. Relics of George and Martha Washington. Unlike tourists, we opened some of the cases. Touched the old cloth. But then we put everything back except for Washington's three-cornered hat which Kalki wore for the rest of the day.

Lakshmi and Geraldine arranged the picnic on the steps of the mansion while Kalki stretched out on the overgrown lawn, Washington's hat pulled down over his eyes.

Giles suggested that he and I pay our respects to the remains of George Washington. They are kept in a stone mausoleum not far from the main house.

"It would be nice," said Giles, indicating the old mansion, "if we could preserve all this."

"We can't. One hole in the roof, and that's the end."

"I know," said Giles. "Too sad," he added. Sincerely? One never knows with Giles.

We often discuss ways and means of preserving for the next cycle of man the best of the old cycle's works of art. But there are too few of us. By the time that there are enough people in the world to do the work of preservation, there will be nothing left but ruins.

In front of the iron grille door to Washington's tomb, I sat on a bench. Giles started to sit next to me. Deliberately, I imagined a wall between us. A high stone wall. Yes, Giles sensed the wall. But then I am a good mason. Something in me loves a wall.

With a sigh, Giles sat cross-legged on the ground. "Do you think that we are," he said, suddenly, "perhaps, too few in number?"

"Isn't it a bit late to worry about that?" I am quick to suspect a plot. I am paranoid. But sly. First Kalki had asked me if I was lonely. Now Giles wanted to know much the same thing. I was certain that I was being tested. If so, a wrong score on the test. . . .

I answered carefully. "I thought that all of you had figured that one out. You are now in possession of two breeders as well as three sterile preservers of the scientific culture. Then there will be nine children . . ."

"I wasn't referring to the next cycle. We have nothing to worry about in that department. Lakshmi and Kalki are genetic treasure houses. And complement each other perfectly. I am sure that if Mendel were here, he would applaud. No, I only meant too few for company. At the moment."

"Why should you care what I think? So far, no one has ever asked my opinion about anything. This is your show, not mine. Of course," I was reasonably honest, "my opinion could never have really mattered since I never thought that any of this would happen."

"Well, it did. And here we are." Giles arranged four thin hairy limbs into a yoga position. In tennis shorts and T-shirt he looked particularly unattractive. Like smudged plastic, his bald head shone. "Because Kalki is Vishnu. He has to be," Giles added.

The addition surprised me. "Do you doubt him?"

"Doubt is human, my dear Teddy. And Perfect Master that I am, I am entirely human."

"Well," I was sharp . . . too sharp? "he may not be Vishnu, but he certainly turned in a very good performance as Siva, the destroyer."

Giles gave me an odd look. I had the impression that he wanted to tell me something; but did not dare. "Yes, he is Siva who is Vishnu who is Brahma who is Kalki."

Giles reached into the pocket of his tennis shorts and removed a gold cylinder and spoon. Shades of Bruce Sapersteen! Thoughtfully, he transferred white powdery cocaine from container to spoon. Then he sniffed. "Would you like some?"

"No, thanks."

"You are an old bluenose, Teddy!"

"The old bluenose, Giles, will be yours, not mine."

Giles's laugh was louder than my little joke warranted. He gets high easily. Turns manic. Talks too fast. And too much. But seated in front of Washington's tomb, nose dripping and eyes gleaming, Giles was unexpectedly quiet. Thoughtfully, he stared up at me.

Pregnant was the silence which, presently, gave birth to an idea. Nothing brilliant. Just an insight. Something I should have guessed when he made his comment about how few we are. "Of course, we are *un*balanced," I said, looking down at him, compassionately. He began, involuntarily, to wriggle. "I mean," I spelled it out, "five is an odd number."

"A holy number." Giles avoided my compassionate look.

"Holy or not, you're odd man out, Giles. Kalki has Lakshmi. I have Geraldine. Why didn't you immunize poor Estelle? After sterilizing her first, of course." I have discovered, late in life, that sadism has unsuspected pleasures. For a moment, I munched on that forbidden fruit. Giles's wriggle changed, dramatically, to an agonized squirm. Yes, I was on target.

Geraldine and I have often wondered how Giles must feel in his solitary state. Kalki and Lakshmi are happy together. We are ecstatic. Only Giles is on his own and—happy? I doubt it. But Geraldine is not so certain. She suspects him of eunuchhood. Thinks that his kicks are got cooking, playing chess, bridge, backgammon; setting up an elaborate delivery room in the East Room of the White House; keeping endlessly busy. Yet at the end of each full and active day, he goes home, alone, to Blair House.

"That is my role," Giles said, avoiding my eyes. He took another snort of cocaine. "I enjoy being alone."

I had tortured him enough. I let fall the forbidden fruit, and changed the subject. I pointed to the snifter of cocaine. "What," I asked, "was the real point to the drugs?" I wanted to see if his answer would tally with Kalki's explanation that cold day in Central Park.

"Point?" A pair of Dr. Ashok-y eyes stared up at me, slightly crossed.

"I never could figure out why it was necessary for Kalki to be involved in a drug ring."

"The money, dear Teddy."

"Of course. But I meant from a religious point of view. I mean, is there any connection between drugs and the end of the age of Kali?"

"None at all. As a matter of fact, we always disapproved not only of drug addiction but also of alcohol and nicotine. Our ashrams were genuinely ascetic."

"But *you* smoke, drink, sniff . . ."

"I was a flawed vessel of grace, dear Teddy. Yet I hate the sinner even as I hate the sin. Or as Warren Drake put it so well, 'My sphincter around me night and day, like a mild breast guards my way. My Exhalation far within Peeps incessantly for my sin.' " I have not yet tracked down this quotation. I think that it is fractured William Blake. Drugs, I decided, were the cause of the Lowell-Ashok metaphasis.

"Lunch!" called Lakshmi.

We rose. Giles put his arm through mine, as though he were very old. He even gave an Ashok-y totter or two.

"Was Senator White being paid for," I asked, "by Kalki Enterprises?"

Giles put long finger next to long dripping nose. "Like most presidential candidates, Johnny took money from everyone. Naturally, we were obliged to contribute a penny or two to his war chest. Nevertheless, Teddy, I personally would have voted for him. Yes. For president of the United States. I really mean that. I'm really serious. Because, fiscally, Johnny White was sound. He was responsible. He would have balanced the budget by the simple expedient of shutting and locking the Treasury door and giving the key to Milton Friedman."

I had got Giles's arm out of mine. "You should have saved him, then. Senator White, I mean."

"Or Milton Friedman. He was the real hero of our era. Happily, we are post-economics. Oh, dear Teddy, how wonderful it is to be at the threshold of the Golden Age where every prospect deceives us and Lakshmi's picnic is divine!"

Dishes had been neatly arranged on the bottom step of the veranda. Kalki leaned against a column and ate fried chicken, Washington's hat resting on his ears. Either Washington's head had been a good deal

larger than Kalki's or the General had worn a wig under the hat.
Lakshmi filled Martha Washington's crystal glasses with beer. Geraldine served potato salad on paper plates.

"Let us drink to the Golden Age!" said Giles. And so we did. He
was now manic. "And to the rebirth of all those who believed in Kalki
and who now reside in all their teeming millions and, yes, putative
billions *in ova* here!" Giles placed his hand on Lakshmi's swollen
stomach.

Kalki grinned up at Giles from beneath the three-cornered hat.
"Hey," said Kalki, "that's my wife!"

"And that's my doctor," said Lakshmi, filling Giles's glass.

The picnic was pleasant. The mugginess was not. I don't like Washington in summer. Or, to be frank, at any time. But it was Lakshmi's
home, and Kalki wanted to indulge her. Particularly now. The thought
that the entire future of the human race was growing inside of her awed
us all. It was as if four billion people had been compressed into a single
ovary, like one of those collapsed suns that becomes a black hole
opening onto a whole new cosmos. A Golden Age? Well, we shall not
live to see much more than the beginning. According to Lakshmi, the
first child will be called Eve.

"That's a strange name," I said, "for a child of Vishnu."

"I am ecumenical," said Kalki, mildly.

"But," Giles was firm, "the true faith of the Golden Age will be
Hindu."

"Why have any faith?" I am still a perfect atheist. Yet I am obliged,
due to circumstances, to live in the presence of god. Although I am
certain that I shall never get used to my situation, the others are
tolerant and think that I am bound to come around. I doubt it. I am
willing to admit that Kelly is Kalki is Vishnu. Even so, there is no true
god in my cosmos. To me, Vishnu is a name, not a fact.

"How can you *not* have faith?" Kalki dried his crystal glass with a
paper napkin. "Everything starts with me, doesn't it? and with what
I have done." There was no denying that, what he had done. "And
what I will do. Since my descendants will people the earth, it is only
natural that they will worship their creator. Don't look so glum, Teddy.
All things human require form. Well, I am that form. I am now the
literal source of all human life, as Lakshmi is the bowl that contains
our race." For no reason at all, I remembered something my rabbinical

grandfather had read me when I was a child. A passage from the Old Testament. He read in English. I don't know why. I can still hear his voice: " 'Then shall the dust return to the earth as it was: and the spirit shall return unto God who gave it.' " I must check that quotation.

White-violet lightning cracked to pieces the slate-dark sky. Thunder rolled toward us from the west. Wind made the tall grass of the lawn lie flat, revealed the bleached underside of leaves.

I helped Lakshmi and Geraldine put away the picnic things. Odd, come to think of it, how we tidied up. In a few years Mount Vernon will be a ruin and it will have made no difference whether or not we had cleaned up the remains of fried chicken and potato salad, the paper plates and beer cans.

A hot rain was falling by the time we got back to the boat. As we went aboard, Lakshmi suddenly said, "Look!"

Two giraffes from the zoo were silhouetted against the stormy sky.

Geraldine got out her movie camera. "I hope there's enough light, because this is wonderful."

The giraffes stared at us. We stared at them. Then as the lightning fell like fire from heaven all about us, the giraffes disappeared behind the mansion. Giraffes on the lawn at Mount Vernon. Well.

The crossing was rough. The wind made high waves. The rain soaked us. Although Geraldine and Giles were seasick, Lakshmi was reasonably comfortable in the cabin while Kalki very much enjoyed the storm. He stood beside me at the wheel, and let the rain lash his face.

As I prepared to dock, Kalki said, "I want you to write down everything that you can remember from the first day you ever heard of me. And I mean everything. Even when you doubted me, which I don't mind. Just write it all down."

I made my usual demur. "That first book was done by somebody called Weiss and the pieces for *The National Sun* were written by Bruce . . ."

"I don't care how it's written, Teddy. What matters is your personal record. What you felt. What you feel."

We were now roaring at one another over the wind. I shouted, "Why?"

"For the future. For my descendants."

"Giles can do a better job . . ."

"No. You must do it."

I had no idea why Kalki was so insistent. I still have no idea. But I agreed. Why not? "It's a bit like writing the New Testament." I made a joke which Kalki took with perfect seriousness.

"But you're a lot better off than the writers of the New Testament. You were there at the end, which they were not. And now you are here, as a witness, at the beginning." On that resonant note, a gust of wind blew General Washington's hat off Kalki's head. The hat vanished in the river's high waves.

All in all, I have enjoyed . . . well, no, not enjoyed: I have found interesting this work of recollection. Cathartic, even. Certainly it has given shape to *my* days.

Each morning I come here to the Cabinet Room. I work for several hours. Midway through, I offered to show Kalki the text but he refused to look at it. "Not until you're finished."

The autumn has been unusually beautiful. Weather is changing for the good. At least in our latitude. The worst of the heat ended a month ago, in early September. Since then the days have been brilliant. Cool. Clear. Clarity contains us like a crystal.

The day after the picnic at Mount Vernon everyone except me was infected with poison ivy. Lakshmi and Geraldine suffered the most. Giles sprayed them with cortisone. Even so, they were in agony.

Except for the poison ivy, the last three months have been uneventful. As it turned out, we never left the city.

Jack and Jill have had a baby. Jill is a lot older than we thought; and pregnant when I found her in India. Jill's first child is a girl, a good omen. We refer to her as The Child.

I have turned over the lobby and downstairs bar of the Hay-Adams to the monkeys. They could not be happier, swinging from lamps, making messes, chattering to one another—to us, too. They very much want to talk or at least communicate with us. At the beginning, Geraldine did not like either Jack or Jill, but since Jill's motherhood, Geraldine has taken a real fancy to her. For one thing, Jill has matured. She is quite a different (I almost wrote "person") creature from what she was before. Unlike me, Jill is a natural mother. She has also given up her old mischievous and destructive ways; she takes motherhood very seriously. Jack is still pretty much an extrovert. He reminds me a bit of Earl Jr. The same insensitivity. He is unbelievably jealous of the baby. But that is normal at this stage.

I am fascinated by how human they are. Geraldine thinks that I am "anthropomorphizing." But I am not so sure. Since monkeys are racially so close to us, there is no reason why we could not teach them a great deal or even let them teach us those things that they know, instinctively—things that we have forgotten in our lunatic dash to remove ourselves from the fact of our common humanity, *sapiens* or not.

Our days are busy. Geraldine works long hours in her laboratory. Lakshmi studies the latest publications in physics. She is constantly working. She would still like to break, successfully, Heisenberg's law.

Giles spends most of his days at the various government bureaus, going through the secret files of the FBI, the DEA and the CIA. He has now collected thick dossiers on each of us as well as on Kalki Enterprises.

"I am putting all this together," said Giles, "to show our descendants the workings of a typical government at the end of the age of Kali." We were all in the Cabinet Room, looking at Giles's documents. They covered the big table like layers of snow.

"But won't it give those future generations bad ideas?" Geraldine tends to be cynical about human behavior. But what I call cynicism, she calls realism. Perhaps they are the same. Unfortunately, I am not realistic. Or cynical. I crashed my plane several hundred miles east of New Guinea. Or did I land on a desert island? No matter. I am the last romantic.

"It will be thousands of years," said Kalki, "before the age of iron returns. By that time, my people will have left this planet for other worlds, in other systems. That's why your job is so important." Kalki gestured; included us all. "You must give the first generation a head start. Geraldine will teach biology. Lakshmi will teach nuclear physics. Giles will teach medicine. Teddy will teach engineering . . ."

"And what will *you* teach?" Lakshmi was teasing.

"The Way," said Kalki. On the wall behind him the painted face of Abraham Lincoln stared at us from its golden frame. Lincoln looked, appropriately, somber.

Then Giles lectured us at length on his latest discoveries at Langley, Virginia. He has broken most of the top-secret codes. He now knows who really killed the Kennedy brothers, and so on. For some reason, none of us is very interested. As the golden autumn elides with winter, the old days have begun to fade for us. Best of all, we have begun to plan for the future. We hold seminars on education. We discuss how best to teach the children. Unanimously, the new math has been rejected.

Occasionally, Geraldine and I go sightseeing. We both like the Smithsonian. I am fascinated by the early aircraft, by the old trains. I also like the collection of dresses belonging to the former first ladies. I grow more and more feminine. Whatever that state is. Incidentally, we have all taken to discussing sexual roles. Like our earliest ancestors, we must now emphasize breeding. But will such an emphasis rule out relationships like mine with Geraldine? Giles thinks that it will. He sounds like Moses on the subject. But then he is deeply jealous . . . like Moses?

Lakshmi thinks that there will be no problem. I do. Meanwhile, Geraldine believes that artificial insemination is the answer to correct breeding. If this should be the case, then romantic sexual relationships of every sort will flourish, and the baby supply will not be endangered. She makes a powerful case. Kalki is enigmatic; he has taken no line.

Yesterday morning Geraldine and I walked to the National Gallery. Another bright, cool day. We no longer notice the tattered remains or the torn paper lotuses that still decorate the odd breeze.

Animals observe us neutrally. So far none of us has had to use a gun. A well-fed animal is almost always peaceful. Good lesson.

The National Art Gallery is now our favorite place in the city. For a time, of course, it was disagreeable: the water in the fountains and ornamental ponds had gone stagnant. But we went to work. Let the water out. Cleaned everything in sight. Now the gallery is a perfect refuge for Geraldine and me. She likes the atmosphere. I like the pictures. I study them. I realize now that I shall soon have a new role. I will be the only one of us able to explain the visual arts to the children. Lately, I've been reading art criticism. Bernard Berenson, Roger Fry, Harold Rosenberg.

Occasionally, I borrow a picture. Yesterday I took home a Mantegna. I find that I can stare for hours at a picture. As I do, I can see the dead hand at work and I can imagine what the dead eye saw and, sometimes, I think that I know exactly what it was that the dead eye *thought* that it had seen so long ago.

I am now caught up. It is October 3. Giles has invited all of us to

Blair House. He is giving his first dinner party. Yesterday he sent out engraved invitations. Black tie. *Black tie!* R.S.V.P.

3

GILES WAS GOT UP AS DR. ASHOK, "FOR OLD TIMES' SAKE, MY DEAR Teddy.

I was mildly disturbed by the gray wig, the brown face, the aura of curry. It was as if instead of five survivors there were now six. I said as much. Giles giggled, in the breathy Indian fashion.

Parenthetical question: Will we tell the new generation about all the other races that once crowded the planet? I suppose we shall have to. But what will the Golden Agers make of such horrors of the age of Kali as Calcutta and New York? I suppose their response will be conditioned by what we tell them.

Geraldine was direct, as always. "Giles likes being Dr. Ashok because of the wig. He hates being bald. Don't you, Giles? And there isn't enough hair at the back of your head for transplants."

Giles pretended to be amused. But then it always amuses him to pretend. After all, he is two people. At least. And I must admit that one of those multiple selves is a good interior decorator. Certainly Blair House has been beautifully done over.

Giles had collected period furniture from every elegant house and museum in the city. He had even made his own curtains, with some help from Lakshmi. The collection from the Louvre is spectacular. The *Mona Lisa* dominates the main drawing room (and not the john, as threatened). The jade is brilliantly lit. A foot-high pagoda, intricately carved from a single block of Imperial green jade, resembles nothing so much as a wave of sea water frozen in the falling.

Geraldine and I must keep our jade in glass cases because Jack and Jill and The Child have a tendency to smash things. In principle, they are not allowed in our quarters at the Hay-Adams. In practice, they always manage to wheedle their way into our rooms. With, sometimes, disastrous results.

I did notice that Giles's collection of French Impressionists was not in the same class as mine. He has absolutely no eye for that period. Although he had not picked the very worst of the Cézannes and Soutines, he had also avoided picking any of the best. We are competitive, I see.

Dr. Ashok, as Giles wanted to be addressed, mixed the driest of dry martinis. We drank, heavily. Unfortunately, my head is the weakest of the five . . . six? Geraldine's is the strongest. That night Dr. Ashok proved to be so much the perfect host that each of us could not help but be somewhat less than the perfect guest.

We sat before a fire (nicely equipped with a Weissean roar against the clammy night). We drank martinis and discussed the *Mona Lisa*. There is something wrong with that picture's color or maybe there is something wrong with the way Giles has lit it. Then, too, there is a good possibility that the Louvre's *Mona Lisa* was a copy. Experts disagree.

As we waited for Kalki and Lakshmi to arrive, Dr. Ashok reported at tedious length on Giles's latest Top Secret findings at Langley and elsewhere.

"What are you going to do with all that research?" asked Geraldine.

"I thought I might use it to compose a new Bhagavad-Gita, describing Kalki's adventures in exactly the same way that the original told the story of Kalki's earlier self Krishna."

"Why not go further back," said Geraldine. I am always surprised at how much of the Hindu religion she knows. I am almost entirely ignorant; and intend to remain so. "Go back to Rama. To Vishnu's incarnation before Krishna. Write a new Ramayana. It could be fascinating. Particularly the love affair between Rama and his wife Sita . . ."

"But," said Dr. Ashok, "where is the analogy? Sita was kidnapped and raped by Ravana, the demon-king of Ceylon. Lakshmi, thank God, has not been kidnapped or raped and there is no contemporary Ravana. Hence no comparable war to recapture Sita. No defeat of Ravana at the hands of Rama and his monkey allies. In fact, we lack all the elements except those damned monkeys of yours down the street at the Hay-Adams."

I was about to defend Jack and Jill. But Geraldine intervened. "You must find symbolic equivalents," she said.

I thought that Geraldine looked dazzling tonight. She wore a stunning gown by Balenciaga, taken from a display of twentieth-century high-fashion masterpieces at the Smithsonian. This particular gown had been made in the thirties for a celebrated beauty named Mrs. Harrison Williams. Although Mrs. Williams had been somewhat taller than Geraldine, each had the same narrow waist. I know. I fitted the dress for Geraldine. Also, in honor of our first dinner at Blair House, Geraldine wore the Empress Josephine's emerald necklace, as well as a small diamond tiara that had belonged to Marie-Antoinette. The effect . . . dazzling.

I wore another masterpiece from the Smithsonian collection. A classic design in red damask, cut by the genius Charles James. Although I have never cared very much for clothes, I will say that tonight I did not look, exactly, my worst.

"There are times, Giles," Geraldine began. But our host interrupted her.

"Dr. Ashok!"

"Dr. Ashok. That I wonder who you really are. I mean, deep down inside. Is Dr. Lowell impersonating Dr. Ashok or does Dr. Ashok impersonate Dr. Lowell?"

"A true mystery, dearest Geraldine! Personally, I suspect that each is really the other and neither one is me."

Geraldine was amused. I was not. Geraldine is always analytical. "Metamorphosis," she likes to say, "is the key joker in the genetic deck, and jokers tend to wildness in science as in poker. So why not in psychology, too?"

"Hello," said Kalki. He and Lakshmi were standing in the doorway.

Giles leapt to his feet, and pranamed. Geraldine and I both got to our feet. We always do when Kalki and Lakshmi enter a room. I don't know why. After all, we know them so well. See them in bathing suits. Working in the garden. Sweating in the sun. Covered with poison ivy blisters. Nevertheless, there is a real sense of—I won't say divinity because that word means nothing to me—but of magic about them. And, of course, they are physically beautiful. Tonight, Lakshmi wore the ropes of pearls that I had brought her from Paris; a royal purple creation from Dior disguised her pregnancy. Kalki looked very young in a black velvet suit.

They admired the jade, the pictures, the furniture. Since tonight was the first time that any of us had been inside the redone Blair House, we were busy, comparing notes. We are all, like it or not, devoted homemakers, interior decorators. Lakshmi has been gradually doing over the White House. Successfully, I think. In the interest of comfort and authenticity, she has pretty much shed the Sheraton Hotel look so much admired by recent presidents. Geraldine and I have done the best job of all (or so I think) because we had to work with the rather poky low-ceilinged rooms of the Hay-Adams, so unlike the splendid proportions of the White House or the Federal charm of Blair House. I think that if I had it to do all over again, I would have found us a proper house in Georgetown. Perhaps Dumbarton Oakes. But, as it is, we are close to one another. That is something.

Giles—not Dr. Ashok—had prepared the dinner. We gorged on a dozen courses served off solid gold plate that Giles had found in London, created for Louis XV. We do live nicely.

The subject of duality came up again at table. Geraldine repeated what she had said about metamorphosis. I was still not sure what she meant.

But Kalki took the argument in stride. "The secret," he said, "is not that each of us has two identities or one identity that changes into something else, but that each of us has *all* identities. Since Vishnu is all things, all things are Vishnu."

"Then," said Giles, "I am Kalki."

"No," Kalki's eyes were particularly lovely in the candlelight. "*I* am Kalki. But physically you and I and all of us are the same stuff and so interchangeable and so heirs to the original atom that broke and caught fire. But though my body may be the same as yours, I am the avatar, and so unique."

"You are also," said Lakshmi, "about to be the father of the human race." With perfect love, she smiled at him across the table. I felt a sudden twinge in my cauterized womb. A real sadness that Geraldine and I could never have children. I don't mean together. I mean separately. But, no, why *not* together? Parthenogenetic birth is possible with rabbits. But even if a woman could be made pregnant with a saline infusion, the child would be entirely hers, and no one else's. The child would also be female. A child born solely of woman can only be woman.

It is a sign of human perversity that the two children that I did have in the normal way, I did not want. Now that I can have none, I cherish . . . monkeys! I was not a good mother. I was also not a bad mother. I suppose that makes the whole matter worse. A bad mother at least is active. I was passive. Did the minimum. Am barren now. But in love. That is more than enough.

Conversation was general. The state of physics, genetics, medicine, engineering as of April 3 this year. This year! I sometimes have the sense that we are now living a light year in the future and that human existence before April 3 was nothing more than Cro-Magnon whisperings from a prehistoric time.

Kalki hoped that each of us would go in for original research, the way that Geraldine has been doing in her laboratory. "Because," said Kalki, "the most important thing that you are going to have to do is to teach the first generation how to be teachers, too."

"Aren't they lucky!" Lakshmi was flushed in the candlelight. "A brand-new race. With nothing in them of the old except the best."

"Well," said Geraldine, always to the sometimes disagreeable point. "They won't be all that new. And they certainly won't be the best. You and Kalki are nothing more than two pools of absolutely run-of-the-mill genes. Your children will be nice-looking. They'll be healthy. But the odds are very much against their being geniuses, no matter how hard *I* work."

"But I am also Vishnu," Kalki grinned boyishly, eyes shining. "Surely that fact alters the genetic pool."

"I agree. You are Vishnu. But you have taken up residence in the body of J.J. Kelly and your children will be his children. They will be Alpha. Otherwise, they won't be so very different from the rest of the dearly departed four billion." Geraldine was hard, tactless. She had had too much wine.

Giles quickly changed the subject. "We must work out a new calendar. What, for instance, shall we call the period before April 3? And the period after?"

During the châteaubriand, we decided to divide human history into two parts: Before Kalki and After Kalki. Not exactly original. But no one could think of anything better.

Giles then proposed that the months should be renamed for us. Lakshmi was delighted. She wants June to be called Lakshmi. Geraldine has taken September, which is what I wanted. I settled, gracefully, for October. January will be called Lowell. The other eight months will be named after the first eight children, starting with Eve.

As of tonight or, rather, early this morning (I am putting the last touches to this record at the Hay-Adams while Geraldine sleeps restlessly in the next room), the date is Ottinger 4, of the first year After Kalki. Or 1 A.K. Well, it looks no odder than A.D.

We took coffee in the drawing room. The fireplace had begun, slightly, to smoke. I promised Giles that I'd clean out the flue. For a doctor, he is surprisingly clumsy with his hands.

Giles produced hundred-year-old brandy, and Cuban cigars. Geraldine smoked a cigar. I drank brandy from a huge Baccarat snifter.

"Mission accomplished!" Giles's favorite phrase had been appropriated by Dr. Ashok.

"Only part one," said Kalki. "Part two is the launching of the Golden Age."

"The children," murmured Lakshmi.

"Of course! Of course! I was hasty! Oh, how I envy you!" Giles was staring at Kalki with somewhat wild bloodshot eyes.

"Is that possible?" Kalki was gentle, as befits god's earthly avatar.

"Well, no, of course, not really. I mean, you can't envy the highest of the high. That would be like envying the sun, the moon, the full tide of creation as it courses through the emptiness of space. No, no. I bow to Siva. Namah Shivaya. But, ah, Kalki, what it must be like to be not only the sole progenitor of a new race but the beloved of the goddess Lakshmi now incarnate as the most beautiful woman the race has yet produced!"

Geraldine and I exchanged a Weissean quick glance, antonym of the Weissean long look. We still wonder just how Giles will eventually adjust to being odd man out. So far, he has shown no overt signs of distress or anxiety. No, that is not quite true. Last summer when the subject of wife-swapping came up, Giles had spoken powerfully in favor of this sort of sexual pavane. But Kalki had swiftly vetoed the notion on the ground that since only he and Lakshmi can reproduce, there is no reason for the rest of us to go through what he called "the motions." To which Giles had made the point that since there was no biological reason for such couplings, then, by the very same logic, there was absolutely no reason for us *not* to go through the traditional motions. Why, he asked, couldn't the one sterile male couple go through the motions with either or both of the two sterile women, or even with the one fertile female?

Kalki had not been moved by Giles's argument. Geraldine thought that Giles was in love with Lakshmi. "Not with you?" I had asked.

"Not in a million years," she had replied.

"Or with me," I added. Well out of it.

Tonight I thought that Kalki handled Giles with unusual tact. "Your role is just as important," he said.

"No, no! How can it be! I'm a mere doctor, and the human race can certainly survive without doctors. In fact, the race might even thrive without us. But there cannot, literally, be a human race without you and Lakshmi. Oh Lakshmi! Oh beautiful one! Oh ocean-born . . . !" Suddenly Giles sounded like Dr. Ashok in the lobby of the Oberoi Intercontinental, one world ago.

"Giles!" I could see that after Lakshmi's first delighted response to flattery, she was annoyed. Alarmed? "We don't want to hear all of my one thousand titles." She made light of an occasion gone heavy.

Giles poured himself more brandy, and Kalki rolled a joint. Kalki looked suddenly wary. Is Giles indeed "the other," as Kalki had warned me in Central Park? And what form does otherness take?

Abruptly, Geraldine changed the subject. She reverted to biology, to her subject. Our subject, too. "I wish," she said, "that we had a biological backup for Kalki. Or even an alternative."

Giles spilled most of his brandy as hand with glass missed mouth. Lakshmi blushed. Kalki's face looked to be uninhabited, as Geraldine proceeded to drop her bricks. Later, she told me that she could not let this opportunity to speak her mind pass. As if she ever did. Or does. I love her candor.

"Speaking as a geneticist, I'm not entirely satisfied with the present arrangement." Geraldine got to her feet. I could almost imagine a blackboard behind her. She must have been the first biologist ever to · lecture in a Balenciaga gown. "I believe that you've all read my paper on inbreeding." Geraldine had given each of us a typescript soon after we were settled in Washington. "If you have, then you know the degree to which a given DNA situation can be manipulated. In general, the odds favor a Kalki-Lakshmi conjunction. Even if they did not, I am able to adjust the odds. To load the dice. To bend the helices. Nevertheless, ideally, there should be at least one other male that could be added, if necessary, to the equation." For ten minutes Geraldine lectured us, blissfully unaware that her audience had turned to stone. When Geraldine finished, she paused . . . expectantly. Rather the way that Arlene used to stop in mid-commercial for the count of five; a pause that would later be filled with canned applause and laughter. But tonight there was neither applause nor laughter. In fact, nobody said anything for the count of five times five.

"Your advice comes too late," said Giles. And he was now definitely Giles. He had sobered up. He took off his Dr. Ashok wig.

When Kalki spoke, he was icy. "Had I intended for there to be another fertile man at the end of the age of Kali, I would have brought him through the plague, as I have brought the four of you."

"Of course. Of course." Giles was oddly humble, placating.

Geraldine chose to ignore Kalki's plain fury. "You missed my point. You don't actually need a man," she said. "There are other ways of impregnating Lakshmi."

"What other ways?" Lakshmi looked slightly shell-shocked.

"Sperm banks," said Geraldine. "There are two right here in Washington. We can take our pick of donors. We can match Lakshmi with any number of desirable combinations. And I highly recommend that at least one of those combinations should be Chinese. It would be a biological tragedy if the Chinese genetic pool was lost forever."

Suddenly, Kalki whooped with laughter. The rest of us laughed, too. Obediently. Then Kalki said, "Geraldine, you are right off the wall! You're a great scientist, no contest. And I'm sure you're right. And if there had been any way to preserve the Chinese wading pool, I'd have done it. All the other ethnic pools, too. I would have assembled a genetic Noah's Ark. But you know as well as I do that that was not meant to be. At the end there could only be five. And of the five only the creator can be the procreator."

"The sperm banks . . ." Geraldine was getting annoyed. If red hair could truly bristle, hers would have been crackling with electricity.

"Have gone broke!" Kalki grinned at her.

"What do you mean, broke?" I asked.

"Bank holiday. Moratorium. No more deposits. No more withdrawals. Figure it out. To live, sperm must be kept at a certain temperature. When the electricity went off, that was the end for all those billions of spermatozoa."

"I hadn't thought of that," said Geraldine. "You're right. Of course." Unlike the rest of us, Geraldine is prompt to admit an obvious mistake. But she was plainly not happy.

"The human race's only future," said Kalki, "is here!" Slowly, he closed one hand over his crotch. We were all startled. And appalled. Not so much by the gesture, as by its demonstrable truth.

"I have just unearthed a cassette," said Giles, smoothing out the roughest spot thus far in the evening, "of the Inaugural Eve festivities held for the last president. Shall we watch? It's great fun."

So we watched television. Then said good night to Giles. He stood on the stoop of Blair House; and waved until the four of us had got as far as Lafayette Park.

There was a full moon. Does the moon in its fullness affect human behavior? Although I am no longer, precisely speaking, a woman whose tidal blood can command the moon to wax or to wane, I do feel, on occasion, the ghost of my body's ancient power stir whenever the moon is full. Tonight I am very much aware of my old, my primal self.

From Capitol Hill, we could hear the wolves. They seldom come near us. But when they do, they are friendly. But shy. They keep their distance.

As we entered Lafayette Park, the wolves stopped their yelping, and our world was entirely silent. Even now, I find the universal stillness hard to get used to. Nor can it be altered, unlike the darkness. At popular request, Kalki keeps the White House illuminated from sundown to dawn. My desk is so placed that I can see that famous portico even now, as I write.

"Do you want to drop in for a nightcap?" Kalki was still in a partying mood.

"No, thanks," I said. I knew that Geraldine was having one of her headaches.

"And I've got to get my sleep," said Lakshmi.

From across the Potomac, a lion roared. We listened for an answering roar. There was none.

"How strange Giles was," said Lakshmi.

"It's not easy for him." Kalki appeared to be sympathetic. But then he is always generous with us. He is quick to accept our faults, and to praise our virtues. But then, perhaps, we really are his dreams, deliberate extensions of his will. If so, what happens to us when he wakes up?

"I should," he said, suddenly, "have saved Estelle." This was startling.

"Oh, really?" Lakshmi's face was stern in the white moonlight.

"You see?" Kalki laughed. "That's why I didn't. You'd have been jealous. But if I had, Giles would have had someone. And things would have been better all around. But five cannot be six. Not even in the new math."

Geraldine kissed Kalki's cheek. "The god Vishnu did what had to be done," she said. "You are always right."

"Not always," said Lakshmi. "When Jimmy is his human self, he makes mistakes just like the rest of us. But when he's god, well, it's a completely different matter."

"A difference," he said, with a smile, "no greater than this flesh I wear."

Since Kalki was not in the least put out by Lakshmi's near blasphemy, I added my own small heresy. "It must," I said, as drily as H.V.W. could have wished, "be a bit like switching from alternate to direct current when Vishnu switches from Kelly to Kalki."

They laughed. And said good night. What a lovely couple, I thought, as I watched them walk slowly up the driveway to the portico of the White House. Kalki's arm was around Lakshmi's waist; her head rested on his shoulder.

As Geraldine and I entered the Hay-Adams, there were riotous greetings from Jack and Jill and The Child. Then, as always, I cleaned up. Jack's latest project is to pull the stuffing out of the various sofas. He is compulsively destructive, despite Jill's disapproval. As a mother, Jill is a born preserver, homemaker.

"I don't think that the new human race could have had betterlooking parents," I said to Geraldine, prying the last bit of horsehair from Jack's tightly clenched fists.

"They're good stock," Geraldine agreed. "And I suppose if there has to be just one man and one woman left to breed, they are as useful a couple as any." The emphasis she put on "has to be" made me put down Jack.

"You really do believe that there should have been others?"

Geraldine didn't answer. She is entirely loyal to Kalki. She started up the stairs. I locked the children in the bar; and followed her.

I helped Geraldine take off the Balenciaga gown, a far more complicated creation than my simple but subtly cut Charles James. I noted again how closely Geraldine resembles the Joshua Reynolds portrait of Perdita which I gave her as a birthday present. The painting hangs over her bed.

"It's a pity," she said, "about us." Geraldine got into bed.

"Because we can't have children . . . with Kalki?"

"Yes. Stupid of me. I know. Because the only reason that he chose us for the Golden Age is because we *can't* have children. Even so . . ."

"Well, we have a good deal to be grateful for."

Geraldine smiled through her headache. "I know," she said. We embraced. Then I went to my own room.

I have been taking Alka-Seltzer and aspirin. I am now entirely sober and wide-awake. Nearby, the wolves are howling. But that is not exact. Except on such rare occasions as the celebration of the full moon, wolves seldom howl. Generally, they yelp. They are yelping now.

This record is now up to date. I have described how the age of Kali ended and how the Golden Age began. From my point of view, of course. There can be, for me, no other.

ELEVEN

O TTINGER 3, 3 A.K.

It has been exactly two years since I last looked at this record. Kalki wants me to write a postscript. I can't think why.

Two days after the dinner party at Blair House, Lakshmi miscarried. The baby—a girl, as predicted—was born dead, and deformed.

Lakshmi went into a deep depression. Kalki was grim. Giles was soothing; he assured us that nothing serious had gone wrong. He was absolutely certain that the next baby would be healthy. He gave his reasons. But then, unknown to Giles, Geraldine did blood studies of both Kalki and Lakshmi.

On a cold, rainy morning Geraldine came into the living room at the Hay-Adams. She was still wearing her laboratory smock. When she is nervous, she develops a slight tic in her left cheek. The tic was in evidence that morning.

"Lakshmi is Rh-negative," said Geraldine. "Kalki is Rh-positive." She sat in the chair opposite my desk.

I knew exactly what she meant. Every mother knows about those incompatibilities of blood that can exist between male and female. In great detail, Geraldine spelled it out for me while rain fell in sheets, made opaque the windows, darkened the room.

Before Kalki, 13 percent of all American couplings occurred between Rh-negative women and Rh-positive men. Although the first child of such a union might be normal, subsequent births would sometimes be disastrous—until the development of a prophylactic serum called Rho-GAM. If an Rh-negative woman was treated with RhoGAM immediately after the birth of her first child, her next child would be normal. Untreated, subsequent children could suffer fetal hydrops, stillbirth, kernicterus. Lakshmi had not been treated.

Geraldine was precise, angry, guilty because, "I should have known their blood chemistry . . ."

"Why?" I tried to comfort her. "After all, you're not their doctor. Giles is."

"Yes," said Geraldine. "Giles is their doctor."

When I saw what was in her mind, I joined her in a state of shock.

From far away, I could hear my own voice saying what I hoped was true. "He must not have known."

"He knew."

"Are you sure? I mean, isn't it possible that he made a perfectly honest mistake?" I chattered, hoping that the truth was not true and that the crime could be expunged with words.

"Giles has known from the beginning that they were incompatible. So . . ." Geraldine stopped.

"Why?" I asked.

"Why," she repeated. Then she telephoned Kalki.

When Geraldine and I entered the Oval Office, Giles was already there. Lakshmi was not. She had taken to her bed. Would not speak to anyone. Had to be forcibly fed.

Kalki sat at the president's desk. For the first time since The End, he wore the saffron robe. Through the window back of his chair, I could see the chickens in the overgrown Rose Garden. They clucked contentedly as they pecked for food.

Giles sprang to his feet, face vivid with energy, intelligence. "Geraldine! Teddy!" He tried to kiss Geraldine. She pushed him away.

Then Geraldine sat in a chair opposite Kalki's desk; opened her handbag; produced a sheaf of papers. "Now," she said, "this is the problem . . ."

Giles interrupted her. He was entirely manic. "There is no problem! How could there be? I have personally studied every blood chemistry report ever done on Kalki and Lakshmi . . ."

"Shut up, Giles." Kalki's voice was without emphasis.

As Geraldine gave her analysis, Giles paced the room, wanting to interrupt but not daring to. Medical words like "erythroblastosis" were used. But despite the elaborate terminology, the meaning was altogether too clear. As was the solution, which Geraldine proposed.

"You and Lakshmi," she said, "can only have children if, within seventy-two hours of delivery, Lakshmi is desensitized with RhoGAM, which contains a high titer of anti-Rh antibody. This will render the killer antigen in the blood ineffective, and make it possible for her to bear normal children."

Kalki got the essential point. There was still time. "Where can we find this RhoGAM?"

"I suppose we can find it at any hospital," said Giles. "But I don't agree with Geraldine. After all, this is my field . . ."

"We'll discuss that later," said Kalki.

The RhoGAM was found, but it was too late. Lakshmi was now permanently sensitized. Any child she might conceive by Kalki would be born dead or, technically speaking, not really born at all.

Kalki broke the news to Lakshmi. I don't know what he told her. She has never mentioned the subject to either Geraldine or me.

For a week, Kalki and Lakshmi went into seclusion. I rang Kalki once. I offered to do my usual chores in the garden. Kalki said that he would rather not see anyone. According to Geraldine, Lakshmi was still in a state of deep depression. She was not the only one.

I now spend most of my time in the lobby of the Hay-Adams, looking after Jack and Jill. The Child has developed into a lively little girl, with a very definite and charming personality. I call her Eve. Yes, obvious connotation. I should note that in the last two years, Jack and Jill have had two more babies, a boy and a girl. I enjoy being with them. Geraldine does not share my enjoyment. She treats them neutrally and they respond, sensitively, in kind. Geraldine still works long hours in her laboratory. Since we never discuss her work, I have no idea what she's doing.

Eight days after the scene in the Oval Office, Kalki suddenly appeared in the lobby. Eve jumped up on his shoulder. She pulled his hair. She is very fond of him, and she does not like many people. In fact, from the very beginning she hated her mother and Giles and, I'm afraid, Geraldine, too. She tolerates Jack. She adores Kalki and me. Kalki is very nice with her.

"We've missed you," I said, helping Kalki get Eve's fingers out of his hair.

"We've missed you, too. We want you to come to dinner tonight." Kalki cleared apple cores off the last undestroyed sofa. I apologized for the mess.

Kalki sat down. He was unshaven, pale. "Giles knew about us all along," Kalki spoke as if this were news.

"So we guessed. But why didn't he warn you? And why didn't he give Lakshmi that serum from the beginning?"

"Because he didn't want to." Kalki stared off into space. Then he spoke with slow precision. "Yesterday I went to see him at Blair House. He told me everything. He told me that he had always known our problem. He told me that he had expected Lakshmi to become sensitized to me. He told me that he had never had a vasectomy. He told me that he loved Lakshmi. He told me that if the human race was to continue, it was now necessary for her to have his child."

I saw what was coming with all the clarity of a pilot about to crash-land a plane. "And when she does, he and not you will be the father of the new human race."

"Yes," said Kalki.

"What did you do?"

"I killed him."

I have brought this record up to date only to please Kalki. I can't think why he wants it. There will be no one to read it in the future.

We continue to see one another. One night the four of us will have dinner at the White House. The next night we dine at the Hay-Adams. Kalki has let his beard grow. We wear old clothes. Occasionally, we try to dress up. But, by and large, we are indifferent to such things. To all things. "The constant work of one's life is the making of one's death." Montaigne.

There is not much talk at dinner. Lakshmi has become almost totally withdrawn since the miscarriage. Kalki is silent for days at a time. Of us all, Geraldine alone continues to be like her old self. But then she has an interest. At Kalki's suggestion, she is continuing her experiments with DNA, cellular manipulation and so on. She thinks that Kalki would like for us to clone ourselves; that is, to reproduce ourselves not from sperm and egg but from a cell transferred to a host body. "Unfortunately," said Geraldine bluntly, "we lack a healthy uterus to nourish that cell. You and I are out of the running, and Lakshmi is permanently sensitized."

Our days are haphazard. I have no idea what Lakshmi does in the White House. I know that she has not left the grounds for over a year. Occasionally, Geraldine visits her. When I ask Geraldine how things are, she just shakes her head.

Kalki spends a good deal of time fishing. He also sees to the henhouse, the livestock, the vegetable garden. I do the weeding. It is astonishing how fast everything grows. Lafayette Park is now a jungle, and grass is splitting the pavement of Pennsylvania Avenue. The wolves are still with us, but the lions and other tropical beasts either died during the first winter or all went south. The stillness is more noticeable than ever.

We seldom talk of the old days. Last year I devoted several weeks to removing the stalled cars and trucks and buses and remains from our part of town. As a result, we can now sit in Lafayette Park and look at the White House (which needs a paint job) and see not a single trace of the world that died two years ago.

We are, according to Kalki, in the twilight period that precedes each new age of creation. I do not know about the new age. But I can testify to the twilight. We are all getting dim. To ourselves as well as to each other. Since we seldom speak of the old days and since we cannot speak of the future as there are no children for us to teach, we have only the present and there is not much in our present worth discussing. We sit at the dinner table, saying next to nothing.

This morning Kalki came into the Cabinet Room just as I wrote the above lines. He asked me to leave this record on the table. "The new people will want to know what it was like."

"What new people?"

Kalki combed his wiry blond beard with dirty fingers. "There will be others," he said. "After the twilight."

"Do you really think that there are other survivors in the world?"

Although we occasionally discuss the possibility, each of us knows that except for us, the human species has vanished from the earth.

"I want you to write," said Kalki, pointing at this record, "that I have known from the beginning that we five would not be able to reproduce." I was careful not to show surprise. Or disbelief. "Write that I have been testing each of the Perfect Masters. And each of you has lived up to expectations, including Giles. I told you that Giles was the necessary enemy. Now write that I knew from the beginning that he was the avatar of Ravana, the demon-king who lusted after the wife of Rama, *my* wife. But with the aid of the monkey hosts, I destroyed him this time just as I destroyed him when I was Rama. Yet he was a formidable enemy. Write that he was tall as a mountain peak, and that he stopped with his arms the sun and moon in their courses, and prevented their rising. And prevented their rising."

I take this last to be a quotation from the Ramayana. But I am not interested in poetry. I asked the hard question: "If you knew what Giles intended to do, why didn't you stop him?"

" 'All things conspire to make my happiness complete,' " Kalki quoted the last line of the tale of Rama. "I am what I am. There is no questioning."

"There is no logic, either." I was bold. I have nothing to lose.

"Creation is without logic. Destruction is without logic. I am without logic. Because I am not human." Kalki spoke in a low voice. He did not look at me. He might have been saying a prayer. Perhaps he was. "But that does not mean that there is no design in my universe. When the twilight goes, I shall begin a new cycle."

"How? Lakshmi cannot have your children. Yet you thought she could. You were mistaken."

"No." Kalki was bleak. "I have always known that it could not be. But I was impatient. I wanted to eliminate the time of twilight. I wanted to go straight to the Golden Age. I wanted it to begin—now —with our children. But Vishnu's plan cannot be altered."

"You are Vishnu."

"I am his avatar. But I wear human flesh. I am limited by every sort of human weakness. As Giles tried to outwit me, I tried to outwit my own design. He failed. I failed. Now I am again linked with the single godhead whose human presence in history I was and am and will be."

"What next?"

"Complete the record as of today. Leave it here. On this table. They will find it useful." Since Kalki did not choose to tell me who "they" are, I did not ask.

Who is Kalki? I no longer know. Before The End, I thought that he was a brilliant actor. After The End, I thought that he *might* be some sort of god or primal spirit made flesh. Since the death of Lakshmi's baby, I have no perception of him. I also have no interest in him.

What more? Geraldine and I are healthy. We talk every now and then of taking a trip. But like those Chekhov ladies in the play, we only talk. We never leave home. Anyway, I would be afraid to fly now. No jet has been properly maintained for a year.

The best part of my long days are when I take Jack and Jill and some of the children on walks. Although they enjoy climbing trees and behaving as monkeys are supposed to behave, they are always eager to get back to the Hay-Adams.

Only this afternoon I took the whole lot of them down to the banks of the Potomac River where I sat on a log beneath a weeping willow tree, with Eve on my lap. We watched the others, as they climbed trees, played tag, chattered constantly in their own language. At times I understand what they are "saying." I am planning to learn sign language. Apparently, monkeys can be taught to communicate in the same way that human deaf-mutes once did, with hand gestures.

This afternoon, sitting on that log beside the river, with Eve snuggled in my lap, I was surprisingly happy. Small things give great pleasure now. Let me list today's delights. Apple-scented air. Bright red birds on the wing. Silver fish that briefly arc above the surface of a river which glitters in the sun like a silver fish's scales. The cold clear clean water of the river that makes no sound as it slides past me to the sea. The Child.

TWELVE

W<small>INTER, 43 A.K.</small>

I am the last as I was the first. Lakshmi dropped her human body twenty-one years ago. Since the death of Teddy Ottinger sixteen years ago, Geraldine and I have been happy together. This, too, was intended from the beginning.

Late last night, Geraldine died. To the extent that I am human, I am sad that she is gone. Yet there was no real point for her to remain another day in the human state. Our work is complete. Presently, I shall join them all in Vaikuntha.

An entire new race of Brahmins is now on the threshold of a most holy epoch. As I sit in this cold and derelict mansion, I can hear the singing and the praying and the sheer joyfulness of earth's new heirs, my loyal allies in the war with Ravana, the descendants of Jack and Jill to whom I now bequeath the Golden Age. For am I not the highest of the high? the lord of songs, the lord of sacrifices?

I am breath. I am spirit. I am the supreme lord. I alone was before all things, and I exist and I shall be. No other transcends me. I am eternal and not eternal, discernible and undiscernible. I am Brahma and I am not Brahma. I am without beginning, middle or end. At the time of the end, I annihilate all worlds.

I am Siva

NOTE: *Yersinia entercolitica* would not have killed everyone on earth as promptly as Kalki wished. Although there are a number of lethal bacteria, viruses and toxins that would have done the job, I have forgone verisimilitude in the interest of good citizenship.

G.V.

About the Author

GORE VIDAL wrote his first novel, *Williwaw,* at the age of nineteen while overseas in World War II.

During three decades as a writer, Vidal has written with success and distinction novels, plays, short stories and essays. He has also been a political activist. As a Democratic candidate for Congress from upstate New York, he received the most votes of any Democrat there in half a century. From 1970 to 1972 he was co-chairman of the People's Party.

In 1948 Vidal wrote the highly praised, highly condemned novel *The City and the Pillar,* the first American work to deal sympathetically with homosexuality. In the next six years he produced *The Judgment of Paris* and the prophetic *Messiah.* In the fifties Vidal wrote plays for live television and films for Metro-Goldwyn-Mayer. One of the television plays became the successful Broadway play *Visit to a Small Planet.* Directly for the theater he wrote the prizewinning *The Best Man.*

In 1964 Vidal returned to the novel. In succession, he created three remarkable works: *Julian, Washington, D.C., Myra Breckinridge.* Each was a number-one best seller in the United States and England. In 1973 Vidal produced his most admired and successful novel *Burr,* as well as his first volume of collected essays, *Homage to Daniel Shays.* His second book of essays, *Matters of Fact and of Fiction,* was published in 1977. And in 1976, thirty years after the publication of *Williwaw,* Vidal wrote *1876,* which, along with *Burr* and *Washington, D.C.,* completed his American Trilogy.